Praise for

DEAD ON THE DELTA

"Everything you could want in an urban fantasy . . . strong, vivid writing, unique world building, and a clever, twisty plot."

—Stacia Kane, author of the Downside Ghosts series

"Relentlessly tense . . . a creative take on fairies, a flawed but sympathetic heroine, and the gritty sense of a disaster-ravaged Louisiana . . . a hard-to-put-down 'rural' fantasy. . . ."

—Fantasy Literature

"An awesome take on fairies and a kick-ass urban fantasy."

—Scooper Speaks

"A super urban fantasy police procedural. . . . The fast-paced storyline is action-packed."

—Alternative Worlds

"Unflinching and unforgettable. . . . Gnawed its way into my heart with writing sharp as fairy fangs."

—Jeri Smith-Ready, award-winning author of
Bring On the Night

"Fascinating . . . the seedy setting and hard-drinking heroine are written with skill and humor and enough quirks to enmesh you in the story. . . ."

—Fresh Fiction

Dead on the Delta and *Blood on the Bayou*
are also available as eBooks

Also by Stacey Jay

Dead on the Delta

Available from Pocket Books

STACEY JAY

BLOOD
ON THE
BAYOU

POCKET BOOKS

New York   London   Toronto   Sydney   New Delhi

Pocket Books
A Division of Simon & Schuster, Inc.
1230 Avenue of the Americas
New York, NY 10020

This book is a work of fiction. Names, characters, places, and incidents either are products of the author's imagination or are used fictitiously. Any resemblance to actual events or locales or persons, living or dead, is entirely coincidental.

Copyright © 2012 by Stacey Jay

All rights reserved, including the right to reproduce this book or portions thereof in any form whatsoever. For information, address Pocket Books Subsidiary Rights Department, 1230 Avenue of the Americas, New York, NY 10020.

First Pocket Books paperback edition April 2012

POCKET and colophon are registered trademarks of Simon & Schuster, Inc.

For information about special discounts for bulk purchases, please contact Simon & Schuster Special Sales at 1-866-506-1949 or business@simonandschuster.com.

The Simon & Schuster Speakers Bureau can bring authors to your live event. For more information or to book an event, contact the Simon & Schuster Speakers Bureau at 1-866-248-3049 or visit our website at www.simonspeakers.com.

Designed by Jacquelynne Hudson

Manufactured in the United States of America

10 9 8 7 6 5 4 3 2 1

ISBN 978-1-4391-8987-0
ISBN 978-1-4391-8989-4 (ebook)

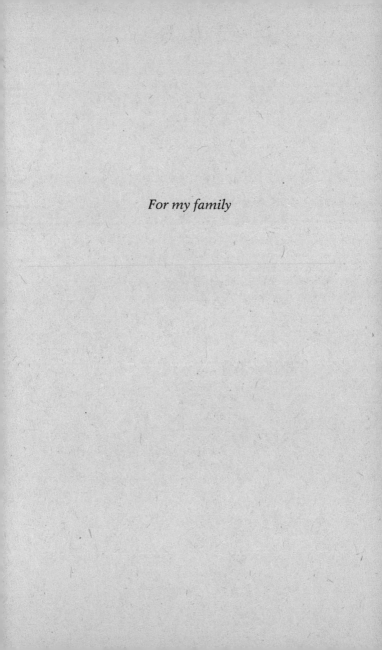

For my family

Acknowledgments

Thanks again to Mike, Grandma Stumpy, Riley, and Logan for being the best family a woman could hope for. Thanks to Jennifer Heddle for the edit—you will be missed! Thanks to Stacia Kane, Jennifer Estep, and Jeri Smith-Ready for their support and their amazing books. Thanks to Rhianna Walker, tireless champion for Annabelle and the series. Thanks to Wendy Richmond, friend and chemist, and to her boss, Perry, for the aid with all things scientific and smarty-pants. Thanks to Susan Wallendal-Held for the chopper knowledge (and for being a hoot and a half—I hope to ride with you someday, Susan!). And a big, big thanks to everyone who has written to share their thoughts about *Dead on the Delta*. From nuclear scientists to Harley enthusiasts to chemists to Baton Rouge strippers to political science majors to grandmothers raising their grandbabies—every e-mail has meant the world to me. I am so honored to tell you stories. Thank you.

BLOOD
ON THE
BAYOU

1

Nightmares suck. Not being able to wake up from one sucks even more.

But that's what happens when you double up on sleep aids the night after an unexpected murder-investigation-inspired visit from your ex-boyfriend.

But maybe I'd be okay right now if I'd had a nice, calm sandwich before bed instead of a few beers and extra-cheesy nachos, topped off with extra-strength Benadryl, in the hopes that Alcohol and Antihistamine would heroically join forces and fight back the evil duo of Jalapeño Sauce and Stupidity, allowing me to snag a few hours of REM sleep.

Maybe I'd *still* be okay, if I hadn't popped a Restalin an hour later, on the off chance that Alcohol and Antihistamine needed some insomnia-crime-fighting help.

All things considered, I earned this. I *deserve* it. And I *know* it's just a dream.

But that doesn't make the solo trudge through the menacing darkness any easier.

I'm walking barefoot through the swamp, mud

oozing between my toes, an unseasonably cold wind reminding me with every step that a T-shirt and bikini panties aren't the best choice for a walk outside the iron gates. I shouldn't be out here after dark without some serious protective outerwear. I'm immune and the fairies will probably leave me alone, but the gators and snakes don't care if my blood kills the Fey.

Ugh. Snakes. *Shudder*.

On cue, the mud beneath my feet spits forth a legion of snakes that slither between my legs, hissing and twitching, baring their glistening fangs, but refusing to go ahead and *bite me* already. Because biting would take the edge off the *fear* of being bitten—the jaw-locking, bone-shuddering, skin-crawling fear inspired by all those hard, reptilian bodies squirming around my ankles. The fear that swells even larger when the moon slips from behind a cloud and I get a good look at the shoreline spreading out in front of me.

Nothing but snakes and snakes and more snakes as far as the eye can see, an undulating carpet of horror that, for a moment, I'm stupid enough to believe is as scary as this dream is going to get.

And then it gets worse.

Of course it does.

Because that's what nightmares *do*.

Grace Beauchamp materializes under a nearby cypress, glowing like she's swallowed a piece of the moon. She looks the way she did the last time I saw her, after her mother-sister and father-brother killed her and dumped her body outside the gates. Her extra-small child's nightgown is muddy, her pink bow lips are torn, peeling back to reveal crooked little teeth. Her white-blond braids are fuzzy and coming undone on one side.

"Your cat ate my hair tie," she says in a bell-ringing-inches-from-your-ear voice that's painful to listen to.

"I'm sorry." I cross my arms and squeeze my legs together, trying to ignore the snakes and pretend her face doesn't make me want to scream. "Gimpy eats crazy things."

"That was my favorite hair tie."

Don't you have bigger grudges to hold, kid? What about the family members who murdered *you?*

Instead, I say, "I'm really sorry." It's tacky to pick fights with dead people. Especially dead children.

"No you're not." What's left of her nose wrinkles. "I'm dead. You think I don't matter."

"No. Of course I—"

"But you're wrong." She drifts toward me, floating above the carpet of snakes. As she passes, they scream and shrivel into black curlicues, as if her moonglow feet are made of blue fire. "Dead people matter, Annabelle. Sometimes, they matter more than the living."

Like Caroline, I think.

"Just like Caroline," Grace says, privy to my unspoken thoughts in the way of dream people. "But you can't see her face anymore, can you? You've forgotten what she looked like."

Yes, I have. "No, I haven't."

"Your own sister." A piece of her ruined lip curls. "That's horrible. You're bad. I'm glad I didn't know you very well when I was alive."

"Thanks." I barely resist the urge to roll my eyes.

"You're *not* welcome."

"You know, I heard you weren't the nicest person yourself," I say, even though I know she's right. I *am* horrible. And I *have* started to forget. I held Caroline after she was bitten by fairies, watched the convulsions of the severely allergic snap her spine and shatter her teeth before she was allowed to die. Even if I hadn't spent sixteen years looking up to my older sister, I never thought I'd forget the pain on her face that last night.

But I have.

"And now you're picking on a murdered kid." Grace sounds like she's about to cry. "I was six years old. I couldn't even tie my own shoes."

"Sorry," I mumble.

"I couldn't use the microwave by myself, except for the popcorn button." She swoops closer, destroying snakes at a rate that would be encouraging if I weren't starting to wonder what will happen to me when she gets close enough to touch. "I couldn't run my bath, or ride my bike without training wheels, or give myself my shots."

The shots. The same shots the invisible people who were running Breeze in the bayou gave me after I was bitten. I'm immune, so was Grace, and unlike 95 percent of the human population, we shouldn't have had to worry about the effects of fairy bite. But both of us were affected, in the form of headaches and messed up eyes and . . . magic.

Real magic. The kind that allows you to manipulate matter with your mind, float objects through the air, and eventually disappear and reappear at will if the rest of the Invisibles are any indication. Both Grace and I were approached by these unseen folks and told to inject ourselves with mystery medicine every four weeks to keep from catching bad cases of crazy.

Grace's mother-sister, Libby, stopped giving Grace the shots months ago, hoping she'd die without them. She didn't. She went off the deep end, killed the bunnies for the Easter raffle, and tried to off Libby by dropping a box of canned pickles on her head. Unfortunately, she failed, and Libby smothered Grace in her sleep, framed my best friend, Fernando, for the murder, and killed her housekeeper—and very nearly myself—in an attempt to cover her tracks.

But Libby got her just desserts. I was there when the leader of the invisible people took care of Libby and her brother, James. I heard the satisfaction in the Big Man's voice as he sent them to their shared hot tub in hell. The pleasure he took in their murders made me hope I'd never have to *not see* the man again.

Then tonight he'd sent Tucker, his right-hand man, with his "present"—the motorcycle he promised me if I survived the anaphylactic shock from Libby's killer shrimp muffin and healed my ex-boyfriend's fiancée's bullet wound. I did both, saving myself, Stephanie, and her unborn child, ensuring Stephanie would live happily ever after with the man I think I'm still in love with.

"That's stupid. Hitch hates you," Grace says. "He's going to marry Stephanie and they're going to have the cutest baby *ever*."

"I know."

"Way cuter than if you and Hitch had a baby." She coasts to a stop a few feet away, close enough that I can feel her ghost power tingling along my skin. "Stephanie's a *lot* prettier than you."

"I know." I fight the urge to step back. The tingling isn't a good feeling, but at least it's scared off the snakes. I'm back to standing in plain old mud, and appreciating it a lot more than I did when this dream started.

"You should call Cane. See if he'll take you back."

Cane *would* take me back. At least I think he would. But not until I'm ready to promise him Forever. As much as I love him, Forever still scares me. What if I can't be the person he needs me to be? How can I vow to love and honor him when I'm still carrying a torch for someone else?

"A pointless torch," Grace says. "That's going to burn you."

I go ahead and roll my eyes. "What are you? My mom?"

"No, your mom wouldn't talk to you this much."

"Thanks."

"Just telling it like it is." She shrugs. "You shouldn't let Cane go. He's nice."

"I know."

"Too nice for you."

"I know."

"Because you mostly suck. Even the FCC isn't sure they want you anymore." She giggles a mean giggle. "I mean, who gets suspended from scooping fairy poop? Can't a monkey do your job?"

"Probably."

She crosses her arms and huffs, sending a piece of lip flapping. "Don't think I'll stop telling the truth just because you stop fighting back."

"You're not telling the truth."

"I am." She floats close enough that the tingle becomes a sting. "I'm a messenger from the other side."

"You're chips with jalapeño sauce and refried beans."

"Really?" Her face snaps into sharper focus and suddenly the air seems colder, the nightmare bigger. A breeze ruffles the bottom of my T-shirt. I fist it in my fingers, needing something to hold on to. "Could chips with jalapeño sauce do this?" She lifts her small, white hands and the glow beneath her skin becomes a blinding light.

I wince and squeeze my eyes closed, throwing my arms up to block the glare as the wind starts to blow in earnest. It blasts in from every direction at once, a twister that rushes through my legs and whips my hair into a wild red tangle. It smacks and patters and beats at my skin and then I feel it—unbearably soft, hot flesh brushing against mine, and the tickle of silky wings.

This isn't wind. It's a swarm of fairies.

My eyes fly open. They're everywhere. The air

is alive with naked humanoid bodies glowing pink and gold, with flat, black eyes, and rows and rows *and rows* of teeth. All of them have their detachable jaws dropped and their layers of sharklike fangs out for show-and-tell. I'm immune to their venom, but I know how badly those teeth hurt when they break the skin, how freely even one bite will bleed.

This many fairies could kill me. They would die after, but if enough of them dig in for a suicide nibble, I'll bleed to death and all the immunity in the world won't matter.

"Dead woman," a voice rasps in my ear. I flinch and scream and brush wildly at my head. I knock the fairy away, but he flies around to hover in front of my nose, his ancient prune face screwed up in a scowl.

He's easily the oldest fairy I've ever seen. About two inches from head to foot, with a concave chest that gives way to bony ribs and a belly that sags like an empty pouch. His skin is more yellow than gold and even his eyes seem duller than the rest of the fairies', but his teeth are just as sharp.

I get an up-close-and-personal inspection when he bares them in a hiss. "Dead," he shouts. "Dead. Dead. Dead!"

Spittle flies into my eyes, but I swallow the scream rising in my throat. My eyes *feel* like they're burning, but they aren't. This isn't real. Fairies can't talk. Grace is dead. And I would never go for a stroll in the bayou in my underwear.

Just a dream. A stupid dream!

"Your last nightmare," the old fairy assures me in a voice like sandpaper scraping down my spine. "Leave the breeding ground of the Slake."

"What?"

"We suffer no more Gentry!" He jabs an angry thumb over his shoulder and the crush of fairies parts, revealing Grace and her glowing hands.

"No. Not me! Not me! You promised!" Her ruined mouth drops open and her eyes fly wide and then they're on her.

The fairy swarm descends and Grace's skin blossoms with red. One, two, three, ten, fifty blooms, like she's being hit with tiny paintball pellets that burst open and soak into her nightgown. She screams and it feels like the entire world will shatter, but I can't close my eyes and I can't take a step toward her. I'm frozen, with the shriveled old fairy fluttering near my cheek, grinning his yellow grin as Grace's skin is stripped from her bones.

"Stop!" I try to shout, but it comes out a whisper, almost unintelligible over the screeches of the feeding fairies.

They're ripping mouthfuls of her away, chomping and chewing and flinging scraps of nightgown from their fangs before going in for another bite and another and another. I'm going to be sick. I can feel it rising in my stomach, a heavy fist thrusting toward my mouth.

"Go." The old fairy pokes my cheek with his hot finger. "Leave the land of the Slake or die like the girl."

"You're not real!"

"We are all that is real."

"No! Stop! I want to wake up! I'm going to wake up!" I scream, loud enough that the nightmare begins to rip at the seams.

Holes tear in the night, and Grace's bloody body smears into a red stain. The last thing I see clearly are the old fairy's cruel button eyes narrowing to slits and then nothing but bright, mind-numbing light.

2

Light. Bright. Sunshine. Eyes. *Argh!*

I curse and jerk my head over to the cool side of my pillow. I must have left the shades open. Half the bed is bathed in redhead-scorching sunlight. Good thing I woke up when I did or I'd have a hell of a burn.

"And probably wet the damn bed," I mumble, rubbing my arm across my sleep-puffy face, trying to banish the last of the nightmare.

"You still do that, too?" a deep voice drawls from the foot of my bed.

I bolt upright, squinty eyes getting squintier. I can't see anyone, but that doesn't mean much these days. "Tucker?"

"You were expecting someone else?" He materializes, going from invisible man to floating smile to six feet three or four of yummy in the course of a few seconds. He's wearing his typical Tucker uniform—a pair of faded jeans and a white wife-beater he manages to make look like a fashion statement instead of something from the cover of *Trailer Trash Monthly*.

His shoulder-length blond hair seems darker than usual, but those bright blue eyes are just as full of trouble and . . . sex.

Jesus. Simply making eye contact with Tucker feels vaguely dirty. In the good way. The *really* good way that I haven't experienced since Cane declared a nookie time-out until I'm ready to Commit.

"I wasn't expecting *anyone*." I sound cranky. But that's fine. Tucker should know better than to mess with me in the morning. "I was sleeping. Alone. In my house, where you are *not* invited to come inside anytime you please."

"You were screaming." His grin fades a watt or two. "Thought you might be in trouble."

"So you were coming to the rescue?"

"What can I say? I'm a knight in shining armor."

"You're a creepy, mojito-stealing Peeping Tom."

"Now, now . . . name calling just turns me on, Red." He winks and my stomach flutters in spite of myself.

I roll my eyes, pretending to be beyond the reach of his charms. "I was having a bad dream. No big deal."

"Some dream." He sits on the edge of the bed, close enough for me to smell the soap-and-sunshine scent of his skin. I let him brush my hair over my shoulder, and try not to think about how almost naked I am under my blue cotton sheets. Only a T-shirt and panties that I'm sure Tucker could make disappear faster than he does. "You okay?"

"Kick-ass awesome." I push images of Grace's

bloodied body to the back of my mind, and narrow my eyes at Tucker's damp hair. "Did you use my shower?"

"Nope."

"So you live close enough to shower and get to my house with your hair still wet." I know nothing about Tucker, and for some reason even a minor discovery feels like a victory. "Interesting."

He smiles. "I thought you gave up on the amateur detective stuff."

"Why would you think that?"

"Libby almost killed you."

"Aw." I purse my lips. "You sound like you care."

"Would have been a shame. You're a fine piece of ass."

"And you're ridiculously good-looking."

He tips his head like a cigarette cowboy and his grin takes a turn for the smug. "Thank you, ma'am."

"No. Really. Ridiculous." I shove his shoulder with the tips of my fingers. "Off my bed."

His brow lifts. "Because I'm too good-looking?"

"Yes." I give him my best deadpan stare, enjoying tormenting him more than I probably should. "The long silky hair and the eyes and the eyelashes and all . . . this." I gesture to his perfectly sculpted body and too-tight jeans. "It's overkill. Not my speed."

"You're such a liar." He leans in, until his mouth is temptingly close, and for the first time I am truly tempted. There's always been an undercurrent of sexual awareness between Tucker and me, but neither of us has made a move. I assumed we never would. But now, with him warming a spot on my bed, looking at me with those smiling eyes . . .

Thank god I know for a fact that I have killer morning breath, or I might give in and see if his lips are as soft as they look.

"You're crazy." I tap a finger to his nose and scoot away.

"Am not. I've seen both those boys you play with."

"I play with no one."

"That window says different."

"Ew." This time my shove is a lot less delicate. "You really *are* a Peeping Tom. That's disgusting. You shouldn't watch other people do it."

"You shouldn't do it with your window open."

"You should leave so I can get dressed." I point to the back door, but Tucker doesn't move. He only bats his long eyelashes and shoots me a predatory look I'm lame enough to find nearly irresistible. "Really. You should go," I say again, but I don't sound like I mean it.

"Maybe you should forget about getting dressed." He reaches out, resting his hand on my hip, warming my skin through the thin cotton of my shirt. He's never touched me like this. He knows it. I know it.

The knowing thickens the air between us, introducing a possibility that's never been there before. But now it is. It *is* and I can feel how easy it would be to run my hand up his arm, to slide my fingers beneath his shirt and hold tight as he pushes me back onto my sun-streaked pillow and his mouth meets mine and—

"I can't." I swallow. Bite my lip. Think strong thoughts.

"You could . . ."

"No, I *can't*." But maybe I *can*. Maybe I *should*. Relationship-death-by-Tucker would certainly put an end to all my angst about Cane. He won't take me back if I've been with another man, and I'd have to tell him I cheated or the guilt would eat me alive.

But is it really cheating if you're not officially together? Does an invisible man count as a man? If a penis you can't see falls in the forest is it really a penis at all?

I close my eyes, blocking out Tucker's hypnotic sex stare. I refuse to let him help me sabotage myself. I care about Cane. I love him, and I'm not going to wreck my last chance before I've had time to decide what to do with it.

"Really, I have to be somewhere." No sooner have the words left my mouth than I realize they're true. I whip my head around to check the clock, cuss, throw off the covers, and dive for a mostly clean pair of jeans on the floor.

I'm supposed to meet Hitch at the restaurant at nine. It's already eight forty-five and it takes five minutes to get to Swallows on my bicycle. I guess I could take my new Harley. If I knew how to get it out of the kitchen. Or how to ride a motorcycle. Or wanted to answer a bunch of questions about why I bought a Harley when everyone in town knows I'm a rabid bicycle-with-trailer-and-room-for-my-blue-cooler enthusiast.

"Listen, Red," Tucker says in a softer voice. "I didn't mean to—"

"Go," I order as I button my jeans and search the ground for a bra. I know I threw a not *too* dirty one down here last night. "And get that bike out of my kitchen."

"I'm not your errand boy." He sounds bristly. Good. Better bristles than possibilities.

"No, you're a pain in my ass," I say. "Get."

"I'm not touching the bike. You need to put those shots someplace safe. Do I need to remind you that—"

"I know, I know. Top secret. Tell no one about the shots. Penalty of death. Blah, blah, blah," I say, shocked to find I'm not as scared of the Invisibles as I was even last night. Maybe it's the fact that Tucker showers like a normal person that's given me comfort. More likely it's that he tried to get me in the sack. He doesn't seem like the type who'd sleep with someone he's going to have to kill in the near future.

Tucker snort-laughs and stretches out on my bed. He props his hands behind his head, making his wifebeater crawl up, baring a tempting inch of tanned stomach. "Blah, blah, blah, yourself. Don't forget to brush your teeth before you go. Your breath smells like the wrong end of Taco Bell."

"I didn't know Taco Bell had a right end." I dig through a pile of definitely dirty clothes, though I seriously doubt my bra slipped under all that on its own.

"I didn't know such a pretty girl could have such ugly breath."

BLOOD ON THE BAYOU ◆ 17

"I didn't know—Oh, whatever." I give up on the bra and throw the dirty T-shirt in my hand at Tucker's head. "I don't have time for banter, Bubba."

"Aw. A nickname. I like that, Red," Tucker calls after me as I grab a black tank top and duck into the bathroom. I brush my teeth, run damp fingers through my frizzy curls, and think about throwing on real makeup, but end up sticking with a thick coat of mascara and some freckle-concealing powder.

There's no time to spare and I don't want Hitch to think I tried too hard. We're meeting to talk about tracking down a cave full of hostages out in the bayou. It's not a social call. Even if it were, it would be a *friendly* social call, and Hitch knows I don't get pretty for friends. He knows me too well, something I need to keep in mind if I want to keep the fact that I've still got it bad for him a secret while spending more concentrated time together than we have since we were a couple six years ago.

With a last fluff of my hair I declare myself decent-but-not-pretty and dash out of the bathroom to find Tucker still lounging on my rumpled sheets. "Go away. You're not sleeping in my bed."

"I'm tired."

"Go sleep in your own bed."

"I like yours better. The sun's nice."

"You should wear sunscreen. You're going to get skin cancer." Tightness flashes in my chest.

I sound like Marcy. She was always riding my ass about wearing sunscreen and eating healthy and taking care of myself like a full-fledged grown-up. It drove me crazy. Until the day she left town and was suddenly not there to nag me anymore. It was like losing my mother all over again. But worse. I didn't meet Marcy until I was sixteen, when she was the social worker in charge of my floor at the group home, but she was more of a mother to me than Mama Lee ever was.

Until she wasn't. Until the day the sweetest, most giving, hardest-loving woman I've ever met told me she'd killed two people, done time, and was afraid the FBI was going to find out she'd helped a father kidnap his daughter.

She skipped town later that day, went on the lam with her husband, Tyrone, and a few suitcases. I haven't heard from her in nearly a month. I don't know if I'll ever see her again. And that . . . hurts. Almost as bad as knowing the man I suspect is my soul mate is starting a family with another woman.

Your "soul mate" is going to kill you if you're any later than you are already.

He won't kill me, but he'll look at me with those eloquently disappointed eyes and decide asking for my help was a dumb idea. I should be glad to bail on an investigation that could get me killed—or at the very least spectacularly fired—but I don't want to let Hitch down. I want to help him find out who murdered his friend. Even more, I want to show him that I'm not a complete waste of living tissue.

"Wake me up before noon," Tucker says, eyes sliding closed. "I have someplace to be."

"Up. Now. Or I get my gun from under the bed."

I grab his arm, haul him up, and push him into the kitchen. After one final sigh, he squeezes past the Harley still taking up 90 percent of the space and heads for the back door, while I grab my purse and keys from the kitchen table and bend to check Gimpy's water bowl. It's still mostly full. As is his food bowl.

Because he's clearly been too busy eating *my bra* to bother with actual food.

"Gimpy!" I grab the strap and pull it out of his mouth, but I'm too late. Half my barely-B cup is gone, scarfed down into the bottomless pit of Gimpy's twisted digestive tract. He yowls and narrows his green eyes as I stuff what's left of the bra in my purse.

I point a warning finger his way. "If your guts get impacted again, don't come crying to me."

The last time Gimpy was at the vet, the doctor had to perform emergency surgery to remove all the crap he'd swallowed from his small intestines. She found— among other usually inedible things—a heart-shaped hair tie. Grace's hair tie. Gimpy must have eaten it the night before her body was discovered.

Despite the hot September air rushing in from the door Tucker's holding open, I shiver. And make a solemn vow not to eat Mexican food late at night. I could do without any more dreams like the one this morning.

"Be good," I warn Gimpy as I hurry out the door, realizing too late that I can still see Tucker just fine.

And so can everyone else, including my nosey next-door neighbor, Bernadette, the old bird single-handedly responsible for spreading tales about my private life all over town. When we step outside, Bernie's already in her back garden picking tomatoes, and I can tell by the pucker of her mouth that she's gotten an eyeful of Tucker.

She makes no secret about being Team Cane.

This perceived misdeed will *not* go unpunished.

"Why didn't you poof?" I ask Tucker through gritted teeth.

Tucker tosses his hair over his shoulder with a cocky grin. "I don't see any need to hide our relationship."

"What relationship?" I hiss before forcing a smile and waving to Bernadette as we pass by. "Morning, Bernie. This isn't what it looks like."

Her mouth gets puckerier. *Great*. I drop the smile and give her the evil eye while scissoring my fingers in front of my face—the universal sign for "I'm going to steal your Sunday paper and cut out all the coupons if you don't keep your mouth shut." Bernie still doesn't speak, but her puckered mouth presses into a thin line. She turns back to her tomatoes with a muffled humph, and I know we've understood each other.

If only all relationships were so easily managed.

Which reminds me . . .

"Who are you supposed to be? How do I know you?" I ask as I unchain my bike from the tree in the front yard.

"I'm an old family friend."

I snort. "My family wouldn't let their friends talk to me, and my family wouldn't be friends with someone like you."

"Why's that?"

"My mom and dad own half of New Orleans. They don't like poor people."

"Who says I'm poor? You're making a lot of assumptions, Red."

"Kind of like people who assume I want them in my house or in my bed or to be seen coming out my back door with them." I strap my purse across my chest and kick up my kickstand. "Just tell me what the cover story is. I'm going to have to tell Bernadette something. I don't want to pull a story out of my ass and get in trouble for breaking the rules."

"I'm an old family friend from New Orleans," he says. "Your parents knew my parents when we were little. If I remember correctly, we used to swim naked in the kiddie pool together."

"My parents don't believe in naked. They wear clothes when they shower." I eyeball Tucker's lightly lined faced. Could be too much sun making him look older, but I'm guessing he's somewhere in his midthirties, while I won't be hitting twenty-nine until May. "And I think you've got a few years on me, Bubba. If we swam naked together when I was a kiddie, you were a teenage sex pervert."

He laughs. "Teenage sex pervert or not, you've been kind enough to offer to help your old friend get settled here in Donaldsonville."

My forehead wrinkles. "I thought you were a top-secret spy. How can you—"

"The Big Man decided I'd be more useful to him as a member of the community."

A sour taste fills my mouth. Could be a hint of the acid reflux Marcy always said I'd get if I kept eating so much fried food, but I know it isn't. It's the mention of the Big Man.

So far, these are the things I know about this guy:

1. He was running Breeze—dried fairy poop mixed with bleach, a lot like crack but ten times more addictive—out in the bayou until he got shut down by the FBI, so he has no problem profiting from the suffering of his fellow man.

2. He's the leader of the invisible people, and rules them with a blood-spattered fist. I can tell Tucker's afraid of him, and Tucker doesn't seem to be afraid of much.

3. He's in control of the shots that are keeping me from going nuts, and is comfortable with threatening to withhold them if I step out of line.

4. He enjoys violently murdering people who get on his bad side.

Even considering he was avenging a little girl's murder when he killed James and Libby, I don't like the idea of a drug-dealing, person-strangling psychopath messing with the people in my town. Whatever reason the Big Man has for wanting Tucker in Donaldsonville, I know it isn't a good one, and I want no part in facilitating his plans.

Unfortunately, I don't have a choice. Keeping the

Big Man happy is necessary to maintaining access to the medication that's keeping me sane. I have to play along, but I don't have to play nice.

"You're a distant cousin, my parents think you're trash, and I've never met you in my life," I say. "You've got a shady past that I'm guessing involves some jail time and I'll be advising my friends not to walk alone with you after dark, or loan you money, or be that nice to you if they can help it."

Tucker laughs. "Sounds perfect." I roll my eyes and push off down the street. "Stay out of trouble, Red."

"Suck it, Bubba," I call over my shoulder. Tucker's still laughing when I reach the end of the block and start past the junkyard.

I smile. Just a little. He's a mess, but I have a soft spot for messes.

I have to. My self-image depends upon it.

3

The good news is that by the time I make it to the town square, the clock above the courthouse only reads five after nine. The bad news is that the street in front of Swallows has been torn to hell and is crawling with construction equipment. There's no way I'm getting through it on my bike.

"Shit," I curse and start around the block to the back entrance. I knew the city was breaking ground on the community center this week, but I didn't think they'd be working on Saturday.

Father Reginald, our parish priest, finally convinced the city council that the citizens of Donaldsonville need something to do with their spare time if we hope to keep people off Breeze and lower the teen pregnancy rate—which is getting downright ridiculous. Not that I can't understand that there's nothing to do that's as much fun as doing it, but we have a teen health center one block off the square and the social workers at Sweet Haven orphanage are proactive about advocating safety first.

So there's really no excuse for the number of

baby girls with baby bumps that I see around town. Of course, it could be that I'm simply noticing the bumps more than I did before. Ever since Cane suggested we start thinking about marriage and babies, pregnant women seem to be popping up everywhere.

Like evil, blood-thirsty clowns in a fun house. Or something scarier.

I really don't get it. Why does Cane think I'd be a good mom? What have I ever done to lead him to believe such a ridiculous thing? I can barely keep my new sod from turning brown and my cat is probably going to get his bowels impacted and die if I don't stop leaving my laundry on the floor.

Ugh. Cane. I can't stop thinking about him. It doesn't help that the building being gutted down the street from Swallows used to be his sister's, Amity's, bar.

Coop's closed down a month ago when Amity was shipped off to the containment camp at Keesler. She was bitten by a fairy while out in the bayou scoring Breeze. She isn't severely allergic, so she'll live at least a few more years, but she'll live them in what amounts to a posh concentration camp. She'll have no autonomy, no privacy, very little contact with her family, and armed guards watching her every move to make sure they're ready with the kill shot when the fairy venom finally destroys the part of her brain that keeps her from attacking people like a flesh-hungry zombie.

I feel so bad for Cane, his brother, Abe, and their mom. I'm not looking forward to my first Sunday lunch at the Cooper house without their sister in attendance. Amity hated my guts, but she's vital to the Cooper family dynamic. Without her, things are going to be even more awkward. I know Cane's mom thinks he can do better than a girl like me. I'm sure he could, too.

But for some reason I'm the one he wants. *Sigh*.

I skid to a stop halfway down Hammer Street, and hurry to lock up my bike at the rack. I'll have to go down the alley behind Swallows to get to the restaurant, a fact Theresa's been bitching about since the vote came through to widen the road and put in a roller rink in the basement of what used to be Coop's. She swears food sales are going to drop if people have to walk past the Dumpster before coming inside. I recommended running more drink specials—especially on pitchers of Blue Moon, my new favorite, and Saturday morning Bloody Marys. Ah, Bloody Marys . . .

Too bad there will be no Bloody in my morning today.

Hitch is a big disapprover of my drinking, to the point that he likes to call my perfectly respectable habit an "addiction" and stage interventions on public sidewalks. Under normal circumstances, this would only make me inclined to order a pitcher with extra vodka and give him the proverbial finger with every sip, but today is not a normal day.

Today we're going to talk about a dead man and the fact that whoever killed him will be after Hitch next if he learns Hitch is poking his nose where some crooked member of the FBI would prefer he didn't.

Hitch's dead friend was part of the task force that shut down the Breeze houses surrounding Donaldsonville. While he was hunting fugitive addicts out in the bayou, he stumbled across a cave—which is plain weird considering our part of Louisiana isn't cave-prone.

Even weirder, he spotted U.S. military–looking types going into the cave with captives and coming out alone. He took pictures and did some digging beyond his clearance level and found out that two of the military types used to work for the FBI in the development of chemical weapons. But they're not working for the FBI anymore, and whoever they *are* working for is willing to kill to keep the cave a secret.

Hitch's friend must have known he was in danger or he wouldn't have sent Hitch copies of all the evidence he'd gathered, but still . . .

Did he suspect he was going to be murdered? Only a couple of days later? Logically, I know agreeing to help Hitch is dangerous, but I don't think I'm going to die. But perhaps I should pause and consider that very real possibility.

I stop next to the Dumpster Theresa's so worried about.

She's right. It stinks. Rotten vegetables, old grease, and sour beer drift to my nose, and I suddenly have no interest in spicy sausage and fresh biscuits. Maybe I have no interest in being here at all.

Why am I doing this? When Hitch has made it perfectly clear he wouldn't fault me for saying no? Justice is great and all, but I don't have to dig that deep to know a hunger for righteousness has little to do with my presence here this morning. I'm here because of what Hitch said last night, that parting shot, that whisper that he "thinks about me all the time."

What does that even *mean*? Is it good thinking or bad thinking or just general bland blah thinking that means nothing at—

"Slut! Wait up!" The shout comes from the end of the alley. I turn before I think better of it. "Ha! Made you look." Fernando claps his hands and throws back his head as he laughs, showcasing shiny white teeth. Half of them are caps, but you wouldn't know it from looking.

Just like you wouldn't know his nose is courtesy of the best plastic surgeon in New Orleans or that this lean, mean, Latin lover with the beefy arms and the six-pack of steel used to be the skinniest kid at Sweet Haven. There was a time—not too terribly long ago—when *I* could have kicked his ass. Instead, I helped him hide from the boys who enjoyed beating him up, punishing him for being the only kid in a small-town orphanage brave enough to come out of the closet.

I was sixteen, he was eighteen, and we drank a lot of vodka in a lot of dark, cramped spaces. By the end of my first year, we knew each other better than we knew ourselves. It was damned hard to leave Fern when I went to college. He's been my best, best friend forever.

"Don't you own a bra?" He stops beside me, surveying my chest with a delicate scrunch of his nose. "The girls aren't going to stay perky without elastic assistance, Lee. I'm already detecting *significant* sagging."

He's also constantly picking on me. Even more so lately than usual, which is bullshit. *He's* the one who was dealing Breeze to his bed-and-breakfast customers and keeping it from his best friend. He's also the one who would have spent quality time in prison if it weren't for my mad sleuth skills. If anyone should be feeling betrayed and cranky, it's me.

I have low standards and a high tolerance for other people's bad habits, but even I can't stomach peddling Breeze. It kills people, plain and simple. There's no using Breeze in moderation. People start and they don't stop until they're out of their minds and too messed up to figure out how to get the money to buy more. It's wrong to do that to another living thing. I thought Fern knew the way I felt about Breeze. What's more, I thought he felt the same way.

Now . . . I'm not sure Fern is the gossip with a heart of gold that I've always believed him to be. Maybe his heart is more gold-grubbing than golden, and maybe he's only been my best friend for so long because no one else will put up with his crap.

"Some of us would like to walk the streets without rogue mammary glands bouncing all over the place," he adds with a disapproving click of his tongue.

"My mammary glands are not rogue," I say. "They're attached to my torso and they're just fine."

"No. Not fine. Especially with a scoop neck."

"I don't hear anyone else complaining."

"You need to start wearing a bra. For reals." He

crosses his arms and lifts his freshly plucked eyebrows. "I say this out of love for you, Slut. Because I care about your continued ability to live up to your nickname."

"That's not my nickname," I say. "And for your information, I was going to wear a bra, but Gimpy ate my last clean one." I tug it out of my purse, showing him the shredded cup, but don't join in his laughter. "So are we okay? Can my tits and I continue to exist in your general vicinity?"

"Wow." He takes a wounded step back. "Somebody woke up on the crabby side of the bed."

"I'm not crabby. I just need you to be a little . . . nicer to me." *And quit making me wonder if you're one of the bad guys.* I don't want to think of Fern that way. I need him to be my smart-ass best friend who's always got my back. I need something to stay the same while everything else I've counted on morphs at warp speed.

"Since when have I ever been nice?"

"You know what I mean." I try to smile, but can't. "Surely, not everything I do is cause for criticism."

"Of course not. Only about ninety percent." He softens the words with an arm around my shoulder. "But that's why you have me. To keep you on track. And today, that means no Happy Saturday Bloody Mary."

"I wasn't planning on having one."

"Oh, you can have one. Or two or three." He turns back toward the entrance to the alley, pulling me along beside him. "You just can't have them *here*."

"Why?"

"Guess who is inside Swallows lurking in wait even as we speak?"

"Who?" I ask, though I have a feeling I know.

"Dr. Herbert Mitchell Asswipe Jerkface McSmuggy Rideau."

I smile. I can't help it. Lingering feelings for Hitch aside, there are times when Fern's descriptions fit him to a T. "I know. He stopped by the house last night." I don't mention that it was while Fern was inside pouring more mojitos. If he knows I kept juicy news like this from him, he'll kill me. "He asked me to meet him to talk about some FCC stuff," I add, experiencing only a slight twinge of guilt as the lie slips out. I can't tell Fern the real reason that I'm here.

Even if he were capable of keeping his mouth shut, I wouldn't risk it. I don't want to put him in danger, or endure the inevitable lecture about offering aid to the enemy. No matter what I decide, as far as Fern's concerned, Hitch will always be the enemy. It took him a while to put two and two together, but he's realized that Hitch is the reason I ended up back in Donalsonville a crankier, sadder, more jaded person than I was before. He'll never forgive Hitch for that. Fernando is like a big brother that way. He picks on me relentlessly, but he'd die before he let anyone else hurt me.

Aaaannd now I feel awful for thinking shitty things about him.

I slip an arm around his waist. "But thanks for the warning. It would usually be muchly appreciated."

"Fairy Containment and Control crap, huh?" He

gives me a one-armed hug. "Aren't you supposed to be suspended until next week?"

"Yeah. He's just following up on the Breeze house stuff," I bluff, resisting the temptation to elaborate. Vague is best. I'll be less likely to contradict myself later.

"I think you should tell him to screw off and come back next week."

"I could. But then I'd have to see him again."

"Right." He shudders. "Better to get it over with. Like a shot."

I stiffen and pull away. I don't want to think about shots or magic or how many things I'm keeping from my best friend. "I should get to it. We still on for supper?"

"Absolutely, but let's do it at your house. I can bring everything over and cook on your sorry excuse for a stove."

"But I thought you were going to ask some of the boys to eat with us." I was looking forward to a tableful of whatever flamboyant guests happened to be staying at The First and Last Chance Flophouse. Nothing to keep your mind off your troubles like heated debates on fashion, politics, musical theater, and the latest gay porn.

"I was, but considering Hitch is one of my 'boys' for the next four days and three nights, I didn't think—"

"He's staying at your place?"

"Tell me about it." He runs a dramatic hand through his hair. "I can't remember the last time someone that straight slept under my roof. It's bringing the fabulous levels in the house *waaaay* down. He left at five o'clock this morning to go jogging. Then he came back to shower and didn't even bother putting any product in that springy clown hair of his. Just walked out frizzy as hell in saggy jeans and a grungy T-shirt. It was like the nineties came back to haunt me, and they were even uglier than I remembered."

"I like the curls." I also like those jeans and grungy T-shirts. They remind me of when Hitch and I would roam the French Quarter on Sunday mornings, hunting down coffee and beignets before going back to his place and gorging on pastry and each other.

Fern raises an eyebrow. "Uh-un. No, you don't. No smiling, or fond remembering or whatever you're doing right now. You don't like anything about him. You don't notice the way he looks like sex on a stick. He's bad for you."

"I know."

"And practically married."

"I know."

"*And* going to be a *daddy* before Valentine's Day."

"I know!" I hold my hands in the air and try to look innocent. "I have to go, okay? I'm going to be late."

"You're already late."

Hitch's drawl. From right behind me.

Balls.

4

Fifteen minutes late," he adds.

I spin with a smile, praying Hitch didn't hear that he was the subject of discussion. The only thing worse than Fernando thinking I still have a thing for Hitch is *Hitch* thinking I still have a thing for Hitch. I shrug. "That's practically on time."

"If you're you." He steps into the alley, breathtaking in jeans so broken in I can feel how soft they are just looking at them and a threadbare blue T-shirt that shows the skin beneath in the really thin patches. His sun-streaked brown hair fuzzes in curls around his head and his face is shadowed with patchy whiskers. Like an adorable dog with a mild case of the mange.

Yum. I have no idea what Fern's talking about. The nineties were a good decade. At least they look good on Hitch.

"But I'm not you," he says, in his new, more-adult-than-thou-wilt-ever-be voice, the one that makes me remember why I was working up a healthy resentment of him a month back.

"Sorry for the wait," I say. "I forgot about the construction and then Fern had some important things to tell me about food. I figured our FCC conversation could wait a few minutes while we decided on fish or steak for dinner."

Hitch's expression loses its irritated edge. I silently congratulate myself on passing the lateness buck onto Fern and the need to pretend Hitch and I aren't up to anything of interest. "Of course." He lifts a hand in Fern's direction and smiles. "I'd go with steak. Nothing like a hunk of meat on the grill at the end of a long day."

"And Annabelle *does* like her a hunk of meat."

I shoot Fern a dirty look, but he's already backing away. "See you at seven," he says. "Buy something red for supper. Cabernet or Syrah. No Merlot."

"Merlot can be good."

"So can cat shit," he says. "If it's buried in the dirt where I don't have to smell it." He waves and turns to walk away, a swagger in his step that wasn't there before.

Fernando can't resist putting on a show, even when he knows the audience isn't interested. Hitch is as straight as a stick, and—if Fern's stories are to be believed—not only in his sexual tastes. The old Hitch considered skinny dipping in the lake behind his house the only respectable form of exercise. Well, that, and other clothing-optional activities that work up a sweat . . .

Activities that I *refuse* think about.

I clear my throat. "Heard you were up at five to go jogging. Intense."

The smile he put on for Fern slips. "I couldn't sleep, and I had some other business to take care of. Thought I might as well do something productive. This whole thing is just . . ."

His eyes scrunch with worry and for the first time I notice the tiny wrinkles around his baby blues. He looks older, tired . . . scared. The only time I've seen Hitch scared was when he was seconds away from being torn apart by a swarm of fairies. He's not immune. Even one bite would have killed him. Maybe instantly, the way fairy bites killed most of his highly allergic family during the initial emergence.

And now he's scared again. It brings home the danger we're facing in a meaningful way, but I'm still not as frightened as I should be. But then I don't have a great job, a beautiful fiancée, or a baby on the way. I have less to lose, and magic on my side.

On *our* side.

That's part of the reason I agreed to help Hitch. I know I have something to offer aside from the dumb luck of being immune to fairy bite. Too bad I can't tell *him* anything about that. Tucker made it clear the FBI is at the top of the list of people who do *not* need to know about the Invisibles or the things I'm learning to do with my newfound magic. Not that Hitch would believe me, anyway. The old Hitch, who came from bayou people and grew up on folktales about fairy lights at midsummer and enchanted alligator men, might have at least considered it, but this new Hitch is all facts and logic.

"This isn't going to be easy, or safe," he warns.

"But it matters to me. A lot. I have to find out who did this as quickly as I can."

"I'm sorry," I say, meaning it. "I should have met you earlier."

He shakes his head. "I really did have some other business to take care of. It's good you pushed us back until nine. And you don't have to be here at all, you know. You can still walk away. I won't hold it against you."

"No. I'm here." Even slackers have codes, and being there for the people I care about is part of mine. "I'll help however I can. As long as you need me."

Relief makes Hitch's shoulders sag. He steps forward and for a second I think he's going to take my hand, but he doesn't. Instead, his fingers curl into fists that he stuffs in his pockets. "Thank you," he says, studying the gum-pocked asphalt. "I'm . . . glad."

Me, too. Glad he didn't touch me. Simply standing this close to him is enough to make my chest ache.

"No worries," I say, voice as light as I can make it. "What's the plan?"

He searches the alley behind me and then casts a glance over his shoulder in true paranoid spy fashion. "I have two supervisors I can trust. If we get the name of the FBI operative involved in this or even a firm location on the cave, I'll feel comfortable turning the investigation over. But I can't risk it right now. Even if they believed me, we'd waste time with preliminaries and give whoever killed Steven a chance to cover his tracks."

I nod. "If someone in the organization killed him,

you can't let them know you're looking into the murder until you have real evidence."

"Right." The tension around his eyes eases. "So I thought you could take a trip out to the docks this morning. In the information Steven sent me, he included the shipping manifests from the Gramercy port, just south of here. They've had a lot of discrepancies in the past few years. At first it was the usual stuff—a few leather coats gone missing, a box of designer purses that fell off the barge, that sort of—"

"I remember that. One of the Junkyard Kings was selling Coach crap last Christmas."

He lifts a brow. "The Junkyard Kings?"

"The men singing down the street from my house last night," I say, remembering the way the Kings' song drifted through the muggy air, weaving Hitch and me closer together. "They live in the junkyard."

"And have delusions of grandeur."

"Don't we all?"

He rewards me with a tight smile. "I don't know. Do we?" His eyes meet mine and I see a hint of the old Hitch, *my* Hitch, the one who didn't have everything in the world figured out and secured with a regulation knot.

"I don't know." I shrug and look away, wishing every other moment with this man wasn't an exercise in extreme discomfort. "But the purses and crap . . . Isn't that part of doing business in the infested states? Don't most companies expect to lose stuff?"

"Sure. Some skimming is expected," he says, nudging a smashed paper cup under the Dumpster with his shoe. "But a few months ago, major shipments of medical supplies started disappearing from the Gramercy port. Over a hundred thousand dollars of product was lost in July and they're expecting higher numbers for August. The dock crew said the goods were gone when the boats arrived, but the captains swear they weren't boarded between Memphis and Gramercy. The supplies had to have been stolen while the dock workers were unloading the cargo for storage until the boats arrived from New Orleans and Galveston."

"Those are FCC operatives working out there." I can't help being shocked. The dock workers make at least thirty grand a year more than I do, and I make enough to have everything I need and a hundred thousand or so left over to donate to Sweet Haven. Pinching a few designer purses I can understand, but hundreds of thousands of dollars worth of medical supplies? "Those guys are getting paid very, *very* well."

"Maybe not well enough."

"Greedy bastards." I may slack and run late and be on suspension from sample collecting, but at least I don't steal from the people I'm supposed to be serving.

Though, really, what would I steal? Vials of swamp water? Fairy corpses? Poop?

"They're more than greedy, they're unexpectedly particular," Hitch says. "They left the morphine and the Percocet and all the other easy-to-sell script drugs. Instead, they took a few thousand glass hypodermic needles and three cases of fairimilus."

"I don't even know what that is."

"It's a rare cyclic peptide derived from a fungus. It's used as a serum in some malaria vaccines." He sounds doctory, but not in the condescending way. This morning, doctor sounds good on Hitch. "It keeps the vaccine fresh longer than synthetic peptides. It's also being used in the fairy venom vaccine research trials."

"Ohhh . . . kay," I say, connecting the dots. "So they've taken a super-rare serum and needles that can hold fairy venom without being corrupted the way metal would." The notion gives me an unpleasant scratchy feeling in my brain, but I ignore it.

The Big Man and Tucker deal in drugs and needles, but they're intensely antigovernment and have a small-time sneaky-criminal vibe. My gut tells me the Invisibles aren't connected to whatever's happening at the cave. If they were, Hitch's friend would have taken pictures of captives fighting someone they couldn't see as they were dragged away.

"You said some of the people involved used to work in chemical weapons development?" I ask.

"Right."

"So you're thinking they're working on a biological weapon. Using fairy venom."

He nods. "If they were working on a vaccine, there'd be no reason to keep it secret."

"And you're thinking someone in the FBI is helping coordinate the operation and keep it off the government's radar so these people don't get caught."

"That's exactly what I'm thinking." His dimple pops, and I find myself grinning back at him. To geeks like us, all this conspiracy talk is practically foreplay.

The thought makes me take an awkward step back. I pretend I'm checking the back door to Swallows for interlopers as I pull myself together. It's like Grace said in my dream: Lusting after Hitch is a good way to get burned.

"Why else would they need the glass needles?" he asks, seemingly oblivious to the way he affects me. "And why else would they set up shop in the middle of the bayou?"

"Well, it's isolated, not a lot of cops risk going out there, and those who do are too busy rounding up infected highwayman types to notice people hiding out in a cave. Even the helicopter patrols wouldn't see them if they're underground most of the time," I say, always willing to play the devil's advocate. "Steven and the Breeze task force were probably the first law enforcement on the ground that far out in the bayou in years. Anyone could be doing anything out there."

"True," he says, though I can tell he isn't buying. "But I think this is about weaponizing fairy venom."

"I think you're right."

"You do?" His eyebrows lift.

"The swamp around Donaldsonville has the highest concentration of egg-laying fairies in the infested region," I say. "If they're looking for a steady source of venom, this is the place to be."

"I agree."

"We agree. Good." I cross my arms and nod, trying to act like Hitch and I being on the same page is business as usual. "And we also agree I should go out to the docks and see if I can figure out who those guys are stealing medical supplies for."

"You can pretend you're interested in a job transfer."

"I'm ready to give up scooping poop and become a thieving scumbag and I need them to tell me how to get in on the action." I smile, starting to look forward to my mission. Dramatics can be fun. As long as they're not of the personal variety. "I'll bring my Coach bag and look greedy."

"Good."

"Good."

"Agreeing." He chucks me on the shoulder with a light fist. "This is nice."

"You sound surprised."

He shrugs. "Well . . . we didn't get along so well the last time I was here."

Right. We didn't get along *at all*. Except for the times when we *did*, like when he tried to save my life and I ended up saving his instead and we made out like randy teenagers in the front seat of my boyfriend's police cruiser.

Cane wasn't there at the time, of course, but he saw the recording. Hitch and I unknowingly activated the camera on the dashboard when he hit the sirens to scare away the fairies. Cane's face after he watched that amateur video was painful, to say the least. The recording, and the fact that I lied about knowing Hitch when he first showed up in Donaldsonville, led to our extended time-out. Cane says he's forgiven me, but sometimes I wonder . . .

Hitch offered to talk to him—to apologize and explain that the kiss was just a reaction to a near death experience—but I declined. I didn't think it would help, and a part of me didn't want Hitch to apologize. I didn't want him to be sorry for a kiss that felt so much like going home.

I glance up at his scruffy face, and for a second I would swear Hitch is thinking about those minutes when we got along so well, too. But then he smiles, an innocent grin without a hint of longing in it, and I feel like a fool. "But I'm glad," he says. "Really glad."

"Me, too."

"I already rented a car for you, a Land Rover in case you need to go off-road. I parked near the bus station." He starts for the end of the alley, but stops when he sees I'm not following.

"Thanks. But . . ." I glance down at my not-trying-too-hard outfit and sigh. "I should run home and change before I go."

"Why?"

"The dock agents are both men. They come into town for groceries and booze every few weeks. They're probably fairly desperate for female companionship, so I—"

"But it's an hour drive. Right?" His forehead furrows and an exclamation point made of stress forms between his eyes.

"Yeah. Maybe an hour and fifteen if the roads aren't in good shape after the rain."

"You should get started," he says. "The sooner you

get there, the sooner you get back, the sooner we can decide on our next step."

"If I can't get one of them to talk, there might not *be* a next step."

"You'll get them to talk. Or I will." His jaw muscle clenches and I can tell he's thinking about how he'll pound the truth out the men at the docks if I fail, but even *I* know what a stupid plan that is.

"Hitch, please." I'm tempted to lay a calming hand on his arm, but know contact between us is never calming. "A few minutes of preparation could save a lot of time in the long run, and spare you a trip out to the bayou."

"I have my suit with me. I'll be fine."

"Yes, but if these guys are working with the people in the cave, it's going to get around that some dude in a superexpensive fairy-repelling iron suit only the FBI can afford questioned them. You may get information, but whoever killed Steven will also know that someone's on his trail. Right now, I think it's safer for everyone involved if you're not seen at the docks."

"I'm not planning on being seen. Not unless I have to be."

"Then let's make sure you don't have to be. Let me go home and—"

"But you look fine."

"Fine?"

"Yeah. Fine," he snaps, suddenly very interested in the brick wall behind me.

"Fine as in, I'm not going to make anyone run screaming? Or fine as in, able to seduce information from men who have no doubt been instructed not to talk?"

He finally makes eye contact, but I wish he hadn't. "Fine as in, you're a good-looking woman in skintight jeans and no bra who looks like you just rolled out of bed after being fucked. Repeatedly."

Woah. That wasn't what I was expecting. At. All.

I don't know how to handle that tone, *that* tone that says he's noticed that I'm not wearing a bra and still thinks I'm good-looking and wonders who's been making me look just-been-fuckedish.

My mouth opens, but I don't know what to say. All I know is that the way he said the F word makes me want to do it. Right now. On the ground by the stinky Dumpster. Screw Cane and Stephanie and anyone who walks out the door. Any sacrifice or embarrassment would be worth feeling Hitch's skin against mine. Just one more time.

"So believe me." He's looking at the wall again. I'm glad. "You'll be fine."

"Okay." I clear my throat and make a serious face and pretend I'm not thinking about my hands on his skin or his hands on my ass or how good it would be to be wrapped up in Hitch so tight he could never let me go again.

You're the one who let go. You're the one who let him assume the worst and walked away.

Whatever. Even if I'd told him the truth, he wouldn't have believed me. His face when he walked in our house that morning said it all. He was positive I'd willingly banged his brother's brains out. He'd heard Anton's version of events; he wasn't interested in hearing mine. Or what I remembered of them, anyway.

That night with his brother is still a blur. A horrible blur, that ends with me waking up bleeding and hurting and so ashamed I can't stop being sick. Maybe it was the Jack Daniel's I drank the night before that made me toss cookies for an hour. Maybe it was something Anton slipped into my drink to make sure I was "the dirtiest lay he'd ever had" that turned my stomach inside out.

I'm guessing the second option, but it's only a guess. And a guess about something that happened six years ago means nothing in the here and now.

No matter how he looks at me or what I feel, there's no future for me and Hitch. We can't even be friends. It's impossible to be friends with a man who makes you want to bang him in front of a Dumpster with a few husky words.

"Are you sure Stephanie's okay with you doing this?" I ask, driving the truth home with a sledgehammer.

"I don't want to talk about Stephanie."

I ignore the warning in his tone. "Why? Because she hates that you're risking your life while she's back in New Orleans knocked up and waiting to see if the father of her child is coming home? How do you think that makes her feel?"

His lips curl and I see the increasingly familiar disgust for me lurking beneath his smile. "And you care because . . . ?"

"Why wouldn't I care? About your wife and baby?"

"My fiancée," he corrects before he realizes what he's doing, that he's emphasizing that his future with Stephanie isn't set in stone.

When he does, I watch the knowledge that he's slipped flicker across his face, followed closely by fear. Fear that I've noticed he has a problem calling Stephanie his wife. That maybe he isn't as thrilled to be promising his future to another woman as I've been led to believe.

"Your fiancée," I concede, carefully, not wanting to make a big deal out of his moment of weakness. We all have them. They don't mean anything. They're a moment, here and gone. "But you know what I mean. Your actions affect your family. They need you alive."

"I know that, Annabelle," he says, with forced patience. "But I have to do this. There is no other option. Stephanie and I are on the same page and frankly, even if we weren't, it isn't your place to comment on my personal life."

Ouch. Right. Because I'm not a part of his personal life anymore. I'm just an immune person he's asked to help him solve a murder. He might have regained a small amount of respect for me, but he doesn't care about me or like me or have any interest in what I might think or feel. My opinion doesn't matter to him. *I* don't matter to him, and I'd be stupid to forget it.

"I apologize," I say. "Again."

"Apology accepted." His gentle tone makes me want to punch him in the face. How dare he? How *dare* he act like he's letting me down easy when *he's* the one who refused to call his future wife his wife and said scandalous things about how bedable I am and all but *penetrated* me with his sex eyes?

He's *impossible*. I remember why I couldn't stand to be around him the last time he was here. Fern is right; Hitch is Jerkface McSmuggy and I've had my fill of him for the morning.

"Keys, please." I hold out my hand, palm up.

"You're sure you know—"

"I know what to do. I'll get something we can use." I cross my fingers and hope I'm right. I need Hitch out of here as quickly as possible and right now the dock workers are our only lead. "In the meantime, you might want to act like you're doing follow-up work on the Breeze investigation. Otherwise, people are going to wonder why you're spending time with me."

"Can't two old college friends spend a long weekend catching up?"

"No. They can't. Not when they're us."

His smile vanishes. "Okay. I'll put on my pretty clothes and make a few business calls. Call me when you're done and we'll arrange a place to meet. But don't say anything important on the phone. Cell signals might not be secure."

I give him a thumbs-up with only a hint of smartass in it, and start down the alley, doing my best to eliminate the wiggle from my walk. Unlike Fernando, I'm not into putting on a show for people who couldn't care less.

"Annabelle?" I think about pretending I didn't hear him, but then he calls again, "Annabelle?"

"Yes?" I turn to find him still standing by the Dumpster, his hands stuffed in his pockets, shoulders bunched, every inch of him screaming "I'm worried, I'm scared, and I'm not holding it together as well as I'm pretending," and I feel for him. He's a bossy, arrogant jerk I'm better off without, but he's also a bossy, arrogant jerk getting ready to put his life and future in serious danger.

"Please be careful," he says. "Really careful."

"I will."

"Careful for a normal person, not Annabelle careful." I'm halfway to an eye roll when he adds, "I won't be able to live with myself. If anything happens to you. Because of me."

Something in my core softens. "It wouldn't be because of you," I say. "This is my decision. I know what I'm doing."

"No you don't," he says, sucker punching my soft spot. "But thank you, anyway."

And what to say to that? Nothing. I've got nothing. Maybe Hitch is right. Maybe I am a clueless idiot, but I'm all he has.

So who's the real *idiot?*

The thought is strangely comforting. I spin on my heel and book it to the end of the alley before he says something so insulting I can't talk my way into feeling okay again.

5

The Land Rover Hitch rented is enormous and baby-poop green and drives like a shoe box on wheels. By the time I reach the iron gate, my bone marrow is rattling and my head feels like it's about to explode.

I curse myself for forgetting to throw ibuprofen in my purse and then curse myself again for leaving my gate remote in the junk drawer. Getting out to punch the button won't take *that* much time, but every second is precious. I can't wait to get to the docks and get back and be one step closer to getting Hitch out of my life.

The more I think about it, the more I realize I'm not clueless, I'm *insane*. The fact that I was even a *tiny* bit excited about working with Hitch proves it.

Just when I thought it was safe to go back in the self-esteem water, too . . .

I've cut back on my daily alcohol intake, thought seriously about trying to beat my Restalin habit, and usually get eight hours of sleep a night. I've spent my suspension from the FCC studying up on the new regs for sample collectors, taking Bernadette for rides in her Mustang, cleaning all the expired food out of my pantry, and stocking the fridge with fruits and veggies that I might actually eat at some point. I've even upped my flossing to twice a day. I'm completely boring and committed to establishing good habits.

"But still crazy," I mumble as I throw the Rover into park and jump out the door. By the time I smash the gate button and head back to the truck, the heat has stickied my skin and my upper lip is beaded with sweat.

The calendar might say it's nearly fall, but in southern Louisiana it still feels like deep summer. The heat is brain-boiling, and the air hums with millions of insects. The flies and mosquitoes have had so many hot, humid months to breed that not even the fairies—who make due with insects and animal blood when they can't get their fangs on the preferred human meal—can keep their numbers under control.

As I pull through the gate at the mandated five miles per hour, I see a few fairies floating in the shade by a knotty cypress, swooping in drowsy circles. One sees me and zips off into the bayou, but the rest keep playing a game that seems to involve kicking the smallest fairy against the trunk of the tree and seeing who can catch him before he hits the ground. A couple of them are into it, but the rest are giving the sport a half-assed effort at best.

The heat makes fairies lazy, listless. The Fey don't care for sunlight and are usually pretty tame during the day, especially in the summer months. It isn't until after sundown that they show their feral, predatory side and will swarm anything warm-blooded like a pack of rabid flying wolves.

Still, if I weren't immune, I have no doubt a couple of the buggers would come whizzing over to force their way in through the Rover's outside air vents. It's only the abnormal concentration of iron in my blood that makes them turn flat, bulbous eyes my way and go back to their game with a few shouted curses about "stupid poison people."

Stupid. Poison. People.

I hear the words, as clear as the squeal of the gate sliding closed behind me.

What the hell? My foot slips, stomping on the gas, making the truck leap forward with a roar. I slam on the brake and the Rover grinds to a stop, but everything inside me is still racing a hundred miles a minute.

I *heard* them. I heard the fairies *talk*. Words that I could understand. Scientists have yet to identify any spoken Fey language. The fairies communicate primarily via body language and scent cues given off during the mating season, with a few screeches and barks thrown in for emphasis. They slap each other around. They stink up the bayou every spring with pheromone spray. They. Don't. Talk.

But they did. I *swear* to god they did. Just like last night in my dream.

The prune-faced fairy's warning to get out of Donaldsonville before I'm a dead woman floats through my mind. I fight for my next breath, then turn back to the road and squeeze the steering wheel so tight it feels like the tendons in my hand are going to snap.

Because *there* he is, there he *fucking* is, floating in the air in front of my goddamned windshield.

I blink and choke and spit out, "What the fucking fuck!" thinking maybe words will make him vanish. But they don't, they only give me an earful of how terrified and foulmouthed I sound.

The nightmare on the other side of the glass smiles, fluttering to the right and the left, grinning like a jaundiced demon, rubbing his paunch belly with one hand and flipping me off with the other. I stare hard at his tiny fingers. That's his middle digit all right, poked up into the air—deliberate, intentional, and so human-looking it makes my stomach roil.

I'm crazy. I really am. I'm out of my bleeping mind and experiencing auditory and visual hallucinations. Symptoms of late-onset schizophrenia and psychotic depression zip through my head, but are quickly discarded by the wannabe doctor within me. There's no history of that sort of crazy in my family. We're a pale, pasty, depressed lot who hit the bottle more than we should; we're not the people at the homeless shelter who think the aliens are lasering our eyes shut while we sleep.

Of course, most of the people I've seen like that are addicts in addition to being bat-shit crazy.

The drugs. *Crap*. It has to be the drugs. Whatever Tucker shot me up with must be making me hallucinate.

Or maybe it's wearing off. Like with Grace. Maybe it's time for another dose before you go off the deep end and start killing fluffy things for fun.

"Okay. Okay," I mumble beneath my breath, wishing I had a phone number where I could reach Tucker.

Hell, I wish I'd taken him up on his offer to roll around in bed. Then I'd be with him right now, able to get immediate feedback on which kind of drug reaction I'm having. Too much or too little, it has to be one. It *has* to be.

I cling to the thought as I reach over to kick up the air-conditioning. Maybe the cold will shock me back to my senses. I close my eyes and think calm, hallucination-banishing thoughts, but when I open them again, the fairy is still there. He's closer now, and taking his obscene gesturing to the next level. His hand is under his paunch, and I can imagine what he's playing with beneath his saggy skin.

"Gross," I say, as much to myself as the fairy.

He's a figment of my imagination after all. I'm the one imagining this. *Why,* I have no idea, since I'm pretty sure I don't have any deeply repressed desire to watch an old man touch himself, but . . .

"Not gross. Slake." His voice is muted by the windshield, which seems weird for an auditory hallucination. Would my mind work in a detail like that?

It must be. There's no other explanation. Don't get any nustier than you are already.

Right on, mental voice. Fairies don't talk, and there's no way I could be seeing a character from a dream in real life. "You aren't real. I'm going to stop seeing you now," I say, hoping it will work the way it did when I was asleep.

"Am real. Am Slake." His jaw drops and greenish liquid oozes from his gums to coat his fangs. Venom. Thicker and nastier than anything I've seen before. "Slake."

"Yeah, I hear you," I say, voice shaking.

"Hear and know." He's close enough to touch the windshield, close enough for me to catch a glimpse of the holes in his left wing and the wrinkles creasing his itty-bitty sunken cheeks. "We are the Slake. Our thirst is great. It will never be appeased."

I watch his lips move, mesmerized by the way they pinch and stretch, forming words. He looks so *real*. As real as the trees behind him and the sky above and the road stretching out through the bayou toward the docks. It's all the same, all as solid and three-dimensional and chock-full of detail. I can't tell the difference between what's real and what isn't.

Shit. I can't. I really can't.

What am I going to do? What the *hell* am I going to do?

"Leave our land," he growls. "Leave. Now."

My breath comes out in a rush. At least I know what this is about. When times get tough, Annabelle hits the road. It's what I've always done. I never stick around to suffer through the hard times. Hard times suck ass and make you want to off yourself and are best avoided at all costs. It was true after Caroline died, it was true when Hitch and I had the fight to end all fights, and a part of me must think it's true now. That's why my drug-addled mind created this freaky little man, to scare me into leaving Donaldsonville and all the hard stuff behind.

The mess with Cane, and Hitch popping back into my life are the least of my problems. Somehow I've fallen in with some very shady people. Invisible, magic people who could kill me before I even know they're in the room. Being able to float a beer from my fridge out to my chair on the porch with my mind power isn't going to protect me. Even being able to heal a gunshot wound won't help if they hit me in the right spot. One bullet to the brain and my mind won't be powering anything anymore. The smartest thing I could do is take a clue from my crazy and leave Donaldsonville before it's too late.

"But what about the shots?" I stare the fairy straight in the eye, willing my subconscious to listen. "I have ten. I could go give myself one right now and hope you go away, but what about when they run out? And what about all the people in town? Fernando and Cane and Theresa and the guys from the bar and Bernadette and Deedee?"

God, poor Deedee. I haven't been out to see her in days. Libby Beauchamp murdered her mom and now eight-year-old Deedee is one of the youngest orphans at Sweet Haven. She begs me to let her come stay with me every time we hang out. I know I'm not foster mommy material, but I can't leave her with no one to visit her, no one to care that her entire life's been ruined.

Not when I played my part in getting her mother killed.

"I can't leave," I say, voice stronger, ignoring the fairy's increasingly pissed-off expression. "I can't leave without knowing what the Big Man is doing, or why Tucker is in town. And what about the cave? Whatever's going down there isn't good. Someone's already dead, and—"

"Die." The fairy kicks the windshield. "*You'll* die."

"No. I'm not going to die." I point a finger at his prune face. "I'm going to stick around and figure things out and make my life work. I am not a clueless idiot! I am not a loser! I am not a child!"

And I don't protest too much. At all.

"We would have killed child if someone hadn't killed her first," he spits, his yellow face flushing red. "We'll suffer no more Gentry!"

It's what he said in my dream, but he's a hell of a lot more pissed off about it now, and I can't even imagine what my subconscious is trying to tell me. The only Gentry I know of live in England, where it's too cold to have to worry about fairy infestation or venom infection or invisible people or magic or iron-gated towns where people are always on the verge of losing their minds with fear.

England. That's where I'll go. Or maybe Ireland. The Lees are Irish. My grandfather traced our ancestry all the way back to medieval times. He even forced my father to name me Annabelle after some ancient relative. I could go there, buy a cottage in a quiet village by the sea, take up sheepherding, and learn to act like I'm not crazy. Or drink enough that the towns-people blame the talking-to-things-that-aren't-there on the alcohol.

"Leave." The fairy points to the gate. "Leave."

My hands squeeze the steering wheel even tighter. Maybe I *should* turn around. I could be back at the house and shooting up another dose of mystery medicine in fifteen minutes. But what if I'm wrong? What if more drug makes me worse instead of better? What if I end up rocking in a corner, slobbering on myself and talking to invisible fairies all day and never make it out to the docks?

Hitch is expecting me to call him in a few hours. If I don't call, he'll come looking for me, and if he finds me at home I'll never be able to explain. If I try, I'll be putting his life in even more danger than he's put mine. The Big Man won't hesitate to kill him if he finds out Hitch knows about the Invisibles or the shots or the magic or anything else. Of that, I have no doubt.

"I have to keep going. I have someplace to be," I say in a calm, even tone.

"Go away!" The fairy's shout ends in a familiar Fey screech. I decide to take that as a good sign.

I slam my foot down on the gas. The fairy shoots straight up into the air, barely avoiding becoming a squishy spot on my windshield as the truck roars down the road. I can't help but be disappointed. It would have been nice to see his guts splattered, even if they are imaginary guts.

I check my rearview in time to see the old man flip me the bird again before whizzing off into the bayou. My hands relax and I breathe a little easier. It's over. And it didn't last that long. Not much longer than the dream, and I had a good hour and a half of normal in between the dream and the hallucination. If I book it and have luck on my side, I can make it to the dock and talk to the guys there before I start seeing things again.

"Better not count on luck," I mumble as I give the Rover more gas, kicking the jostle into a full-on bone rattle.

Lucky isn't a word that applies to my life. I need to think of a Plan B. They have to have toilets out at the docks. If I start seeing things, I'll fake a potty emergency and go hide out in the lav until I talk myself down from the edge. Then, as soon as I get back to Donaldsonville, I'll go on a hunt for Tucker. I know he's living somewhere close enough for him to get to my house with wet hair. If I have to, I'll search every formerly vacant house in the town until I find him and—

My thoughts are interrupted by a high-pitched screech and then another and another, until the screech becomes a roar, a wave of sound that smacks into the truck hard enough to make it vibrate. I scream and slam on the brakes, hunching my shoulders, squeezing my eyes closed, smashing my hands over my ears as hundreds of rocks thud against the side of the truck.

Thud, thud, thud-thud-thud-thud-thud-thud!

Not rocks. Rocks don't thud; they ping or crack. But what else could it—

I slit my eyes—still afraid of shattering glass—in time to see another fairy hit the window. And another and another and another, pink and golden bodies slamming into the Rover's side until they block the sunlight and hundreds of tiny shoving hands become thousands of tiny shoving hands and the world tilts on its axis.

No, not the world. The truck. They're lifting a *two-ton* truck off its wheels. They're trying to tip me over.

I whip my head toward the other window to see water rising all the way to the side of the road. The bayou's deep here. If the truck flips, it's going to sink until it's submerged. Then I'll have two choices: stay in the cab until it fills with water and I drown, or get out and make a run for the iron gate.

I'll never make it. There's no way. It's like I was thinking in my dream last night. If enough of this swarm decides to bite me, I'll bleed to death and immunity won't matter.

"It was just a dream," I shout as I hit the gas pedal. The truck rolls forward on its two right wheels, but the fairies don't miss a beat. They fly alongside, pushing hard enough that the Rover's center of gravity begins to shift. I slam on the brakes, surprising enough of the Fey that the left side dips back toward the ground.

Last night might have been a dream, but this is real. I'm not hallucinating the two tons of steel shifting and rocking around me. There's no way the truck could be moving except—

"Me!" I shout, hope exploding in my chest like a firework. I can move things with my mind. I must be doing this. I must be hallucinating the fairies and—

The Land Rover lurches to the right and the fairies scream in anticipation of their victory and there's no more time left for coming to logical conclusions. I force fear away and lash out. The part of my brain I've come to associate with supernatural phenomenon sparks to life, humming and sizzling, making the place where brain meets spinal cord hot enough for sweat to break out on the back of my neck.

I imagine the wheels moving back toward the ground, the truck righting itself, and for a second, I think it's going to work. I'm moving in the right direction, I'm taking control. But then I see him—the old fairy, hovering behind the rest, his angry raisin face barely visible through the crush of wings and tiny fingers pressed tight to the glass. He lifts his arms and let's out a series of barks that summon a round of howls from his army.

Suddenly I *know* this isn't a hallucination. That old geezer is real. So is his army, and so is the death waiting for me as soon as the truck rolls over.

The fairies surge forward with renewed strength and the truck is going, going, going, and I know there's no way I'm going to stop it and I'm already bracing myself for the impact with the water when the thought whips through my head.

The fairies. If you can't move the truck, stop the fairies.

I talked Stephanie's lungs back together. If I can heal; I can also hurt.

I lean into the window, pressing my hands against the glass, feeling the heat from all those burning Fey fingers against mine, and send everything I have out into the swarm. I imagine my energy spreading like poison gas, seeping into their bones, turning them to jelly. Visions of limp, useless arms and wings shoot from my mind, and before I have time to wonder if my last-ditch effort is going to be good enough, they're dropping like feral, toothy flies.

Screeches become squeals of pain and the hands glued to the glass fall away.

Plop. Plop, plop, plop-plop-popalop-plop.

Dozens hit the dirt and the shoving comes to an abrupt stop as the fairies still left alive flee into the bayou. Still, for a moment, it seems my reprieve has come too late. The Rover teeters on two wheels—caught between upright and up and over—while my heart leaps in my throat and my thoughts jerk from the fairies back to the vehicle just in time.

Down! Down!

The truck slams back to the ground with enough force to send me bouncing into the ceiling. My head hits with a crack and my teeth knock together and I taste blood, but it tastes amazing because I'm alive and whole and then my hands are on the wheel and my foot is on the accelerator and I'm peeling down the gravel road so fast that by the time I get up the guts to look in the rearview mirror, I can't see anything but my own dust.

But I'd be able to see the fairy glow through the haze. If they were following me, I'd know about it. I'm safe. For now.

As safe as any person can be whose nightmares are coming true.

6

The bridge over the muddy Mississippi is the first smooth stretch of road. I hit the graying pavement and the rattle inside the truck becomes a high-pitched whine that threatens to kick my migraine into skull-shattering territory.

I know fairies can't follow me onto a bridge made entirely of iron, but I don't pull over. I grit my teeth and ignore the pain like I've ignored every terror-filled thought that's raced through my mind since I left the turn in the road past Donaldsonville. I can't think about how close I came to dying. I have to focus and get the information Hitch needs.

Then I can start stressing about an army of fairies out to kill me and the insanity of dreaming something that came true and the throat-clutching fear that grips me every time I think about having to drive back the way I came.

I'll have to. There's no other way back to D'Ville. The only other bridge close by was blown up three years ago. The self-declared cotton baron of Louisiana—an immune man who took over several plantations and the historic mansions on them after their owners died in the fairy emergence—destroyed it to get a leg up on his competition. Now, the only way to get cotton out of this part of Louisiana is via the river dock on Baron von Greedy's property.

"Greed, greed, and more greed," I mutter, narrowing my eyes as the dock's main building comes into view.

The structure crouches in the shadow of a long vacant petrochemical plant and has a charming view of the barbed-wire fence the FCC installed on both sides of the river last year in hopes of deterring pirate attacks on the barges. But if you ignore the post-apocalyptic scenery, the facility is downright swanky. It's about four thousand square feet, a three-story iron building with glass walls that sparkle in the sun. It's big enough for half the town of Donaldsonville to live in, but houses only two men. I know the dudes who man the dock work long hours—punching in the commands for the robots who do all the loading and unloading of the ships that pass through—but do they deserve this kind of luxury? Simply because they won the immunity lottery?

It doesn't seem right. But if the government didn't pay the immune well, most of us would quit working for Uncle Sam and find someone willing to pay a better wage. There are independently owned companies doing business in the Delta, too, and they always need immune employees, especially ones who are qualified to do more than not get infected.

My premed degree has earned me cushy job offers

from several private research facilities. I've turned them all down. I'm too lazy for the long hours, and the salaries were scandalous. I didn't see how anything I'd be doing would be worth millions of dollars per year. Most people don't have that problem. I'm definitely in the minority when it comes to feeling bad about scarfing down more than my fair share simply because I can get away with it.

It's too easy to get away with it these days. With so many people dead and 95 percent of the fairy-infested states living in mortal fear, the immune can get away with murder.

Maybe even literally, in this case.

I wonder if the dock workers know that their black-market dealings led to at least one person's death. I wonder if they would care if they did. After all, isn't one life an acceptable price to pay when it comes to getting rich and living large?

"One life." My foot eases off the gas and inspiration strikes like a Zeus-hurled lightning bolt to my brain.

Hitch's friend wasn't some random murder. He was killed because he knew too much. He was a threat that had to be eliminated for the safety of whatever shady business is going down in the cave, a threat serious enough for the high-ranking FBI traitor in charge to risk exposure to take him out.

To date, scientific observations of the Fey have shown them to be nonverbal, antisocial creatures incapable of complex thought. But what if that's a smoke screen? What if the little bastards are way smarter than we've given them credit for? What if they've been hiding in plain sight, using the fact that we underestimate them to their advantage, secretly planning some kind of fairy uprising?

If so, what humans don't understand about them would be the fairies' biggest strength. They wouldn't tip their hand unless they had a very good reason, a serious threat that had to be eliminated.

Like, say, an immune woman with the ability to take them out with a thought.

Holy shit. I've been so busy trying not to think, I've missed the single most important aspect of what went down on the road.

The fairies lost. I beat them, with a highly effective, nontoxic weapon that might be able to succeed where chemical companies have failed. So far, the only pesticides capable of killing the Fey are deadly to everything else—humans, animals, even plants and trees. The Fey are crazy hard to kill, damned near indestructible.

But maybe they're not. And maybe they know it.

And maybe they're willing to risk revealing their true intelligence in the name of eliminating a person who could maybe—just maybe—take care of the Delta's fairy problem once and for all.

Holy crapping shit crap.

Could I? Could I really? The fairies by the truck looked dead when they fell, but even if they weren't, they were definitely incapacitated. I could have gathered them up in an iron box while they were passed out. I could go out into the bayou and keep stunning and gathering until they're gone. All of them. Until every adult is captured or killed and every egg sac collected. Until, someday, it might finally be safe for people to walk outside the iron gates again.

Hope hits me in the gut, so fierce it's painful.

We've all spent so many years thinking there's no going back, that we have to live with the constant undercurrent of terror because there's nothing that can be done. But maybe there is, maybe—

"Stop the truck!" An amplified voice shouts. I look up to see a man with a megaphone. And a mean-looking rifle. "I'll shoot!"

I'm so wrapped up in my thoughts that—by the time I spot him—I'm almost on top of him. I slam on the brakes, but I don't know if it's going to make a difference. He might still decide to shoot me. I can read the temptation in the twitchy eye peering down the barrel of his gun.

Jin-Sang, my boss at FCC headquarters in Baton Rogue, is a douche canoe. He's also a religious fanatic, a control freak, a tight-ass teetotaler, suffers from a severe case of OCD, a superiority complex, and misuses the English language in a fashion that should be criminal in someone who thinks he's so much better than everyone else.

In addition to his many faults, he's also responsible for my monthlong suspension from work, despite the fact that Stephanie—Hitch's fiancée and the FBI agent in charge of my review—recommended I be reinstated with a warning.

To put it mildly, Jin-Sang and I are not best bud-dies. In fact, I think I could come to *hate* Jin-Sang if I had the energy to walk around hating people I don't see every day. So to say that I'm surprised to hear him reaming the dock agent who held the gun on me via speakerphone is an understatement.

"This is unacceptable! Agent Lee is a valuable association of our team. Disrespect her further, and there will be the supreme high price for your pay-ment. Supreme!" There's enough heat in his tone to make the agent slumping behind the desk flinch.

A little.

Ferret Face, as I've dubbed him—because his pointy nose, rodent teeth, and shaggy brown hair are ferretlike, and because he didn't bother telling me his name before shoving me through an oversized garage and into his second-floor office with the business end of his rifle—isn't super responsive to stimuli. Judging from the glassy eyes and slightly slurred speech when he demanded I call my boss and prove I'm FCC, I'm guessing he's stoned.

Which is *really* comforting in someone who's pointing a gun at your forehead.

"He's still got the gun, Jin-Sang." I try to sound as bored as Ferret Face looks. I've met his type before. With a man like him, apathy is power.

"Down your weapon quick time! Super quick time!" Jin-Sang's English is deteriorating rapidly. It's as if he actually *cares* whether or not I get killed.

Aw.

"Don't bust a nut." Ferret Face tips back in his chair,

summoning a groan from the springs as he leans the rifle against the bookcases behind him. "Sorry."

His expression couldn't be more flagrantly unapologetic. So much for finding a desperate, horny man willing to spill secrets in hopes of scoring with the first woman he's seen in weeks. I'll just have to hope the other guy shows up soon, and is in more of a welcoming mood.

"Sorry is inadequate," Jin-Sang says. "You threatened Ms. Lee with a loaded weapon."

"I never chambered a round." FF yawns, showcasing a mouth full of yellow teeth. No wonder this guy is okay with living almost alone in the middle of nowhere. He's repulsive.

"That is not significant." Jin-Sang's volume begins to build. "What is significant is that your tone is unacceptable and your mouth is in bad, bad shape." If he only knew. "I am your superior. You do not speak at me with words like *nuts* and—"

I lean over and grab the receiver, muting Jin-Sang as the speaker cuts off. "Hey, Jin. It's me," I say. "You're off speakerphone. I'm fine. Thanks for the positive ID."

"What are you doing, Annabelle?" he snaps. "The road out to the docks is dangerous."

"I live for danger."

"This is not the time for jokes." I can hear his V-shaped frown. "There are criminals on that road. Highwaymen who kidnap women and children."

"They'd bring me back," I say. "I'm more trouble than I'm worth."

Jin-Sang sighs, but doesn't rush to agree with me, which makes me feel sort of bad. I'm not in the mood to give him shit right now, but old habits die hard, and I can tell my lousy attitude is winning me a point or two with Ferret Face.

Or maybe half a point. With the zombie eyes it's hard to tell.

"I wanted to take a look around," I say. "I'm thinking of applying for a transfer."

"A transfer," Jin repeats, like I've said I'm thinking about sprouting tusks and going to live with the wild boar.

His obvious lack of faith in my transferable potential makes the smart-ass come easier. "Yeah. I think I'm tired of scooping poop. But maybe I've just forgotten what worthwhile work it is. You know, since I've been suspended from my life's calling for nearly a month and all."

"Your suspension was necessary." He's starting to sound tired and cranky. Either the fear for my life has passed, or he's remembering why he shouldn't care if I get shot at close range. "The rules are the rules."

"Maybe I like the rules for dock workers better."

"Annabelle, this is not good to hear." His response blows my mind. I thought he'd be thrilled to get me out of his hair. "We'll discuss this when you return to work."

"Why don't we discuss it now?" I push. "Ferret Face thinks I'd make a great coworker. Don't you Ferret Face?" I smile, a sarcastic twist of my lips that makes something in FF's eyes come to life for the first time.

"Sure," he smirks back. "Break up the sausagefest around here."

Sausagefest, indeed. Maybe he's not beyond the reach of feminine wiles.

"See." I lean over and steal a piece of candy from his desk. "The Ferret is on board."

"What are you talking at?" Jin-Sang asks.

"I think it's pretty clear. I'm talking at a transfer to—"

"No. No, no, no. I can't have discussions on this. I have instructions."

What? I stop unwrapping my stolen butterscotch. "What kind of instructions?"

He pauses before stating, "My advisor told me not to have talks until you return to work."

My feigned cool slips. *"What?"*

He sighs. "He sent paperwork on you last week."

"What kind of paperwork?"

His sigh becomes a grunt. "I can't tell you."

"What the hell, Jin?" I can't believe this. I can't *fucking* believe this. What have I done? I've been a good little suspended agent. At least until I agreed to help with an illegal investigation. But there's no way the people at Keesler knew about that last week. *I* didn't even know about that last week. "This is total—"

"I can't tell you that you will be drug tested on your first day back at work," Jin says in a quiet voice that is, nevertheless, quite effective in shutting me up. "I also cannot tell you that the drug tests will continue every other week for the next six months.

And I most certainly cannot tell you that testing positive could result in you being taken into military custody and held in isolation at Keesler's Biloxi base, pending a second internal review of your conduct."

What the . . . ?

Who knew Jin had it in him to make sense for so many consecutive sentences?

Who knew that the FCC could become so completely whacked?

This is nuts. I've never heard of anything like this. The FCC doesn't drug test their employees or pull them into military custody for a little drug use. After the emergence, Keesler Air Force Base in Biloxi was fortified with iron and redesigned to make room for the families previously living off base. Most military operations were moved to the National Guard base in Gulfport, where immune air force personnel work with the FCC to supervise the camp for the infected. The Keesler camp keeps everyone plenty busy. They don't go looking for FCC ops to arrest. Only the worst of the worst end up in solitary in a Biloxi prison cell. It's like I was thinking on the bridge—immune people can practically get away with murder. I know I messed up when I tied up that Breeze addict and left her in the bayou in August, but the FBI found her a few days later. She's fine, I've been reviewed by a respected member of the New Orleans FBI, and all the hand-slapping should be behind me.

But it isn't behind me, and this is a lot more serious than a slap on the hand. I don't do any recreational drugs that would show up in a test, but what about the injections? Will they show? Will my cure become my curse when I'm forced to pee in a cup in a few days? If so, how will I explain what I'm on without breaking the promises I've made to the Big Man? Even locked up in a military installation, I won't feel safe. If I break my word, he will find me and kill me. I know that. I *know* it.

"This is not fair," I whisper.

In another rare display of compassion, Jin-Sang says, "It will be all right." He must think this is bullshit, too, or he wouldn't be giving me the heads-up. "Don't hurry to come in on Wednesday. Take as much time as you need to make sure you're clean."

"Of course I'm clean." I try to muster up some righteous indignation, but I don't sound very convincing.

Ferret Face smirks another knowing smirk.

"Good." Jin-Sang doesn't sound convinced, either. "Then you will do what the people are asking for some weeks, show everyone this is unnecessary precautions, and I will petition to discontinue the testing."

"Okay," I grumble.

"And then you will move on to your future. Hopefully, that will be here with us."

"You really want me back?" I ask, no longer able to keep my surprise at this lovefest concealed.

"My cousin's maternity leave ends in three weeks," Jin says. "She is very excited to show all the baby pictures. She would be sad to learn I let one of her field agents leave the office without protest."

"Oh . . . well . . ." I've missed Min-Hee; I want to see the baby pictures. I never wanted a stupid transfer, but now I might have no choice. I have to find out if that shot is going to screw me.

I add another burning question to my list of things to drill Tucker about and tell Jin-Sang, "Thanks. For . . . yeah. See you soon."

I hang up the phone to find an eager-looking Ferret Face leaning across the desk with a handful of tea bags. "Tea time? Do you have any scones?"

He grins, the nicest grin I've seen from him so far. "This ain't just any tea. It's caterpillar fungus from Tibet. They only make a hundred pounds of this shit a year."

"Caterpillar fungus. Yummy." The deadpan delivery works its magic on FF, who graces me with a grunt-laugh.

"It tastes like ass flakes. But it works. Haven't had a positive piss test in six months. We got a fresh shipment in about an hour ago. I bagged it up myself." He motions for me to hold out my hand and tips the tea bags into my palm. There are five. "Let a bag sit in boiling hot water for ten minutes and then chug it as fast as you can. You'll pee clean for at least six weeks."

"Wow. This is generous."

His expression takes on an ugly edge. "Fuck yeah. I'm on your side. I mean who the fuck do these people think they are? I've worked for the FCC for four years and never had a goddamned drug test, and now, all of a sudden there are dickweeds in iron suits out here every few weeks making me piss in a cup? That's bullshit." He emphasizes the point by kicking his desk hard enough to make the phone rattle. "I do my job *fine* when I'm high. Shit, I do it *better*."

So he's being tested, too. It eases my mind. A little.

At least this isn't an Annabelle-only policy. They must be cracking down on all the people they suspect of having a habit. Jin-Sang thinks I drink too much and knows I occasionally take more Restalin per night than recommended by medical professionals. If he put that in his monthly report, it could have been enough to get me on the drug-abuse radar. But I'm cutting back on the Restalin and alcohol isn't going to show up in a test. Unless I'm drunk at the time, which doesn't happen during the day anymore.

At least . . . not as often.

Still, there's no way I'm going to turn down Ferret Face's tea bags. I might need them, and besides, drug abuse is bringing us together.

I lift my hip and tuck the bags into my back pocket. "So is that why you met me with a gun? You decided to shoot the next asshole who comes looking for a pee sample?"

He grunt-laughs again. "We just don't like unexpected company. You know how it is."

"Sure. I heard there were highwaymen on this road."

"Fuck them. I ain't scared of them."

"Then what are you scared of?" The second the question's out, I know I've pushed too hard. Ferret Face's mouth hardens and his eyes start to glaze over.

He shrugs. "Nothing."

"So this is a safe place to work?" I ask, trying to steer us back into lighter territory. "I'm serious about that transfer. You seem cool." I gesture to the pocket where his tea is snuggled in tight. "I could use a change. Sample collecting sucks it and the money is shit."

"Oh, the money's good out here."

"How good? Like FCC good, or like . . . serious cash good?"

"I don't get you."

"I've got debt. I had some problems a few months back," I say vaguely. "I owe a few different people. I'm not going to be able to pay unless I get a better job." I sigh and pick at a frayed seam on my jeans. "At this point I don't even know if I can stay with the FCC. I'm thinking about going downriver, seeing if the guy running the cotton plantation needs a pair of hands."

"I heard his people do pretty good."

"Yeah. It just stinks. I feel like I should stay with the FCC, but how do they expect us to make a living?" I ask with a tortured bat of my eyelashes. "They don't pay us half what we're worth. I swear, this is why people turn to a life of crime."

Ferret Face smiles an ugly, yellow smile. "Don't try it."

"Try what?"

"Don't try to work me."

"What?" I lift my eyebrows and feign innocence.

"I know why you're here, and it ain't because you want a transfer." He leans back in his chair, hand drifting closer to his rifle. "I don't like being fucked with."

"Okay." I let my eyes go as cold as his. "I know you're skimming the shipments. I want in."

"Fuck you," he says with a laugh.

"Fuck you," I say, finding it easy to take offense with his dismissal. "I'm immune, I've got connections in this parish, and I'm a hell of a lot more motivated than the homeless men you've got selling your shit right now. I could help you expand your business."

"Is that right?"

"That's right, Ferret Face."

He grins again, less ugly than before. "Lance."

"Annabelle."

"Annabelle." Recognition flashes in his eyes. "I've heard of you. You're the one who left the Breeze head tied up in the bayou."

"I did. I'm a total badass." I don't wait for him to finish laughing. "You should let me in on this. I'll transport product to Donaldsonville or wherever you need it delivered and I'll only ask for thirty percent of the cut."

He stares at me down the long slop of his rodent nose for a minute. Maybe two. Maybe three. All I know is the eye contact goes on way too long and I'm starting to feel uncomfortable in an I-could-be-dying-soon kind of way when he finally says, "Fifteen percent."

"Twenty-five," I counter, not wanting to betray how relieved I am.

He grunts. "We'll see. I gotta talk to Jose. He's the one with the major connections. I mostly do purses, designer clothes, shit like that."

"Okay." I shrug. "So Jose's in charge."

"I didn't say that. He works out the deals, but I know who he's working with and what she wants. She's the one who gets the biggest deliveries so . . . maybe that could be something we talk about. If we decide we can trust you."

"Don't I look trustworthy?"

"You look like trouble," he says in a way that leaves little doubt he has a thing for trouble. "But we'll see." He flicks a pen over to my side of the desk. "Give me a number and I'll call you tomorrow."

I scribble my cell number on a Post-it, and rack my brain for some way to keep the conversation going. What I've managed to learn so far only eliminates 48 percent of the population as a suspect. I need more. "So it's a woman I'd be delivering to? Is she cool?"

"She's a bitch. Even Jose doesn't fuck with her."

"Oh." I take a moment to look appropriately intimidated and second-thought-filled. "But I could handle it, right? She wouldn't like . . . shoot me or something?"

"I don't know what she'd do. I don't talk to her. I watch the meetings on the computer to make sure Jose doesn't end up dead while that bitch takes her needles without paying."

Needles. Score. And I could score even bigger. "You watch them on the computer. So you film them?" He nods. "Do you keep any of the footage?" I ask, hurrying on before the suspicion in his expression can fully flower. "It would be nice to see who I'd be dealing with. Right now I'm imagining someone with laser vision and fangs and flaming farts."

He laughs. Fart jokes. Gets 'em every time.

"Yeah. I've got video. I don't care if you get a look at her." He leans over and stirs the computer to life with a wiggle of the mouse. He clicks a folder and scrolls down through a long list of files. If they're all of this woman, she's a regular customer. "The camera Jose wears is small so the footage is grainy, but . . ." He clicks once more and swivels the screen my way. "There she is."

He's right. The picture quality is crap and if I weren't very familiar with the woman in question there's no way I'd be able to place her.

But, I am familiar. Gut-twistingly familiar. It's Marcy, my sweet, loving, takes-groceries-to-shut-ins second mama. *She's* the bitch buying black-market medical supplies, and this investigation just got a hell of a lot more personal.

7

I park the Rover behind the bank at the end of Railroad Street and head toward Swallows on foot. Most people in D'Ville walk or bicycle around town, so I probably could have scored a closer parking spot, but I need time to pull myself together. I need to walk, put one foot in front of the other until I talk myself into my lying headspace.

I'll have to be at the top of my game. Hitch can smell a fib at twenty paces. Just thinking about his narrow, I'm-looking-through-your-skin-and-see-your-filthy-lies look makes me feel vaguely ill. I don't want to lie. But I can't tell him about Marcy. I *can't*. Not until I know for sure what's going on. She's like family to me. No matter how bad this looks, I can't throw her to the FBI wolves until I give her a chance to explain.

Hopefully Lance will convince Jose I'm the woman for the delivery jobs, and I'll be able to have a long conversation with Marcy. In person. Until then, I'll stick to my cover story: I talked with Lance, got confirmation on the skimming, but nothing solid. I'll tell

Hitch I'll have to go back again and keep trying. He'll understand.

No he won't. He's risking his life and his future. He's going to be devastated, his investigation will be quagmired, and it'll be all your fault.

Anxiety prickles along my nerve endings, making me itch. *Shit.* I could really use a beer. Too bad Hitch suggested Swallows for our meeting place again this afternoon. If we were meeting somewhere else I could sneak in for a quick Blue Moon before facing the music. Beer is a well-known lying-effectiveness enhancer. And maybe it would calm me the fuck down. Between the fairy attack and watching Marcy broker a black-market deal, I feel like I'm about to crawl out of my skin.

And I'm *thirsty*, dammit. Really thirsty. I can just imagine how good that first explosion of cold, carbonated hops will feel as it swishes through my mouth.

Without conscious agreement from my brain, my feet veer sharply to the right, heading for the entrance to the Quik Mart. They have beer. And they sell it by the can—a lot of people around here don't have enough loose change lying around for a six-pack. I'll grab a Sapporo, duck into the alley behind the store, and chug some liquid courage before meeting Hitch. As long as I pop a stick of gum after, I should be fine. It's not like he's going to get close enough to smell my breath.

The bell above the door tinkles as I shove inside. Even with the window air-conditioner chugging away, it's only a few degrees cooler in here than it is out on the sweltering sidewalk. I can tell J.J. isn't thrilled to be working behind the counter. He greets me with a limp wave and a drowsy "S'up?" as I grab a pack of gum.

"Same old, same old."

"Hear that," he mumbles as I head to the coolers at the back of the store. I go straight to the single can beer section, tug open the sticky door, and am about to pluck my beverage of choice from the bottom shelf when I'm attacked.

Tiny arms wrap around my waist and squeeze hard enough that my "Holy shit!" comes out more grunt than scream. I have a full-body startle-spasm and barely resist the instinctive urge to shove my attacker into the CornNuts display. Luckily, I see the carefully plaited braids with their collection of white bows, and pull my hands back to my chest in time.

"Shit, Deedee! You scared the *shit* out of me," I gasp, forgetting to watch my language. But it's not like Deedee hasn't heard me say worse. On several occasions.

Child friendly, I am not.

Deedee tips her head back to give me a crooked grin. "I snuck up on you. Like a spy."

I take another breath and will my heart to stop racing. "Yes. Just like a spy. But don't do that again. You almost made me wet my pants."

She giggles, and I can tell she's going to pounce me again as soon as she gets the opportunity, on the off chance that she might make a grown-up wet herself. "Where's your cat?" she asks, still hugging on me. She's been clingy lately. Not that I mind. Her smallperson hugs are surprisingly nice.

"Gimpy's at my house." I tuck a braid behind her ear, and worry about the dark circles under her eyes. "I had work to do today."

"He's home all by himself? With no one to watch him?"

"He's a big boy. He'll be fine."

"You know," Deedee says, propping her fists at her waist and throwing out a hip. "I know a few things about cats."

"You do?"

"They've got six cats at Sweet Haven. They live in the barn with Mrs. Malky's goats. I go out and pet 'em all the time, and I only got bit twice and it didn't bleed very much and I didn't even cry for more than a minute."

"Wow." Only Deedee would think that story was something to brag about. "You're such a little weirdo."

She grins. "Just like you."

"No. You're a much cuter weirdo."

"You're cute, too. *I* like you," she says, with such a sweet blinky look that I see her coming a mile away.

Still, I say, "I like you, too."

"Then why don't you take me home with you?" She drops the sugary act with a stomp of her foot. "I can help you out. I can watch Gimpy while you're at work and when school starts I'll do all my homework by myself without asking for help. I'm smart. I can do it by myself."

"Deedee—"

"And I can cook for you, too," she hurries on. "I know how to make Macaroni and Cheese in the microwave. And hot dogs. And bologna and cheese sandwiches. Those are really good. If you heat 'em up just a little the bologna gets all puffy around the edges like a spaceship."

"That sounds awesome."

"It is. All you need is bologna and you can get it right here at the Quik Mart! We could go make space-ship sandwiches right now!"

"Listen, Dee. I want to have you over for spaceship sandwiches, and I promise we'll do that soon," I say, summoning up my firmest big-person voice. "But you can't come live with me."

"Why not?" Her face scrunches, but thankfully she looks more angry than sad. If she starts crying the way she did the last time we had this conversation, I might have to chug my Sapporo right here in front of the cooler. "You took Gimpy home for keeps. Why not me?"

"You're not a stray cat. You're a kid, and you need things I can't give you."

"No, I don't. I'm low maintenance. Mrs. Malky said so."

Speaking of Mrs. Malky . . .

"Does Mrs. Malky know you're here? When I was at Sweet Haven, you had to be at least twelve to get an afternoon pass."

"I don't need a pass." She crosses her arms and lifts her stubborn chin. "Mrs. Malky's always off doing her goat business. I climb the gate whenever I want."

"Deedee Jones! You can't do that. You have to follow the rules." Said the woman who has broken most of the rules and several federal laws in the past two months alone.

"I don't want to follow the rules. I hate it there," she says, tears pooling in her big brown eyes. My hands ball into fists, fighting the urge to reach for liquid relief. "All the kids are mean to me. They make fun of my dresses and one of the girls peed on the fancy satin Mama got me for Christmas last year. Mrs. Klein helped me wash it, but I swear it still smells like pee and I hate Tonya Trace for putting her pee on my dress and I want to kill her every time I see her stupid skinny face!"

"Well, sh—Sorry," I correct at the last minute. "I'm really sorry, Dee." Sweet Haven hasn't changed much, then. I should have known better than to think that it had. I should have guessed the other girls would be jealous of Deedee's nice things. Before her death, her mama worked for the richest family in Donaldsonville. They paid her well and she spent half her salary dressing up her baby girl. She loved Deedee so much.

And now she's dead, and Deedee is learning what it's like to be a kid that nobody treasures.

"Take me home, Miss Annabelle. Please." Deedee leans her forehead into my stomach, all the fight going out of her in a rush of breath. I put my arm around her thinner-than-they-used-to-be shoulders, feel her exhaustion and desperation seep into my skin, and for a second I think about it.

Maybe it could work. Maybe Deedee and Gimpy and I could be a team.

Maybe even a family.

And then I look over her shoulder at the cooler door. It's still open, ready for me to snag that two o'clock beer I was planning to chug in the alley before I lie to my ex-boyfriend about a murder investigation I've somehow become a part of and then go looking for an invisible man—who is no doubt a killer himself—to ask him why a fairy army is determined to get me out of town. Or kill me if they get another chance.

I can't be there for Deedee. I can't handle my own life, let alone take responsibility for hers.

"I'll come visit you tomorrow," I whisper. "I promise."

She sighs. Doesn't move her forehead from my stomach. Sighs again. "Okay."

"I'll bring you anything you want to eat, too," I say, even though I feel lousy about bribing her to accept her shitty lot in life with junk food. "How about a cheeseburger and fries from Swallows?"

She stands up, expression brighter than it was before. "How about a dozen buffalo wings with extra spicy sauce and blue cheese on the side and a triple order of celery?"

"We'll make it three dozen wings and six orders of

celery and we'll both pig out until we're sick." I reach out and close the cooler door. There's no time for a beer now. Which is probably a good thing. Probably. "But I've got to run. You go sneak back into Sweet Haven and follow the rules and I'll call for a visitor's appointment tomorrow afternoon."

"You could call now." She digs in her dress pocket. "I've still got minutes on the phone you gave me."

"I've got a business meeting in like two minutes," I say, edging toward the front of the store. "I'll call as soon as I get home. Okay?"

"Okay." She stands still, watching me go.

I think about ordering her out the door in front of me and watching until I see she's headed back in the right direction, but that would be acting like I have authority over her behavior. Like a guardian or a foster parent or a fully functional adult. Which I obviously am not.

So I just give one last wave, toss J.J. a couple of dollars for the gum, and hurry out into the glaring sun. It is hellishly hot. Again. It feels like this stupid summer is never going to end. By the time I reach the entrance to the back alley behind Swallows, my armpits are fighting through their protective deodorant shield and sweat pools between my bra-free breasts. It's too hot to be outside unless you're submerged in water. Or naked.

Naked. Holy. Christ.

Not fifteen feet away, outside the back entrance to Swallows, my ex-boyfriend is pulling his faded red

T-shirt over his head, revealing ebony skin and his ruthlessly chiseled eight-pack. (Cane has a habit of taking things to extremes, and his body is no exception.) I freeze at the end of the alley and step quickly to the side, pressing myself into the shadows behind the big blue recycling bins. I don't want to see Cane right now. I'm on my way to meet Hitch, and I know that won't go over well. I wouldn't want to see him if he were alone, and I especially don't want to interrupt him while he's stripping down with another woman.

I watch Theresa Swallows—owner of Swallows and a woman I consider one of my closest friends—pull off her gray and white Swallows T-shirt, revealing a black string bikini top that leaves *nothing* to the imagination. Theresa is five feet two in heels and probably doesn't weigh much more than my cat. She's a cute-as-a-button Latina who gets mistaken for her twelve-year-old daughter's sister all the time. With her tan skin and walnut brown eyes, I've always considered Theresa pretty, but never sexy.

But then, I've never seen her in nothing but a string bikini and a pair of ripped-up short shorts, either. Theresa may be petite, but she's *nicely* proportioned. I'm a straight woman with pretty close to zero interest in women sexually, and *I* can't stop looking.

So I shouldn't be surprised that Cane can't keep his eyes off her fingers as she rearranges the itty-bitty triangles to make sure they're covering her not nearly so itty-bitty boobs. Men like boobs. Men *will* look at boobs—even if they're in love with another woman, as Cane still professes to be in love with me.

If this were the community pool and Cane and Theresa happened to cross paths while they both happened to be scantily clad and Cane happened to ogle Theresa's chest and Theresa happened to reach a flirty finger out to poke Cane's stomach, I might not be bothered by what I was seeing.

But this is *not* the community pool. This is a back alley and I can't imagine any innocent reason for the pair of them to be getting seminaked together. Yeah, it's hot. But it's cool inside in the air-conditioning. They could be in there, cool and *fully clothed*. Instead, they're throwing their discarded shirts over their arms and moving closer. Theresa's head tilts back to gaze into the much taller Cane's face, and Cane smiles that smile that makes his eyes crinkle and his teeth flash and pulls women's lips to his mouth like a sex-powered tractor beam. I watch Theresa give Cane's stomach a second finger poke and Cane run his hand over his shaved head the way he does when he's thinking naughty things, and I'm really glad I didn't chug that Sapporo.

Because I would be tossing it back up all over the pavement.

I feel sick. Sick, sick, sick. My stomach is freefalling and my ribs are contracting in a viselike grip of misery and my mouth fills with the burnt-plastic taste of loss.

I've lost Cane. I've dicked around too long deciding if I'm ready for the long haul and now he's found someone else. He and Theresa will probably get married and Cane will be the best stepfather in the world to her two kids and they'll have more babies—because Theresa had Dina when she was only seventeen and is still young and undoubtedly fertile and Cane is dying to have kids—and I'll have to pretend to be happy for them because Theresa is my friend and Cane was my friend, too, before he became my lover. And I can hardly fault them for finding happiness with each other. I had my chance, and I screwed it up.

But he said he'd wait. Just last night he kissed you good-bye and called you Lee-lee. What kind of man does that, and then turns around, strips off his shirt, and flirts with another woman?

A man who's thinking about other options. That's who. At least *thinking,* and maybe even acting. Who knows how much further this smile-and-finger-pokefest is going to go?

I don't know, but I know I don't want to stand around and watch.

I take a slow step back and then another, easing around the corner without being observed by the pair still canoodling by the Dumpster. As I hurry away, I whip out my phone and stab out a text to Hitch: "Can't meet. Bernie called. Gimpy sick. Can meet first thing tomorrow. Six a.m. at Piggly Wiggly. They have coffee and donuts. I'll buy."

As soon as I hit Send, I feel the weight in my chest ease.

My insides still hurt like evil leprechauns are pummeling my guts with their fists, but I can't bring myself to get angry. How can I? I've been tempted. I've stared into Tucker's dreamy blue eyes and had impure thoughts. I even kissed Hitch the last time he was here. I'm in no position to play the woman wronged, but that doesn't make imagining what Cane and Theresa might be doing right now any easier. The thought of his arms around her, her hands resting on his chest, her lips kissing those lips that once were mine . . .

I suck in a breath and surprise myself with a sob. I'm actually *crying*.

Crying over losing Cane and with every shuddery breath it gets harder to imagine feeling okay again. This is what it felt like the day I walked away from Hitch, like there was nothing in the world worth reaching out for because everything I touch turns to shit.

That's why I decided never to love anyone again. But it looks like I broke that promise like I break everything else. I love Cane. I knew I loved Cane, but I'm not sure I knew I loved him like this. It's only now that he's slipping away that I realize how much he means to me.

But then, men are always more attractive once they've had the sense to reject me.

I resist the urge to call myself names like *stupid* and *pathetic* and *chronically incompetent* and *unlovable*. That way lies madness, and I refuse to let Low Self-Esteem win. Low Self-Esteem is for teenagers who haven't realized that everyone else is just as lame as they are.

And who don't have the cash or necessary ID to buy something to numb the pain.

Whiskey. Whiskey is perfect for a good, angry drunk, and I'd much rather be angry. I swipe the back of my hand across my face, smearing away the worst of the emotional leakage and start toward the liquor store at a jog.

8

I go in for a fifth of whiskey, but come out with two two-liter jugs, a six-pack of generic Coke, and a sleeve of plastic cups.

There's no need to drink alone, especially when my drinking buddies might prove useful. The Junkyard Kings know more about what's going down outside the iron gate than anyone in Donaldsonville. Even with easy travel between towns restricted by poisonous fairies, the vagrant gossip network manages to keep up with the news we average roof-over-our-heads people are unaware of.

The Kings know which towns are cracking down on the homeless population, which people give out a free dinner if you show up on their back porch, where the bands of highwaymen are moving, and who needs what contraband distributed for what price. Some of the homeless men living in the nonperishable waste dump down the street from my house are bleary-eyed drunks who spend their days digging through Dumpsters for recyclables and their nights pissing all over their grungy mattresses.

But some of them are black-market goods dealers or drug pushers or middlemen brokering information to whoever will pay for it. Some say last year's breach of the iron gate in Baton Rouge and the subsequent theft of ten top-of-the-line metal-plated motor homes by Vlad the Inhaler—the leader of a band of highwaymen known for the pink and yellow inhalers he wears around his neck to combat a nasty case of asthma—wouldn't have been possible without information provided by some of Donaldsonville's own Junkyard Kings.

I figure there are worse places to start looking for answers. Besides, the Kings are always happy to see me. Especially when I come bearing alcoholic goodies.

This afternoon is no different. I'm greeted with catcalls and hugs and an impromptu serenade about good redheaded women who bring home the bacon.

And by "bacon," we all know they mean booze. Bacon—though tasty—wouldn't have generated nearly as much excitement.

We settle down around the cooking fire, where Stan is poking a pot of what smells like chili, but most certainly contains some breed of rodent meat, and get our drink on in a serious fashion. By the time the sun slinks low in the sky, we're all comfortably wasted and the mounds of trash and rusted-out cars are starting to look artistic and meaningful and the laughs are coming easier and even Gerald—a relatively new King with ashy skin and yellowed eyes who doesn't blink often enough to be anywhere close to sane—is singing along with some of the songs.

So when Eli and Nigel finish up their duet and Stan starts dishing out chili con rat, I decide the time has come to ask questions. Before I forget what the questions are.

"So, Eli, seen any good movies lately?" I casually drop the code phrase rumored to be the way to initiate off-color business in the dump.

Eli—an ancient black man with steel gray hair that sticks up all over his head like an electrified Brillo pad and surprisingly beautiful muddy green eyes—drops his spoon into his bowl and pins me with a hard look. "You know there ain't no movie theater around here, girl."

"I know that." I take a sip of my drink. "I know a lot of things. But I'd like to know more about some other things, if you know what I mean." I don't bother trying to sound sober. It'll be easier to pull this off if the Kings assume I'm too wasted to be a threat. My boyfriend is a cop—as far as the King's know, anyway—and no matter how much they appreciate my gifts in clear bottles, it isn't going to be easy to get them to trust me.

"I can know you more, girl," Nigel shouts from the other side of the fire, a leer in his rheumy voice. "You come sit on old Nigel's lap and I'll know you all kinds of good things."

"Nigel, you ain't seen pussy since before this girl was born." Stan leans over and nudges me with his beefy elbow. "I'm the only one of these stinkers who can still get it up, and that's the damned truth. You need some seeing to, you come see me, Miss Lee."

"Thanks, guys." I manage not to gag at the thought of any of the Junkyard Kings naked. Just barely. "But I have questions that can't be answered by a penis."

"Sound like stupid questions to me," Nigel says, inspiring a burst of raucous laughter from the circle at large.

It's a man joke and I get that and I normally wouldn't let the laughter throw me, but tonight it makes me uncomfortable. There's an edge to it, a sharp edge that warns me to take a step back. For the first time, I feel a hint of danger whisper through the sour-smelling air, and I wonder if maybe Bernie is right and the Kings aren't as harmless as I've always believed.

"Might be." I keep my eyes on Eli, the only one of the pack who didn't find the joke funny. "But stupid questions still need answers and you know I can pay for them. In drinks or cash. Your call."

Eli scoops a bite of chili and chews. His tightly coiled beard makes his pink lips look like the underside of some menacing sea creature. He takes his time swallowing, but I don't break eye contact, and the other Kings don't say a word. They're all Kings, but Eli is the ruler of this yard. Finally, he says, "All right."

"You know anything about a cave out in the bayou?" I ask, not missing the tightening in the air as soon as the words are out of my mouth. I scan the circle, but no one is looking at me anymore. They've all become very interested in their drinks or their chili or the fire.

Except Gerald, who is staring at me with an I'm-thinking-about-what-you'd-look-like-without-skin look that makes me turn quickly back to Eli.

"I don't know anything about that." Eli enunciates each word more clearly than any I've heard him speak. "And neither do you. That's what's good for you, girl. You listen to Eli."

Well. Dead end there; no doubt about it. Whatever Eli knows, he's not going to tell me, for any price. But at least it seems like he still cares what's good for me. It makes me ballsy enough to try avenue of questioning number two. "What about Marcy? Do you know anything about her?"

"What kind of anything?"

"Just . . . anything. About her past or where she went or what she's doing now . . . anything." I pause, but Eli doesn't say a word. "Listen, somebody else wanted me to ask about the cave, but this is for me. Marcy was family to me, and all of sudden she disappeared. I don't believe she's gone to take care of a sick relative. If she were only out of town, she would have called me and told me when she was coming back. But now . . . I'm afraid she's never coming back and I . . ." I swallow, surprised by how easily tears have risen in my eyes. I let them sit there, hoping they might convince Eli to take pity on me. "I miss her. A lot. I want to know she's all right."

"She's all right," he says, his voice a hair gentler than it was before.

"Then I want to know why she thinks it's okay to run off and leave everyone who loves her," I say. "Because right now, it seems like bullshit."

Eli nods and chews with that same steady, stern look on his face. I've about decided to call it a night when he says, "Marcy is a good woman, but she's got a past."

"I heard she killed her old man," Stan adds, taking the cue from Eli that it's okay to spill. "Slit his damned throat while he was sleeping."

"She ain't killed Traynell." Nigel coughs up a wad of phlegm and spits perilously close to the leftover chili. "I saw him last week down in N'Orleans, creeping round the Superdome flea market, buying scrap metal."

"Was Marcy with him?"

Nigel shakes his head. "Nope. He was by his own sorry self. And looking it. A man should never live with a woman as long as that man has. Makes him weak. And after that woman leave your ass, you get all skinny and your skin goes saggy and your hair starts falling out."

"More proof you ain't never had a woman, you fat, hairy bastard," Stan says, summoning another circle-wide laugh. Nigel joins in, ruffling his mane of kinky gray hair, sending a few insects jumping for safer ground.

"I wasn't talking about Traynell or his skinny ass," Stan continues as the laughter dies down. "I was talking about her *old man*. Her Daddy." Stan turns his full attention my way. "I heard she tied him up in his bed and cut his throat, real slow, so he could stay alive to know he's being kilt as long as possible."

I nod, and try not to let on that Stan is fucking

with my head. "I heard she killed two people, but I didn't know who they were. Or why."

"One was her daddy because he deserved a killing," Eli says. "And Marcy was the first of her sisters brave enough to do it. The other was her own baby girl."

"What?" My stomach twists, sending up a nose-scalding gurgle of whiskey and cheap soda. "That can't be true. Marcy would never. Never."

"I lived in Lafayette around the time it happened. Read all the papers." Eli stretches out his stick legs, wiggling them at the ankles. "They said it was an accident. The little girl was supposed to be at her grandma's house across the field, but came back looking for her mama in the middle of the night. She must of snuck in the back door just after Marcy rigged the gas stove. Exploded her right up and burned what was left of Marcy's daddy down to the bone."

The circle falls silent. Not even Stan or Nigel have any sarcastic commentary to offer. A woman murdering her father and accidentally taking out her baby girl in the process isn't funny. It's sad. So, so sad. Marcy was fifteen, trying to escape some kind of abuse, and she ended up killing her own kid. A kid she shouldn't have even had at that age. If the girl could already walk and open doors on her own, she must have been at least two or three. That meant Marcy was pregnant when she was . . . twelve.

God. I want to go back in time and take care of the terrified kid she must have been. But I can't. All I can do is try to help her out of whatever trouble she's in now.

"But she served her time, didn't she?" I finally ask, my voice thin. "Why is she running now?" I know what Marcy told me—she helped a father kidnap his daughter from her abusive mother—but I want to know what the Kings know. Marcy clearly left out several *major* details in her version of the story.

Eli shrugs. "Who knows? Maybe those old demons are still hauntin' her."

"After forty years?" I lift a brow, letting Eli know I smell bullshit. "All of sudden she has to up and run after being a part of this town for decades? When everyone here thinks she's a saint?"

"I never thought that woman was a saint." Nigel grunts and crosses his arms with an arthritic hitch of his shoulder. "She was a tough bitch. That's what she was."

Marcy? A tough bitch? Tough, yes. But Marcy has the kindest heart. I've never seen her lose her temper, not even when two of my bunkmates at Sweet Haven tried to set each other's hair on fire during the spring barbecue.

"Marcy wasn't a bitch. She was a mama bear." Stan throws his arm around me and leans in to whisper in my ear. I smell rat chili and whiskey with an undernote of diseased gums and rotted teeth and I try not to shudder. "She didn't want us messing with her baby. The day you moved in down the street, she was up in here with that bulldog face of hers warning us to stay away from you. Said she was going to bring down the wrath of hellfire upon our place in the sun if we didn't keep you safe."

"But she ain't here anymore," Nigel says, a shade meaner than I'd like. "Guess we can be as bad as we want to be."

I look to Eli—the only one of the Kings who seems like a decent excuse for a human being—but he has his face in his chili, slurping up the sauce at the bottom of his bowl. No help coming from there. Guess he's done offering me good-natured warnings. I grit my teeth and think uncharitable things about him and men in power in general. They always turn a blind eye when the going gets tough.

"Nah. We love our little Lee. She's good to us." Stan hugs me closer, pressing me against his sweat-soaked fat rolls. I can feel the stink of him seeping into my skin and want to shove him away. But I don't. I have to watch myself. Closely.

That feeling of potential danger is stronger now. It lifts the hairs on the back of my neck, crawls skeeter feet along my arms. It's the feminine instinct kicking in, reminding me that I'm the smaller, weaker member of the species. Modern society tells women we have equality with men—and some women never have cause not to believe it—but in moments like these, when you're a woman alone and a man's good nature is the only thing keeping you safe and you know his "good nature" isn't that good, the fear kicks in. These are the times when the threat alone keeps you quiet and submissive and in your place.

A place Marcy didn't want me to be. So much so

that she came to the dump to make sure these men never gave me a reason to be afraid. It makes me love her even more, and I swear to myself that I won't betray her to Hitch or anyone else.

I stand, throwing off Stan's arm. "Thanks for the chili."

"You didn't eat none."

"I'm not into rat." I grab my purse and the bottle that still has a few inches of amber liquid at the bottom. I'm done drinking, but I want the Kings to know they don't get to keep my leftovers anymore. The bastards.

"It's not rat. It's pig," Nigel says. "And we know you like them. That pig boyfriend of yours was over at your place just last night."

"But he don't sleep there no more." Harlan speaks up for the first time, in a soft voice that, despite the heat, makes me shiver. I've always thought of Harlan as the sweet, slow, silent type. But he doesn't sound sweet now. He sounds eager. Hopeful. About things I *know* I don't want him to be hopeful about.

My feet tingle, itching to run. Instead, I take a slow step back and then another, resisting the urge. If I run, I'll never be able to stop. I'll have to run by this stretch of road every day and these hard-eyed men with their stink and their mean will know they've won.

"No, he doesn't." Nigel shifts his belly and loops his hands together underneath. "Maybe she don't like pig, either."

"Or maybe pigs don't like her." The man next to Harlan—Jake or Juke or something that starts with a *J*—smiles, showcasing a mouth full of black spotted teeth.

"Could be." Nigel clucks his tongue. "That ain't good, girl. This ain't a good town for people on the wrong side of the pigs."

"Seems like you rats do okay." I sound tougher than I'm feeling.

"We pay for our safety," Eli says, speaking up for the first time since the vibe in the yard started going sour.

He's got to be kidding. Cane and Abe wouldn't take graft from the Junkyard Kings. They're not crooked. The internal affairs investigation found nothing. They were led astray by false evidence when they arrested Fernando, not taking the law into their own hands. And they're certainly not strong-arming people into paying for their safety.

"You've been paying for yours, too." Eli plunks his bowl onto the ground by his feet. There's red sauce in his beard, but it doesn't make him look silly. He's too intense to be silly. "You stop paying, and you'll learn things you don't want to learn."

"And maybe I'll be the one to teach you," Nigel says. "I'd like to—"

"Shut your mouth," Eli orders. Nigel does. Immediately. Which makes me wonder just how mean Eli is underneath the relatively pleasant facade.

Pretty mean, I'm guessing, to keep this bunch in line. Pretty damned mean, and I've been pretty stupid to think I live in an idyllic small town where everyone loves one another and gets along and me and the crazy homeless guys are BFFs because I bring them booze. Maybe I've only been "getting along" because I had Marcy and Cane on my side. Maybe, now that I don't, things will change. Maybe I won't feel as driven to protect the people of Donaldsonville. Maybe it will be okay to leave them to the Invisibles and get the fuck out of town.

Deedee. Sweet, weird little Deedee with her fuzzy braids and her skinny arms wrapped around my waist and all the need in her eyes. There's no excuse to abandon her. Especially if D'Ville is even less child friendly than I've thought.

"Go home, Annabelle," Eli says. "We don't have anything else for you."

"Nothing else you're willing to give, anyway," I say, still doing a decent impression of not being intimidated. "That's fine, Eli. But you're not the only one with information. Remember that when things start happening that *you* don't understand. Maybe then we can have a real conversation."

Eli doesn't nod or raise his eyebrows or look in any way interested in my bluff that's not a bluff but might as well be.

Fine. *Asshole.*

I take another step back and mumble "Whatever," under my breath before turning and picking my way back through the mountain range of trash, gripping the glass handle of the whiskey bottle tight, refusing to look over my shoulder. I won't show fear, even if every nerve ending in my body is sending out run-for-it flares that sizzle as they shoot up my spine.

I keep a slow, steady pace as I weave around a huddle of half-crushed trucks and a tower of old office furniture one of the Kings must have used to play blocks. There's no other explanation for why every rusted desk in the junkyard is gathered in one location. I stop and stare at the tower for a long moment, looking for a weak spot, thinking about pulling one of the desks out and sending it crashing down just to be childishly vindictive. I've had enough whiskey for that to seem like a good idea. But I've also had enough whiskey to be too tired to bother.

"Fuck you, desks." I flip off the tower. It's easier to be angry at a bunch of inanimate objects than bitter and sad and confused by my failed attempt at information gathering.

It wasn't a failed attempt. You learned that Marcy killed her dad and her kid, Cane and Abe might be crooked, and the Junkyard Kings are dangerous assholes who find it amusing to scare the shit out of the hand that's fed them. Or drunk them. Or whatever.

And Eli knows something about that cave—that it's dangerous, bad news—but won't spill the details.

"So many good things." I weave on my feet as I twist the cap off the whiskey.

Another drink is starting to sound like a good idea. A few more swigs and maybe I'll be able to stumble home and pass out instead of looking for Tucker or answers or thinking about all the scary stuff that's gone down today. It will all still be here tomorrow at 6:00 a.m. When I'll have to drag my ass out of bed and tell Hitch I'm a failure. It's okay to forget.

It's okay. Everything's going to be okay. I repeat the mantra as I tip the bottle back with both hands and chug cheap whiskey.

It only burns a bit. I'm good at chugging things. It was my parlor trick back in my college days. The amount of hard liquor I could take down without passing out or throwing up was legendary, and every new person at a party would want to see the legend in person. I can't count the times I woke up in my narrow dorm bed with no memory of how I got there. Enough that I should have stopped chugging things.

But I didn't. I never stop. I never learn. And things are never okay. Never.

I know this.

So I'm not really surprised when I round another pile of trash and find Gerald waiting for me, an ominous light flickering in his dead eyes.

He comes for me.

I drop my purse and swing the whiskey bottle at his head, but he ducks a second too soon. I adjust and go for a backhand, but he snatches a handful of tank top and stomach skin and squeezes tight.

Tight, tight, tight. So tight the pain makes me scream and my fingers spasm and my makeshift weapon thuds to the ground. I lift my hands to scratch his face, but he's already on the move, knocking me to the ground, landing on top with that ropey body that feels so much heavier than it looks.

My breath rushes out, but his other hand wraps around my throat, keeping me from pulling in another. And then he's tugging at my jeans and I'm kicking my legs and slamming my fists into his head, but he doesn't seem to notice and I feel the button on my jeans pop open and panic smashes through all the protective barriers in my mind, blowing me open like a hurricane made of screams.

Not again. I can't. Not again.

I squeeze my eyes shut and thrash and kick like

I've been set on fire. I won't look at him. I won't look up into his gray face and watch his eyes fill up with the satisfaction or victory or violence or whatever it is he's going to feel while he does this.

I'll fight him until I black out, but I won't look. I won't. I won't. I won't.

I won't remember another man this way. I only have fleeting glimpses of Anton, but they're enough. I see him sometimes when I'm really smashed, in those seconds just before I black out, when everything I've forced myself to forget comes surging to the surface. I see his red face, jaw clenched, veins standing out. He's so angry, but pleased with himself at the same time. What he's doing seems to hurt him, but it hurts me more—*so* much more—and that's what he wants. The hurting is better than the fucking, better than the release that comes at the end, better than—

Thunk! There's a burst of sound—metal hitting flesh and bone with some serious force—and I can breathe.

Air rasps in as Gerald goes limp and I scramble out from underneath him, scuttling like an insect; a small, filthy thing that can't think beyond getting away from the danger and the pain and the hands.

"Don't!" I scream and bat the new hands away.

They're clean and I recognize them, but I can't let them touch. I'm not safe. I'm never safe. *Never*. Because all the things I've tricked myself into thinking I've put away are still there and I will never forget them and I will never remember them and I will never know the truth. Because Anton took that away, too.

Whatever he slipped into my drink that night blurred the edges of the nightmare, until I can't even say for certain that I have the right to feel like a victim.

Maybe I'm just a drunk. Maybe it's all my fault.

"No." Suddenly I'm crying. Or maybe I've been crying for a while, and just suddenly become aware of it. As I become aware of Hitch beside me, pulling me close, pressing my head into his chest, whispering that he's got me, asking me if I'm okay.

It's the worst thing he could have asked. I've already answered that question, and the answer is "No." I push him away and wrap my arms around my knees, squeezing tight, staring at where Gerald lies unconscious—but still breathing—on the ground a few feet away. Looks like Hitch hit him with a piece of an old fender. He's bleeding a lot, but I don't care. Not happy about it, not sad, not . . . anything.

Just empty, except for the raw feeling inside, almost like it happened. Even though Hitch stopped it.

This time.

Last time, he assumed I was a willing participant, assumed I'd jumped into bed with his brother without even asking me what happened. The disgust on his face tore me up all over again, made me feel like I was back on the bathroom floor, bleeding and puking and helpless while Anton stood grinning down at me, smug in his victory over his golden boy big brother.

What he'd done wasn't about love or lust or hating women or hating me. It wasn't about me at all. It was about proving that he could have what his smarter, better-looking, more successful, mommy-loved-him-best brother could have.

And that only made it worse, made it impossible to look into Hitch's accusing eyes and defend myself. Because I shouldn't have had to. Because Hitch should have known what a waste Anton was and given me the benefit of the doubt. At least. At the very, very least.

"I remember it sometimes," I find myself saying, words spewing without permission. I think about slapping my hands over my mouth, biting my tongue until it bleeds—whatever it takes to stop what's coming—but I can't. Not anymore. I just *can't*. "I remembered it a second ago. What his face looked like . . . during. So angry. Why would I remember that, if it wasn't true?"

"What are you talking about, baby?" He puts a gentle hand on my back.

Baby. He hasn't called me baby in forever. Not since the night he found out that I slept with his brother while he was pulling an all-nighter at the hospital. His brother. His fucking brother.

"Anton." I spit out the name, hating the way it feels in my mouth.

Hitch's hand turns to stone. I can feel how much he wants to pull away. I save him the trouble and scoot on my ass through the dirt. His fingers slide down my spine and contact is severed.

It feels better. And worse.

I grit my teeth and hunch around my legs, digging my chin into the top of my knees. "I remember being scared and trying to scream for help," I continue, voice wavering up and down as I try to get a grip. I've never said any of this out loud. Not even to the therapist I talk to once a year during my FCC annual training, not even to myself. "But I couldn't. I couldn't move and I was already fading out again."

I sniff and my entire body shudders in response. My arms are shaking and my heart is racing and it's getting harder and harder to speak, but I'm not done yet. I'm going to finish this, get it all out to the only person who ever cared and maybe then it will be done. Maybe then Anton's face will fade from even my buried memories.

As long as I don't look at Hitch, as long as I keep my eyes on the slow seep of blood from Gerald's head, I can do this. "But for a few minutes, I was there. And I know I didn't want to be. I *know* it. No matter what Anton said. I didn't want it. I didn't want *him*." Deep breath, hold it tight for a second, will down the pressure rising in my guts. "And when I woke up the next day, I was bleeding."

There. It's done. My next breath comes easier.

But I still can't look at Hitch. I can't. Not now. Maybe not ever. Maybe I'll never look at anyone ever again. Maybe I'll sit on the ground in the junkyard forever, staring at the second man who tried to rape me. At the moment, it sounds like an okay idea. I can sit here, curled up and hugged tight, the danger behind me, refusing to stand up and walk back to my house or go on with my life or admit the possibility of living through any more of this same damned shit.

Shit.

My life.

There are moments when it's good, but there are so many more when it's bad. And maybe that's my fault, too. I don't know. All I know is that I wish I were like Tucker and could go invisible at will. I don't want to be seen anymore. I don't want to meet Hitch's eyes and know what he sees when he looks at me.

He doesn't say a word for a long time. A really long time. But I know he understood me. He sits so still. Frozen. As if he, too, has decided that stopping time right here, right now, is for the best.

He's probably right. Where do we even go from here? What was the point in telling the truth?

"Because it's the truth," I whisper, shocked to find I believe it. I used to think the truth only mattered if it made a difference, but maybe the truth matters simply because it *is* the truth. People perceive things differently, politics and opinions come into play, there are shades of gray and alternate points of view, but sometimes, a thing is just *true*.

Marcy didn't deserve a father who terrorized her. True.

Grace Beauchamp and Deedee's mom didn't deserve to be killed. True.

Fernando didn't deserve to take the rap for a murder he didn't commit. True.

I didn't deserve what Gerald tried to do. I didn't deserve what Anton did all those years ago. I didn't deserve a boyfriend who thought so little of me that he didn't stop to consider I might be innocent.

True. True. And true.

"I don't know what to say." Hitch sounds empty, hollow. I can't tell if he's angry or sad or feels anything at all.

"You don't have to say anything," I say, realizing that's the truth, too. "I just couldn't lie about it anymore."

"Why?" Hitch's voice cracks. I risk a peek at him out of the corner of my eye and watch him . . . shatter. Lines that I've never seen before crease his face, like what I've said hit him so hard it made permanent slivers of brokenness across his skin. "Why didn't you *tell* me?"

"You didn't ask," I say, angry for a split second.

And then he pulls in a breath and says, "You're right," and buries his face in his hands. And cries.

Hitch is crying. Not the angry tears he cried the night he screamed for me to get out of his house. Not the happy tears he cried the time we found a bunch of kids alive and safe in the back of an iron-plated eighteen-wheeler after Hurricane Katrina wrecked the gates around New Orleans.

Sad tears. Hopeless tears. Tears that come from deep inside where I can tell he feels as lost and wrecked and afraid as I do. A person can't cry like that if they have real happiness, real hope. Despite the perfect education, the perfect job, the perfect fiancée, and the promise of a perfect family, Hitch isn't happy. He's not even okay.

I put a hand on his knee. A part of me shouts that it's stupid for *me* to be comforting *him*, but the rest of me knows feelings don't play by the rules. Some things may be black and white, but emotions are always red. Messy, sloppy red that bleeds outside the lines and stains and stings and doesn't care about labels like *accuser* and *accused*.

"I was waiting for it to happen," he says, rubbing the back of his hand across his face. "Since we first went out."

"Waiting for me to cheat on you?" Now I'm angry again. "Why? What did—"

"No. It wasn't—" He makes a frustrated sound and his hands clench. "I don't know. I guess I was . . . You were so beautiful. And smart. And you didn't give a shit what anyone thought. You'd do crazy things. And you were never afraid. And I was . . ."

"So ugly and stupid." I shake my head, floored by what I'm hearing, by the truth I see in his face. Cocky, ambitious, brilliant, sex-on-a-stick Hitch had doubts about whether he was good enough for me. *Me*. The fuck up Sweet Haven kid who only brushed her hair every other day, wore the same pair of jeans to class for a week, and lived on frozen fish sticks and beer. It's . . . dumbfounding.

"And you loved me." He catches me with those soft blue eyes I used to see every morning. It's Hitch without barriers, all the sweet, wicked, messy, perfectness of him. "All of me. Even the parts I hated. It felt . . . too good."

Too good. It's crazy. Because I felt the same way. About *him*. And now . . . about Cane. He's too good. At least for me. I really believe that, but maybe . . .

Maybe . . .

I thought I was afraid to commit to Cane because I was still carrying a torch for Hitch. But maybe I'm simply carrying the baggage I've always had, the same baggage that ruined my first relationship. *Helped* ruin it, anyway. It takes two to kill something like what Hitch and I had. If I were a normal person, I would blame him for thinking the worst of me and be done with it. If I stay true to my own destructive bullshit, I'll blame myself and my innumerable flaws and keep loathing myself enough to make sure that a bottle continues to be the most significant attachment in my life.

But maybe there's a third option, something between blame and responsibility. Maybe there really is such a thing as forgiving and forgetting. Or at least moving on.

"What happened with Anton . . . What I *thought* happened, was confirmation of what I was afraid of. I was too ready to believe and . . ." He swallows and his left eyelid does that twitchy thing it does when he's really upset. "I would say I'm sorry, but that doesn't come close to what I am."

"Me, too." I scoot closer. "I should have told you the truth."

"I probably wouldn't have listened. Not right then."

"I still should have tried." I lean my head on his shoulder. "We're too much alike."

"You think?" The familiarity in his voice twists things in my chest, makes me want to start crying all over again.

My arms find their way around his neck, threading

through that curly hair that was once one of the most familiar, comforting textures in my world. "I don't want you to hate me anymore."

"I never hated you," he says, fingers digging into the small of my back. "Ever."

"And I don't want to hate you." I force myself to look up into his eyes, to ignore how close we are and how badly a part of me wants to be closer. "But even more, I don't . . ." I swallow, try to force my tongue to form the words. But it's so hard to sit here and be defenseless in front of this person whose love and loss has defined nearly a decade of my life.

"What?" he whispers.

"I don't want to love you anymore. I can't. It hurts too much. But I don't know how to stop."

I expect him to pull away, for the sadness in his eyes to turn to pity as he tells me it will simply happen someday, the way it did when he fell in love with Stephanie. But neither of those things happens. Instead his arms tighten until I'm pressed against him and his mouth finds mine and we kiss like we kissed that night I saved him from the fairies.

No. Not like that.

That kiss was as full of pain as it was pleasure. There's pain now, but it's different. It's not sadness or hatred. It's the desperation of two people trapped in the dark waiting for the bombs to explode. Terrified and almost hopeless, but grabbing hold of the only person who offers comfort. The person who understands, the person who's as lost as they are, but in whose arms they are found.

His tongue slips inside my mouth and I taste Hitch—hint of garlic and mint and cherry ChapStick and that spicy saltiness that has always been the sexiest taste. My arms twine around his neck and the smell of him spins through my head and I'm twenty years old again.

We're on our third date and we're naked in the pond behind his house and every place he touches me is alive in a way it's never been before and I finally know what all the fuss is about. I know what I've been imagining I feel with other boys isn't even close to how good a man and a woman can really be. *This* is desire, *this* is a feeling worth killing for, dying for, burning up in the flames because annihilation by pleasure is the only way to go.

Even after what happened with Gerald, even with his limp body lying a few feet away, even with the memory of that night with Anton so fresh and the smell of the junkyard so very *un*fresh, it's so easy to be pulled back. Back to Hitch. Back to the source, the start of the first road, the beginning of the person I thought I could be with him, *because* of him, back when loving him was the answer to every question.

But I didn't become that person, and my answers turned out to be lies. Because we lost each other, and we can't find our way back. And because I think I meant what I said.

I don't want to be in love with Hitch. Not anymore.

I stop returning the kiss and push at his chest. He lets me go so quickly I almost tumble backward and he has to catch me and let me go all over again.

Afterward, we sit staring at each other, lips damp, breath fast, question marks stabbing into the air all around us.

Finally Hitch says. "Anton's in prison."

"Yeah?"

"If he weren't, I'd kill him."

"No, you wouldn't. He's your brother. And he's not worth it."

"But you are," he says, a hint of the old passion-before-reason Hitch in his eyes.

I look at the ground. "You still wouldn't kill him. That's not who you are."

"Maybe it's who I should be." He sighs. "But you're probably right."

"I know I'm right." I stand on shaking legs and brush off the dirt, reach down and grab my purse. "And I know that you and—"

Gerald moans and shifts on the ground, preempting some strong words from me about knowing Hitch and Stephanie and the baby are going to live happily ever after.

For the best, really. I have no idea if Hitch is going to live happily ever after. If he were *that* happy with Stephanie, he wouldn't have kissed me the first time he was here, let alone a second time. If he were *that* happy with Stephanie, he wouldn't know how to cry like there's no chance of a better life.

But Hitch isn't my problem. I can't let him become my problem, even if some part of me or of him thinks getting tangled up in each other again is a good idea.

"I have to get home."

"We need to call the police." Hitch stands beside me. "We can give a statement and get this guy locked up. At least for a night or two."

I shake my head. "No. I don't want to go to the police."

I don't want Cane to know what happened. I don't want him to feel sorry for me, and I don't want to get too close to the police until I figure out what Eli was talking about. If someone on the Donaldsonville police force is crooked, they could have their finger in all kinds of sketchy business. Maybe the black-market dealings down at the docks. Maybe even whatever's going down at the cave. "There are some things I have to figure out first."

"Like what?" he asks, eyes sharper. "Is this about—"

"I'll tell you everything in the morning." I need time to pull my shit together even more than I did before. "Six a.m. Piggly Wiggly."

"Yeah, I got your message," he says, ignoring another moan and arm flop from Gerald, who I'm no longer sure is getting up tonight after all.

He certainly had his share of whiskey. He might end up sleeping it off in the dirt and wake up tomorrow with no memory of his last hour of consciousness. But even if that's the case, I can't pretend this didn't happen. Gerald's a menace. He doesn't need a night in jail; he needs to disappear. He's a problem best solved by the Invisibles. Hopefully a few threats from a man he can't see will send him on his way.

If not . . .

Well, I'll cross that bridge when I come to it, when

I'm sober and this night is a memory and murder doesn't seem like a reasonable solution.

"I was on my way to your house when I heard you scream," Hitch says. "We can't afford to wait. I got nowhere today. I'm no closer than I was before I came to Donaldsonville. I need to know what you found so I can plan our next move."

"I didn't find much, and I just want—"

"Please, Annabelle." Hitch grabs my hand, so fast I can't avoid contact. "Please help me. I don't have time for games or—"

"I'm not playing games."

"Or nerves or . . . strangeness between us, whatever this is." He brings his other hand into the mix, making my fingers into sandwich filling. I try to pull away, but he holds tight, a squeeze with a tremble that brings home again how serious this situation is. Especially for him. "I'm sorry I kissed you. I'm sorry I don't know what to say or what I feel and . . . about everything and . . . Honestly, I'm a fucking mess right now. But I don't have time to be a mess. This is so important and—"

"The man at the docks wasn't friendly, but I did learn a few things." I have to give Hitch something or he'll never leave me alone. But I have to be careful what I share. No matter how much I want to help him, I can't betray Marcy, not without a lot more proof. "They're definitely stealing from their shipments and selling the stuff on the black market. They have a regular customer for the glass needles and some of the other medical supplies. I got the guy I spoke with to show me a video of one of the meetings with her, but it was too blurry to get a positive ID."

"I can get a buddy of mine to hack into their files," Hitch says, making my stomach drop. "We can search the tapes and enhance the quality. Maybe that will be—"

"I wouldn't do that. The guy's a computer geek," I say, scrambling. "He'll know he's been hacked and I'll never get him to trust me. Give me some time. He's talking to his partner tonight. They're thinking about offering me a delivery job. If that happens, I'll be able to meet the woman connected to the medical supplies in person."

Hitch nods. "And I'll come with you."

Shit. This is why I needed time to plan! I can't have Hitch tagging along. I need to speak to Marcy in private.

I shake my head. "The deliveries happen out in the bayou, Hitch. I don't—"

"I brought my suit. I'll suit up and hide in the back of the truck. I'll keep out of sight until you find out everything you can from this woman. Then I'll come out and help convince her to take us to the cave."

"If she knows the way."

"She'll know the way," he says, a determined smile on his lips. "You did great."

"I don't have the job yet," I remind him. "Lance is going to call me tomorrow and let me know. That's why I thought this talk could wait. I'm not going to know anything else until tomorrow so . . ." I take a step back, sensing this is my chance to escape before I say anything else to trap myself.

"I'm glad we talked. It's good to know we're getting somewhere." He takes a mirror step toward me. "Really. Thank you so—"

"Don't worry about it." I lift a hand and turn to go. "See you tomorrow."

"Let me walk you," he says, falling into step beside me.

I cross my arms and clutch my purse strap, disliking the feeling of him next to me. I need some space, some time, and I certainly don't want to work my way through a "good night" at my screen door. There's something about Hitch right now. He doesn't want to be alone. I can tell. But I can't be with him. Not as friends, and certainly not as anything else. "I'd kind of rather . . . go alone."

"No. It's not safe."

"It's fine." I gesture toward the sidewalk that's already in sight. "I can see my house from here."

"No. I could taste the whiskey on your breath, I don't—"

"I'm not drunk." I'm not. Not anymore. And the reminder that Hitch *tasted* me is enough to make me even more uncomfortable. I stop dead, making him stumble. "Let me go, Hitch."

"I will. I just want—"

"Please, Hitch," I whisper. "Let me go."

"I . . . I . . ." He swallows. "I'm sorry."

"I know."

"I don't want you to be alone tonight," he says, in

that honeyed drawl that makes my bones melt. "Let me sleep on your couch. I'll make sure you're safe."

"If you sleep on my couch, neither of us will be safe." Even the thought of Hitch shirtless in my living room is too dangerous to touch. "And if you hurt Stephanie you'll regret it. Forever." I don't know how I have the guts to say it, but I do, and the look in Hitch's eyes leaves no doubt that I'm right. "Good-bye."

His hands fist and his eye twitches, but when I take another step back and then another, he doesn't say a word. He lets me go. Finally, I turn and walk away, wondering if this is it, if this is really the end of a certain breed of possibility between me and the first man I ever loved. I wonder if I truly want it to be.

Then I can't stand any more wondering and break into a run, sprinting for my front door with everything in me.

10

Fernando is *pissed*. The note on my front door confirms it:

> *You are half an hour late. You are not answering your phone. You are also a selfish bitch, and I hate you. I am taking my steaks and going home, where I will eat them both and get fat and it will be all your fault!*
> *Sincerely, Fernando, former best friend.*

Crap. Dinner with Fern. I completely forgot. I pull out my phone. Three missed calls. One from him, two from Hitch. I turned off my ringer while I was in the junkyard and didn't realize anyone had called. I could tell Fern that, and explain that I was busy being attacked around seven o'clock tonight, but I don't want to talk about that anymore. Or think about it.

I'll call Fern tomorrow and apologize profusely. Hopefully it will be enough. If it isn't . . . well . . . who gives a shit? He can mope and pout and give me the silent treatment for a few weeks. At least then I'll get a break from the constant criticism.

I snatch the note off the door and crumple it into a ball, planning to throw it into the trash can by the door. But when I open the door, the trash can is across the room by the two potted plants I've managed not to kill. The two potted plants that are now *unpotted* all over the floor.

Gimpy is *also* pissed. Or he *was* pissed at some point in the day.

Even in the dim light streaming from the kitchen, I can see that my antique chintz sofa cushions have been ripped to shreds. Clouds of tacky brown stuffing litter the room. Trash and potting soil make a mess in the corner and the curtain I nailed up to offer some protection from Bernadette is sporting a few claw marks, but the sofa definitely took the worst of the abuse.

"You little bastard!" I stomp through my mercifully intact bedroom and throw my keys, purse, phone, and the smashed tea bags from my back pocket on the kitchen table before squatting down by Gimpy's bed. "What did you do?"

"*Rrrreow*." The Gimp greets me with a lazy purr-growl and a smile. I swear, the wee terrorist *smiles* at me, pleased as shit that he's gotten the desired reaction.

"Bad!" I point to the front room. "No treats for you tonight."

He yawns, stretches, and pops his claws, as if to emphasize how little he cares for my stupid treats.

He's already had his fill of couch stuffing, *thank you very much*, and is completely stuffed. Ha, ha, ha.

"You're lucky I hated that couch." I plop down on the floor cross-legged beside him, and pull his bed close enough to reach the sweet spot behind his ears without working too hard. "I still shouldn't pet you." I start to scratch and Gimpy's purr-growl becomes a rumble of pleasure. "You don't deserve my sweet love."

My sweet love. The smell of Hitch lingers on my shirt, but there's only one face that keeps floating through my mind. Cane. I keep seeing the way he was smiling at Theresa, and remembering all the times he smiled the same way at me. I'm still not jealous or angry, I just . . .

"I want to see him," I mutter as I pull Gimpy onto my lap. He stiffens for a moment—not being the snuggly sort—but eventually gives in to the double ear and jowl scratch. "I miss him."

I saw him yesterday, but it seems like so much longer. I may have talked to him, held his hand, and kissed his lips, but we didn't connect the way we used to. Our time-out is becoming a chill-out. The spark between us is cooling. Not only the sexual spark, but the way we used to talk and laugh and be ourselves without any threats lurking in the dark future.

We used to have a sunny future. Or at least partly cloudy, small chance of rain.

But then Hitch showed up and changed everything and now things are . . . complicated. Even if we live through this investigation and Hitch heads back to New Orleans and I get the situation with the

Invisibles and the fairies under control, I'm not sure that things will be less complicated. Not after tonight. Despite the fiancée and the baby, Hitch might come back. For me. *To* me.

"And I might want him to," I whisper. "But it would only go bad again, wouldn't it? If it were meant to be, it would have been the first time around. Right?"

Gimpy gives me a slitty-eyed look that expresses what he thinks of "meant to be."

Right. Nothing is meant to be. Meant to be is crap, the philosophy of fools and smug, happy people trying to justify why they're getting an easy ride while everyone else fights and hurts and bleeds and struggles to get up after being slapped down again and again. There is no benevolent hand of fate guiding my life.

Shit happens. The only thing I have power over is how I deal with the shit.

I can change the way I do business. I can be better. Or at least different. And maybe different will be better.

"Or I could pack a bag, steal Bernadette's car, and drive out of here and never look back. That would make the fairies happy." Gimpy growls and digs his claws into my jean-clad leg. "Don't worry. You can come, too. At least as far as St. Louis."

Gimpy growls again and narrows his eyes at the front of the house. I turn to look, a shivery dread working down my spine. No one comes by my house this late anymore. Not even Tucker. He's a morning person. And a back-door kind of guy.

Which means the heavy footfalls climbing my porch steps belong to someone else. Maybe Hitch, determined to protect me. Maybe one of the Kings, determined to show me I need protection. Maybe the Big Man come to tell me he's seen me chatting it up with the fairies or the dock workers or the Kings or the FBI agent and has decided it's best I die after all.

"Two out of three," I whisper. I sit Gimpy back on his bed and crawl toward my bedroom, grateful, once again, that I live in a shotgun shack not much bigger than a shoe box. I'm out of the kitchen and sliding my safe from under my bed in less than a minute. I haven't had my gun out to play since the mess in August, but a two-thirds chance of danger is good enough for me. I spin the combo and pull out the small silver handgun as the knock comes at the door.

It's soft. Too soft. More of a test than a summons.

Whoever's out there is hoping I'm not home. Or asleep. And I get the strong feeling that—should I refuse to answer the door—the knocker is going to come on in. They won't even have to break in in order to enter. Thanks to Gimpy's acts of senseless destruction, I forgot to lock the door behind me.

As the knock comes again and, seconds later, the doorknob begins to turn, I curse beneath my breath and vow to make Gimpy an outside cat. Assuming I still live here tomorrow. Assuming I don't have to kill the person creeping into my house and go on the run from the law because I can't handle a trial. Even a justified homicide trial. The thought of sitting under the cold, judgmental stare of a court official makes me want to stab myself to death with a fork.

I crouch behind the end of the bed, aim at the tall shadow easing inside the darkened living room, and try to breathe past the fear clutching at my chest. "I'll shoot you," I say, stopping the shadow in its tracks. "It's legal to shoot to kill for breaking and entering."

"But it's not legal for you to keep a handgun without a current license," a deep voice rumbles. "And I know that one is expired."

"Cane." I'm relieved. And surprised. And so happy that I find myself laughing hysterically as I put the gun back in the safe and stand on shaky legs. "You scared me."

"Sorry," he says. "I guess I forgot . . . I'm so used to coming in." He shrugs, that familiar bunch of his broad shoulders that makes me want to throw my arms around his neck and squeeze. Instead, I fidget, trapped between what I want and what Cane's refused to give until I make my big decision. "What happened in there?" he asks, motioning over his shoulder.

"The Gimp."

Cane nods, knowing enough about my new cat not to be surprised. "Might want to consider declawing that bad boy."

"Declawing would only take away one of his weapons, not the evil within. I can't de-tooth him, so I figure . . . yeah . . . What's up?" I wince at how awkward I sound.

"I needed to see you." He stops in the doorway to the bedroom, and leans against the frame. He's wearing a pair of dark jeans and that same T-shirt I saw him strip off earlier today and he looks . . . good. Long and lean and strong and safe. Cane is a big man, but he's never made me feel anxious. Not physically, anyway. Emotionally, it's a whole different ball game, one Cane plays with a big stick.

Hm. Big stick.

I didn't mean *that* particular stick, but now that I've thought about sticks I can't keep my eyes from dipping down and back up again, or my thoughts from wandering. A part of me insists that feeling lustful about a man I love is the best revenge for what Gerald tried to do. And I miss Cane's stick. A lot. Sex with him is easy and shameless. Silly and intense, mind-numbing and soul-freeing. I miss his friendship, but being naked with Cane is what I miss the most. Our relationship isn't all about sex, but we do our best connecting when we're . . . connected.

I clear my throat, and try to ignore the X-rated montage flitting through my mind. "Why? What's going on?"

"Nothing. Does something have to be?" He props his almost comically large hands on his hips, and I think about the way they feel wrapped around my waist, almost completely encircling it as he urges my body in all the right directions that feel so. Damned. Good.

I lick my lips. "No. I wanted to see you, too. I

was just thinking about you. The second before you walked in."

"That's good to hear." He smiles that sexy smile I saw this afternoon, and I'm reminded of my other reasons for feeling awkward. I don't believe for a second that Cane is part of any police force corruption—if something like that is going on I'd bet on Dicker or even Dom or Abe before Cane—but there's no doubt he was flirting with Theresa. Full-fledged flirt, with a side of smolder.

"Is it?" I lift a brow.

"Of course it is." He takes another step into the room, but I stop him with a dubious grunt.

"I saw you this afternoon."

"You did?"

"I did. Outside Swallows. With Theresa. *Without* your shirt." I still don't sound angry, and I think that confuses Cane.

It takes several seconds before he says, "Oh," and a couple more before the *"Ohhhh"* comes again, longer and slower. I expect him to start making excuses. Instead, he smiles, teeth glowing white in the semi-darkness. "Jealous?"

I smile back, weirdly turned on by his refusal to explain himself. "Should I be?"

"Probably not." He takes a step closer and then another, until I can feel the furnacelike heat of him. His skin is always hot to the touch. In the winter, I don't need any heat but this man in my bed. In the summer, he sighs when my cool skin presses against his. With relief. Pleasure.

I sigh, thinking about it, and sigh again when his arm wraps around my waist. "But I'd love it if you were."

I tip my head back to stare up into his face. So familiar. More familiar than Hitch's, though I spent three times as many years as one half of Hitch's whole. But I fell so hard and fast for Hitch. It was sparkly and epic, filled with high drama and higher feeling, filmed in glitter vision from day one. And now, so much time has passed, and he's not the same person he was before, so much so that I'm beginning to wonder if I ever saw the real Hitch. Maybe all I saw were the sparkles.

With Cane, the love crept up on me. He was a friend before he was anything more. He was always handsome, but one day I woke up to find him still asleep beside me and he was beautiful. Love had made him beautiful, but I could still see the face of my friend behind the sparkle.

I *know* Cane. I love Cane. And it could be so simple, if I'd only let it be.

Why can't I let it? Why? My eyes burn *yet again*, but I blame the whiskey for the sting and the way my voice cracks when I ask, "Do you still . . . love me?"

He cradles my head in his big hand. "I'll always love you, Lee-lee. You should know that by now."

"I'll always love you, too." The stupid tears spill over, tickling my cheeks. I brace my hands on his chest, the feel of his muscles dipping in all the familiar places making me want to cry harder. "I miss you so much."

"I'm right here." He guides me back to lean against the wall and kisses me. Just once. Soft and sweet, but it's enough to make my entire body ache. "I'm always here. Whenever you want me."

"That's not true." I fist my hands and press them into the pec muscles he spends way too much time perfecting in the DPD weight room, banishing my tears with critical thoughts about how obsessive compulsive he is, reminding myself how annoying I find his healthy eating habits and his ten cans of whey protein shake mix taking up all the counter space in my kitchen. "Not. True."

"Why do you say that?"

"You put us on a time-out."

His lips press together. "Guess I did."

"You're such a girl." I give his chest a one-two punch. Hard, but not hard enough to break free of his arms. "Withholding sex is a girl trick. You get that, right?"

"A girl trick?" His bemused smile makes me punch him again.

"Yes." *Punch.* "Withholding the pussy until you get what you want is the oldest manipulative tactic in the history of female kind." *Punch, punch.* "But it never works! Because how is anyone supposed to make a rational decision when their mind is all fucked up from pussy deprivation?" *Punch, punch.* "And it's even less acceptable coming from a man." *Punch.* "Women have been oppressed for centuries and were forced to use sex as a way to gain power." *Punch.* "Coming from you." *Punch.* "This is just." *Punch.* "Gross!"

I pull back to punch his chest again, but he catches my wrists in his hands, holding them still. "You're right," he whispers to my fists. "I'm sorry."

"You are?" The fight drains out of me, my fingers go limp, and I'm suddenly very aware of his heat and his touch and the certain light in his eyes that says I'm not the only one who's very aware.

"Yes. I am." Slowly, deliberately, he pulls my wrists over my head, pressing them into the wall above me. My lips part, and my breath shudders out with a sigh. "I'm not your father." He shifts closer, pressing that sculpted body against mine, making my insides turn to electrically charged radioactive goo. "And I don't want to be." One hand slides down my arm, over my elbow, down, down, until his hand's on my breast and I've got free fingers to curl around his neck, and pull his lips down to mine.

So I do. I curl. I pull. "I don't want you to be, either," I whisper into his mouth, kissing him with the words, pulse pounding faster as he pulls the neck of my tank top down, eliminating the thin barrier between my skin and the rough pads of his fingers.

Currents of deliciousness sizzle through my body and the ache inside becomes a need that gnaws at my frayed edges, eliminating worry and fear, banishing the awareness of everything but this man and his strong body and soft lips and . . .

God . . . his lips. Skilled and perfect, melting me from the inside out. By the time he gives me a moment to breathe, I can't. I don't want to. I want to drown in him, sink into the warm ocean of Cane and never rise to the surface.

"I just want you," he whispers, his other arm wrapping tight around my waist. "Naked. On that bed, with your legs wrapped around me, and me so deep inside you I don't—"

I stop him with another rough kiss and shove him back toward the bed. I can't take the dirty talk right now. Not until we're both wearing a lot fewer clothes and his skin is hot on mine and his big hands are everywhere.

He falls back onto my rumpled covers, and I go for the bottom of his T-shirt, ripping it over his head before going for my own tank top and finding his hands already there. I lift my arms, blood whooshing in my ears as he rips it up and over my head and I feel his breath hot on my skin and his tongue teasing the sensitive flesh where his fingers were a second ago.

So good. So wickedly good.

I suck in a breath, digging my fingers into his arms as my head falls back and the ceiling spins. "I missed you."

"I missed your tits," he murmurs as he kisses his way up my neck.

"Bet Theresa doesn't let you call them tits." I find his lips, and kiss him hard, refusing to let him pull away. My hand dips between us and I find the button on his fly and then the zipper and then he's pushing me back onto the bed and I'm shoving his jeans down his legs with my toes, moaning with triumph when I free the hot, hard length of him.

He's burning up, rigid, but so soft at the same time. For a moment, I'm reminded of the scalding softness of fairy flesh and my rhythm falters long enough for him to pull his mouth away.

"Theresa and I were starting up the sprinkler in the alley." He unsnaps and unzips my jeans, pulling them down my legs with a swift *shush*, throwing them into the pile of clothes on the floor. "The air-conditioning at Swallows blew and she wanted people to have a way to cool off."

"You two looked pretty cool," I say as he slips his fingers under the sides of my panties and pulls.

He pauses, meeting my eyes with a look that's as serious as sin on a Sunday morning. "Nothing's going on with Theresa and me. You're the only woman I think about." His hands fist in my underwear. "You're the only woman I've been with in almost two years."

I realize it's the same for me. I haven't been with anyone else since Cane and I went on our first date. But before I can wonder what that means—why I've stayed faithful when I didn't have to, after I promised myself I wouldn't be sucked into another pointless exercise in monogamy—my panties are gone.

And Cane's hands are on my thighs, pulling them apart, and his body covers mine and he's telling me that I'm the only woman he wants to be with. And then he's pushing inside me, and my entire body strings tight before breathing a giddy, pleasure-infused sigh of relief.

Finally, finally, *finally*, he's with me again, and I'm not alone in the way that only Cane can make me feel not alone, and he fills every aching inch and all the other aching places that no dick can touch. But his love can. And his words can, and the way he whispers my name like it's the sweetest word he's ever known can.

And they do. Again and again until I'm crying and laughing and coming so many times I lose track and decide counting is overrated.

And hours later, when we're sweaty and sticky and worn the eff out from effing and my head is on his chest and my fingers are brushing back and forth across the springy hairs there and he's sleeping the heavy, solid sleep of strong men and healthy animals everywhere, I am still not alone.

Even in his sleep, I can feel the heart of the man I love beating in time with mine. "I'd bet my left tit you're dreaming about me," I whisper into his skin, smiling when he gives a sleepy grunt that sounds like an admission of guilt. At least to me.

And then my eyes slide closed. And I sleep, and dream of very scary things.

11

This time, the old fairy doesn't bother with words. He goes straight for the shock and awe. My dreams are a relentless, bloody assault on my sanity, filled with images of Grace being ripped to pieces by the fairies, Cane being ripped to pieces by the fairies, Hitch and Marcy and Fernando and Deedee and Theresa and everyone else I've ever cared about shredded before my eyes.

I can hear them screaming, feel how cruelly they're suffering as they die, watch their eyes fly wide and their hands reach for me like I'm the only person in the world that can stop the agony. But I can't. I can't move. I'm buried in the mud, cold, trapped. I can't even close my eyes to block out the misery of the people I've destroyed.

Me. *I* did this.

Deedee howls as a strip of her scalp is peeled away and blood rushes into her eyes, and her pain is my fault. If I'd left Donaldsonville, the people I care about would have been safe. The fairies would have left them alone. If only I'd run away. Run away, run away, r—

"Rnnn way," I mumble as I throw off the dream, pushing it back with an exhausted shove of my thoughts. But it's hard. *So* hard. An incredible effort that leaves me limp, my brain a wad of dough that's been pounded too long. Lumpy, rubbery, useless.

"Blerrr." I curl onto my side and bury my face in my hands, shivering.

I'm covered in a full-body sweat, my head is pounding, and my stomach is full of acid. I could blame the whiskey, but I wasn't drunk when I went to bed. It's the dream that did this. The damned fairy is eating my brain from the inside out.

That has to be it. Somehow, he's sending these dreams. It's the only explanation that makes a lick of sense. That's why I saw him in my head and then on the road in real life. He's trying to scare me away, and he's going to play dirty until he gets what he wants.

I can't blame him. If there were someone around who could control my behavior and kill me with a thought, I'd want them gone, too. I haven't had much time to consider the greater implications of what I did to those fairies yesterday, but the old guy obviously has, and he's determined not to let me fulfill my fairy-destroying potential.

More than my own suspicions, more than the dead Fey I saw squished on the road when I drove back by the scene of yesterday's attack, my nightmare-filled sleep convinces me I'm onto something big. Huge. Maybe life-altering for everyone in the Delta.

What if I can get rid of the fairies? Forever? What if I can take back everything we've lost, and make things the way they were when I was sixteen, before the terrorist attacks on the petrochemical plants and the chemical spills that mutated the fairies and the constant lingering terror that has left so many people shadows of who they could have been if fairies had stayed the stuff of story books and legends?

The idea should be intoxicating, exhilarating. I should be filled with hope and wonder and the fire of Things to Be Done. But all I feel is . . . dread. Big, black, nameless dread hovering over my bed, making me want to hide under the covers.

I don't want this responsibility. I don't want to decide the future. I don't want to be held accountable for changing the fate of every soul living in the infected Delta. Because a part of me wonders if getting rid of the fairies will make things better, if it might not, in fact, make some things worse.

I don't care for spiders or rats or snakes—especially snakes—but they have their place. If the snake population was suddenly wiped out, we'd soon be overrun by mice and rats and all the other disease-bearing critters the snakes used to kill. The fairies are a part of the bayou, too, and have been for hundreds, maybe thousands, of years. Yes, they're larger now and they kill people as well as insects, but that doesn't change the fact that they're a part of our world. I can't know what ripple effects eliminating the fairies would have on everything else living in the infested states.

I suppose I shouldn't care. My sister was killed by fairy bite, so were Hitch's mom and sisters, so were countless other people, and more die or are infected every year. Cane lost his sister to a containment camp a few weeks ago. He'll never hug her again. Because of fairies. Screw upsetting the ecosystem, I should be gearing up for a mass extermination.

But it still doesn't feel right. In the beginning it was so clear—I wanted the fairies dead. I wanted them all burned alive as payment for Caroline. But now . . . when I think about the world before and the world after . . .

There are things that were better then, *hell yes* there were, but there *are* things that are better now. People pull together. Racism and classism and sexism and homophobia still exist, but not with the same raging intensity. People connect because we are all people, united by our common enemy.

"Like Hitler." I jab myself in the eyes with my thumbs, rubbing until I can stand the invasion of gray morning light cutting through the curtains.

Tolerance created by a common terror isn't worth the terror. And who am I to decide if life is better or worse than it was? I'm immune. I've got a free pass, at least for myself. I live in fear of losing the people I care about, but I can wander outside the gates whenever I want.

Or at least I could. Now, the rules are changing, and all this thinking is probably going to amount to nothing. It's going to come down to them or me, and I'm not going to choose the fairies' lives over my own.

I drag myself into a seated position and find the cool hardwood floor with my toes, shivering in the blast of the window air-conditioner, feeling vaguely uncomfortable in my own skin. The air in the house is different this morning. Thicker, but lighter at the same time. I glance at the clock, see that it's only five forty-five, and decide the hideously early hour must be to blame. Then I hear a low rumble in the kitchen and it all comes rushing back to me.

Cane. Me. The bed. The nookie. The lovey-dovey feelings and going to sleep certain the future was going to be brighter this morning.

But it's not. The nightmare made sure of that. The fact that Cane isn't snuggled up beside me right now isn't helping. What's he doing in the kitchen? And who is he talking to before six in the morning?

I stand, careful not to step on the squeaky place in the floor as I tiptoe on bare feet toward the kitchen. I stop when Cane's rumble becomes words I can understand and stand perfectly still, straining my ears not to miss a single word. I know I'm doing a bad thing. I shouldn't eavesdrop on my lover. I am violating his privacy and I feel bad about it.

Just not bad enough to alert him to the fact that I'm no longer asleep.

"I have the money," he whispers. "In cash, all different serial numbers, like you said."

Money. What the . . . ?

"Make sure you've got what you promised." Cane's voice takes on a razor edge I've never heard before. He sounds mean. Scary. I think about tiptoeing back to the bed and hiding under the covers, but before I can move he speaks again. "I'll be in Gramercy at noon. I'll be wearing my suit, and I will be armed."

He pauses. Grunts. "I don't care what he said. I'll be armed, and I'll be able to see anyone else who's armed from the old dock. You come alone, give me what I want, and you won't have to worry about my gun."

The docks. Oh god. Why is Cane going to the docks? With a gun? And a big batch of cash? Even wearing the DPD's iron suit, he won't be completely safe from fairy bite. Why risk his life like that? Why, unless he's involved in something illegal?

Maybe it's an undercover job. Maybe he's trapping a bad guy.

But I know the hopeful thoughts are bullshit. Cane is a man of many talents, but he couldn't act his way out of a paper bag—even in the name of serving and protecting. I always know what Cane's thinking and feeling and so does everyone else. He's an open book, and right now that book is a story about an angry man with a gun who's threatening to shoot whoever's on the other end of the phone if they don't deliver what they've promised to deliver.

"You leave right after, and don't come back through—" He breaks off, and when he speaks again his voice is even harder. "I don't give a shit about your deliveries. You take the money and disappear or I'll *make* you disappear. I don't have anything left to lose."

He has *nothing* left to lose. What am I? What was last night?

"Noon," Cane says again. The phone snaps shut. I spin, heart leaping as I tiptoe-dash to the bed. I ease back onto the covers and throw an arm over my eyes just in time. Cane is by my side a few seconds later, smoothing his hand over my hip.

For the first time, his gentle touch makes my skin crawl. "Lee-lee? You awake?"

I moan, but don't move my arm. I can't look at him right now. Not yet. I can't let him see that anything's changed. I don't want him to suspect that I heard his conversation, not until I show up at that dock today and find out exactly what kind of shipment he and his gun are going to be collecting.

If he'd stopped before that last sentence, I'd be tempted to talk this through right now and do whatever I could to keep him from risking his life outside the iron gates. But I felt the truth in his words. He really believes he has nothing to lose, and I'm tired of feeling like nothing.

"Lee-lee?"

"Wha?" My sleepy voice is so convincing that Cane laughs beneath his breath. *Laughs*. How can he laugh at me? How can he pretend he finds my sleepy morning self adorable when he's planning to put our future at risk?

Maybe he's a better actor than I thought. I certainly never suspected he was involved in the alleged DPD corruption. But he must be in it up to his thick, weight-lifting and whey-protein-shake-guzzling neck. What other reason is there for him to be hanging out on the old dock with a bag of cash?

"I have to go, girl." His hand smoothes up, sliding under my tank top, tracing the curve from my hip to my waist.

I barely resist the urge to bat his fingers away. How dare he? How dare he lie to me when I'd finally started to believe in Us? In me and Cane. Against the world. Filling up each other's emptiness and being something better together and *blah, blah, blah*.

Ugh. I don't have to fake my nauseous moan. "I feel . . . yucky." I push up into a seated position and bring a hand to my forehead, figuring playing sick is the best way to avoid a mushy good-bye.

"You look beautiful." He kisses the nape of my neck, making me shiver. His lips still feel good, even knowing they're the lips of a traitor. "You were sweet in your sleep this morning. Like an angel."

I snort. "An angel of death."

"If death looks like you, it can come for me anytime." He tries to pull me into his arms, but this time I can't stop myself from shoving him away.

"Bathroom. I must go to it." I stumble toward the bathroom, pretending I don't notice the hurt on his face. "Call me?"

"We still on for later? Mama's expecting you."

I lean heavily against the bathroom door. "Right. Lunch. Noon, is it?" I ask innocently.

"No. We decided to have dinner instead. Around five. Abe has to work and I've got errands to get done before the week starts."

Black-market-business-on-the-docks types of errands. Grrr. What a *liar* he is. It makes me want to punch him in the chest and demand the truth.

Instead I smile. "I'll be there. I'm sure I'll feel better after a shower."

"Okay." Cane rises and slips on the shoes he kicked to the floor last night. "You want to pick me up? I'd love to see your new ride in action."

"What new ride?"

He smiles and motions toward the kitchen. "You realize you've got a Harley in your kitchen, right? When did you get that? And why—"

"I didn't want to park it outside until I built a shed." I cut his questions off at the pass, cursing Tucker and the Big Man and their stupid gift that I haven't had time to figure out how to dispose of. "I know it's a pain in the ass in there. I'll figure something out."

"I can build you something," he says, making it even harder to pretend. How can he stand there and act like everything is hunky-dory, when he's getting ready to risk his life? How can he look me in the eye and smile like he loves me when he's got nothing left to lose?

"Thanks, but I know you're busy." My tone is more cutting than I would like. I cover with another smile. "See you at your mom's. Five o'clock."

He nods, obviously confused. "All right." He turns toward the door, but turns back almost immediately, a softer look in his eyes. "Hey. I love you."

"Love you, too." I do. But that doesn't keep me from glaring at his back as he walks to the door.

I love him, but he's made that immaterial. The only thing that matters is what goes down at noon. If he gives me proof that he's one of the bad guys, I'll have no choice but to end things. Just because he's the man I love doesn't make it okay for him to be a criminal, any more than being my surrogate mom makes it okay for Marcy to traffic in black-market drugs.

Jesus. First Fernando, then Marcy, now Cane. Who's next? Who else is going to prove to me that I'm a trusting idiot without the sense god gave intestinal bacteria?

Hm. Intestinal bacteria . . .

I really *don't* feel well. My stomach gurgles sickly and the weak morning light feels like it's stabbing me in the eyeballs. Shower. It needs to happen.

I head into the bathroom and reach past the faded green shower curtain to turn on the water. I strip off my dirty tank top, throw it in the already overflowing wicker basket, and consider forcing myself into the water before it's warm in the name of shocking myself awake. Then I catch sight of myself in the mirror.

Beautiful, my ass. I look like *hell*. My hair is sticking out in a thousand different directions, dark circles purple the skin beneath my eyes, and my pupils are as dilated as they were the morning after I was first bitten by fairies. I lean over the sink, getting as close as I dare to my troubling reflection.

I look like a creepy doll with black button eyes. Good thing it was dark in my bedroom and Cane was too preoccupied to bother looking too closely or I would have been on my way to the emergency room. I'm going to have to wear my sunglasses all day or risk seriously freaking people out. I grab my toothbrush with an angry grunt and set to vigorously brushing my teeth.

Shit! Why is this happening? Am I getting sick again? Is the shot wearing off a few days early? Should I give myself another? If I do, is it going to show up on my drug test at work? Is the shot what's making me able to control the fairies? Are the Big Man and Tucker aware that we can do this kind of thing? Can they control them, too? And where the hell is Tucker and why hasn't he moved the goddamned Harley out of my kitchen?!

"Argh!" I kick at the sink, groaning as my bare toes crunch against the cabinet. I spit out my toothpaste, stab my toothbrush back into the holder, and hop toward the shower, cussing beneath my breath, lamenting the state of my life, cursing all the gods human beings ever imagined into existence.

And then I pull back the shower curtain, forget my less pressing troubles, and scream like the heroine of a 1950s horror movie.

Because there is someone in my shower.

A small, paunchy someone with damp wings, and a very nasty—very toothy—little smile.

12

I stumble backward, covering my bare chest with my arms for a moment before I realize I don't care if the old fairy bastard sees me naked. He's practically an insect, for god's sake.

Besides, he's naked, and *he* doesn't seem to care.

In fact, he appears pretty damned pleased with himself. He's smiling like the cat that ate the sofa, sliding his ass back and forth across my damp bar of soap, leaving a trail of light green behind.

"That's my soap!" I point a serious finger at his face. "Don't poop on my soap!"

His grin grows another layer of fangs and more green oozes onto my Ivory. I glare at him, trying to focus over the jackhammer of my pulse drilling away in my head. There is a *fairy* in my *bathroom*. Somehow he got inside the iron gate, through the iron grid, and all the way to my house without shriveling into a fairy nugget from overexposure to deadly metal.

"Crap." My heart works even faster. What if the

gates are down? What if the town is filled with fairies? What if—

I spin to the tiny bathroom window and rip apart the blinds. Outside, the morning light is starting to turn pale yellow and the world is the picture of peace and quiet. Bernadette's flowers nod in a gentle breeze and what I can see of the street is empty—of people *and* fairies.

Still, I have to be sure, and this thing obviously understands English.

I whip back around, pinning him with my toughest look. "How did you get here? Are you the only one, or are there others?" He responds with a screechy cackle and another wiggle of his bare ass. I step closer and turn off the water with a swift twist of my wrist. "Answer me," I demand in the new silence. "Answer me, or I'll do to you what I did to your friends." Yesterday, I was focused on the fairies closest to the truck and missed this guy, but that's a mistake that can be remedied. Quickly.

The fairy's nasty grin falls away. His jaw unhinges and he bares his ancient teeth in a royally pissed-off hiss. His tiny hands fist at his sides and his skin glows a faint yellow, but he doesn't attack, and when he's done with his tantrum, he actually answers my question. "I come alone!"

English. He's speaking English. It's still blowing my mind.

"How did you get in?" I ask, trying not to lose my shit. Yesterday, I was protected by the suspicion that he was a figment of my imagination. Now, I know he's real. As real as the iron gate that should have kept him in the bayou where he belongs. "Why isn't the iron in the town killing you?"

"Slake are strong." He flutters into the air, hovering a few inches above eye level. "Slake will have the town and all the food in it. When we want it, we will have it."

I shiver, knowing he isn't talking about the food on the shelves at Piggly Wiggly. He's talking about my friends and neighbors. "You're a liar. The gate keeps the fairies out. I've seen what happens when they get too close. They die."

"The young ones. Not we who lived through the growing time." His chest puffs up and his shoulders roll back, as if he's expecting to start growing again any second. "We learned to drink your poisons and survive. We will learn to live in your metal towns and feed."

He must be talking about the mutations. That the fairies that lived through the mutations aren't as sensitive to iron. But that still doesn't hold water. "It can't be only the newborn fairies that can't cross the gate. We've always used iron to keep from being attacked. Way before eggs had time to hatch we—"

"Second growing time."

"Second growing time?" I squint at him. He doesn't look any bigger than he did the other day, or any bigger than the average fairy. If anything he's smaller, shrunken and pruned in the way of the very old.

"Nothing a human would know." He smiles and scratches his stomach. There's no belly button—

fairies are hatched from eggs, so no umbilical cord. It makes it even stranger that, otherwise, his body could belong to a miniature geriatric. Fairies are remarkably humanoid in appearance, except for the wings and the shark teeth and the black, bulbous eyes.

With my eyes as dilated as they are today, all I need is a pair of wings and some fangs and I could be this dude's much larger, much younger cousin. He even has a few wisps of red hair on his head that aren't too far from my color.

I cross my arms over my chest, suddenly not as okay with continuing this discussion naked. This fairy isn't an insect or even an animal. He's a creature capable of thought and language and plotting things that will be bad for everyone I care about. I inch back to the dirty clothes basket, grab my discarded tank top, and jerk it over my head. Even with only panties on bottom, I feel better. "Why are you here?" I hope my tone lets Grandpa know I'm not going to be satisfied with vague answers.

"You know why."

"You want me to leave town. If I don't, you're going to keep trying to kill me."

He grins another mean grin. "Maybe not so stupid."

He made a joke. Employed sarcasm. It makes it hard to swallow or think of what to say. Fairies having language is one thing; having a smart-ass sense of humor is another entirely. It makes them even more human. And more evil than I ever imagined.

They aren't mindless killing machines driven by

instinct. They are thinking, feeling, humor-possessing creatures, who have simply decided they should be at the top of the food chain. And that people are their preferred meat.

"I'm not leaving," I whisper, the sick feeling in my gut worse than ever. "Especially not knowing you can get inside the gates. I'm going to stay here and I'm going to kill every single fairy who dares to flap a wing in Donaldsonville."

"You can't kill us all." His eyes narrow. "You don't have the strength."

"I'm tougher than I look."

"Not when your mind is gone." He flutters closer, until our noses are only inches apart. "I will come to you every time you sleep. I will fill your mind with blood. You will wake one morning and never stop screaming."

What small sense of victory I feel for my spot-on deduction is banished by the reality of his words. He really *is* coming to me in my dreams, filling them with horror. And he'll keep doing it until I'm exhausted and sick and crazy, and, if for some reason that plan fails, I know he'll move on to killing people, creating more loved ones that I've failed to protect. If he can sneak into my house, he could as easily sneak into Cane's or Fernando's. Or slip into Sweet Haven and find Deedee on her narrow cot. One bite and their lives will be over. Literally, if they're among the severely allergic.

Which means there's only one thing to do.

Grandpa must read the decision in my eyes. He flits away, darting back so quickly that his wings hit the tile with a soft *thwph* before he slides back down to the poo-streaked soap. "If you kill me, there will be others to take my place!"

I shrug and step closer, until my toes touch the cool claw foot of the tub. "Guess I'll have to kill them, too."

"If you kill me, the Slake will take this town." He puffs up his chest again, trying to look fierce. But I can see the fear in him. Guess he didn't expect me to fight back. Guess I really am smarter—or at least more murderous—than he gave me credit for. "They will not suffer the death of their king."

"Like you won't suffer Gentry." This is it. My chance to get some real information. "What are Gentry?" He opens his mouth to hiss, but I stop him with a finger in the air. "Tell me, or I'll kill you right now." He closes his mouth, presses his lips together. I shrug again. "All right. I would say it was nice knowing you, but you're a filthy, mean bastard who pooped on my last bar of soap. And you tried to kill me, so I figure it's only—"

"The Gentry rule," he says, arms beginning to tremble. I'm guessing with rage, but he could be cold. It's cooler in the bathroom than the rest of the house and he *is* naked and wet. For a second I think about offering him a washcloth to wrap up in, but decide that would affect the credibility of my death threat and settle for another glare.

"And?"

"They are the most powerful Fey folk," he says. "They lived long ago. We were their slaves."

"How long ago?"

He crosses his arms, stilling the tremble. "Longer than you can imagine."

"So you're . . . thousands of years old."

"I am time itself." His chin lifts, and his nose pokes proudly into the air. "I am of the first. I am a god."

I roll my eyes. "You're an egomaniac."

"I am a father to my people. I will not see them slaves. No new Gentry will rise."

"You said the Gentry were fairies." I point over my shoulder at my bare back. "In case you haven't noticed, I'm not."

"Not all Fey folk have wings."

"I'm not a Fey folk. I'm a person."

"It doesn't matter." He sniffs, scrunches his face into a pout. "You grow too powerful."

"And whose fault is that? Your people are the ones who bit me and infected me with their stupid magic in the first place. I never wanted this."

"The young ones are fools. They are forbidden to touch the poison people. But children never listen." His proud head dips. Ruling a bunch of bloodthirsty kids can't be easy. "Few will live to see a hundred years. Fewer a thousand."

"Few of them will live to see next week if you don't stay out of Donaldsonville, out of my dreams, and away from anything with two legs. The next time— the *very* next time—I hear about a person getting bitten in your territory, I'm going to come out there and kill every last one of you."

He chuckles, but when he lifts his eyes he doesn't look amused. Or scared. He looks . . . defeated. "You kill the Slake; you kill yourself. Your magic is the magic of the Slake."

There's a very serious, very human expression on his tiny face. He isn't the gross old geezer or the gleeful monster anymore. He's realized that act isn't going to work. Now he's trying something new, something that sounds like the truth.

"Your power comes from the lesser Fey," he says. "It is why we must obey your magic. But we have our own power. Long ago, the Gentry slaughtered us to protect the humans they loved. But when the Slake died, the Gentry died, too. All but the strongest, who used the last of their magic to make the Slake so small it seemed we had ceased to exist."

"But you didn't," I whisper, awed by the story he's telling. What if it's true?

"We did not." He stands on top of the soap, managing to look dignified despite the fact that his own excrement squishes between his toes. "We formed hunting parties to kill insects for the blood we needed. We survived in a world filled with predators. We endured until the poison came and our bodies grew large and the birth of new Slake led us into a second growing time. We will survive the challenges of the new world. And you, Annabelle Lee."

"So if I kill too many of the Slake, I kill myself?" I ask, trying to sort out his logic.

"And your Gentry friends."

Hm. "But shouldn't that go both ways? If we have some kind of symbiotic magical relationship, shouldn't you suffer for killing me?"

He grunts, and I detect a hint of respect in his beady eyes. "Slake will die when you die. But if you refuse to leave, it is a price we will pay. This is our breeding ground, the only place where Slake eggs survive."

Well then. We're back to this. He needs me gone, and I refuse to leave. That means one of us has to die, and I don't plan on it being me. I should kill him now. Fast, like lightning striking, before he can fly away. Instead, I find myself asking, "Do you *have* to eat people? I mean, it sounds like you survived on insects for a long—"

"Mosquitoes."

Ah. Mosquitoes. They've been getting their human blood second hand, but they've still been getting it. I should have guessed. I know fairies have a taste for the bloodsuckers.

"But we could go without," he says, surprising me with the freely offered information. "We fed on other beings before humans walked the earth."

"Then why don't you go *back* to feeding on other beings?" I know reasoning with this man is pointless, but I can't stop myself from trying. "Leave people alone. If you do, there's at least a chance we could—"

"Declare a peace?" The fairy laughs, a grating screech that makes me wince. "Humans don't understand peace. Or balance. They fight nature with bombs and medicines and poison. Now their poison has created a solution to the human virus. The Slake will feed and the earth will reclaim the rotted bodies of the dead and sigh with relief."

"You make it sound so poetic." My tone is dry, but inside I'm feeling anything but cool or unaffected. He's talking about a fairy apocalypse. All-out war between the human and the Fey.

"It is justice. But you can be spared. For a time. Leave. And live."

"I can't."

"Can't?" He crouches on top of the soap and runs a thoughtful finger over a patch of dried suds. "I have seen your sleep thoughts. I know your desire. I could show you the way to the cave of screams." Something inside me perks up. He's talking about the cave Hitch's friend found. He has to be. "The man would leave. You could take the little girl and—"

Something crashes to the floor in the kitchen with an epic *scraa-bam!*

The second my focus splits, Grandpa Slake shoots into the air, rushing for the window. I dive back, getting a hand on the crank handle and spinning it closed seconds before his body hits the glass. He bounces back into the bathroom, tumbling into the sink with a hiss.

Scrambling to keep him from bolting a second time, I grab a towel from the rack and throw it over the entire sink, then upend the trash can by the toilet and slam it down over the towel. Hopefully the towel and metal trash can will be enough to keep Grandpa trapped until I decide what to do with him.

Right now, I need to go take care of whoever is in my kitchen.

I back out the door to the bathroom and slam it

closed, then drag my bedside table in front as an extra barrier, not caring if the person snooping around in my house hears me. I hope they do. I hope they hear me and get the hell out. I'd be happy to avoid a confrontation with an intruder in my underwear and dirty tank top.

Of course, there's a good chance this is an intruder I know. Maybe Tucker decided to pop in for another visit. If so, he's going to regret sticking his handsome nose in my business today. I need answers and it's past time Tucker gave them up. I'm not even going to try asking nicely. I'm going straight to threatening at gunpoint and see how far that gets me.

I grab my gun from the safe I didn't bother closing last night, and stalk toward the now silent kitchen. "Who's in there?" I demand, but the only response is more silence.

Grr. I am so *sick* of people sneaking into my house. Whatever happened to respecting people's privacy? Whatever happened to *asking* before you let yourself in or lurk in wait to stab people with needles or steal their frosty beverages or dump a Harley in their kitchen or hide out in the shower and poop on the soap?

"I've got a gun," I say, louder this time. "And I will shoot the shit out of you and I will enjoy it because I'm in *that* kind of mood this morning!"

Still no response. If the hairs on my arms weren't standing on end, I'd think Gimpy had knocked the coffeepot off the counter or something. But I can *feel* another person breathing my air, taking up my space, smelling their smell in my . . .

"Hitch?" The verification that the Hitch smell is indeed attached to my ex comes as I step into the doorway. Hitch stands at the far edge of my kitchen, wedged into the corner by the Harley, which is now lying sideways on the floor.

I should have known that crash was too big for a coffeepot.

He doesn't look up when I speak his name. He keeps staring at the hog at his feet and the leather storage compartment that has popped open, spilling syringes out onto the floor. Syringes. Glass syringes. Like the ones that were stolen from the dock, that are somehow related to the death of his friend. Syringes I haven't bothered to tell him I have in my possession because I'm forbidden to speak of them. Because the Big Man will kill anyone I tell and then kill me for telling.

But here we are. With Hitch bending down to pick a needle up from the ground and me standing in the doorway with a loaded gun that can do nothing to protect us from the danger that's been unleashed in my kitchen.

13

He looks up, tragic blue eyes meeting mine. He looks so hurt, so utterly betrayed. I expect him to start hurling accusations, to ask what I was really doing down at the docks, to ask how much I know about the missing medical supplies and the cave and all the rest of it, but instead he asks, "Are you going to shoot me?"

I startle, arm shaking as I realize I still have the gun aimed at my "intruder."

"No. Jesus. Of course not." My breath rushes out and the weapon falls to my side. "I thought . . . I didn't . . ."

I take a shaky step into the kitchen and drop the gun on the table, wishing Gimpy were still in his bed underneath. I could use some fluffy support right now. But Gimpy's already up and about. He must have decided to make use of the cat door I installed in the kitchen. Or maybe Hitch let him *out* when he let himself *in*.

Which raises the question . . .

"What are you doing in here?"

"We were supposed to meet at six o'clock," he says, his voice flat.

I shake my head. "No we weren't. I . . . I told you everything last night. I assumed the meeting was off."

"I assumed it was on," he says. "When you didn't show up, I thought something had happened. I came to the back door because I remembered you said your neighbor spies on people who come to the front. I saw the motorcycle and I know you don't have a motorcycle, so I . . . came in."

"And knocked it over?"

"It fell over," Hitch says. "I didn't touch it."

"It's been sitting there for days and it didn't fall over." I huff, wondering if it's possible to keep arguing about stupid things and never get around to talking about the needle Hitch clutches so tight his knuckles have gone white.

"What are you doing to yourself?" he whispers.

"I'm not doing anything to—"

"Heroin or Breeze?" he demands, in his no-nonsense, I'm-a-doctor-and-have-my-shit-infinitely-more-together-than-you-do tone. The tone instinctively pisses me off, even before I get the meaning of what he's asking.

He's asking what I'm *on*—heroin or Breeze. Both highly additive monster drugs only fools think they can use in moderation. I know better. I worked in the emergency room and saw firsthand what happens to people who stick needles in their veins. I'd have to have a death wish to get involved in that level of drug use. I'd have to be insane.

But I guess Hitch doesn't find that so hard to believe.

I should be grateful that he jumped to the druggie conclusion instead of the involved-in-conspiracies conclusion, but I'm not. I'm hurt. And angry. I want to slap that sad, pitying, disappointed look from his face.

Instead, I point to the door. "Get out."

I have a fairy locked in my bathroom. I don't have time for the drama, and the longer Hitch stands there, the better the chance some invisible person will wander by and see that he's found my shot stash. I need to get him out, and then I need to hide those shots somewhere none of my visitors—invited or uninvited—will find them.

Then I'll track Hitch down, and make sure he doesn't talk about what he saw on my kitchen floor. Ever. After all the favors I've done for him, he can do that much for me.

"Out," I insist again, when he makes no move toward the door.

"No." His jaw tightens. "I won't let you kill yourself."

"I'm not killing myself! God! Of all the self-righteous, preachy, conclusion-jumping—"

"Why are you doing this?" He steps over the handlebars of the fallen bike, needle still clenched in his hand like a smoking gun. "Why are you throwing *everything* away?"

"I'm not," I snap. "You have no idea what's going on."

"I know what you told me last night." His words hit me in my already rotten-feeling guts. I don't want to think about what I told him. I don't want to think about how we kissed afterward. And I certainly don't want to think about it while standing in front of him in nothing but panties and a tank top.

"Please, leave." I angle myself behind one of the kitchen chairs, hoping it will offer some cover.

"I care about you." He crosses the kitchen with obvious purpose, only stopping when his knees hit the legs of my chair. "I want to help you."

I would roll my eyes, but he's too close and I'm too semiclothed and vulnerable and angry and frustrated.

Instead, I try to snatch the needle away, but Hitch won't let go. He holds tight with one hand and grabs my wrist with the other. Before I can think about pulling away, he's kicked the chair out from between us and pulled me close, until our tangle of arms is the only thing keeping my body from his and I can feel his jeans against my bare legs and his fingers brush my chest, making my skin heat in spite of all the awful emotions swimming inside me.

"I can get you checked into a treatment center by lunchtime." His mouth is so close to mine that I can smell the hint of coffee on his breath. "I know some great people. Therapists and doctors who can save your life if you'll let them. If you'll let *me*." He drops his voice to a whisper. "Please, let me . . . Please."

I look up, blinking, shocked by how much he wants to save me. Too bad I don't need to be saved.

Well, maybe I do. But not from anything as "easily" solved as a drug addiction. Double too bad that I find the fact that he's jumped to Annabelle-damning conclusions again after our talk last night absolutely enraging.

Absolutely. En. Rage. Ing.

"Jesus," he mutters beneath his breath. "Your eyes . . ."

"I'm not high," I say through gritted teeth. "And I find everything you've said in the past three minutes very, *very* offensive."

"I'm not judging you. I'm only trying to—"

"Yes you are." I jerk my wrist free and stumble back a few steps, half-falling against the wall. "You've been judging me since you showed up last month in your fancy new suit with your stupid new hair and your perfect new life. But trust me, Hitch, you have no idea what's going on in this town. Or with me."

"I helped with the Breeze investigation. I think I know how prevalent drug use is in this part of Louisiana." He props his hands on his hips, holding up his saggy shoulders, looking so weary it's all I can do not to scream.

"Listen to me."

"I am lis—"

"Forget all the things you think you know and really *listen*," I whisper. Bernadette is probably awake next door. I can't afford to have her popping over to check on me. The fewer people who see the shots, the better chance we all have of living through the day. "There are bad things happening in Donaldsonville that have nothing to do with drugs. And I'm involved in them, whether I like it or not."

I take a step closer, curl my fingers around his arm and hold tight. "And unless you give me this needle and walk out of here and pretend this morning never happened, you will be, too. And then you'll be dead." I meet his gaze without flinching, willing him to look into me and see the truth the way he once could. "Because that's what the bad guys do when you break the rules. They kill you and they kill everyone else they think might know their secrets."

Hitch's eyes go wide. "You know what's happening to the medical supplies."

It's the other logical conclusion, but it's still not the *right* conclusion and it only proves that Hitch is determined to think the worst of me. Even though it makes sense for him to think the things he's thinking, I hate him for thinking them. I hate him for pitying me and for the hard suspicion creeping across his face. I hate him enough to open my mouth and let the dangerous truth spill out.

"No. I don't." I tighten my grip on his forearm, letting my nails dig into his skin. "I was bitten by fairies while I was saving *your* life. And all that stuff they say about the immune not being affected by fairy bite? It turns out that's not true. At least not around here."

He pales. "You mean you—"

"I'm not infected, not the way a nonimmune person would be." I'm still not quite angry enough to let him fear the worst. "But I started having reactions.

Dilated pupils and horrible headaches and . . . other things."

"What other—"

"I can move things. With my mind," I blurt out before I lose the courage. Hitch can give me his she's-finally-lost-it look all he likes, but in the end I can *prove* what I'm saying. I can lift that Harley off the floor; I can snatch the gun on the table up with a thought and bring the butt down on Hitch's thick skull.

"Move things," he repeats carefully. *Too* carefully.

He's probably wondering who he'll have to call to have me forcibly admitted, but that doesn't stop me. I've started the story; I might as well finish it. As angry as I am, it's still a relief to finally tell *someone* what's really going on.

"Yes. With my mind. And I can manipulate matter at baser level, too. Like when Stephanie was dying." My heart beats faster. "I know it sounds nuts, but I healed her. I fixed the hole in her lung."

Hitch's eyebrows lift and I see the Delusional Disorder, Grandiose Subtype, with possible Schizophrenic Overtones diagnosis flitting behind his eyes. "Annabelle, I—"

"I saved the-woman-you're-too-chickenshit-to-call-your-wife's life," I say, losing what's left of my temper. "But the only way I was able to do that was with this."

I shake his arm, making the needle bounce between us before he flexes his muscle, stopping it cold. He's stronger than he used to be. All those crack-of-dawn runs and manly push-up and sit-up sessions have paid off. There's no way I'll be able to physically overpower him and take the needle.

Unless I call my own bluff and see how strong my mental workouts have made me. I moved a two-ton truck yesterday. I could force Hitch's fingers open with a thought. To prove myself, I might have to. But not yet. The honest to god insane part of me still hopes he might listen. That he might believe.

"There are other immune people who have been bitten and had the same reactions," I say. "They created the medicine in this injection. As far as I know, it helps control the negative side effects of immune infection and keeps me from going crazy like Grace Beauchamp did before she was murdered. She was immune and had been bitten, but her sister stopped giving her the shots."

Hitch's eye twitches.

"But that's another story."

It twitches again, a prolonged quiver that would be funny if anything were funny right now.

I screw my courage to the sticking point and push on. "Libby and her brother didn't follow the rules. So the man in charge of handing out the shots killed them." I lower my voice. Just thinking about the Big Man is enough to scare the crap out of me. "And he'll kill you, too. Unless you give me this, walk out of here, and never say a word to anyone about what I've told you."

Hitch sighs. The frustration and sadness in the noise says it all. I know he doesn't believe me, even before he mutters, "Annabelle . . ." My name is the first note of the saddest song ever sung.

My fingers slip from his wrist and my gaze drops to the ground. I study my bare feet and the long knobby toes Hitch used to make fun of back when all my parts were a source of endless fascination. Now all my parts add up to nothing. At least in his eyes.

Maybe he's right. Maybe I *am* a crazy person who's throwing her life away. I shouldn't be standing here explaining myself to a man who's proved he doesn't have any faith in me. Or planning to spy on a man with lying on his Sunday to-do list, or imagining that I might be better for Deedee than the group home, or that Fernando would miss me if I left, or that I might be able to change the course of the Delta's fairy-plagued history.

I should be in the car on my way out of town, with the wind in my hair and my cat in the passenger's seat.

I'm *seriously* thinking about it. Seriously considering grabbing a pair of jeans, my sunglasses, and a pair of flip-flops, and heading next door to "borrow" Bernadette's Mustang with no intention of bringing it back.

And then Hitch whispers, "I love you," and my heart stops beating.

14

A choking sound gurgles in my throat. "What?" I must have heard him wrong, I must have—

"I love you," he says, soft and sure, his expression telling me he's been thinking about saying those words for a while. "I never stopped loving you. I thought I did, but I . . . I was so angry. And hurt . . . I'm not angry or hurt anymore."

The light in the kitchen is getting brighter and my headache never really went away, but that isn't why I blink. Then blink again. And again. He loves me. I love him, too. But what difference does that make? And more important—

"What's love have to do with telekinesis?" I cross my arms, huddling against the weird vibe he's giving off.

"What is love if *not* telekinesis?"

"Um . . ." Maybe I'm not the crazy one.

"The direct influence of the mind on a physical system." Hitch's hand moves to rest on the same hip Cane touched less than an hour ago. "A force that makes your heart beat faster because one person is standing next to you instead of another."

His head dips closer to mine, but I keep my eyes on his chest. I'm not ready to look up. I have no idea what's happening here, but I'm sure it's not a good thing. "I'm not talking about pheromones," I say. "I'm talking about lifting the banana out of my fruit basket and floating it across the room."

"And yet you chose the banana."

He's got to be kidding. I pin him with a tough look. "Really? Now?"

"You're the one who brought up the banana."

"Is that a joke?"

"Not a very good one. Sorry."

I blink again, befuddled. "This is not how I expected this conversation to proceed."

"The expected is overrated." His arm wraps farther around my waist. I waver, torn between leaning in and pulling away. Finally I settle for a hand on his chest, contact with a degree of resistance.

"What about everything I just told you?"

"What about it?"

"Do you believe me?" I don't bother trying to hide how much I need him to believe. If he can . . . if he does . . . it could change everything. Absolutely everything.

"I don't know what to believe," he says. "There are a lot of things I don't understand."

"Are you going to try?"

"Try to believe that you have superhero mind powers and that similarly powered immune people have provided you with medicine to support your ability, but will kill you if you share that information?"

I laugh. A sad laugh. "Of course not." Stupid, Annabelle.

But in a way it's a relief. That moment of blinding hope was exhausting.

"How did we get here?" His arm tightens, hugging me close, tempting me to drop my head onto his chest. "You and me?"

He's not talking about this cramped kitchen with the motorcycle on the floor. He's talking about being so close, but still so out of reach. Of knowing so much about each other that we're worse than strangers. We're people who knew older versions of each other too well to ever see the new person standing in front of us.

"I don't know," I whisper.

"Will you let me take this?" Hitch holds up the shot with his free hand. "I can send it back to New Orleans. A good friend of mine works at a lab."

"No." I shake my head. "Absolutely not."

"He'll keep the results confidential. Just between him and me. And you, of course. And then we won't have to—"

"No." I push at his chest, slip out of his arms. "The people who gave me the shots know how many I have. If one goes missing, they'll find out. And then I'll be dead."

"Annabelle, I—"

"Do you want me dead?" I snatch at the shot. Hitch jerks it away, up over his head. "Do *you* want to end up dead?"

"I don't think it has to—"

"And what about Stephanie?" I cross my arms. "How can you say what you said to me when you have a beautiful, smart, successful, kind woman who's pregnant with your child waiting for you in New Orleans? Who you have asked to marry you? *Marry*."

His lips thin. "The pregnancy wasn't planned."

"Does that matter?"

He ducks his head, but the shot stays up in the air, out of reach. "No. It doesn't."

"How can you do this to her?"

He laughs, a sound as desperate and confused as I feel. "What *am* I doing? Can you tell me? *I* don't even know what I'm doing. I love Stephanie. I'd do anything to keep her and the baby safe, but I . . . I don't know." He breaks off with a curse. The shot falls to his side as he runs a frustrated hand through his hair, but I don't reach for it. I feel frozen, so completely repulsed and excited that I think I might be sick.

"You shouldn't be saying these things to me," I warn.

"I shouldn't be promising the rest of my life to someone when I can't . . . I just can't . . ."

I don't want to ask him, I don't want to say a word, but I can't keep myself from whispering, "Can't what?"

He looks up, taking my breath away. "I can't forget you. Ever." His eyes meet mine and all the bullshit he's shoveled to cover up the real Hitch is flushed away. It's him. It's *my* Hitch, the one who remembers what is was like to be us, who's still a part of me no matter how I try to deny it. And he isn't lost or erased and I'm so happy to see him that it makes me miserable.

Because what can we do? Where do we go from here?

"But I think you're insane." His voice is heavy, thick.

"I know." But it doesn't make me angry anymore.

Hitch would be crazy *not* to think I'm crazy. And he's not. But he *is* conflicted. And he loves me. He said the words. That he wasn't sure he was ready to promise his life to someone else. Because of me.

Way down deep inside where my happily-ever-after wishes are locked away in a prison made of hope-resistant stone, I've been dreaming about this. About Hitch realizing he's made a mistake and coming back to me. But now that it's actually happened, all I feel is . . . sad. Sad for me and Hitch and Cane and Stephanie and the baby and all the people who will be hurt if Hitch and I let our feelings get the better of us.

And sad about the feelings, too. They shouldn't be here. They had their moment and that moment is over. Letting love be a possibility in the here and now is—

"Crazy," Hitch says, as if he's been reading my mind, following my thoughts through the maze of pointlessness and gloom. "You're crazy. You always have been. And I'm tired of pretending I don't find crazy sexy as hell."

Oh dear. There's *that* look, the sex eyes that make

me take a step back even as my heart beats faster. "Hitch—"

"I don't want to be the man I'm becoming, and I can't be the man I was," he says. "I don't know what to be or believe anymore. But I know I love you and I want to help you. If this is drugs, you can beat it."

Aaaannd we're back to this. Again.

"And if it's not," he continues. "You can still beat it. They have some great medications on the market right now. People with mental illness can be well without losing who they—"

"Jesus!" My shout turns to a burst of hysterical laughter. "I don't have a mental illness! Okay? I really don't."

"You don't have to lose yourself. You'll still be Annabelle. I wouldn't want you to be anyone else."

I grit my teeth, muffling my scream of frustration. That's it. I can't take this anymore. I need Hitch to wake up and smell the magic.

I turn my attention to the bike on the floor, willing it to rise. To tilt back onto its wheels and poke out its kickstand and stand upright and shove the truth in Hitch's face. If he thinks he's troubled now, wait until he gets an eyeful of what's *really* going on around here.

I have some very vivid, very brief, fantasies about Hitch falling to his knees and begging for my forgiveness for being such a close-minded fool. And then I realize the motorcycle isn't moving.

Not moving. Not at all. Not a wiggle, not a twitch. What the . . . ?

Hitch starts talking again, but I silence him with a hand in the air as I step around him to get a better view of the bike. It's on its side, but it doesn't seem to be caught under the counter or stuck on anything. There shouldn't be any problem. I mean, it's a heavy bike, but I moved a *Land Rover* yesterday.

I squint and flex my base-of-the-brain muscle, but the only result is a flash of pain behind my eyes.

Oh my god. Oh. My. God. *Ohmyfuckinggod*.

My pulse kicks into a rapid-fire beat that would make the drummer of Fairies Will Die proud. I'm broken. My mind powers aren't working. And proving to Hitch that I'm not crazy is the least of my problems.

I can avoid the bayou for a while, but I'll eventually have to venture outside the gates. And when I do, I'm going to die. If I can't control the fairies, they're going to kill me. Violent, skin-peeled-from-my-flesh-while-I'm-still-alive kind of kill.

And then there's the fairy in my bathroom that I smugly assumed was mine to control. But here I am. No control. And the only thing that might help me gain it is being held captive by my ex-boyfriend. There's no way Hitch is going to let me pick up a shot and inject myself.

I have to change the plan. I have to play nice. With Hitch and, more important, with Grandpa Scary, who I've already royally pissed off. "Shit!"

"Annabelle?"

"Don't tell me you love me again." I run a shaking hand through my hair, wincing as fingers catch in tangled curls. "I can't do that right now."

His hand brushes my shoulder. "Can I ask if you're okay?"

I shrug him off and stumble toward the bedroom. "I need a shower." I stop in the doorway and spin back to pin him with a shaking finger. "Wait right there." I hustle into the bedroom, grab the safe I use for my gun, and carry it back to the kitchen, dropping it on the table with a clank. "Put all the needles in there, lock it up, and stick it under the sink. We'll talk about where to put the shots that's agreeable to both of us later. But there is *no way* I'm letting you send them to a lab or anywhere else. That's not an option. Do you understand me? This has to stay a secret."

He nods. "Okay. For now."

I want to tell him "for forever," but I don't. He doesn't understand the danger. I do. My best hope of keeping him safe is to get the shots hidden and then come back and get them when he's distracted by other things. Like investigating that cave . . .

If I can get the fairy to talk, there's a chance . . .

"After the shots are locked up, pick up the bike and make yourself some coffee. I'll be back in ten minutes." I start to go again, but then I think about Hitch and his total lack of respect for my privacy and personal space and his driving need to catch me using drugs and I spin back around. I cross the few feet between us and cup his chin in my hand, bringing my face uncomfortably close to his before whispering, "If you hear me talking to myself in the bathroom, do *not*, under any circumstances come in to check on me. No matter *what* you hear, or I swear to god, I will kill you myself. If something else doesn't get you first."

He lifts an eyebrow, but says, "Okay," in a way that makes me believe he means it. That's going to have to be good enough because we're running out of time. Today's to-do list is getting longer by the minute.

"When I'm clean and dressed, we'll go get your suit."

"Why?"

"I'll know more after my shower," I say cryptically, not worrying about making sense. That's the nice thing about talking to people who think you're crazy. It relieves so much of the pressure.

I head toward the bathroom, hoping my captive is still in the mood to bargain. If I can get him to tell me more about the cave of screams, I'll have a way to keep Hitch distracted while I spy on Cane. And if I promise to leave town as soon as my business with Hitch is through, maybe the old fairy will honor his word and keep me safe from his winged hordes in the meantime. As long as I don't let him catch on to the fact that my fairy controlling powers aren't working, I should be good.

Maybe I'll even buy myself enough time to find Tucker and get some answers and a shot and be back in matter-manipulating shape by the time the moment rolls around for me to break my promise to Grandpa and elect not to disappear.

As I dash into the bathroom—locking the door behind me—and turn to face the rattling trash can, I actually feel a pang for what I'm about to do. I don't enjoy making promises I don't intend to keep. But this isn't a normal lie; this is a lie to a monster that eats people, tortured me in my sleep, and thinks the human race should be wiped out and left to rot.

"And he pooped on my soap," I whisper as I reach for the trash can, preparing to make a deal with the devil.

15

Hitch and I take the back way to Fernando's bed-and-breakfast, hoping to avoid further interaction with my friends and neighbors. We've already received a double humph and a tsk from Bernadette—who responded to my second coupon-stealing threat by announcing that she's signed up to get her coupons online and "won't be putting up with any more of my shenanigans."

Hitch thought this was funny. And smiled at her. And waved. And offered to help weed her flowers and check the oil in her Mustang if he gets the time before he leaves town.

He stops smiling as we're walking away, when I tell him, "Bernadette thinks I should ask Cane to move in with me."

"Really?" He shrugs. "Cane seems . . . nice."

I almost tell him that I thought Cane was a lot more than *nice* last night and explain that, while I'm not engaged, I *am* confused, but bite my lip. Hitch said he loved me, but he's still engaged *and* confused. I don't know if he's planning to call things off with

Stephanie, but even if he is, I don't owe him any explanations. I don't know what to do about his confession, and I don't have time to even *think* about my feelings.

If I don't get myself sorted, people are going to die. Soon. Maybe very soon.

Grandpa Slake gave me until sundown tomorrow to find the cave, do whatever I'm going to do out there, get my affairs in order, and get out of town. After that, he's sending an assassin for someone I care about. He didn't even bother threatening me. He went right for my friends and surrogate family, as if he knew they were my weak spot.

But then, he's been in my dreams, poking around in my subconscious. He probably knows a lot about me, way more than I want a monster to know, that's for sure.

It makes me wonder what he'll learn if I fall asleep tonight. Will he read my intention to stay in D'Ville? Will he learn that my powers aren't working? Will he begin to doubt that we have that symbiotic relationship he talked about if I can't control the fairies? Will he decide it might not be a liability to kill me after all?

I close my eyes for a moment, blocking out what sun is getting through my darkest pair of bug-eye sunglasses, and take a calming breath. I won't sleep. I'll stay awake for the next forty-eight hours and figure this out and everything will be fine. I am the master of my own destiny.

"Isn't that your cat?" Hitch stops beside me.

Gimpy's signature *yeowl* sounds from the other

side of the fence. I slit my eyes. It's him all right, rolling around between the vegetable rows, wreaking havoc.

Right. Not the master of my own destiny, not even the master of my own cat.

"Gimpy, get *out* of there," I hiss, motioning him toward the Hogans' back gate.

My summons is answered with an amorous *preow* as Gimpy flops on his side, nuzzling the root vegetable trapped between his claws. He lets out another husky moan and gives the veggie a love bite, dragging his teeth over the skin. I've never seen him so worked up, even about his blue cooler.

"Is that a carrot?" Hitch asks.

"Or a sweet potato," I mutter. "Gimpy! Here!" I point to the ground at my feet.

"I didn't think cats ate vegetables."

"I'm not sure he's eating it." As if to emphasize my point, Gimpy hitches his arthritic leg around the carrot-tater and rolls through the dirt, coming to a stop in a row of spinach, where he proceeds to writhe obscenely. "Even if he is, at least it's not jewelry. Or a fishing lure. Or my bra."

"Is that what the feminists are doing with their bras these days?" Hitch pokes me in the side with a finger that I brush away with a stabby elbow. I refuse to joke with someone occupying such a prominent place on my shit list.

By the time I came out of my powwow-with-fairy/shower, Hitch had hidden the shots. He says they're in my house, but that no one, including me, will be able to find them, and that we're good to "stick a pin" in that conversation for a while.

Which made me want to stick a pin in *him*. A *sharp* pin.

Unless I can read Hitch's mind and figure out where he stashed those shots, I'm going to have to tell Tucker that I've lost them. Call me crazy, but I don't think he's going to be cool and slip me a few extras behind the Big Man's back. Not after he warned me ten jillion times to keep them safe and secret.

No. I can't ask Tucker. If it comes down to it, I'll have to tie Hitch up and stab him with knives until he tells me where the shots are. Or pins . . .

"Gimpy, come on. Kitty, kitty," I call, but Gimpy only rolls on his back and hugs the large carrot/skinny potato between his legs, licking it like he's found his soul mate. I resist the urge to flip him off—the Hernandez family next door has kids under the age of obscene-gesture-viewing who could be peeking out a window—and stomp off down Perimeter Road Five. It's already hot as hell. My head can't handle standing around in the sun yelling at my stupid cat. Even in light olive cargo pants and my thinnest brown tank top, I'm already starting to sweat.

"You're going to leave him there?" Hitch catches up to me on the dirt path.

There's no sidewalk here. The perimeter roads were created right after the emergence, lanes of iron-fortified cabins with oversized backyards for families with gardening skills. The city council hoped these gardens would provide the town with food we weren't sure we'd be getting from the outside. The yards are almost an acre each, with a dirt foot path weaving around the edges. Sometimes there's no path, and we have to pick our way over rock-lined gardens.

"It looked like he was doing some damage," Hitch adds. For a man with real problems, he's awfully worried about my cat.

"I'll send some money to pay for what he eats," I say. "But he's probably safer in their garden than at my house. You're not the only person who likes to drop in unexpectedly, and some of my visitors aren't as relatively harmless."

"Like who?"

"You wouldn't believe me. And I can't tell you, anyway, so . . ." I sigh, feeling the weight of the day drag at my feet. So many pieces have to fall into place before tomorrow. If they don't, I'll have to warn my friends about the danger of a fairy attack, kidnap Deedee from Sweet Haven, and head north. I can't have any more blood on my hands, especially innocent blood. My part in the deaths of Libby and James is sufficiently haunting, and they were murderers who deserved to die.

I sigh again, and wish I'd tucked more Tylenol in my purse. The two pills I popped before Hitch and I left the house aren't going to last long. I can already feel the headache creeping up the back of my neck.

"You okay?" Hitch asks.

"Peachy."

Hitch's fingers brush my hand. "Stay at the bed-

and-breakfast tonight. The room across from mine is empty. I'll feel better if I can keep an eye on you."

Before I can tell him what a bad idea that is, or explain that I'm already risking severe torment from Fernando for walking Hitch into the lobby of the B and B to get his suit, my phone buzzes. I wiggle it out of the pocket of my cargo pants—expecting Cane or maybe Fern if he's up early and eager to yell at me for standing him up—but the number isn't one I recognize.

I stop at the end of the path and edge into the shade of an oak at the corner of Perimeter Five and the far end of Railroad. The First and Last Chance Flophouse is catty-corner across the street, and I don't want anyone overhearing this conversation who doesn't have to.

What if it's Tucker or the Big Man? What if they saw Hitch in my house with his hands all over their precious, secret shots, and are calling to tell me to expect a bullet to the brain in the next few seconds? Big Man, at least, would do something like that. He likes to savor a victim's fear before he kills them.

"What's wrong?" Hitch asks.

I shake my head and turn my back on him, hoping he'll get the hint and give me some privacy. With a tremble in my finger, I hit the green button. "Hello?" My voice is tremblier than my hands.

"Hey. What's up?" I recognize the sleepy—or stoned—voice and my next breath comes easier.

"Hey, Lance. Nothing much," I say. "Heading to breakfast. Then I figure I'll go home and change into my supersecret-life-of-crime clothes, make sure I'm ready for any deliveries that might need to be made."

He makes a snuffling sound that could be a laugh. "You're confident."

"I am. You're too smart to let a chance like me go to waste. Did you talk to Jose about letting me in on the action?"

"Yeah, he wasn't into it at first, but I made him see the light. We can move more product if we have someone else doing deliveries while we organize the warehouse. But here's the thing . . ."

"I don't like 'things.'"

He snuffles again. "Jose wants to start you out at ten percent."

"Ten percent?" It's easy to sound pissed off. I'm obviously not doing this for the money, but still— they expect me to risk my life for ten measly percent? "That's bullshit, Lance."

"You can earn your way up to more. After you prove yourself. And if you *really* need the money . . ."

I grunt. "It still sucks." I pause, as if weighing the offer. "But I *guess* I can live with it for a while. How long am I going to be at ten percent?"

"I don't know . . ." There's a scratching sound and I hear a muffled Lance mumbling to someone else. They go back and forth, and finally Lance comes back on the line. "Twenty deliveries."

"Twenty?! Fuck Jose in his cheap pink asshole. Five. I'll do *five* deliveries at ten percent, then you bump me up to twenty five." Lance makes a skeptical sound. "Or you keep doing the face-to-face work with scary people on your own. I have other options."

Hitch, who has circled around and is hovering uncomfortably close, bulges his eyes. He knows I have directions to the cave—allegedly obtained from a secret source I met late last night—but he still thinks we should meet the person delivering the supplies. I'm counting on the fact that he'll be on his way back to New Orleans before that meeting happens, but he can't know that.

I pat his arm and turn my back on him again. If I'm too eager to take a crappy deal, it's only going to make these guys suspicious. "That's my final offer. Take it or leave it."

"We'll take it. Five jobs is fair," Lance says, triggering some mumbling in the background. But it isn't angry mumbling, and I get the feeling that Jose would have agreed to 25 percent from job one if I'd pushed harder. "There's a delivery today."

Great. Today. It *had* to be today.

"You ready to jump in and get your feet dirty?" Lance asks.

"I'm always willing to jump in and get my feet dirty. Or my hands dirty and my feet wet, what have you." Another sound from the background, a real laugh this time. I'm guessing Jose is listening in on another line. "What time do you want me out there?"

"Two o'clock. We'll have the load ready. Bring your truck. It's a big one."

"Where am I taking the stuff?" I lower my voice as the front door to the flophouse swings open. Hitch and I are still pretty far away, but there's no need to take chances. "How far from the—"

"We'll have a map when you get here."

"Can you at least tell me how long it will . . ." Words escape me as I get an eyeful of the people stumbling out Fernando's front door. One of them is Tucker.

This would be enough to short-circuit my brain— what's he doing at Fernando's? why isn't he heeding my warning to stay away from my friends?—if he were alone. But he isn't. He's snuggled up to a blond woman, his manly arm looped around none other than *Barbara Beauchamp*.

Barbara Beauchamp, grandmother of the murdered Grace and mother of her murderers, Libby and James. Barbara doesn't know that James was Grace's father as well as her brother, but she knows that the children she loved were killers. She lost her entire family to violence in less than six weeks' time. I know we all grieve in our own way, but the woman with the goofy smile and her hand straying down to get a handful of Tucker's ass does *not* look like she's grieving.

She looks like a cougar with a claw full of man meat.

"You there?" Lance asks.

"Yeah, I think the phone cut out for a second." I force myself to pull it together and end this conversation before Tucker gets any closer. "One question: Is this delivery going to the woman from the tape? If so, I'm bringing my gun."

"You should always bring your gun. But yeah, it's her."

It's her. A fresh wave of pain flashes behind my eyes. "See you at two."

I end the call as Tucker and Barbara stumble by on the sidewalk across the street. It's not quite eight, but from the weave factor, I'm betting they've already had a few. For a moment I don't think Tucker's noticed me, but then he turns and lifts a hand. "Cousin! Morning!"

"Sure is." I grit my teeth. Hitch takes a long look at me, before shifting his curious gaze to Tucker. I never introduced him to my family, but I did talk about them from time to time, and I never talked about a male cousin close to my age.

That's because I don't have one. All of my cousins are girls, a fact I think I mentioned to Hitch at some point. But whatever. The lies I'll have to tell him will be worth it. I need a powwow with Tucker. Now.

"You got a second?" I shout. "I wanted to talk to you about that shed you were going to build."

"Well . . . we're kind of on our way somewhere important," he calls back, a leer in his voice I've never heard before, a leer that leaves no doubt where he and Barbara are headed. He's bound for Camellia Grove and some plantation-house sexy time with Barbara in her big brass bed.

My nose wrinkles. I don't like the thought of Tucker rolling around with Barbara, and not just because she's old enough to be his mother. Barbara has aged well and can afford all the lotions and creams and injections of deadly viruses that keep a middle-aged woman looking younger than she is. But she's an elitist snob who's always treated the people of this town as members of the servant class. I have no doubt she's using Tucker.

But maybe he's okay with that. Maybe he'll sleep with anything with boobs—even if they're fake and once nursed a child only a few years younger than he is—and I shouldn't have been even a little flattered that he tried to get into my panties yesterday.

"It'll only take a second." I ignore a disapproving grunt from Hitch, who doesn't realize that "building a shed" is code for "I'm in deep shit and need your help immediately."

"If I don't get a place to store that motorcycle, I'm going to go *crazy*." I hit the word like a mallet upside a gong. "Really crazy."

Tucker laughs, but he smells what I'm cooking. Tension creeps into his shoulders and he stands up straighter. "All right," he drawls. "I guess I can spare a—"

Barbara interrupts him. Her whisper is too soft for me to hear, but I see her artificially plumped lips move. Tucker turns to whisper something back, but Barbara only gives a delicate shake of her head and fluffs her hair with pink-tipped claws. She doesn't look my way, or give any sign that she's aware there's anyone else on the street.

Ever since it came out that her daughter tried to kill me with a shrimp muffin, the woman's been giving me the cut direct. When I see her on the street, she sticks her nose in the air and turns around to walk in the opposite direction. As if *I* committed some unforgivable social faux pas by daring to be almost murdered. I never expected an apology—it isn't *completely* her fault that she raised a homicidal maniac—but this blaming the victim crap is crap.

Tucker turns back to me, but makes no move toward my side of the street. "Let me shout at you later, Cousin. We've got an appointment. The massage therapists are coming at eight-thirty."

Massage therapists? He's blowing me off for a couples massage with Barbara Beauchamp?

"I've got work stuff lined up all day," I say, hating how desperate I sound. "Are you sure you can't—"

"I'll call you." Tucker lets Barbara tug him farther down the sidewalk. "Later, Red!"

"Suck it, Bubba," I shout. Tucker laughs, making me want to race after him and punch him in his pretty face. "For real. You totally suck. I have a major, *pressing* need!"

But he doesn't turn around. He's *that* committed to being Barbara Beauchamp's boy toy. I shake my head in disgust and imagine all the really mean things I'm going to say to him the next time we're alone. Like the fact that he could have been born from the vagina he's so hot to get into, and how totally gross and unprofessional it is to blow off a fellow magical person in need to get his daily dose of Frigid Rich Bitch with a superiority complex.

"Who's that?" Hitch asks.

"My cousin," I mumble.

"That man is not your cousin."

I turn back to Hitch with what I hope is an innocent look. "He is. Unfortunately. On my mom's side. A real loser jerk asshole. Don't ever loan him money."

"Wouldn't think about it." Hitch leans down to whisper in my ear. "I don't like seeing you so eager for another man to build you a shed."

Hm. Maybe my code did not go as unnoticed as I assumed. Time to lie a little harder. "I'm not eager for Tucker to do anything. I just don't like seeing my cousin with a woman like Barbara."

"I'm not stupid, Annabelle." He turns his head. His lips brush my cheek, and my breath rushes out. "If that man's your cousin, I'm your Aunt Floe."

"That's what women call their periods," I say, angry that Hitch can still make my stomach do that fluttery thing, even when he's topping the list of people I want to smack with a dead fish. Or at least he was until Tucker strutted down the sidewalk. "That's disgusting."

"I'm hurt," he says, ignoring me. "You never gave me a nickname."

"Your name *is* a nickname, Herbert Mitchell. It's stupid to nickname a person who already goes by a nickname. And besides." I step away and start across the street. "You never gave me one, either."

"Red is hardly original," Hitch calls after me.

I don't respond. I keep gunning for Fernando's front door, knowing Hitch will follow. He has to come get his suit and whatever else he needs to head out into the bayou. Until then, I'll spend my time pumping Fern for information about what the hell is going on between Barbara and Tucker. Hopefully he'll be hot enough for gossip that he'll forgive me for standing him up last night because I need the dirt on those two. The sooner the better.

I've got a bad feeling Tucker's relationship with Babs isn't purely about physical pleasure and gigolo-type treats. I smell an agenda, an invisible-person agenda.

16

I push through the front door of the flophouse into the gently wafting air-conditioning and even gentler wafting jazz music. Except for a few men lounging on the lobby's vintage couches, sipping free coffee out of a mishmash of midcentury china cups, the place is pretty quiet.

Way too quiet for Fernando to be close by. I peek into the bar area, anyway, just in case, but Barry, one of the bar backs, is the only one there.

He stops chopping limes to shoot me a smile. "Hey, slut! What's up?"

I try not to roll my eyes. It's one thing for Fern to call me a slut, it's quite another for him to spread the use of the moniker. Still, I know Barry doesn't mean any harm. He's a sweetheart and it's not like he doesn't get around. He's a delicate, boyish type with skin so dark it's nearly black, and a goatee so cute it makes me want to pinch his face and other gay men want to pinch all his other parts. He and Fernando had a brief thing a few years ago, but parted amicably. Fern isn't the type to hold a grudge with his exes . . . only his best friends.

Ugh. I need to find him, and head the pout off at the pass.

"Fern around?" I ask Barry as Hitch breezes into the lobby. He spies me, but doesn't stop to say hello. He starts up the stairs to his room, pulling his key from his back pocket. I've only got a minute or two.

"Um . . . yeah. Somewhere," Barry says. "He's not in the laundry room because I was just there, and he's not in the kitchen because the limes were in the big fridge and I had to—"

"Never mind, I'll find him." I cut him off before he can complete his list of all the places Fern is not. The bed-and-breakfast isn't that big, and I'm not afraid to head up to the top floor and breach Fern's inner sanctum if I have to. It'll be faster to start looking.

I head up the stairs, but change my mind on the third step and turn back around. It's so early—barely eight o'clock. I can think of only two places Fern might be at this hour. He's either upstairs in bed, or out on the back patio watering his flowers before it gets too hot. In the name of avoiding climbing unnecessary stairs, I slip through the lobby and out into the back garden.

The dark red tiles on the patio are already damp and the flowers in the planters dewy and dripping. Fern's definitely been here, but maybe he—

There.

I spot him at the far end of the garden, by the clutch of potted palms he brings out to give the hot tub area a tropical feel in the summer. I'm about to call out when I see the arm around his waist. Fern isn't alone. I step back and prepare to flee the scene—unlike Tucker and Bernadette and everyone else in Donaldsonville, I don't make a habit of spying on other people's liaisons—when curiosity gets the better of me.

Fern hasn't been dating much lately. At least no one he's felt the need to tell me about. But something in the way he's standing—so relaxed, leaning into the man in front of him with such familiarity—tells me this isn't a quick slap-and-tickle session. This is someone he cares about, who he's been involved with for a while. And if that's the case, why hasn't he said anything to me about it? We're best friends.

I've had my share of things I can't share with him lately, but that's because lives are at stake and unusually strange shit is going down. Back in the good old days, I never would have kept anything from him, and he usually can't wait to dissect every aspect of his latest love affair.

I pause, easing far enough into the shadows of the arbor of grapevines to hide myself, while giving me a clear view of Fernando and Friend as they kiss. And kiss. And kiss. And then there's a little groping and hips shift and I'm starting to get uncomfortable enough to sneak back through the door without discovering Friend's identity, when Friend pulls away and shoots a wary look around the garden, as if he can sense his private moment is being observed.

I smash back against the bricks, holding my breath, hiding behind the grape leaves, praying I haven't been seen. Because I know Fern's friend, and

I know why Fern's been keeping their relationship under deep cover. Friend is *Abe*, Cane's older brother, captain of the DPD, a man assumed to be straight as a willow switch by everyone in town.

Holy crap. I always thought Abe crossed the street when he saw Fern and me coming because he was a homophobe. But he's actually one of the "homos"— albeit a deeply closeted one. Cane and his mom certainly have *no* idea that Abe is gay, and I have a feeling his mom would experience a cardiac event if she knew Abe was never going to give her grandbabies.

Dozens of questions rush through my mind—how long has this been going on? Why has Fern pretended to think Cane is such a hot piece when he's been scoring with his almost equally hot brother all along? How could Abe let Cane arrest Fern for a child's murder last month? How could he have so little faith in his lover?

Because they *are* in love. I can see it in the way Fern reaches for Abe's shoulders, in the way Abe lets Fern whisper him back into his arms and pull him into the shade of the palms. In the way they move together, touching with such careful deliberation.

Poor Fern. He must have been ordered to keep this a secret.

Abe knows our town better than anyone. He knows homosexuality is tolerated, but not truly accepted, and that being "the gay cop" wouldn't give him street cred with the criminal element. Abe and Fern may never be able to be openly together, and Fern's crankiness suddenly makes more sense.

So does his disapproval of seeing me with anyone other than Cane. Abe has never been my biggest fan, but he knows that his brother loves me and wants to build a life together. And Abe wants whatever his brother wants. Usually, anyway. It makes me wonder if Abe knows what Cane's doing in the bayou today, if he's in on the sketchy business, or if, for once, Cane is acting as a solo agent.

Maybe Abe has something left to lose. A tall, sexy, something who is even now pushing him back against the brick wall surrounding the patio.

I wait until the two men start kissing again and slip quietly back into the lobby to find Hitch standing by the front desk. He has the case containing his iron suit in hand and has changed into a tight brown T-shirt, the better not to bunch beneath his holster. The sight of his gun snuggled against his chest makes me think of my own weapon. I almost grabbed it before we left, but I'm kind of glad that I decided against it. I don't want to be armed for a meeting with Marcy.

Marcy. *God*. I'm going to see her this afternoon. I have to find a way to ditch Hitch before two o'clock. Hopefully our trip this morning will lead us straight to the cave and Hitch will need to hightail it back to New Orleans to arrange backup for an FBI raid.

"You look ready." I shove my glasses on top of my head. My eyes are feeling better, at least good enough to do without protection indoors.

"Past ready." His voice is distant, brisk, the teasing Hitch of this morning vanished without a trace. "Stephanie called while I was out. We need to get this done. I have to get back to New Orleans as soon as possible."

It's exactly what I wanted to hear. At least the part about him leaving. Still, it hurts to see the wall thrown back up. Romantically, Hitch and I are a hot mess waiting to happen, but I was enjoying feeling like his friend again.

"Sounds good." I turn away with a stiff nod. Simona's working the front desk. I can trust her to give Fern a message. "Will you tell Fernando I stopped by to apologize, and ask him to call me when he gets the chance?"

"Sure thing," Simona says, swiping off a sheet of official flophouse stationary—yellow and purple with Fern's signature at the bottom—and writing a note. "Anything else I can do for you, Miss Annabelle?"

Hmmm . . . well, since she's offering.

"Yeah. I was wondering if my cousin was staying here this week? His name is Tucker? I saw him leaving a few minutes ago with Bar—"

"We don't have time for this," Hitch says, a surprising degree of heat in his tone. For a man who was teasing me about nicknames a few minutes ago, he's awfully testy.

"This will only take a—"

"Let's go." He grabs my elbow, making Simona's pencil-thin eyebrows shoot toward her braided hairline. We're not close, but she knows me well enough to know macho demands don't go over well.

I tense my arm and give Hitch's hand a cool look. His fingers tighten for a moment before sliding away with a sigh. "Sorry." He takes a step back. "I apologize. I'm . . ." He pulls in a breath, fighting for a gulp of air. "I need a cigarette. I'll meet you outside."

He turns and charges away, nervous energy pouring off him in waves. The man at the cream-and-sugar station flinches as Hitch flings open the door.

"He doesn't seem like the smokin' type," Simona says, dropping her formal tone now that there are no guests close enough to overhear. "I mean, he gets up to run before the chickens, you know?"

"Yeah." I shake my head, wondering what Hitch isn't telling me. There's got to be something. Even the double threat of going out into the infested marsh to hunt bad guys and facing the wrath of Stephanie when he gets home couldn't have made him this rattled.

"You okay?" Simona asks.

I force a smile. "I'm fine. And he's harmless. Just having a hard time with his fiancée."

Simona nods and leans over the counter, looking both ways to make sure we're alone before whispering, "I could tell. She's called the front desk like six times a day since Mr. Rideau checked in."

Well. Stephanie is either very concerned for Hitch's safety or she realizes that—despite the fact that they're having a child together—Hitch isn't completely ready to make her his Mrs.

"Any woman who's checkin' on her man that often is trouble," Simona says. "Or she's *expecting* trouble . . ." She lifts a scrawny brow, silently inviting me to share the dirt.

"Is there something on Fern's employment application that says all employees must have a lust for gossip?"

Simona smiles. "No, he talks about that during the interview."

I'm laughing when the door to the garden opens and Fernando breezes in, fresh and unrumpled in a tight gray polo and battered black jeans I know he purchased already roughed up. He doesn't wear anything often enough for it to become battered. Looking at him, no one would guess he's been outside mauling his lover in the garden.

I meet his amber eyes and try to hold on to my smile as my laughter fades. I don't have time to confront him about the secret he's been keeping, and I don't know if confronting is even the best call. Maybe it's natural for people to grow older and more secretive. Maybe the intimacy we've shared since we were teens is the unusual thing, a part of life we'll leave behind as we choose significant others and they become the shoulders we cry on.

Sniff. It's . . . sad.

No matter how rocky our friendship has been the past couple of months, the thought of a distant, superficial relationship with the man who's been like a brother to me makes me want to pull Fern into my arms and squeeze him until he promises we'll always be family.

And then he opens his mouth.

"What the heck do you think you're doing?" he hisses, leaning up against the desk, cutting his eyes at Simona in a way that—after a sympathetic look in my direction—makes her turn and busy herself at the other end of the reception area.

"Good morning to you, too." I knew he'd be pissy, but I can't help but be embarrassed that he got snarky with me in front of someone else.

"It's not a *good* morning." His voice acidic, but his expression remains calm for the benefit of the guests milling about the lobby. Fern's a drama queen, but he's also a good businessman and host. You have to be to lure clients into the fairy-infested boonies for a weekend break.

"Listen, I'm sorry about last night," I say. "I didn't mean to stand you up. I ran into some trouble and—"

"Barry came to tell me you were here." Fern crosses his arms, erecting another barrier to letting me back into his heart. "He said he saw you walking up the road with Hitch. Arm in arm. Cozy as pigs in shit."

Barry. What a rat fink. He must have been spying on me out the window for a good twenty minutes before I came inside. I'm going to have to seriously rethink my opinion of him as sweet or cheek-pinch worthy.

"You have nothing to say for yourself?" Fern asks.

I fight the urge to tell him to mind his own god-damned business. I *did* bail on him, and there's nothing he hates more than being abandoned. "Hitch came over to my house this morning. We were—"

"Noticed he wasn't here," Fern says. "Just like he wasn't here last night when I got back from lugging two pounds of prime steak meat and marinated sweet potatoes and zucchini over to your house and back."

"I'm sorry I wasn't there. But I swear I'm not making some lame excuse. I really did run into some trouble. I was in the junkyard and—"

"So what did Cane say?"

My explanation stumbles and falls into a pile of What the Hell. "What?"

"Cane was here last night. When I got back, he and Dicker and Dom were drowning their cop sorrows at the bar. He took one look at me and knew we weren't having dinner." He leans against the desk and sticks out a hip. "He asked me where you were. I said I didn't know, but that I hadn't seen Hitch lately, either, so . . ." He lifts one shoulder, lets it fall. "I told him he might want to check your place. *Later* in the evening."

My lips part and a pained sound slips out. How could he? "You sent Cane to my house?"

"I didn't *send* him anywhere."

"To try to catch me with Hitch?"

"Listen, girl, it's not my fault if—"

"It *is* your fault," I snap. "You don't do that kind of a thing to a friend. Especially not because you're pissy that you got stood up for dinner."

"I didn't do it because I was pissy, I did it for Cane," he says, a noble note in his voice that makes me want to puke. "You're never going to love him the way he loves you. He needs to move the fuck on."

"You . . ." I swallow. I feel scorched inside. Like Fern's set fire to the underbrush of our friendship and is standing there watching me burn. "Who the hell are you to decide that for me? Or Cane?"

"He loves you, Annabelle. And you treat him like crap. It's not right."

"I don't treat him like crap, and since when are *you* in the place to judge what's right and wrong?" I ask, grateful for the anger knotting in my belly, banishing some of the sickness. "Less than a month ago, you were dealing hard drugs, junk that *kills* people."

"And you're never going to forgive me for it, are you?" Hurt tightens the skin around his eyes. "No matter how many times I say I know I screwed up. No matter how many steak dinners I make. You're always going to look down your nose at me, like I'm trash that belongs in a Breeze house."

"I never—"

"You've been looking down on me ever since I got out of jail. You've been judging me every single day. I was just returning the favor."

I bite my lip. He's right. I *have* been judging him, but that doesn't give him the right to try to sabotage my life. "You're supposed to be on my side," I whisper. "I have *always* been on your side. *Always*."

For the first time he looks guilty, but not nearly as guilty as I need him to look. "I'm sorry," he says. "But I care about Cane. He's almost forty, and he wants a family."

He reaches for my shoulder but I step back, lifting my hands in silent warning. If he thinks we're going to hug this out, he's crazy.

"You're never going to want the same things he

wants," Fern continues, clearly frustrated that I'm not seeing how *right* he is. "It's criminal to lead him on. Let him find someone else. While he still has time."

I cross my arms and clench my jaw. "Okay." I breathe in. Breathe out. "Maybe you're right. But it's not your place to decide. Just like it's not my place to do anything to damage your relationship with Abe."

His expression is priceless. I've never seen him so completely at a loss, so exposed and panicked that he can't figure out what face to make. Too bad I don't get off on pulling the rug out from under my best friend. But enjoy it or not, I'm not backing off until Fern realizes how far he's overstepped his bounds.

"Abe will never come out of the closet and live Gaily Ever After with you. *Never.*" I hit the word hard enough to make him flinch. "I know that. As a friend, I know it would be better for you to move on and find someone who isn't ashamed of who he is or who he loves."

"You don't know anything about me and Abe." His protest is weak. He's still too thrown to put up much of a fight. What's more, he knows I'm right.

"But I have too much respect for you to do something like that," I continue. "And you know what? Even *that* hypothetical doesn't work. Because if I did something to break you and Abe up, I'd still be thinking about what's best for *you*. Not Abe." I look up at him, throat so tight it hurts to speak. "You've been my best friend for almost half my life. You're the closest thing I have to family since Marcy left, and you tried to screw me over."

"Annabelle—"

"Don't Annabelle me." I shake my head. "Don't speak to me. For a while. A long while."

Maybe forever.

I turn to go, but spin back before I've taken two steps. "And so you know, I was alone last night when Cane let himself in. I almost shot him. I thought he was a burglar."

"Shit," Fern whispers, going pale beneath his golden tan. "I—"

"But I didn't. I fucked him instead," I say, hating the tremble in my voice. "And I told him I loved him." I take a deep breath, but it doesn't make me feel any more in control. It's not only Fern who's betrayed me. "Now I know he only came over because he was trying to catch me with someone else. So I guess he's as big an asshole as you are."

Ferns eyes shimmer. "Now come on. I'm sorry. You know I love—"

"No. I don't. I really don't."

"I was trying to do what I thought was best for everyone," he says. "You included."

"No. You were trying to punish me." I take another step back. "And you succeeded."

I turn toward the door, ignoring the curious stares of the couple camped out on the paisley couch who've obviously overheard at least part of our conversation. We were quiet, but we weren't that quiet, and emotional outbursts don't go unnoticed in the court of the drama queen.

Hitch is waiting for me outside the door, his clove

cigarette burned nearly to the filter. I see him quickly notice that I'm upset and even more quickly decide not to appear to notice. He crushes out his cigarette in the dirt-filled wine barrel, keeping his eyes on the collection of butts. "You ready? Truck's in the parking lot."

"I'm ready." I knock my glasses back down onto my face and hold out a hand. "Keys and a cigarette please."

He obliges, handing over his keys, fishing a fresh clove from the pack on the other side of his holster and lighting it with matches from his back pocket, happy to give me whatever I want in the name of ignoring my fragile emotional state.

I'm glad about that. I'm mad about it, too. I'm angry and confused and so hurt that I want to turn around and stab Fernando with this cigarette. But that wouldn't make things better, and I'm already choking so hard I wouldn't be able to stand up straight long enough to stab him, anyway.

"Been a while since you smoked," Hitch remarks as we head for the parking lot.

"Master of observation." I hack, wincing at the burning in my lungs.

His long fingers drift in front of my face. "Maybe you should give that to someone who can handle it."

"You're not supposed to chain-smoke. Stephanie would be pissed." At the mention of his future wife, Hitch's arm drops to his side. I throw the cigarette on the ground and stomp it out. I think about picking it up and throwing it in the trash like a good citizen, but then I realize I'm still on Fernando's property and leave it to clutter his sidewalk. "And you need to spend the ride to the gate getting into your suit, not smoking. I'm not going out into the swamp until you're suited up."

"I hear you," he says. "I *do* learn from my mistakes. Sometimes."

"I don't." I kick the base of the antique streetlight, cursing it for being another reminder of Fernando. He could lobby the city council for three years about these stupid streetlights and "beautifying Railroad Street," but he couldn't give me more than a month to make a decision about where to go with Cane.

And now I don't have a decision to make. Because Fernando handed Cane the apple and Cane gobbled it right up. Even if Cane's meeting in the bayou turns out to be something innocent, or at least forgivable, it's over. I can't be with a man who came creeping into my house to try to catch me with someone else. Even reminding myself that Cane would have had something to catch if he'd happened through the junkyard thirty minutes earlier doesn't make what he did okay. I've made mistakes and had moments of weakness, but I've never tried to pin a romantic crime on Cane or anyone else. I've always believed that trust was synonymous with love.

Obviously I've been wrong.

"I keep trusting people." I squeeze the keys until the ring digs into my skin. "When *no one* should be trusted."

"That's not true. There are people worth trusting.

Lots of people." Hitch makes an effort to sound sincere, but I know he's lying. Either to me, or to himself.

I stop by the Land Rover's dusty bumper and face him. "Name one."

His eyebrows lift. "One what?"

"One person I should trust."

"You," he says, a soft look on his face that makes me dizzy. "You should trust you. I trust you."

"You shouldn't." I refuse to give in to the spinny feelings he inspires or the warmth creeping into my chest at the unexpected compliment. I don't have time for bullshit. Even sweet-smelling bullshit.

I lift my chin, pinning him with a glare I hope he can see through the dark lenses of my glasses. "I'm lying to you. About several things. But I'm going to give myself a free pass. Because A: I tried to tell you some of the truth and you refused to believe me. And B: I'm not the one who came to you and asked you to risk your life to help me out.

"But you? You don't get a free pass, and I want to know what you're hiding." I step closer, and continue in a whisper. "So I'm going to get in that truck and drive, and you are going to tell me everything you've neglected to tell me. Everything. If I believe you're being straight with me, I'll keep driving and we'll find this cave and you can run back to New Orleans and send the FBI to save the day and you and Stephanie can try to fix your life. If not, I—"

"If I don't find the cave in the next week, there won't be a life to fix," Hitch says, his voice rough in a way I know has nothing to do with the clove. "Stephanie's in the hospital. If I don't find the cave and destroy it, she's going to lose the baby. And it will be my fault. She'll never forgive me."

And then his face crumples and his body sags and I'm left with a *much* bigger mess than I was anticipating.

17

Hitch and I get in the truck and drive. He pulls himself together quickly, but doesn't say a word during the drive to the south gate.

I wait as patiently as possible, stealing glances at the passenger's seat as he slides on the iron mesh overshirt of his suit, then unbuckles his seat belt to step into the pants. He zips the top and bottom of the suit together before moving on to the mesh footies and gloves. By the time we reach the gate, he's suited up, save for the hood piece with the breathable iron face mask, which he leaves in his lap.

Deciding he's suitably protected—he could have the hood on in a few seconds—I hop out and hit the button to raise the gate. As the gears turn and the heavy iron lifts, I scan the world outside. There's not a fairy in sight. No pink and golden glow under the trees, nothing fluttering above the water on either side of the road or hunting mosquitoes in the shadows.

Hopefully that means Grandpa Slake made it back to the swamp, issued the cease and desist order to his hordes of flesh-hungry minions, and it's safe for me to take this drive.

If not, at least Hitch is protected. If the fairies roll the truck off the road, he'll be able to crawl out and walk back to town without fearing a bite. The new suits look more fragile than the bulky iron shell Cane wears when he ventures outside the gate on police business, but iron mesh is about a hundred times stronger than iron plate. The fairies could try gnawing their way through, but they'd be dead of iron poisoning long before they made it to Hitch's skin.

Trying to take comfort in that and not let myself worry about trusting another person—or monster—that I shouldn't, I walk back to the truck. Worry won't accomplish anything, and I've got no choice but to trust Gramps. His information is the only thing we have to go on, and we *have* to find that cave. Our mission is even more urgent than I'd assumed. I believe that, though I'm going to need *a lot* more explanation before we get where we're going.

I slide into the truck, shift into drive, and ease through the gate at a creep, searching for the perfect prompt. As if sensing I've reached the end of my patience, Hitch speaks.

"Someone broke into our house while I was working late at the office," he says, in that familiar I-am-an-FBI-agent-in-control-of-my-destiny-and-vocal-tones voice I've come to know and hate. But I can't hate him for it right now. I know it's something to hide behind so that he doesn't lose it again.

Watching him cry for his fiancée and unborn baby—even if it was only for a minute or two—changed the way I see him. He said he loves me, and I think he means it, but he also loves her. Being a member of the torn-between-old-and-new-love club, I can sympathize, but I can also resent him for hiding how much he loves her.

Though maybe he wasn't intentionally hiding. Maybe he's as messed up and confused as I am.

"Stephanie was alone, napping on the couch, waiting for me to get home," he continues, the glimpse into their lives stinging more than it should. "She didn't wake up until the guy was on top of her. He pressed something over her face and she passed out. I found her unconscious, with a note pinned to her shirt."

"*Shit*." And now I feel awful. I'm not a Stephanie fan, but . . . *shit*.

"It said she'd inhaled an undetectable biological weapon that would progressively elevate her blood pressure until she lost the baby." Hitch relates the information without a great deal of passion, but I can feel how hard it is for him to speak. I bite my lip, holding back the stream of questions until he's finished. "She'll recover after the stress of the pregnancy is eliminated, but the baby is going to die. Unless I find the cave Steven found and destroy it."

"Oh my god." I know I should say something better, but I can't think of anything. It's too horrible. Stephanie's only a few months along, but she's already in love with that baby. This will devastate her. And maybe Hitch, too, judging from his haunted look.

It makes me grateful I have to keep my eyes mostly on the road. No matter how conflicted I am when it comes to Hitch, I don't enjoy seeing him hurt. I *really* don't.

"If I shut down the lab inside the cave within a week—maybe two if Stephanie's immune system fights off the initial effects of the toxin—the person who wrote the note promised they'd deliver the antidote to her bedside, and turn themselves in to FBI custody."

I cast a skeptical look his way. "Really?"

He shrugs. "Allegedly they used to work at the lab, and only want the experiments stopped before more bioweapons are created."

"And they're using an unborn baby to force you to do their dirty work."

"That's about the size of it."

"Jesus, Hitch. I'm so sorry." I risk another glance his way, but he's staring out the window at the still fairy-free bayou.

"I called an ambulance as soon as I found her, but she woke up before it got to the house. We decided not to panic until the doctors ran some tests, but . . ." He turns back to me, a hopeless expression on his face. "The note was telling the truth. The toxin screens came back negative, but Stephanie's blood pressure kept spiking. All night long. Nothing her doctors did made a difference. In the morning they moved her to a private room and assigned a high-risk pregnancy specialist. I left her with a guard and came here. That was . . . Friday." He blinks and runs a hand through his hair. "I can't believe it's only been two days."

"How is she doing now?"

"The same. Her pressure keeps spiking, none of the conventional fixes are working."

"What are her doctors advising? Because you know it's not only the baby at risk. Stephanie could suffer kidney damage or . . . something worse."

"I know. I explained that to her," he whispers. "She promised me that she'd let the doctors terminate the pregnancy if they thought her life was in danger. But . . . the message I got this morning was from her doctor. He's a friend of mine. He wanted me to know Stephanie's refusing to talk about the possibility of an abortion."

"She could die," I say, unable to help myself. I wouldn't be in Stephanie's place for anything, but if it comes down to losing the baby or losing both the baby's life and her life, there's only one choice to make. Her death won't help the baby survive. It would be a senseless waste. "You have to talk to her. Explain that—"

"I've explained. She won't listen. She's waiting for me to do what the note said. She thinks the person who poisoned her is really going to bring the anti-dote."

"But you don't?" I come to a fork in the road and take a left, following Grandpa Slake's directions, praying that he was telling me the truth.

"I don't know what to believe. If this fuck is okay

with poisoning a pregnant woman, I'm sure he'd be fine with a lie or two, don't you?" Hitch pinches the bridge of his nose and let's out an exhausted sigh. "I'm sorry I didn't tell you the truth. The note said anyone I told would be killed, and that if I tried to get help from the FBI the man would let the baby die. I'm not sure he won't, anyway, but—"

"Even a chance is worth it," I assure him. "You have to at least try." I search the side of the road, looking for the hidden path the fairy said would be on my right side about a mile past the fork. "But . . . you know what I don't understand?"

"What?"

"Why didn't the person who wrote the note tell you where to find the cave? Why make you look for it? If he or she used to work there, they have to know where it is."

"Apparently it moves around a lot."

I ease my foot off the gas, seeing a break in the trees that could be a road. "The lab moves around? It's not always in—"

"The cave moves around. It's a mobile unit."

I brake in front of a rough-looking dirt road almost hidden behind a pair of cypress trees, but don't turn down it. Instead I slip my glasses to the end of my nose, needing Hitch to see the confusion in my eyes. "How can a cave be *mobile*?"

"Tunnels. Really big tunnels. Under the swamp."

"Really big tunnels under the swamp," I repeat, a nasty feeling getting started in my stomach. I shove my glasses back on. "That's an enormous project."

Hitch nods. "Yep."

"It would have to have been around for years. At least a decade."

"Yep."

"Maybe more than a . . ." My words trail off as the full weight of my suspicion thuds inside my brain, squishing so hard I wouldn't be surprised to feel gray stuff oozing out my ears.

"I did some research," Hitch says. "I couldn't find anything in the county records, but I did find an old newspaper article in the *Baton Rouge Gazette*, talking about oil found near Donaldsonville and the possible environmental impact of a digging project starting in the bayou that summer. It was sixteen years old."

Before the mutations. "Fuck."

"Yep."

"Would you say something other than 'yep'?"

"Why? You know what I'm thinking."

I do. He's thinking that sixteen years is almost four years before the mutations. If someone was creating a secret mobile cave/lab way back then—and continued to move forward with it after the fairies emerged—then there's at least a chance, "They knew about the fairies."

"Or worse." Hitch shifts in his seat, not seeming surprised that I've stopped in the middle of the road. "Maybe the terrorist attacks and the petrochemical spills aren't responsible for the mutations."

A sound—half gasp, half gag—escapes from my mouth. "Who was digging for oil? What company?"

"Robusto Chemical. A subsidiary of Gamut 9."

I close my eyes and hang on to the steering wheel, as if it will keep me grounded in a world that's being flipped like a sloppy omelet. I make it my business to know as little as possible about politics and politicians—this country's government is a joke, and not that funny kind I enjoy—but even *I* know about Gamut 9.

After the mutations, there was an ongoing investigation into then President Rush's association with Robusto Chemical and *its* associations with Gamut 9, a Middle Eastern–owned oil company that allegedly helped finance the terrorist attacks that poisoned the Mississippi River delta and caused the fairy mutations. There was never any connection made between the president and the attacks, and no one could find a money trail connecting Gamut 9 with the terrorist organization, but that didn't matter to most Americans. Especially those of us living in the Delta.

The head of the terrorist organization responsible for the attacks said Gamut 9 paid the tab for destruction of the chemical plants and we believed him. And wanted him, and Gamut 9, destroyed. Everyone living in the Delta—and a lot of people in the noninfested states—boycotted gas stations carrying Gamut 9 oil. Within a few years, the company disappeared from the United States.

"But the federal investigation into Robusto Oil didn't find anything." I open my eyes. There's nothing to see behind my lids except fleeting glimpses of Caroline's face the day before she died, before she was bitten by monsters someone might have deliberately created.

"What was there to find?" Hitch asks. "Robusto pulled out their drilling equipment after the mutations. As far as a satellite can see from outer space, they left nothing behind."

"Nothing but some tunnels underground and a mobile cave being used as a biological weapons lab."

"Maybe," he says. "Maybe not. There isn't enough evidence to know one way or another."

"And the person who wrote the note couldn't give you any idea where to start looking?"

"Maybe they could have, but they didn't." He tosses his headpiece into the cup holder between us. "Now it's your turn."

"My turn to what?"

"Who told you where to find the cave?"

"It was one of the Junkyard Kings," I improvise, knowing Hitch will never believe a truth involving talking fairies. "They meet with the local highwaymen at the gates and exchange supplies and information. One of their contacts said they heard screaming in this corner of the swamp and went to check it out. They saw the entrance to a cave, but didn't go inside. They didn't want to borrow trouble."

"How long ago was this?" Hitch asks.

I shrug. "I don't know. I didn't ask. I didn't think that would be important. You don't usually think of a cave as something that's going to move around."

"S'all right," Hitch drawls. "At least we've got

something." His gloved hand comes to rest on my knee. "But I'm going to ask a favor."

"Another favor?" I try for a joking tone, but fail. Nothing is funny right now.

"When we get within a mile or two of where we're going, I want to park and go the rest of the way on foot."

"Okay, that sounds—"

"Alone."

I shake my head. "No. What's the point in me helping you if—"

"The point is that we may have found what we're looking for and I have training you don't," he says. Not in his holier-than-thou way, but in a rational tone that reminds me Hitch isn't the same man I knew in many ways. The man I loved wasn't a federal agent, with training in sneaking and spying and deadly breeds of intrigue. "Hopefully, I'll be able to get inside unnoticed, plant the explosives I brought in my case, and get out before they know I'm there."

I eye the case his suit came in with new respect. It's black—not the clear number he carried the last time he was in town—and not much bigger than a carry-on bag, but I know there's room in there for an explosive device serious enough to blow up a building. Amazing how tiny bombs are getting these days.

Jesus. There's a *bomb* in the truck. Mere feet from my feet. I've never been this close to a weapon like that. It makes me squirm, and Hitch pull his hand from my leg.

"So you're just going to do what this guy who poisoned Stephanie told you to do?" I ask, a tremor in my voice. "Without taking the time to surveil or whatever it is you—"

"I don't have the time to 'surveil,'" he says. "And I don't see that I have a choice."

"But Hitch," I say gently, understanding that his thinking is probably pretty muddled right now. "What if there are innocent people in there? Those people Steven saw being pulled inside obviously don't want to be a part of this. They could be victims like Stephanie and the baby."

"Then I'll do my best to get them out."

"Your best." My skin suddenly feels colder, though the air-conditioning in the truck is still on low.

"Yes. My best."

I shift the car into park. I don't trust my wobbly leg to keep tension on the break. "Hitch . . . This is crazy. What if your guess is wrong? What if this guy is lying about what's going on at the lab?"

Hitch starts to protest, but I barrel on before he can argue with me. "And even if he's not, and you're right, and only good can come from destroying the weapons being developed, who knows how many people you're going to kill doing it? It could be a lot. And you're still a doctor. You swore to protect *all* life."

"I know. " He drops his gaze to the seat. "But I . . . This man isn't someone I can afford to cross. I can't make an enemy who can . . . do the things he does. Stephanie and the baby will never be safe."

"Why? What kind of—"

"There are things I absolutely *can't* tell you. Please."

I dig a fist into my flip-flopping stomach. "You've met this guy, haven't you? It wasn't just a note. You—"

"Stop." He rubs a hand down his face, as if he can wipe our conversation away. "I *can't* say anything else. I have no idea who could be listening."

The hair at the back of my neck prickles. "Why?" I ask, then mouth silently, "Are you wearing a wire?"

"No. I'm not wearing a wire," he says out loud, eliminating the possibility that the truck is bugged.

I relax. A little. "Okay . . ." I scan the area outside, but see nothing but road and trees and bayou and a single nutria slinking through the tall weeds and into the water with a slick splash. "So . . . I don't get it. Who's going to be listening? We're in the middle of nowhere."

"Yep."

"And we're alone."

"It appears that way."

My brow furrows, and the seed of a wonderful, horrible suspicion plants itself in my mind. Horrible, because the thought of Hitch being a player in the Invisible Drama is horrible. Wonderful, because I might not be alone. There might be someone I can talk to about all this. Someone who, unlike Tucker, is not the enemy.

At least I don't *think* he is.

"I need you to explain," I say.

"I can't tell you anything else." His jaw clenches,

and a hint of his usual stubbornness hardens his expression.

"You can," I insist.

"It's too dangerous."

"I don't care."

"You should care."

"I need to—"

"No you don't."

"Tell me, goddamnit!"

"I can't!" he shouts. "And you wouldn't believe me, anyway!"

"You don't know that. Think about this for a second, Hitch. I told you I can manipulate matter with *my mind*. And I really *can*. My game is off today, but I swear I'm telling the truth."

"Annabelle—"

"I can work *magic*." I refuse to let his pitying expression divert me from my course. "And I've seen other people do even wilder things. So please . . . try me. You might be surprised what I'll believe."

He hesitates, but only for a second. "This is different."

"How?"

"I can't," he says. "You have to drop this, or I can't promise you'll be safe."

"It's too late for safe. It was too late the minute you asked me to help you."

"I'm sorry." A hint of guilt creeps into his voice. "I needed someone who could get information, and I didn't have time to find someone else I could trust. I swear I would never have put you in danger if—"

"I don't care," I say, simultaneously touched and confused by his "trust." How can trust exist amidst all the lies we've told each other?

Unless . . . maybe . . .

Maybe trust isn't inextricably tied to truth. Maybe trust is like faith, something you believe in without necessarily knowing all the facts. Something that feels right and real, even when the supporting arguments are weak and the evidence sketchy at best.

Maybe I should trust Hitch, and quit pushing. Maybe I should trust in how good it felt to be with Cane last night, and mark spying on him off my schedule. Maybe I should don a habit and devote my life to the church and swear off meat and potatoes and liquor and men and lead a life of quiet contemplation as the bride of a god I've never seen and rarely felt on the off chance that heaven is real.

For some people faith is enough, but I know myself better. I need facts.

"I'm fine with being in danger." I turn the key in the ignition, shutting down the Land Rover and our forward progress until I get what I'm after. "The truth is worth a little danger."

Hitch sighs, and I see the war he wages with himself played out in the wrinkle between his eyebrows. Wrinkle, smooth, wrinkle, smooth, and then finally he says, "Whatever this man gave Stephanie isn't the only biological weapon he developed before he left the lab."

"Okay."

"He has others. And one of them . . ." He breaks

off with a frustrated sound. "This is pointless. We're wasting time. You're never—"

"What's the weapon do?"

His looks up, resignation and misery mixing in his eyes, and I know I'm about to get the goods. "It makes people appear . . ."

"Yes?"

"Not . . . there."

My heart lurches. "You mean . . ."

"Invisible." His laughter is tight, breakable. "It makes people fucking invisible."

The world does another sloppy omelet flip, but this time Hitch and I are on the same side of the pan, sizzling together, trapped in the same hot bed of insanity and magic.

There's only one question left unanswered.

I open my mouth to ask him who he's been in contact with: the Big Man, Tucker, another Invisible I've yet to meet—because I've been assured there are more. But before I can speak, a shadow falls across the hood of the car. A shadow with a head and arms and manly shoulders, but no body attached.

None that we can see, anyway . . .

18

The shadow shifts and stretches as whoever's standing in front of the car circles around to the driver's side. I instinctively reach for the keys to start the truck and get the hell out of here, but Hitch's hand whips out, grabbing my wrist. "Don't. Let me talk to him."

"You know this person?"

"If it's the person who's been following me since I left New Orleans, yeah."

"And what if it's not?" I hiss, cringing away from the window as the shadow spills across my lap. "There's more than one of them."

I feel Hitch's surprise in the flinch of his fingers, but before he can say a word, the shadow knocks at the window and a familiar voice drawls, "Come on out, girl."

Tucker. I pull in a ragged breath, but don't know whether to trust the relief rushing in my chest. Tucker has been friendly lately—more than friendly—but that doesn't mean he isn't going to kill me. And maybe Hitch, too. Why else would he be out here?

How is he out here? I didn't hear a car behind us

and there's no way he could have followed us on foot all the way from Donaldsonville.

"Is this the person who's been following you?"

"No," Hitch says. "But the man I talked with said he'd send someone else to take care of me if—" He breaks off with a curse. "I knew better. I should have kept my mouth shut."

"You should have," Tucker pipes up from outside, proving he could have heard every word we've said. "But that's all right. Annabelle's a friend of the cause. Aren't you, Belly-welly?"

Belly-welly? I can understand him skipping "Red" on the off chance Hitch remembers my "cousin" called me Red, but really. *Belly? Welly?* He should be shot. For the crime of uttering that nickname alone.

"I don't even know what 'the cause' is." I can't hide how angry I am. How could Tucker do this? Threaten the life of an innocent child?

"You *know* him?" Hitch shifts closer to the passenger's-side window. The atmosphere in the car shifts perceptively, shock and horror swelling like a balloon about to pop.

I face him, knowing turning my back on Tucker for a few seconds won't get us in any more trouble than we're in already. "Don't freak out on me," I warn. "I tried to tell you the truth. I would have told you more, but you kept trying to have me committed! You thought I was crazy."

Hitch's eyes slide from me, to the window where Tucker is still patiently waiting, and back again. "What was I supposed to think?"

"You were supposed to *believe* me," I say, exasperated. "You knew all about these weird bioweapons and invisible people and you still couldn't connect the—" I almost say, "the shots and the people threatening to kill me if *I* talk, to the weapons and the invisible people threatening to kill you if *you* talk," but bite my lip at the last second.

I'm not sure Tucker knows I've spilled the beans about the shots. On the off chance that he doesn't, I can't risk saying too much. Instead, I settle for, "You still couldn't connect the dots?"

Hitch's gaze flickers again, but I can feel him starting to relax. "Guess I couldn't."

"Well I guess you're not as smart as you think you are."

"No, I'm not as smart as *you* think I am." Hitch nods his head toward the window. "This person is a friend?"

"No, not a friend," I assure him, not wanting Hitch to think I'm buddy-buddy with the people who have put his child's life in danger.

"Aw, Belly-welly, that hurts." Tucker's easy laugh makes me want to strangle him. On some level I've acknowledged that Tucker is a dangerous man, but I honestly never believed he'd kill *me*, let alone a *baby*. He's going to have to make this right. *Now*. Not after Hitch blows up this stupid lab.

I meet Hitch's eyes and make him a promise. "I'll do whatever I can to convince him to help Stephanie and the baby."

"Thank you."

"But you have to promise me you'll stay here in the truck until I get back."

Hitch shakes his head. "No. I'm not letting you go out there without backup."

"Hitch, please, I—"

"Just because I can't see this guy, doesn't mean I can't make him bleed."

"Now I'm startin' to feel offended." Mean frosts Tucker's tone. I've always guessed he could pull off menacing. Now I know. And fear. For Hitch, mostly, but I have to admit I'm not looking forward to getting out of the truck.

What if Tucker's talk about being a friend of the cause is pure bullshit? What if he's planning to kill me as soon as I open the door?

"He only asked *me* to get out, and this will go a lot better if it's just me and him." I know better than to say Tucker's name. Hitch hasn't connected this voice with my "cousin" and it's better if it stays that way. The less Hitch knows, the safer he'll be. "I don't think he'll hurt me."

"Now I'm flat-out offended." Tucker's drawl is humorless. He's genuinely angry, and I need to get out there and do damage control before he gets any angrier.

"Stay," I warn Hitch. Before he can say a word, I'm out the door and slamming it closed. Tucker steps back a pace or two, but he's still close enough for me to smell his salty, grassy, sun-baked scent. He always smells like the best of a summer day, but right now it's not comforting.

I can feel how angry he is; hear it in the stiff scuff of his boots as he leads me away from the truck. I follow his creeping shadow and the puffs of dust rising from the road, refusing to look back and give Hitch any encouragement to come after us. Still, as the road bends and Tucker keeps walking, I start to worry. There's no way Hitch will stay in the truck if I walk out of his line of sight.

"We've gone far enough." I stop. "He won't be able to hear us."

Tucker's shadow pauses and shifts in a circle as he turns around. "But he'll be able to see us. Won't he, Red?"

I shrug. "So?"

"And he'll be able to *shoot* me if he gets the mind to."

"He won't shoot you."

"You sound pretty sure of him." Tucker's footprints puff closer, and his shadow falls across my face. "Why don't you sound that sure of me?"

I look up, guessing at where his eyes would be if I could see them. "Why should I sound sure of you? The first time we met you broke into my house and stabbed me with a needle."

"For your own good."

"And since then all you've done is sneak around, spy on my private moments, and make lying to me your new hobby."

"I've *never* lied to you." He has the balls to sound hurt. Like this is about his feelings or my feelings or that feelings matter when a woman and a baby's lives are at stake.

My lip curls. "You're even crazier than I thought you were."

"I'm not the one telling secrets that aren't mine to tell, or inviting the FBI into the Big Man's business. Seems to me you're the—"

"Hitch is *already* involved in the Big Man's business, and you know it," I say, voice shaking with anger. "How could you be a part of this?"

"A part of what?"

"Don't bullshit me, Tucker. I want to know who did it." I cross my arms, dig my fingers into my strangely cool skin. "Did the Big Man do the job himself, or did you drive down to New Orleans and attack a pregnant woman in her own home? And poison her? And maybe *murder* her and her baby if Hitch and I don't find this stupid cave in time?"

"You're not going to find a cave down that road," he says, bypassing my questions. "That's the way to the Big Man's compound. You drive into the middle of that, and he'll kill you."

"What?" My arms fall to my sides. This can't be right. It *can't* be.

"Maybe he'll kill you now. Maybe he'll decide to let you and the spook go about your business for him first, and kill you later. But you'll be dead. He doesn't want you knowing any more about his operation. Not anytime soon. And he sure as hell doesn't want the FBI knowing where he's based."

"That's . . ." A part of me wants to keep pushing about the poisoning, but I can't, not if what he's saying is true. I point back over my shoulder. "Someone told me that was the way to the cave. Down that road, and then right, and then the second left."

"Someone told you a lie. Keep to those directions and you'll land in the middle of the Big Man's secret hideaway."

"Fuck." That fucking fairy *bastard*. He was trying to get me killed. No wonder he called off his winged assassins. He set me up to walk into the jaws of death on my own two feet.

"Who was it?" Tucker asks. "I can arrange for him or her to feel really bad about lying to you."

I pull off my sunglasses, ignoring the faint pain that flashes through my head. "Don't ever offer to hurt anyone for me," I whisper. "It makes me sick. I hate what I've learned about you today. *Hate* it."

"You haven't learned anything about me," he says. "I didn't hurt that woman. And I won't—Hold up."

I feel his fingers on my chin and flinch away. "My eyes are messed up again. Like right after I was bitten. That's one of the *many* things I was trying to talk to you about while you were busy fondling Barbara Beauchamp." Which reminds me . . . "Why are you even here? Did your *massage therapist* call in sick? Or did you decide to skip the rubdown to come spy on me?"

"Barbara passed out on the couch in the parlor," he says, confirming Fernando's stories about Barbara's taste for Kendall Jackson Chardonnay for breakfast. "I could tell you wanted to talk, so I came looking for you. I saw you and Hitch headin' through the gate, and I followed you on my scooter. I wasn't—"

"You ride a scooter?"

"Hybrid scooter. Goes forever on a tank of gas. Quiet, too."

Guess that explains why Hitch and I didn't hear him following us. "I'll keep that in mind the next time the Big Man offers me a present. You know, if my eyeballs don't explode before then."

"You'll be fine," he says. "You're just burning through the injection too fast."

"Why?"

"Probably need to lay off the hard alcohol. It interferes with protein absorption near the end of a cycle. You should start feeling better once your body processes whatever you've drunk, but you'll need another shot sooner than later."

"So it's a protein." I decide it's not the best time to bring up the fact that I've lost track of the injections. Hopefully, now that we're on the same page, I'll be able to convince Hitch to tell me where he hid the shots and their loss will be a nonissue.

"Yeah. It's a protein. Partly," Tuckers says. "So?"

"Just good to know. I was starting to wonder if I was shooting up some kind of bioweapon," I say, taking a stab at confirming Hitch's theory. "Like the one that makes you invisible."

Tucker snorts. "Your doctor friend really is dumber than you think he is."

"Yeah?"

"Yeah. Blinking out is part of being what we are," Tucker says. "Has nothing to do with bioweapons."

Okay. But then . . . "So why can't I disappear?"

"I don't know if we're ready to talk about that yet."

"Jesus, Tucker." I kick the dirt at our feet, making it swirl around his legs and settle in the folds of his jeans, giving him shape from the knees down. "Why don't you grow a set?"

"I have a set. I also have orders."

"Right." I roll my eyes hard enough to make my headache worse.

"Damn right, that's right."

"Really, Bubba," I say, voice oozing contempt. "Can you even take a shit without the Big Man leaning over the toilet telling you it's coming out okay?"

His hands are on my face again, but this time I can't pull away. His fingers dig into my neck, holding me still as his blue, blue eyes swim into focus. Only his eyes, like an overgrown Cheshire Cat. "If the Big Man wants to own someone, he owns them, Annabelle." It's the first time he's ever said my name, and it makes me shiver. "He's got no moral shame. If anything or anyone gets in his way, or even *thinks* about gettin' in his way, he takes care of the problem. Do you understand me?"

"No," I whisper.

"Don't ever love anyone more than you do right now." His grip gentles, becoming more caress than capture. His fingertips trace the line of my jaw with a tenderness that makes me ache for him, for whomever it is he loves, for the person I'm pretty sure he doesn't get to touch like this anymore. "Don't ever let him have that on you." His floating eyes are full of pain, and I want to offer some kind of comfort.

But you don't hug a man who does the things Tucker does.

No matter what his reasons.

"If Stephanie or the baby die, I won't keep quiet anymore. I'll tell everyone—the police, the FBI, Fairy Containment and Control, doctors, scientists. I'll tell them everything, and I'll keep talking until someone believes me."

His hands fall from my face. "That would be suicide."

"I don't care. This is too much." I pray Tucker will realize that I'm right. "These are two innocent lives."

"That woman is FBI. I'm sure she's nowhere close to innocent." There's something personal behind his words. Tucker definitely isn't a member of the FBI fan club, but I don't have time to figure out why.

"It doesn't matter," I say. "The baby hasn't even been born. It's as innocent as—"

"So is it even a baby yet?"

"What?"

"It's still within the time limit for a legal abortion. Some people would say it's not even technically alive."

His words leave a sour taste in my mouth, but not as sour as if I thought he believed them. "It's alive to Stephanie. It was the first day she found out she was pregnant. This should be her and Hitch's choice," I say. "I need you to make this right."

He sighs, frustrated, but weakening. "I can't."

"Why not?"

"The Big Man's the only one with the antidote."

"So there *is* an antidote?"

"There is," Tucker says. "I promise he'll be good to his word. If the doctor takes care of the lab, the Big Man will take care of his wife and baby."

I wish his promise made me feel better, but it doesn't. "Why Hitch? Why does he have to do this? Why doesn't the Big Man blow up the cave himself?"

"He doesn't know where it is anymore. They've changed up the locations."

So what Hitch heard about the lab being mobile must be true, otherwise Tucker would have said "location" not "locations." Still, that leaves the question: "Why not have you or one of the other invisible minions find it and get the job done?"

"I'm nobody's minion."

"You know what I mean."

"We need a fed," Tucker says after a moment. "The Big Man wants the lab shut down permanently and those people out of his territory. The doctor is supposed to download a few files before he rigs the place to blow. Once he turns those over to his superiors, there's no way the people behind this will be able to bring the project back to life."

"Because they're FBI, too?"

Tucker's eyes dip as he nods. "They'll know how close they are to exposure and back off, and the Big Man will be able to move on with his own plans."

"Which are . . . ?" I know I'm pressing my luck, and I'm not surprised when Tucker answers my question with a question.

"Who told you the way out here, Red? I need a name. If someone in our organization is trying to get you killed, I need to know about it."

"It's not someone in your organization."

"You can't know that," Tucker says. "The Big Man has other people in town, people you'd never think are part of this. People you might think you can trust."

"Interesting." I refuse to start imagining who else among my friends and acquaintances might not be what they seem. "But I know it wasn't one of the Big Man's people."

"You can't—"

"It wasn't a person." I take advantage of his stunned silence to spill the entire story—starting with the dreams, through the attack yesterday, and finishing with the fairy in my bathroom pooping on my soap. I tell him about the Gentry and Grandpa Slake's threats and I've just gotten around to my deal with the fairy and his helpful directions out to the Big Man's compound when Tucker starts cussing a blue streak.

"I know, right?" I say. "He's a motherfucker."

"Motherfucker," Tucker repeats.

"But you don't sound surprised." I shift into the shade of his shadow, direct sunlight too much to take without my glasses on even if my head is feeling better. "Why didn't you tell me fairies can speak English? I thought I was losing my mind."

"They can't speak English."

"Beg to differ."

"Take a listen to yourself next time you think you're speaking English to one of those critters," he says. "Think you'll find it pretty interesting."

"Interesting how?"

"You're speaking their language; they're not speaking yours."

"*What?*" Could he be right? When I came out of the bathroom after my bargaining session with the fairy, Hitch *had* asked if I was feeling okay. He'd said he heard me coughing a lot. I dismissed his concern—thinking Bernadette must be getting a cold—but fairy noises are pretty guttural. At least they sounded that way to me before . . .

"But how's that possible?" I ask. "How could I speak fairy without—"

"You moved a truck around with your mind yesterday, and you're asking me how something magical is possible?"

Right. One point for Tucker.

"Grace could do it, too," he says. "Talk to the fairies, understand what they were saying."

Grace. I forget sometimes that Tucker knew her, cared about her. The sorrow in his voice when he says her name sounds real at least. But how can he have feelings for one little girl and then turn around and let the Big Man put a baby's life in danger?

Whatever the Big Man has on him must be some serious shit. It makes me wonder who he loves, and what the Big Man has threatened to do to them if Tucker doesn't perform up to expectations.

"Grace and I, we're the only ones?" Tucker's eyes

get fuzzy around the edges and threaten to disappear. "Don't fade out on me." I reach out, tangling my fingers in the invisible fabric of his shirt. As soon as I touch it, a wad of white appears in my fist, a development so surprising that I pull my hand away and stumble back a step.

"Shit. So if I touch you, I—"

"My clothes," Tucker corrects. "You can touch me all you like and I'll stay out of sight, but clothes are different. That's why I patrol naked if I'm worried about brushing up against someone on the street."

Naked Tucker. Roaming the streets. Normally that would be a distracting thought, but not today. Now it only makes me wonder . . . "How can you make your clothes disappear? They're not part of you or infected by fairy magic. So why—"

"Are you going to stand here being nosy all day?" he asks. "Or are you going to help that man find the cave? I'm sure the Big Man would appreciate you facilitating—"

"Fuck the Big Man. I need answers, Tucker," I say. "I'm not going to keep playing nice if I'm not kept in *some* part of the loop."

He grunts, and I sense I've nearly pushed him too far.

"At least tell me what's so different about me and Grace." I soften my tone, and add an eyelash bat or two into the mix. "Why can we talk to them?" He doesn't say a word, but his eyes are slowly joined by a hint of nose and chin. "Please, Tucker. I need *something*. I can't do this if—"

"It might be a girl thing." Tucker breaks under pressure more easily than I assumed he would. "You and Grace—*You* are the only female in our happy family."

"You're kidding me," I say, genuinely surprised. "Why? There have to be other women who were bitten, right? I mean—"

"I'm going to tell you some things," Tucker says, in a loaded way that makes me doubt the wisdom of pursuing more answers. "These are things you need to know, but if you ever open that pretty mouth of yours, you'll get me killed. And not only me. There are innocent people on both sides, Red. Can I trust you to keep mine safe?"

I nod.

"You tell *no one*. Not your boyfriend, not Mr. FBI, not—"

"I promise," I say, meaning it. "I get that the Big Man has something on someone you love. I won't put them in danger. I swear."

Tucker's eyes close and stay closed as he starts his story. "Big Man used to work at the lab. When he left to start his own facility, he didn't go alone. Two other scientists came with him. Women. They were all part of the team working on the medication to help immune people bitten by the Slake."

"So where are they now?"

"I'll get to it, Red." His eyes open, and are joined by a smiling mouth. I'm glad to see he looks amused by my impatience. The super intense Tucker was freaking me out. "They knew the fairies around here had special venom that caused some pretty kick-ass side effects in people usually immune to fairy bite."

"Magic."

"Yeah, magic. But also crazy. Slake venom is tough on the nervous system, even for immune people. In the early tests, the negative side effects were too intense. The infected didn't last long."

"They died?"

"Or were killed. I don't know for sure," Tucker says. "Wasn't around back then."

He wasn't around . . . I want to ask him when he joined the Big Man—and why and how—but bite my lip. Tucker's history isn't as vital to my existence as the history he's telling me right now.

"The Big Man's team developed a protein they thought would protect the nervous system," he continues. "It was supposed to keep people from going crazy while allowing the infected immune to enjoy the magical side effects of Slake bite. But after they left the lab they had a hard time getting their hands on human test subjects. So all three of them—the two women and the Big Man—decided to infect themselves."

"Wow. That's . . . extreme."

He shrugs. "They were immune. Guess they felt they were close enough to an answer to risk it."

"So what happened?" I ask, sensing where this is going.

"The official story is that, in the long term, the cure didn't work for the women, and the Big Man honored his promise to his partners and shot them when they started to lose their minds."

"But you don't think that's the true story."

"I did," he says. "Until Grace. She could talk to them like the Big Man said the other women could. She could also control the bastards, make them fly around in circles or bring her baby alligators from the swamp—whatever she wanted."

"What did the Big Man say about that?"

His lips curve in a hard grin. "He said her power was a new development, and Grace was just an exceptional kid. All of us have different strengths and levels of ability, so that made sense to most people. And the few old-timers who've been with the Big Man since back when his partners were alive never said anything different."

"But you smelled a rat."

"I started to wonder if maybe his partners didn't have the same powers Grace did. If maybe the Big Man killed them so he'd keep on being the one in charge."

I think on that for a moment. If the Big Man's partners were able to control fairies, that wouldn't make them any more of a personal liability—they could have killed him in his sleep with a regular old gun if they'd wanted him out of the picture. But that kind of power would pack a punch when it came to impressing the troops. I think for a minute about whom I'd follow—the Big Man, or a lady scientist with the power to communicate with the fairies and the mojo to bend them to her will.

She'd have the ultimate bioweapon, a tool to terrorize 95 percent of the population. If I were the sort to voluntarily join a terrorist group, I know which leader I'd pick. The Big Man must have figured most of his troops would feel the same.

Which means . . .

"I'm guessing I shouldn't tell anyone else about the latest development in my personal magical journey."

"I wouldn't. Unless you've got a death wish I don't know about."

I sigh. Just when I thought I was less alone, I've become more isolated than ever. "Then what am I supposed to do about the Slake? The old fart said he'd start killing people I care about if I don't leave town by tomorrow night. He can get through the gates. And he'll do it; I know he will. He already tried to kill me today. If I don't come back dead from this trip, I—"

"Kill him," Tucker says, like the no-nonsense assassin he is. "Make sure you're alone and use what you can do. Take care of it."

"I can't," I say. "My head isn't right. I woke up this morning and I couldn't even move my cat out of the neighbor's garden. The fairy doesn't realize it yet, but he will."

"You need another injection. I'll bring you one. Five o'clock. Your place."

"But I still have a bunch at home." I blink as innocently as I can manage and flip my glasses back down on my face, the better to conceal my lying eyes.

"Yeah, about that . . ." Tucker sighs. "You're going to want to throw those away."

"Why?"

"There's nothing but salt water in those shots," he says. "I figured I'd see how reliable you were before I gave you a real stockpile."

"You're a shifty character." But there's no real heat in my tone. How can I be angry when he's saved me from further shot angst? Now I won't have to worry about explaining the lost injections to Tucker, or pushing Hitch to tell me where he hid the needles.

I turn and cast a glance back at the Land Rover. Even from this far away, it's obvious Hitch is getting twitchy. He'll be out of the truck before too long. Tucker and I have to finish up, even if I do have a hundred more questions and no idea what to do with Hitch now that our directions turned out to be so much fairy poo.

"What should I do? How can I find the cave?"

"I'd head back out to visit those boys working the Gramercy port," Tucker says. "I bet they know more about where the medical supplies are going than they're letting on."

"Yeah?"

"They do their share of snooping. Last month the skinny one got close to the compound. The team on guard had to shoot him with a tranquilizer and dump him a couple miles away. Guy didn't wake up for hours."

"He could have died," I say, telling myself I should feel bad for Lance—it has to be Lance he's talking about. I can't imagine his partner being skinnier than the man I met yesterday. "Or been bitten by Slake."

"He could have. But he didn't, and he wasn't," Tucker says. "The Slake don't bite the immune often. Once they figured out what was happening with the protein, they've kept their teeth to themselves. You and Grace are the only two I know who were bitten. The rest of us got infected with a needle."

Grandpa Slake. He probably put the kibosh on biting the immune. He's smart enough to sort out cause and effect. Hm . . .

I wave to Hitch, then hold up a finger, indicating I'll be one more minute. "If the Big Man and the people at the lab and a bunch of crooked FBI know that Slake venom is special and does things to the immune, how come everyone else doesn't know? How has this stayed a secret?"

"Who says it's a secret?" Tucker's eyes fade, followed by the hint of nose and lips, until it feels like I'm alone when he says, "I'd think twice about peeing in a cup if I were you."

"You would?" My stomach drops.

"Sometimes the injections show up in a urine sample. People with a positive test like that tend to disappear."

I don't even bother asking him how he knows about my new FCC-mandated drug tests. Tucker apparently knows everything, and I—despite the dirt he's shared—feel like I know less than I did before. But I get what he's hinting at. Someone in Fairy Containment and Control knows about the Slake and the

Big Man's protein and the magic and all the rest of it. Maybe a lot of someones.

And those someones think I'm a person of interest.

And if they find out I've been injected with the protein, I might become one of the people who disappear.

19

Peeing in an iron suit—while keeping all the necessary parts covered and safe from fairy bite—is an involved bit of business, a fact I'm grateful for when we stop for Hitch to take a trip into the swamp about a mile from the bridge leading to the docks. While Hitch finds a tree, I pace around the Land Rover, doing my best to pull myself together.

Hitch hasn't given me a *second* to think.

The questions started the moment I settled back in the driver's seat, and didn't let up until I turned the Johnny Cash XM station on at top volume. Hitch has a deep, unnatural love of Johnny Cash, and I think by that point he finally realized I'd said all I was going to say. There are some things I *have* to keep from him.

Which makes me wonder what he's still keeping from me . . .

The FBI and the FCC work together in many ways. The FBI is, in fact, often given the job of policing FCC officials. The one time I saw an FCC operative hauled off to jail, it was an FBI agent who did the hauling. Which means there's a chance—no matter how small—that Hitch knows more than he's letting on about the injections he found in my kitchen. Maybe knocking my bike over wasn't an accident, but a way to justify his snooping. Maybe he's not only working for the Big Man; maybe he's here on Uncle Sam's behalf as well.

The thought makes my head feel like it's about to explode.

"No," I whisper.

I can't believe it. I *won't* believe it, not until the day he slaps a pair of cuffs on me and reads me my rights. I'm having trust issues with almost everyone right now, but I believe that Hitch genuinely cares about me. That "I love you" this morning was coming from a real place, and what happened in the junkyard isn't the kind of emotion anyone can fake.

Emotions, emotions, emotions.

Mine are in knots. It's ten o'clock. Only two hours before Cane meets his mystery caller. Depending on how things play out, I may not have time to spy on my lover at the old Gramercy dock. Even if there is time, I'll have to bring Hitch along—there's no way he'd sit patiently in the car a second time—and I know that's a bad call.

Hitch says he thinks Cane is a nice guy, but Hitch was also the driving force behind the ethics investigation of the Donaldsonville Police Department. He thought Cane and Abe were crooked cops once. It wouldn't take much convincing to bring him back around to that way of thinking. And if he witnessed Cane committing a crime he'd have no choice but to take action. He could potentially even take Cane into federal custody.

"Right before he blows some stuff up," I mumble.

Hitch is operating so far outside the bounds he'll be lucky if *he* doesn't end up in federal custody. He'll blow that lab up with people still inside if he has to. I know he will. I saw the look on his face. Stephanie and the baby are all he's thinking about. Maybe there will come a day when he'll look back on this decision and hate himself for it—I know he has respect for life, no matter how he's acting right now—but either way, he's in no position to be enforcing the law.

Maybe he realizes that. Maybe not.

My best bet is to keep Hitch away from Cane and—assuming we get a location on the cave—convince him to let me join him on his mission. I can get my stealth on, I know how to use a gun, and maybe I can help evacuate the lab before the *boom boom* starts. I know most of the people inside are probably not good people, but issuing death sentences without taking the time to investigate feels wrong.

Now, what to do about Marcy? If we get a solid lead from Lance or—

My phone vibrates, making my butt cheek hum for the fifth or sixth time in the past half hour. I pull it out—to make sure it's still Deedee riding my ass for neglecting to schedule a visit—and find an animated cat crying crystal blue tears, with the message, "Ur cat needs ur love and u r not here for him," underneath.

As if this is about my cat.

We both know what this is about, but I'm the only one who knows what a *horrible* idea it is for her to care about me, for *me* to care about *her*. An image from my nightmares—the one of blood running down Deedee's face as her flesh is ripped away—floats through my mind, making my hands shake.

What the hell am I going to do? How can I make sure she's safe? How—

The phone jumps in my hands and another text—this one of a different cartoon cat shivering in the snow—pops up on the screen, along with, "Gimpy outside Swallows. Acting weird. Plz come help him and show u really care."

"Subtle, Deedee." I curse myself for buying her a phone in the first place and start a text asking her how she knows my cat is outside Swallows if she hasn't snuck out of Sweet Haven again, when a rustling behind me makes me spin around, phone held in front of me like the weapon I wish I had.

"Going to text me to death?" Hitch climbs up the shallow ravine next to the road, his curly hair sticking up and his iron hood clutched in his hand. "Who's that?"

"What are you doing?" I stuff the phone back in my pocket with the message unfinished. "Put your fucking hood on!"

"Relax." He ambles toward the truck as if he's not exposing himself to early death or insanity with every second he spends unprotected. "There are *no* fairies around today. Have you noticed?"

"Um . . . yeah. I guess." No good will come of telling him about Grandpa Slake. The best thing I can do for Hitch is help him get in and out of that lab without killing a bunch of people, and get him on his way back to New Orleans.

"I've never seen anything like it, even before Katrina hit." He turns in a circle, scanning the tops of the trees. Above our heads, puffy gray clouds drift in from the west, threatening to pull together and make some rain. "Maybe this storm is going to be more serious than it looks."

"Hitch, I—" I'm about to tell him something close to the truth, but then I hear it, a faint rumble-crunch from the direction of Donaldsonville. "Is that . . ."

"A car." Hitch grabs my arm and starts back to the truck, moving fast for a man wearing thirty plus pounds of iron. "Is there a place to pull off the road?"

I fumble the keys from my pocket as I throw open the driver's-side door. "Yeah, by the bridge. There's a place to pull down by the river, but I don't know how much cover we'll have if—"

"We'll have more than we have here." Hitch slams his door closed and grabs the "oh shit" handle.

I slam on the gas, stirring up a cloud of dust the person behind us will see if it doesn't settle before they reach the place where we were parked. But there's no help for it. On a gravel road, dust is going to happen, no matter how slow I go. Might as well gun it and hope I get the Land Rover hidden in time.

We don't know who this is, but I'd bet good money it's someone Hitch and I don't want to see. There are only so many people who will risk driving a deserted road outside the iron gate. Maybe it's the FCC "dick-weeds in iron suits" Lance was talking about yesterday. Maybe it's the highwaymen I've been warned to fear—though the whole point of taking a gravel road and avoiding the old highway is to avoid said *highway*men. Maybe it's people looking to move some black-market goods. All of the above are best avoided.

I hit the first turn going fifty, and the second going sixty. Our back end loses traction and the Land Rover skids toward the ditch, but the wheels catch and hold after a second and I guide us back onto the road.

"You drive like a maniac," Hitch says, but he doesn't sound afraid.

"I'll take that as a compliment."

"You should. As long as we don't die."

"We won't . . ." The trees open up and the end of the bridge comes into view. "Oh my god."

Hitch tenses next to me and I know he's seen what I've seen.

A sky filled with fairies. Hundreds of thousands of fairies. More fairies than I knew were in this swamp, more fairies than I knew were in the state of Louisiana. They form a shimmering, undulating wall of bluish green that seems to fill the world.

My foot eases off the gas as my jaw falls open. It's like facing down a giant. But worse. A giant would be big and slow and something smaller and faster would have a chance of finding a place to hide. There will be no hiding from this megaswarm. They'll hit us with the force of their numbers, then break up into tiny killing machines to finish us off. We're screwed. We're dead. We're—

"Don't stop! Don't stop!" Hitch's hands join mine on the wheel. "Hit the gas!"

My knee jerks and my foot smashes the gas pedal to the floor. Beneath us, the truck rumbles and groans as it regains the speed we lost and keeps going. Faster and faster, hurtling toward the wall of fairies so fast there isn't time to worry about what's going to happen if they don't get out of the way. There's barely time to scream before we break through.

Starbursts of blue and green splatter the windshield, but it doesn't break and the road on the other side of the wall is clear. We gain another ten miles per hour as the gravel transforms to pavement, ensuring we're halfway to the other side of the river by the time the megaswarm realizes we haven't frozen in the face of their display.

I watch them swirl and reel in the rearview mirror, forming paisley shapes in the sky as they change direction.

"Hit the wipers," Hitch says. "There's something on the windshield."

I glance down to see the fairy splatters on the glass beginning to smoke. I tug the wiper lever, giving the windshield a shot of fluid before pulling the lever down. The smoke vanishes, but before I can ask Hitch what he thinks it was, he shouts—

"Faster! They're following us." He lets go of the wheel, turning in his seat to stare out the back window. "Over an *iron* bridge."

"That's impossible. How in the—"

"Some are dropping, but not enough." Hitch reaches for his gun, but a gun isn't going to do us any good. Shooting at the swarm would be like jabbing a toothpick into an elephant's toe. Stupid. Pointless. And I don't even know if elephant's have toes, and the fairies are gaining on us like cheetahs on crack and—

"Faster!" Hitch shouts.

"I'm *going* faster!"

"We're only going to have a few minutes." He spins back to face the front, scanning the rapidly approaching end of the bridge and the FCC building glittering in a patch of sun. "Is there anywhere we can drive straight in? A warehouse or a loading dock or—"

"There's a garage," I say. "It's big and it was empty yesterday."

"Go there."

"But I don't remember if there's a door to close it up," I say, adrenaline overload making my hands sweat. We're going ninety and I can't risk slowing down if we're going to make it into the garage before the fairies get to us, but I don't know if this is the best call. "And even if there is a door, I don't know if we'll have time to close it."

"It's okay."

"And even if we close it, what if they force their way through? The building's made of iron, but so is the bridge and—"

Hitch's fingers curl around the back of my neck and his face drifts closer to mine. "Don't think so much. You think too much."

And then he kisses me—a feather of his lips at my cheek that's over in less than a second—but for some reason the kiss breaks through the creeping hysteria. Or maybe it's the fact that Hitch pulls on his iron hood, making me worry less about the future of his lips.

All I know is that my racing pulse slows just as we rocket off the end of the bridge, hanging in midair for a heart-swallowing moment before crashing back onto the gravel on the other side. The Land Rover's rear end does another fishtail as I turn toward the garage, but—thank god for sturdy English engineering—I keep control and send us charging across the short distance separating us from the only possible safety. I keep the gas pedal on the floor, waiting until we're under the overhang to brake and spin the wheel to the left.

The truck spirals, tires squealing and a burnt-coffee smell rising in the air. Before we've come to a full stop, Hitch's door is open. He spills out, landing on his feet and sprinting for the control panel next to the door leading into the building. I jam the truck into park and rush for the entrance to the garage. If Hitch can't find a button, I might be able to bring the door down manually. The ceiling is too high for me to reach the bottom of the door, but maybe there's—

I spot a pulley system to my left and go for it, trying to ignore the killer swarm sweeping toward the garage. There are fewer fairies than there were before—the iron bridge must have deterred some of them—but there are still too many to believe. Every inch of sky is filled with blue and green glowing bodies and bared teeth and so many beating gossamer wings they create a wind that lifts my hair from my neck, sending it swirling around my face as I grab the iron chain and pull.

Why blue and green? a part of me wonders. *Why not gold and pink? Why not—*

"No time!" I pull the iron chain harder and have the door headed in the right direction when it jumps in my hand and the door starts to rise. "Wrong way!" I scream over my shoulder to Hitch, but he's already figured that out. A second later, it starts to close again.

But it's slow. So, so *terrifyingly* slow.

I stumble back from the entrance, hands shaking, unable to look away from the monsters drawing closer with every second. Teeth and more teeth and this isn't going to work. The door won't close in time. At least some of them are going to get inside.

I turn, looking for a weapon—something, *anything* I can use to beat back the ones that make it through— but there's nothing. *Nothing,* not a tire iron or a baseball bat or even a big freaking stick. I spin back to face the fairies, heart jumping in my throat, slamming against my jawbone, the sudden rush of blood banishing the headache that's nagged me all morning.

Headache. No headache. Maybe that means—

The first of the fairies makes it through the still partly open door, and I get the chance to test my half-formed theory.

Hitch fires his gun at the same time as I lash out with my mind and for a second I can't tell which one of us dropped the first one. Then the others start to fall, one after another, plopping down to writhe on the floor as I pour everything I have into keeping them from getting any farther into the garage. I imagine my own wall, a wall of electricity and heat and pain shimmering in the air in front of me, stinging and biting and shocking fairies senseless as it gets thicker and stronger, taller and wider.

A few of the Fey manage to get through and zoom past me to the edible man behind, but Hitch keeps firing and I know he's wearing his suit. It won't be easy for the fairies to get through that kind of iron. There'd have to be a lot more than ten or twenty to nibble a hole before they dropped dead of iron poisoning.

Finally the door closes with a thud, followed by a few hundred thunks as the fairies at the front of the swarm slam into the heavy metal. But the door holds and eventually the thunks are replaced by an angry humming sound as the Fey fall back to bitch and moan and, presumably, plan the next phase of attack.

I turn to check on Hitch. He's still on the steps leading into the building, swatting a few remaining fairies to the ground and crushing them beneath his steel booties. "You okay?" I ask.

"Fine. You?"

"Good," I pant, blinking as dizziness curls around my eyeballs and squeezes. I'm gobsmackingly drained. Good thing the door closed when it did. I don't know how much longer I could have kept my energy wall up. I need that shot Tucker promised to bring me. Bad.

But how I'm going to make it back to Donaldson-ville by five o'clock tonight with *The Fairy Apocalypse, Part Deux: Curse of the Killer Swarm*, waiting outside is anybody's guess.

"Not going to think about that now," I mutter.

"What?" Hitch asks.

"Nothing."

"Make sure the rest of them over there are dead," he says, stomping another fairy that's trying to crawl down the steps. "Then we should get inside and tell these guys what's going on, see if they have access to an armored vehicle."

"Right." I have to shout to be heard over the increasingly loud buzzing outside.

I can't understand what the fairies are saying for some reason, but there's no doubt they're mad as hell and not ready to give up and fly away. The drone—punctuated by feral screeches—only gets louder as I dash around the garage, squishing any fairies that have survived my psychic attack.

I'm preparing to crush my tenth or eleventh Fey—an older male with a touch of blue hair on his chin—when I begin to suspect why these fairies aren't making any sense to me.

"Hitch, come take a look at this." I squat down beside the fairy, shocked again by how human they look when their jaws are closed.

Hitch appears next to me, hood in hand. "You okay?"

"Yeah, but look at that." I point to the thing's face as it struggles to sit up despite a nasty-looking burn mark on its stomach. "Have you ever seen blue facial hair on a fairy?"

Hitch's knees crack as he squats for a better look. "No. You don't see facial hair of any color too often, but I've never seen—"

The fairy opens its mouth and hisses, letting out a stream of bright green fluid that sparkles even in the dark garage. Hitch and I flinch away, and the fairy's spittle lands on the concrete between us. And starts to sizzle. And smoke. And eat a hole in the floor the size of a roll of quarters.

"What the—"

"Watch it!" Hitch pulls me back as the fairy's jaw drops and a gurgle indicates he's gearing up for another corrosive loogie. But this time, the spit only dribbles down his chest and soaks harmlessly back into his faintly green skin. He's fading fast, which is the only thing that gives me the courage to lean forward and take a look in his open mouth.

"See that?" I point with a pinkie finger. "What the hell is that?"

"Careful," Hitch warns, but he's leaning in along with me.

"There's only one row of teeth."

"And the inside of the mouth and gums are blue."

He's right. The gums are especially bright, almost fluorescent. A normal fairy's mouth looks a lot more like a person's mouth—pink, aside from a touch of green at the gum line when venom is produced.

"Take a look at the wings," Hitch says.

The fairy lies on his back, but I can still see his

wings. They're smaller than most, and thicker, with clear bulbous growths at the tips and a glistening, wet, greenish look that reminds me more of a sea creature than an insect. Fairy wings resemble butterfly wings. They're just bigger and made of sturdier stuff.

"It's a new species." Hitch scans the floor, taking in what's left of the fairies I've already stomped. All of them have the same weird wings. In the adrenaline free fall after the door closed, I hadn't noticed. "It has to be a new species."

"One we had no idea existed," I mumble. "But whose population numbers in the hundreds of thousands. At least."

"Yeah."

And the nightmare gets bigger. How is this possible? When there have been people like me out in the bayou collecting fairy related biological samples for years? Someone should have seen one of these guys. Or some sign of them—a wing or a breeding ground or something killed by their acidic spit—*something*. "Shit."

"Yeah." He nudges the fairy over onto its stomach with his shoe. It doesn't put up much of a fight. The greenish glow beneath its skin is fading, and it's starting to turn as blue as its facial hair. The longer we look at it—taking in the horned ridge on its back—the more alien it seems. The normal fairies are so much more humanoid in comparison. "I wonder why the ones who attacked me didn't spray the corrosive liquid," Hitch says. "If it eats through concrete, it would have eaten through my suit."

"I don't know. But think about what these fairies and our fairies could do together."

"One group to destroy the iron fences, one group to infect or kill everyone still living south of Hattiesburg."

"Guess we'll have to hope these fairies don't like the other fairies."

"I just hope their venom doesn't make us crazy," he says. "Or dead."

"Those are good things to hope."

He stands with another knee crack that makes me wonder if all that running he's doing is sitting well with his joints. "Let's go see why no one is coming to check who's in their garage."

I nod. "I wonder what happened to the car we heard coming?" I make a mental note to text Cane the second I get the chance. I have to warn him to stay out of the bayou.

"Hopefully it turned around and made it back to town." Hitch turns away from the fairy dying in front of us.

Or the dying . . . whatever he is.

"Hitch," I call, unable to take my eyes off the creature as it pulls in its strained final breaths. "What if they're not fairies?"

"What do you mean?"

"What if they're something else? What if there are other things out there? Things that are only now mutating that we have no idea how to protect ourselves from?"

"Remember what I said about thinking too much?" He appears at my side again.

I think about his words in the truck, and the kiss he gave me after. "I don't think too much. I don't think *enough*."

"That's part of the cycle. You think too much, until you drive yourself crazy with anxiety. Then you shut thought down and go on a bender until you're too messed up or hungover to think any more."

Hm. Well. Apparently he does know me fairly well, even after the years apart.

"I've been drinking less." I avoid comment on the validity of his theory.

"I've noticed. I'm proud of you." He grins his Hitch grin, the one that always makes me feel like one of the people who gets the joke. "I bet that makes you want to drink more, doesn't it?"

One side of my mouth crooks. "Already thinking about whether I've got margarita mix in the freezer."

Hitch laughs. Actually *laughs*. But then, what else is there to do? We've both done our share of crying the past couple of days.

I glance back at the blue-chinned fairy, but he's not breathing anymore. I'll have to come back and collect a few of the bodies for the FCC before we leave. Lance and his partner will have something I can use to carry the dead fairies in. Some Tupperware, an empty sour cream container, something. Assuming Lance and Friend aren't dead.

Hitch is right. It's strange that no one's come to check on us. The garage door made a significant amount of noise, and then there's the swarm that continues to roar outside.

"Come on," Hitch says. "Let's go."

I stand to follow him and nearly jump out of my skin as my phone buzzes in my pocket again.

God. Deedee. She's driving me *nuts*. I fish the phone out with a sigh, intending to send Cane a quick text and then turn my ringer to silent, but my latest messages stop me cold.

The first unread text is from Theresa, warning me that she had to take my cat to the vet, but that everything will be fine and to give her a call at Swallows when I get the chance. The second is from Deedee. It's a picture of a sickly looking Gimpy, and beneath it Deedee's written, "Me and Gimpy r at vet w/Miss Theresa. I'm staying w/him today. He got his stomach sucked, but he still mite die. And u don't care. I mite live w/Miss Theresa. She says I'm a good head in a crysis."

Theresa already has two children she can barely afford and doesn't see as much of as she'd like because she works so much. But maybe she *will* take Deedee in. Theresa's a good mom and no doubt better for Deedee than I could ever be. Hell, Sweet Haven is probably better for her.

Despite the fact that my cat has nearly died—yet again—it's good that Deedee's getting over her fixation with living with me. So I don't understand why the screen looks blurry as I text Theresa a quick thank-you and a promise to call as soon as I can, then Cane a warning not to come into the bayou because of a code-red threat I'm about to call into the FCC.

It's probably the smell of the weird fairy bodies

stinging my eyes. They have a noxious odor—sulfur and rancid lemon juice, mixed with freshly chopped green onions. By the time I shove my phone back in my pants pocket, tears are rolling down my face. I swipe them away with the back of my hand and start toward Hitch through a cloud of stink so powerful it feels like I'm swimming in it.

"Guess we know why we've never found any corpses," Hitch says as I climb the steps to join him.

I follow his nod, scanning the garage where the weird fairies' bodies are turning to greenish-blue mush that burns a fist-sized hole in the floor beneath them. I lift my imaginary pen and make an *X* in the air.

"Blessing the dead?" Hitch asks.

"Marking collecting samples off my list."

"That makes more sense."

"You know I'll never find religion."

"Godless heathen." Hitch pulls his gun from its holster, and pushes through the heavy white door.

20

Inside the building, the hallway with the red tile floor is weirdly quiet. It was quiet yesterday, too, but that was a different kind of quiet, a quiet that hinted at people breathing air in other rooms, of meals recently prepared and toilets recently flushed and other recent happenings that accompany the living of lives.

Today, there's nothing but an eerie stillness, underlined by the hum of the fairies gathered outside.

As Hitch and I climb the stairs to the office, we get another look at our attackers through the glass walls of the stairwell. The swarm is massive—a biblical plague that fills the sky and blocks out what sun peeks through the gathering storm clouds. I swear it looks nearly as big as it did on the other side of the river.

"You're sure you saw some of them falling on the bridge?" I whisper, not wanting to draw the fairies' attention to the fact that we're no longer inside the garage. If they can't make it through the garage door, they probably couldn't force their way through thick, industrial grade glass, either, but I'd rather not test that hypothesis.

"I think I did," Hitch whispers back. "But it doesn't look like iron affects them the way it does other fairies. Good thing that garage door is thick."

"Good thing." I swallow and keep climbing the stairs, trying not to imagine the Donaldsonville gates falling and this swarm spraying skin-melting bile over everyone I care about.

"I wonder why they're gathered in a swarm like that?" Hitch steps off the top step and we move down another red tile hallway, away from the glass. "It was almost like they were waiting to attack whoever came down that road."

I stop halfway down the hall. Attack. *Waiting to attack*.

"What's wrong?" Hitch asks, stopping beside me.

"Did you see me making the fairies fall? With . . . my mind?"

His brow wrinkles. "When? In the garage?" I nod, and his brow smoothes. "No, but I was wondering how you took down so many of them. Guess your superpowers are working again?"

I cross my arms and shoot him a narrow look. "Are you making fun of me?"

He rolls his eyes. "Honestly, Annabelle, you think I have time to—"

"So you believe me, now?"

"I thought we established that on the drive over."

We did? Maybe I should have turned down the Johnny Cash and focused on the conversation. "Well, yeah. Okay. So I figured out yesterday that inanimate objects aren't the only things I can move. I mean, I knew I could work with living tissue because of what happened with Stephanie in the basement, but—"

"Thanks for that," he says. "By the way."

I wave his thanks away. "You don't have to thank me." I hurry on before I lose my nerve or Hitch tells me we don't have time for chitchat. "And I want you to know I don't plan on doing anything to get between you and Stephanie. Even if you want me to." Now that I know what's going on with Stephanie and the baby, it's even harder to imagine the tension between Hitch and me leading to a good place. It's time to cut the cord. Once and for all.

Hitch's eyes drop to the tile as he gives a single nod. "Okay."

"So no more love or lips or . . ." I clear my throat, surprised by how tight it feels. "Other stuff."

"All right."

"I mean it."

Hitch looks up, sadness in his eyes, but a hint of that unsinkable smile curving his lips. "Message received."

"I know this isn't the time," I say, seemingly unable to quit babbling. "I just . . . I . . . I needed to—"

"I understand. You're right. I'm not in any place to—"

"And also, I can control the fairies. Make them do what I want."

Hitch blinks.

"And kill them by thinking about wanting them dead. And it works on normal fairies and the new fairies and I'm probably going to get better at killing them once I get another shot. My first shot is wearing off early because I drank too much whiskey last night."

It takes Hitch a second to adjust to the change in gears, but when he does I see the implications of what I've said rise in his eyes, popping up like targets in the interactive shooting range he liked to visit when we were in college. "Holy shit."

"Yeah."

"They're trying to kill you before you can kill them."

I nod. "Though how the new fairies found out about what I can do is anybody's guess," I say, mind spinning. "Maybe they saw what happened? When I killed the other fairies? Maybe that's why they were waiting for me here, since this is the route I took yesterday?"

"They're intelligent," he says with a numb shake of his head. "And they've been fucking hiding it, those fucking, sneaky little—"

"They are sneaky bastards." I'm trying to think of the best way to break the whole "they can also talk and I can talk to them, and I made a deal with one to find the cave, but he lied and tried to get us killed, and now I'm pretty sure that he's going to keep trying to kill me, while venting his spleen on the people I care about in the meantime" news, when we hear the first non-fairy-buzzing sound since we entered the building.

A faint metallic crash, like a cookie sheet dropped on tile, echoes through the hall.

"That wasn't on this floor." Hitch turns back to the stairs. I grab his arm and point down the hall toward the office.

"There's a back staircase. It comes out in the kitchen."

Hitch nods, following at a trot as I jog down the hall. I peek into the office and the break room as we pass by, but both are empty. Lance and Jose must have seen the fairies outside and decided to take cover in the kitchen. From what I saw of their sprawling bachelor pad yesterday, it's the only room without glass on at least one full side.

We hurry down the stairs, my sneakers virtually silent and Hitch's booties making only the slightest *skinking* sound. It's possible that Lance and Jose won't hear us coming, and I don't want to surprise them. I stop on the last landing, and turn back to Hitch.

I'm going to tell him I think we should announce our presence, but I don't get the chance.

"Come down the stairs. Slow," a voice announces from the other room. "With your hands on top of your head."

"Cane?" I stumble off the landing and would have ended up surfing the stairs, but Hitch grabs my arm and pulls me back beside him.

"Annabelle?" Cane's voice is noticeably softer, but when he steps through the archway, his gun is raised. Raised and propped up with his left hand and aimed uncomfortably close to my heart.

For a split second, I'm afraid. Not afraid of being seen with Hitch or caught lying to Cane or any of the normal things I'd usually be afraid of in a situation like this. I'm afraid that Cane is going to *shoot* me; that the man who told me he loved me last night is going to pull the trigger and end my life this morning.

And he knows it. I see the second he recognizes my fear. It hits him hard, making his next breath come out ragged and his breastbone sag. His jaw clenches and his elbows bend with a rusty-looking jerk, pointing the gun toward the ceiling. "What are you doing here?" he asks in a hurt whisper that makes me feel rotten.

I should never have been afraid.

But then again, he shouldn't have given me reason to be.

"What are *you* doing here?" I ask. "I thought you weren't supposed to be out this way until noon."

He pales. I'm not sure I've ever seen a black man do that, but Cane manages to pull it off. The golden flush in his cheeks vanishes, leaving him gray, drawn and washed out. His eyes shift between me and Hitch. I see him wondering how much we know about his illegal errand. It *has* to be illegal. He's not in uniform, he's carrying a gun I've never seen before, and he looks. So. Fucking. Guilty.

"My meet time got moved up," Cane says. "Currents weren't strong today."

On the off chance that he hasn't already dug himself so far into a hole that there will be no climbing out, I say, "I haven't told Hitch anything. Watch what you say."

Hitch stiffens and his hand slides from my arm. "What?"

"I'll explain later. Maybe." I wonder how far I can take this bluff. Can I trick Cane into telling me what he's doing out here? If I can get him alone, maybe I—

"I don't give a shit what you tell Hitch." The venom in Cane's voice makes me flinch. "I'm not leaving my sister in that camp. She doesn't deserve that. No person does. I'm bringing her to a place where she'll be taken care of by good people, which I should have been able to do from the beginning."

Comprehension dawns, loosening the knot of suspicion in my chest. Amity. He's paying someone to smuggle Amity out of the infected camp at Keesler. He's committing a crime, but he's doing it out of love for his sister and his family. I should have guessed it was something like this. Cane's weakness has always been loving people too much. He can't let go. Even when the law tells him he has no choice.

"I'm sorry." I wish I could go to him and wrap my arms around his waist and rest my cheek on his big barrel chest. But I can't. He's angry. And I am, too. "Why didn't you tell me?"

"You . . . I . . . ." His voice trails off and his gun drifts to his side as he realizes I've tricked him. I expect him to get angrier, but instead he shakes his head and motions over his shoulder. "We've got two men down in the kitchen. I'm not sure what killed them."

"What?" Hitch's hip knocks against mine as he

hurries down the stairs, but he doesn't acknowledge the contact. Guess he's angry, too.

Good. He might as well get angry and stay that way. He's only going to get angrier when I ditch him to go find Marcy. I can't leave her out in the bayou with no protection from the megaswarm, and I can't risk bringing Hitch or Cane along until I know what's going on. If Lance is one of the dead men, I'll have to search his office until I find out where I was supposed to meet Marcy, and then find some way to get away from the men in my life and past the swarm.

But first. The bodies. The dead bodies.

"The first guy was dead when I got here." Cane leads the way back into the kitchen. I follow, but stop in the doorway to cover my mouth and nose. The smell is awful, an acidic rotten stench that makes the dead fairies upstairs smell almost pleasant.

It's the bodies. It has to be. Except for the two men on the floor, the kitchen is immaculate, and no greasy stove or trash basket could smell *this* bad.

My eyes flit from the closer body—Jose, I'm guessing, though I've never seen his face—to the form huddled in a fetal position by the oven. It's Lance, looking even more ferretlike in death. His wide, empty eyes emphasize the sharp angle of his nose and his mouth hangs open, exposing the tips of his rodent teeth. I try to make myself go to him, to close his eyes and give the poor bastard some small bit of dignity, but I'm afraid I'll lose control of my stomach if I take another step into the room.

Turns out dead bodies still make me want to puke,

even the dead bodies of people I didn't like that much when they were alive.

Cane crosses the expanse from the door to the double oven in a few large steps. "This guy was rolling around a little. At first I couldn't tell if he was in pain or . . . something else," he says, an odd note in his voice.

"Then he started choking. I tried the Heimlich, but it didn't help." Cane squats beside the body. Hitch joins him, crouching down on Lance's other side, peering into his lifeless face. "There wasn't anything stuck in his throat."

"Was he foaming at the mouth?" Hitch asks. "It looks like there's something here, around the lips."

He gestures to Lance's mouth with two fingers, but doesn't touch him. He's in professional investigation mode. So is Cane. Both of them are in their element, focused on the body, ignoring the fact that Cane confessed his intention to commit a federal offense and that it's completely awkward for the three of us to be in the same room after the Captured on Police Camera Kiss Fiasco.

Not to mention that Cane knows I've been sneaking around with Hitch behind his back. At this point he may think it's purely professional sneaking, but then again, maybe not. He's already suspicious or he wouldn't have come to spy on me last night.

Remembering my other reasons for being angry with Cane makes me feel better. And worse. Better, because our lack of trust is mutual. Worse . . . for the same damned reason.

Cane cocks his head, considering Hitch's question. "Yeah. You know, now that I think about it, he was. A little. You thinking poison?"

Hitch nods. "But I'm not sure what would take them both out so quickly."

"Were they eating or drinking anything?" I finally manage to take a step into the room, but keep my eyes on the countertops.

The kitchen is an oversized galley-style, with a double oven and refrigerator on one side, sink and dishwasher on the other, and massive granite countertops between each appliance. The counters on my right, close to where Hitch and Cane are inspecting the body, are bare, but there are a few plates by the sink. I pad over to get a better look, but there's nothing to see but a few crumbs, a greasy butter knife, and a wadded up napkin.

"Anything?" Hitch asks.

"Looks like some kind of pastry." I lift the plate on top to peek at the one beneath. "Only crumbs left so it's hard to tell."

"Tough to get a significant amount of poison in a pastry," Hitch muses aloud. "Especially something that wouldn't start affecting the body until the person had eaten the whole thing."

"As someone nearly taken out by a shrimp muffin, I have a different opinion." I tug open the dishwasher, hoping the dirty dishes might offer up a clue.

"But that was a rare, severe allergic reaction," Hitch says. "What are the chances both of these men had the same—"

"Wait a second." I pull out the top rack of the washer, and pluck a teacup from inside. I lift it up and sniff, wrinkling my nose against the familiar smell. "The tea . . ."

"You think someone poisoned their tea?" Cane asks.

"No, I think . . ." The tea. Oh god. The tea I left out on the table last night like a dumb-ass. The tea that wasn't on the table this morning. "Gimpy! The tea!"

Cane's forehead wrinkles.

"I got a text from Deedee," I explain. "Gimpy was sick and she and Theresa had to take him to the vet to get his stomach pumped. Yesterday, when I was here, Lance gave me some tea bags. He said they were a rare caterpillar fungus that's supposed to clear out your system before a piss test. He's been drinking it for months. That's how he kept the FCC off his back about what I assume was his pot-smoking habit. I took the tea home and left it out on the table and—"

"Gimpy ate it," Cane finishes, because he knows the ways of my cat.

"I bet he did. And then, when I saw him in the Hogans' garden, he was acting really weird, even for him." Remembering Gimpy's performance makes me guess why Cane sounded funny when he first talked about seeing Lance. "You said Lance was rolling around when you came in, right?"

"Right."

"And you couldn't tell if he was in pain or something else." He nods. "Like hot-and-bothered kind of something else?"

Cane looks relieved. "Yeah. I thought maybe he was on Ecstasy or something."

I turn to Hitch, holding up the cup in victory. "It's the tea. It must be poisoned." But Hitch isn't impressed. Or pleased. In fact, Hitch kind of looks like it's his turn to fight the flight or puke response inspired by the stink of the dead men's soiled pants. "What's wrong?"

He stands, backing away from Lance with a small shake of his head. "Nothing."

"Bullshit." I put the cup on the counter and cross the room. I don't stop until I'm close enough to smell the sweat breaking out beneath Hitch's iron suit. "This has to stop, Hitch. We can't keep—"

"I poisoned it."

"What?"

"I poisoned the fungus," his says, shock and misery mixing in his tone. "That was the business I had to take care of yesterday morning." His throat works. "I drove up to St. Gabriel, boarded the barge upriver, and contaminated the compound."

"Why?" I ask, the word barely escaping past the acid rising in my throat.

"It's one of the items that keeps disappearing from the barges. It's the source of fairimilus, the peptide I was telling you about yesterday." He runs a shaking hand across his mouth, wiping sweat beads from his upper lip. "I thought if the test subjects got sick it would make the staff at the lab disorganized, and it would be easier for me to get in and out."

"Jesus, Hitch." I sway on my feet, the enormity

of what he's confessed making me dizzy. "That's . . . murder."

He shakes his head. "No. I had no idea this would happen. The man who gave me the poison said it made people nauseous, that's it. I didn't—"

"You almost killed my cat!"

"He almost killed you." Cane is suddenly by my side, his arm around my shoulders. "If you'd drunk that tea, you'd be dead."

21

Dead.

I glance down at Lance, his soulless husk hitting me on an entirely new level. Cane is right. I *would* have drunk the tea. I definitely would have, especially after what Tucker said this morning about the injections showing up in drug tests.

"Right." My breath comes out a shaky hiss.

"I'm sorry," Hitch whispers.

"I don't think that covers it when you've killed people." Cane's voice is so deep I can feel it vibrate in my chest, the way it does when he's really, *really* angry.

"I'm so sorry." Hitch ignores Cane, eyes only for me. "I was trying to save Stephanie and the baby. I didn't know what else to do. I—"

"You can remain silent," Cane says. "And know that anything you say can and will be used against you in a—"

"Don't Mirandize me!" Hitch turns on Cane, vein pulsing at his temple. "You don't understand what's happening here!"

"I understand these men are dead, and you con-

fessed to maybe havin' something to do with that."
Cane angles in front of me, not intimidated by Hitch
or his anger or the fact that Hitch is an FBI agent. In
that moment, my respect for Cane grows a few sizes,
though I'm not sure hauling Hitch down to the station is the right thing to do.

But he definitely needs reigning in. He's not thinking clearly. If someone doesn't knock some sense into
him, more people are going to die.

"Yes, these men are dead. And maybe it's my fault,"
Hitch says. "If so, I'll have to live with that for the rest
of my life. But I was only trying to protect my family,
like you're protecting your sister."

Cane shakes his head. "Not even close to the same
thing. I'm not hurting anyone. I'm not killing people."

"I don't think the Center for Disease Control would
agree," Hitch counters, stepping closer to Cane, chest
puffed out in a primitive display of aggression. "Neither would the federal government. Smuggling an
infected person out of a camp carries a mandatory
ten-year sentence."

"And manslaughter, even involuntary manslaughter, could get you ten to *life*." Cane mirrors Hitch's
stance, puffs up his own bigger, meaner-looking chest
and glares down at the shorter man. "And I mean to
see you answer for—"

"Okay, y'all. Let's just calm—"

"Fine!" Hitch shouts, interrupting my attempt
to take the testosterone in the room down a notch.
"Arrest me. What the *fuck* do I have to live for, any-

way? These men are fucking dead." He stabs a trembling finger toward the body at his feet. "And they were my last chance to find the fucking lab before it's too fucking late," he shouts, his fragile sanity thread snapping. "My baby is going to die and my wife might die, too, and even if she doesn't, she'll hate me for the rest of her life for failing her when she needed me the most. I know I've fucked up. But what the *fuck* was I supposed to do! I didn't want to hurt anyone, but what the—"

"Stop it!" I shout, moving between Cane and Hitch before Hitch explodes or Cane pulls out his cuffs. I lay a gentle hand on Hitch's chest, feel the pounding of his heart through his bones. "You've got to calm down. This isn't helping. We should go search the office. There might be something there that will help us find the cave."

I turn back to Cane, who's trying very hard to act like he doesn't notice that I'm touching Hitch. "We don't have time to explain everything right now." We don't. Not about the cave or about what's going down here personally. "But the basic gist is that Hitch has to find a mobile lab out in the bayou where dangerous people are doing bad things, and shut it down, or someone is going to kill his family. Stephanie's been poisoned, and the person who did it won't deliver the antidote unless Hitch does as he's told."

Cane's eyes soften. "We can't tell you anything more or it will put your life in danger," I continue. "And you can't say anything about this to anyone. If you do, you'll be risking our lives as well as yours. Just let us go and we can all sit down and talk about the rest of this . . . later."

Or *never*, if I get lucky.

I don't think these men deserved to die, but it was an accident. And they only ended up ingesting the toxin because they were stealing, because they were habitual thieves and supplying criminals of a more deadly variety. They weren't citizens it's going to hurt our world to lose. They took the gift of immunity and exploited the people they should have helped.

Maybe I'm a sociopath, but I can't work up a lot of righteous anger for their deaths. And I don't think this accident—no matter how horrible—should lead to Hitch spending the rest of his life in jail.

Cane sighs, a long, labored sigh that doesn't inspire much hope that he agrees with me. "Annabelle, I can't do this. If Agent Rideau is being blackmailed, we have to report it to his superiors. And I can't—"

"My superiors can't be trusted." Hitch sounds like he's backing slowly away from the edge. "At least some of them can't, and I won't know which ones until after I find the lab."

Cane pauses. I pounce on his moment of doubt. "Please. I'll go with Hitch and keep him from doing anything stupid, and you can go get Amity and take care of her."

"If they've got an armored vehicle, he can," Hitch says. "None of us are going anywhere without armor. An iron-sided vehicle won't be enough. If the swarm starts spitting acid it will eat right through."

"What?" Cane turns to me, a look in his eyes that says he suspects Hitch has lost his mind. He must not have seen the swarm.

"Come on. We'll show you." I tug the edge of Cane's shirt as I walk by. After a second's hesitation, he follows me out of the kitchen and up the stairs. I fill him in on what's happened with the new fairies—minus the fact that I can control them. Cane isn't ready for that information and, even if he were, I'm not willing to spill any more of the Big Man's secrets.

I know Cane believes the only way to deal with terrorist tactics is not to deal with them at all. But I wonder if he'd feel the same way if someone he loved were in danger and the only way to keep them safe was to keep his mouth shut and do as he was told.

You shouldn't shut up. Or do as you're told. You should take your next dose of medicine and use your fairy weapon to take out the Big Man and Grandpa Slake and Gerald and anyone else—human or fairy— who's a threat.

I shiver at the thought. I'm already headed down the road to Sociopathville. I've pretty easily justified Jose's and Lance's deaths. How easy would it be to justify a few more, a couple three murders in the name of making the world a safer place? But if I keep walking this way, it's going to be hard to turn back, and my gut tells me I'm not going to like who I am at the end of the road.

"What do you think?" I stand beside Cane in the door to the stairwell, watching the new fairies circle and dart, their movements growing more agitated.

Above them, the puffy, gray clouds have grown black and swollen. Thunder rumbles through the air. I'm hoping it's the storm that has the fairies all worked up, and not something else. Like psyching themselves up to attack the building.

Cane observes the teeming Fey with a cool eye, but I know this must be hitting him hard. The swarm represents a terrible new threat to the people he's sworn to protect. "I don't know what to think," he finally says, sounding so sad my arms are around his waist before I can think twice about it. I hug him, ducking under the elbow he lifts to let me in, and squeezing tight.

"I'm sorry."

He looks down at me, expression still unreadable. "You were listening to my call this morning."

"Yes. I wish you'd told me the truth."

He nods. "Maybe I should have."

"And I wish you didn't feel like you have nothing left to lose," I whisper. Because I don't know if there will be a better time to say it. And I mean it.

Emotion flickers in Cane's eyes, but before he can speak, Hitch slams out of the office behind us and comes rushing down the hall. Cane pulls away. I cross my arms, missing his warmth already.

"I've found something," Hitch says, holding out a set of blueprints. "These are almost twenty years old, but they're from Robusto Oil and Chemical."

I take the prints and hold them up so Cane can get a look over my shoulder.

"They called it a subterranean office environment," Hitch says.

"The mobile lab." Hope sparks inside of me when I see Donaldsonville's Railroad Street on the plans. "If they used these, we should be able to find the first lab station about . . ." I check the legend. "An inch is equivalent to ten miles, so . . . about five miles from town? Maybe a little more?"

Hitch nods, his cheeks flushed red and his hair standing up in damp clumps. He must be getting hot in that suit. "I think it's a good place to start." He takes the plans and rolls them into a cylinder. "After that, I'll track east. If I hurry, I can hit every lab stop before the end of the day."

"You mean *we* can hit every stop before the end of the day," I correct. There's no way I'm letting him go alone, and Cane certainly won't stand for it. If he weren't otherwise engaged, I know he'd insist on joining Hitch on his hunt.

"We should all go," Cane says, proving I know him fairly well. "Two armed people will be better than one. It's not safe to bring Amity this far upriver with the swarm outside, anyway," he continues. "Let me call my contact. I'll have him stop wherever he's at and tell Abe he needs to take over the pickup. We wanted one of us to stay in town, but . . ." He shrugs and pulls out his phone. "I'll tell him to call in a report to the FCC and the CDC about those things outside, too. Unless you've—"

"No, I haven't had the chance," I say. "But I'll text Jin-Sang." Calling Jin would be faster, but I don't want to get into a conversation with my boss right now. I don't have the time for the freak-out that will follow this news.

Cane nods. "Okay. Give me a minute, and we'll go. I drove the armored cruiser. I'm parked by the back door so we should be able to make it to the car safely. I've got my suit downstairs and Agent Rideau is covered, so . . ."

"Right." I pull out my phone. Cane walks down the hall, getting some privacy for his calls. I'm so busy jabbing out my message to Jin that I don't notice how weirdly quiet Hitch is until I'm about to hit Send. "What's up with you?" I ask.

"Nothing," he says, edging subtly closer. "Your eyes look better."

"They feel better." I lift my phone to my chest. "For real. What's up?"

He sighs and gives my phone a pointed look. "As soon as you and Cane start spreading the word about the swarm, the sky is going to be full of FBI helicopters. The FCC will want to see what's going on, and they go to the New Orleans FBI when they need someone in the air. Maybe the invisible people will see the swarm and realize that's why the copters are here. Maybe they'll think we talked and start killing people we love."

I hit Send on my message to Jin, refusing to have this debate with Hitch. "I'm sorry," I say. "This is my job. If the swarm heads toward Donaldsonville, the new fairies might be able to get through the gates and we have no idea what contact with people will mean. If they're like the others, the entire town could be wiped out or infected in a few hours. People need a heads-up to find a place to hide. I should have done this twenty minutes ago."

Hitch drops his eyes. "I understand."

"Thank you."

"Maybe I'll be able to take care of things before the helicopters arrive." He stares out at the churning sky. "I'll have time to get to a few of the lab stops before the copters get here from New Orleans. Maybe all five if the clouds stick around and make flying dangerous."

"Hitch, I don't—"

"This is another reason I should go alone." His eyes plead with me to understand. But I can't.

"You remember the last time you were here, when you kept trying to stage an intervention and keep me from throwing my life away?" I wait until Hitch nods before continuing. "Well, I'm staging an intervention now. You're not thinking clearly and you're making bad decisions and I can't—"

"I *am* thinking clearly," he interrupts. "If I'm spotted from the air by an FBI friend, they won't question seeing me. If I'm spotted by someone else, at least I'll be the only one on their hit list."

"No." I hold up a warning finger as he starts backing toward the stairs. "You don't get to decide this. We agreed that—"

"You made the right call, Lee-lee," Hitch says, using Cane's pet name for me. "You two love each other. I hope you'll be happy." And then he turns and runs down the stairs, sprinting like a track star despite the heavy suit.

Guess all that damned running is paying off for him after all.

"Hitch stop!" I scream, before spinning to warn Cane. "He's going for your car!"

Cane flips his phone shut. "He doesn't have the keys."

"He'll hotwire it. He's fast. Go!" I shout. "Take the back stairs and see if you can beat him to the door."

Cane sprints for the staircase. I turn and dash after Hitch, though I know it's pointless. Unless he falls down the stairs, there's no way I'm going to catch him. I'm fast, but I'm a *former* athlete, not a current one. My plan to get back in shape hasn't progressed past the thinking-about-making-a-plan-to-start-getting-back-in-shape stage.

Sure enough, by the time I reach the bottom of the stairs, Hitch is nowhere in sight. I take off in the general direction of the back door, hoping Cane reaches it before Hitch. If not, I have a feeling Cane will take this chase outside, and he probably won't take time to put on his iron suit.

The thought makes me run faster. And curse myself. And wish I had a gift for thinking things through on the turn of a dime. I never should have said anything to Cane! I should have gone after Hitch myself, or let him steal the car, or—

"Both of you hold up. Right now. You're going to hurt yourselves," comes a firm voice from around the corner.

I'm not expecting that voice. *Really* not expecting it. Even though I knew there was a chance I'd be seeing the face it belongs to today. My leg muscles go wobbly and I trip over my feet as I stumble to a stop.

I smash myself against the hallway wall, pressing my lips together to silence my gasps for breath.

Around the corner I hear Cane rumble, "Marcy?"

"Marcy?" Hitch echoes. "Are you—"

"I don't go by that name anymore." Her tone is a strange mix of the old firm-but-loving Marcy and chilly stranger. "Now I need you boys to put your guns on the floor and hand over the keys to the armored car outside. Should you refuse to do so, I'm afraid my colleague and I are going to have to kill you."

22

My insides go cold and all my assorted gut parts cramp and squirm. Marcy just threatened to kill Cane and Hitch.

I honestly don't know if I can take this.

How can this be real? How can the woman I've idolized be another wolf in sheep's clothing? I've seen the real Marcy. I've eaten at her table a thousand times, I've worked in her garden, I've let her force me into the church and down to the old folks' home to visit the shut-ins and stayed up until three in the morning cleaning up after her annual Mardi Gras party.

I've *known* her. I've loved her. A month ago I would have died for her, without a second thought. She's been like a mother to me, and at times the only friend who made it worth sticking around to see how this whole "life" thing is going to work out.

When I had faith in nothing, I had faith in Marcy. And I'm not going to let *anyone* take Marcy away from me. Not even Marcy herself.

I have to stop this.

For a second, I desperately wish for a gun, but then I realize I wouldn't know what to do with one. I don't want to shoot Marcy, and I don't want to shoot her accomplice and have Hitch or Cane shoot Marcy, either.

I need a distraction, not a gun, something to pull the focus off Cane and Hitch and—

"Fire! Fire! Fire!" I scream, as I turn and take off running back the way I came. *"Fiiiiiiire!"*

I hear a pair of sprightly footsteps I'm guessing *don't* belong to Marcy—there's no way she's lost those last thirty pounds and made her own fitness plans a reality in barely a month—chasing after me and fight the insane urge to laugh. This is *not* funny. I am probably about to get my damned self killed, a truth brought home as the person behind me fires and a bullet whizzes by my left arm.

"Shit!" I hurl myself down the hallway leading to the back stairs, hoping a Really Great Idea comes to me sometime between now and—

Another gunshot, this time so close it zips between my arm and my hip and I smell burnt cloth. It grazed my belt loop. This person is shooting to kill, not to frighten or maim, and I'm an easy target in this long, white hall. I can't keep running straight or one of those bullets is going to hit me before I reach the stairs.

I dive for the next door on my right, but when I push down, the handle won't move. Locked. *Locked!*
Shit!

I fall to the floor just in time, seconds before

another bullet buries itself in the door where I was standing.

My chin snaps up to see one of the skinniest men I've ever seen in real life prowling down the hall. His skin is dull obsidian and his one-piece jumpsuit the same faded black. He looks like a shadow come to life, the only spark of light in him coming from the whites of his eyes, which narrow as he takes aim at where I crouch on the floor.

I'm debating whether to make another break for the stairs or dive for skinny guy's legs and hope I can knock him off balance—he looks strong, but I'm taller and outweigh him by at least twenty pounds—when Marcy appears in the hall behind him. She's wearing a matching faded black jumpsuit in a much larger size. She's still her round, huggable self, even if the rest of her looks very different.

Instead of the usual course, gray-streaked, carefully tended baby Afro, her jet black hair is slicked back tight to her head. She must have dyed it. She's also wearing a touch of makeup—something the old Marcy would have laughed about having time for—combat boots, and a shoulder holster that boasts an impressive variety of weapons. I see another gun, two knives, and something in a round pouch that looks an awful lot like a grenade.

A *grenade*. The information skips across the surface of my brain, refusing to compute. Marcy plus Grenade equals error, error, error.

"Don't shoot her, Billy." Marcy's own gun is held loosely at her side. "She's immune. We'll need someone to carry the supplies from the car to the cave if the swarm doesn't clear out in the next few hours."

I stand on shaking legs. "Where are Cane and Hitch?"

"I shot the men," she says, turning my core to toxic jelly.

What? *No*. No, she couldn't have. She *wouldn't*!

"The big one's down." She stands beside Billy, glancing at him as she speaks. As if I don't even exist, as is she doesn't know that she shot the man I love, the man she herself advised me to *marry* a few weeks ago. "The one in the suit is still awake, but he won't be getting up for a while. I used the maximum setting on the Taser."

Ohmygod. My knees nearly buckle. A *Taser*. Not a gun. Not dead. "I knew you wouldn't kill them," I breathe, voice shaking with relief.

"Keep your mouth shut, girl." Marcy shoots me a look more deadly than the gun in her hand. I glance at it again. Definitely a real gun, not a Taser. Why did she pull that out before coming after Billy and me? She said she didn't want me shot, so . . .

"Why are—"

"Shut your mouth," she repeats, nipping my question in the bud. "Keep your peace and follow directions, and we *might* let you live."

"You're not going to kill me."

"I will," she says, in that chilly voice that makes me want to scream and shake her until the ice melts and the real Marcy floats to the surface. "I promise you that, princess. So don't do anything stupid."

Princess? What the . . .

"Impossible," I spit. "I was born to do stupid things. Stupid *fucking* things. Like loving people who are liars!"

"Girl . . ."

I ignore Marcy's warning tone and step forward, stopping only when Billy lifts his gun. "You're the one who taught me that actions speak louder than words," I say. "And none of your actions up to this point did *jack* to prepare me for this. You take care of people; you don't threaten to kill them. You make homemade chicken and grits; you don't buy black-market medical supplies and—"

"If you don't want her dead, get out the stun gun. We have things to do." Billy's flat, emotionless words kick my anger up a notch. Or four.

I take another step forward, eyes on Marcy but my focus on Billy's weapon. I'm going to rip it out of his hand and bash his skull in with it. I think I can do it with my mind, but if I can't I'll jump him and do it with my hands. And Marcy will let me. She's *not* going to shoot me. She's not one of the bad guys. I will *never* believe that. *Never*.

"If I stun her, she won't be able to help with transport." Marcy slips the gun into her holster and fetches the Taser from the other side. Like she's going to do it. Stun me into silence, and risk killing me when she does it. Stun guns can kill. I know she knows that.

She was living in Donaldsonville when one of the Sweet Haven kids was killed trying to break into the Piggly Wiggly. The rent-a-cop on duty hit him with a stun gun, thinking he'd immobilize him long enough for the real cops to come handle the situation. Instead, we'd all gotten to skip class that Monday to attend Theodore's funeral. He was fourteen.

"Can't trust her, anyway," Billy says. "Better to do it ourselves."

"Except we don't know about those fairies." Marcy lifts the gun, aiming it at my chest. "They might be able to get through the suits."

"Chance we got to take, I guess."

"Chance *you've* got to take," Marcy says. "That's why you're here, son. My back is shot. I'm not carrying anything anywhere." Her finger tightens on the trigger and my entire body breaks out in a cold sweat. She's going to do it. She's going to shoot me.

I lash out with my mind, but I'm still focused on Billy's gun, not Marcy's. His weapon jerks from his hands and clatters onto the red tile. He cusses and goes for it and I take my own dive to the floor, hoping to avoid Marcy's Taser fire long enough to get Billy's gun and figure out what to do with it.

Shoot Billy? Then Marcy? Marcy? Then Billy?

Can I shoot Marcy? I don't think I can, I really don't—

The Taser sizzles and a blast of electricity arcs across the hall, hitting Billy as he lunges for the gun. I'm close enough to feel the charge in the air, a sting that makes me pull my hand to my chest and lean back on my heels.

Billy moans and squirms. Marcy hits him with another blast of electricity and then a third. Finally, he lies still on the ground, looking like a crime-scene body drawing in his black suit. His weapon is only a foot from my knee. I could reach for it and be armed before Marcy tries to shoot me, but I don't make a move.

Marcy didn't Taser me. She Tasered her partner. And when I look up at her, all the chill has left her eyes.

"What the heck are you doing out here, Mess?" she asks, love and frustration and a hint of pride in her voice. Her normal Marcy voice, using her normal words.

"Mess" has never sounded so good.

"Trying to help the FBI shut down a lab that's making bioweapons and experimenting on unwilling captives," I say in a rush. "What are you doing here?"

She sighs, thinks about it for a second, then says, "CIA."

She's got to be kidding. "What?"

"Central Intelligence Agency."

"No way."

"Way." She nudges Billy with her boot. He doesn't move. She slips her Taser back into her holster.

"You're a spy." My brain flashes the error message again. Marcy plus spy doesn't compute much better than Marcy plus criminal. "For real."

"Traynell and I have been working this area since the eighties, when the oil company first moved in. We were deep cover, long-term engagement." She sighs again. "I knew it was a bad idea to have me back in the field so close to Donaldsonville. I'm too old for this running and shooting crap," she says, rubbing the small of her back. "And I know too dang many people."

"You left Donaldsonville to go undercover." I think through my last conversation with Marcy before she left. "So you didn't really help Kennedy's dad kidnap her or—"

"No, I did. And I killed two people a few weeks after my fifteenth birthday," she says. "I met my first boss in prison. He felt bad that I'd been tried as an adult, thought I deserved a chance to put my life to better use."

Oh. Well. "I didn't know the CIA recruited out of prisons."

"There's a lot people don't know about the CIA."

True that. At least I'm guessing.

"But you're one of the good guys," I clarify, easing back to my feet.

"I'm supposed to disable the lab," she says. "But I didn't realize the FBI had their own thing going on. Think they'd like to communicate that to—"

"It's not an official FBI thing," I confess. "Agent Rideau and I are investigating off the record. He thinks some of the higher-ups in the FBI might be involved with the lab. So if you could maybe *not* say anything about him being out here . . ."

Marcy nods. "Makes sense. I don't see how this could have stayed secret all these years otherwise. Not without someone in the government working to keep it that way."

"And Agent Rideau is Hitch, by the way," I add,

strangely compelled to overshare now that I have the real Marcy back. "You know Hitch? From-when-I-was-in-med-school Hitch?"

Marcy's eyes get bigger. "Good lord."

"Yeah. But it's okay now. I think. Better, anyway."

"You're running around with him *and* Cane?"

"Not running around running around," I say, "I'm working with them both. I guess. We were going to go look for the cave together before you shot them." I suck in a panicked breath. How could I have forgotten? "You shot them!" I leap over the fallen Billy and start down the hall.

"They'll be fine," Marcy says, stopping me in my tracks. "I didn't hit them as hard as I hit Billy. I wouldn't have hit them at all, but I wasn't sure I'd blown cover. I thought there was a chance . . . even though Cane recognized me."

"He's going to be very disturbed."

"He and I are going to have a talk," Marcy says. "I need that boy to keep his mouth shut. This isn't something that can go through official channels. Not *his* official channels, anyway. He needs to learn being a good man doesn't always mean following the rules."

"You still think he's a good man?"

Marcy lifts her brows, giving me her "How stupid are you?" look. "He's a great man. And no man ever loved a woman more than he loves you."

I nod, fighting the tears rising in my eyes. "And you . . . we . . . you and me . . ."

Marcy's mouth softens and her arm comes around my waist, hugging me to her side. "I love you like my own flesh and blood. I wouldn't break cover for just any fool who ran screaming fire."

"Yeah?" I risk a look down at her beautiful eyes.

"Yes, baby."

"I'm so glad you're not a bad guy." And then I burst into tears. *Burst*. My eyes go from zero to gushing in a finger snap and sobs shake my ribs and my stomach feels like it's going to be sucked into a vortex of relief.

"Hush now. It's all right." Marcy pulls me in for a real hug. I fold over her shoulder, trying to ignore all the various weapons gouging into my chest. Grenade in the boob or not, this is still a Marcy hug.

"I've missed you so much," I say.

"I've missed you, too."

"Come back home. Don't leave us again."

She pulls away, carefully, gently. "I can't promise that, baby. It's going to depend on what happens out here, and—"

"Freeze!" Cane's voice echoes down the hall, deep and commanding and totally scary, but neither Marcy nor I flinch.

"It's okay," I say, motioning him over. "She's on our side."

Cane doesn't respond. He moves smoothly down the hall, gun trained on Marcy's forehead. "I need you to unstrap your holster and lay your weapons down."

"Cane Cooper, get that gun off me," she says. "Would I leave your gun by your hand if I was intending you real harm?"

That makes Cane hesitate. I take advantage of the

moment to fill him in on what Marcy told me. I've gotten to the part about her looking for the cave when he interrupts with a grunt.

"Well, you'd better hurry." Cane slides his gun back into his holster. "When I came to, Agent Rideau was gone. So was his map."

"Dammit!" What the hell is Hitch thinking?

And why didn't he come looking for me? He had to have heard the gunfire and the shouting. But he just . . . left me. Decided I was a necessary loss and moved forward with his true goal—doing whatever it takes to save Stephanie and the baby, with no regard for how much havoc he wreaks in the lives of others. Or how many people he kills.

"We have to go." I lay a hand on Marcy's arm. "Hitch is going to blow up the lab. Maybe with people inside if he thinks he has to."

Marcy's brow furrows. "Why would he—"

"He's being blackmailed. But I saw the map and I remember the location of the first lab stop." I start down the hall. "I'll explain in the truck." We're going to have to take the Land Rover and hope we make it through the acid-spewing fairies still teeming outside.

"I think we should try the tunnel," Cane says, making me turn back around. "I'm not sure we'll make it through the swarm without armor."

"What tunnel?" I ask.

"There's a tunnel system under this building," Cane says. "One arm leads to the old docks. That's why I was here. The guy bringing Amity upriver said the FCC agents would take me through the tunnels for a price. He said it was safer than driving a cop car so close to the water. There's been a lot of pirate activity the past few months. They shoot cops on sight. I found the tunnel entrance at the back of the kitchen. I was going in when I heard you and Hitch coming down the stairs."

"But the first lab stop is on the other side of the river." I hesitate. "All the way up by Donaldsonville. Do the tunnels—"

"According to the guy I talked to, they run up to Donaldsonville and on to Baton Rouge in one direction and New Orleans in the other."

"But that's *hundreds* of miles. Through marshland. How in the—"

"It makes sense," Marcy says. "The people who designed the lab have been out here a long time. And they have the technology."

"How long have they been here?" I wonder if Hitch's hunch is correct, if Robusto Oil played a part in the fairy mutations. "You said the eighties?"

Marcy nods. "That's when I was assigned to Donaldsonville."

"Because of the oil company? Robusto Oil?" She nods again. "But Hitch's information said the company only starting digging out here about sixteen years ago."

"That's when they started digging for oil," Marcy says. "They started buying up land in 1984."

"Plenty of time to dig tunnels," Cane says.

Tunnels they might have thought they needed

to survive. They must have known making the Fey larger would make them deadly, but they might *not* have known about the fairies' allergy to iron. They might have thought going underground was the only way to protect themselves.

"Before the emergence, the company owned a good chunk of riverbank land." Marcy starts down the hall behind Cane, giving me no choice but to follow. "The government came in and bought them out a few years later, but Robusto could have owned this parcel originally. I think it's worth a try. We were waiting downriver when the swarm came in," she says, tone sobering. "I've never seen so many fairies. And they look different, don't they? I know my eyes aren't what they—"

"They are different." I drag my feet as Cane gets closer to the stairs. "They also spray a corrosive liquid. Hitch and I took out a few in the garage, but I couldn't collect a sample. Their bodies disintegrate after death. Hey y'all, wait—" Marcy and Cane turn back to me with identical looks of frustration. I'm slowing things down, I get that. But I'm also attempting to be the voice of reason. A new role for me, but surely they can see this isn't the best plan. "Even if we find a tunnel going in the right direction," I say. "It's going to take hours to walk back to Donaldsonville. We'll never make it to the first lab stop before Hitch."

"They had a couple of scooters down there," Cane says. "They're small, but you and I can ride one, and Marcy can take the other."

"Okay. Sure . . . okay." But what I mean is No. Not sure. Not okay.

A pair of scooters versus a speeding police car with a crazy man behind the wheel. We'll never get to the cave in time. Even if we figure out where the hell we're going while zipping around in the dark with no compass and nothing but our guts to keep us going in the right direction, we'll be too late. But if I insist on taking the truck, Cane's and Marcy's lives will be in danger. I'm pretty sure the fairies are after me, and I can't guarantee the safety of anyone in my company.

There's only one answer.

I wait until Cane and Marcy step into the stairwell before running as quickly and quietly as I can down the hall in the other direction. I'm halfway back to the garage—leaping over Billy's fallen form like a spastic gazelle—when Cane calls my name.

I land and look back—long enough for him to hopefully see how much I wish this could go differently—and then sprint for the exit. I hear his footsteps pounding down the hall behind me. He's fast, but after his Tasering, it seems I'm faster. I keep my head start.

By the time he makes the jump over Billy, I'm already at the door leading into the garage, hurling it open and slamming and locking it behind me. I jab a few buttons, and finally find the one that lifts the garage door. As it slides open, I run for the truck. I've got no way to close the door after I drive out, but hopefully the fairies will follow me across the bridge and leave Cane and Marcy alone. Surely Cane will have the sense not to come after me, even if he finds a way to bust the dead bolt.

I turn the keys still dangling in the ignition and slam down the gas, zooming out the door into the fairy swarm as the clouds break and a merciless summer rain begins to fall.

23

Rain batters the windshield, so hard and fast the wipers can't hope to keep up. When I hit the bridge going sixty—as fast as I dare given the sudden lack of visibility—I can barely see the road two feet in front of me.

The good news is that the fairies are following me, moving away from the FCC building in a swirling, undulating mass. The better news is that they don't seem to care for the rain. As I zip down the bridge, lightning flashes and Fey sputter and fall to the ground on both sides of the truck without any help from my mind powers.

Thank the wrath of Zeus.

I don't want to use the only weapon at my disposal unless I absolutely have to. I don't know what I'll encounter at the cave, but I'm sure supernatural mojo will prove helpful and I don't know how much I have left. I seem to have recovered a certain degree of power after the worst of my hangover passed this morning, but I can't afford to risk burning out before I reach Hitch.

Hitch. What an idiot. Guess I'm an idiot, too, but I'm doing this to keep Cane and Marcy safe. There's no sense in all of us getting killed. Maybe Hitch is thinking the same thing, but that doesn't explain why he left Cane and me to the mercy of what he had to assume were deadly criminals. He's never met Marcy, and even if he had, she and her partner were certainly acting like threats to our well-being.

"Not a nice person," I say out loud, testing the words. "Maybe he's just not a nice person." I punch the gas, sending the Land Rover leaping forward, hurtling off the end of the bridge, landing on the gravel road with a wet crunch and a whirl of dirt.

New Hitch is a lot different than the old Hitch—I realized that the day he arrived in Donaldsonville—but deep down I thought the basic components were the same. Hitch may be an arrogant bastard at times, but at his core he's always been a lover and protector of humanity. He worked tirelessly at the hospital, driven by the need to heal, not score a paycheck or social status or follow in Daddy's footsteps like some of the other residents. He risked his life after Katrina, going out in a borrowed iron suit and pulling people from the wreckage, helping the immune teams get to hundreds before they were infected by the fairies swarming through the hurricane-damaged gates.

The old Hitch would never have so easily defended one life over another. Being caught between saving his wife and child and hurting other people would have ripped him apart.

But now . . . maybe that's not the case. Maybe he's decided other people don't matter as much as *his* people. Just like my parents and their wealthy neighbors, who erected their own iron gate around our Garden District neighborhood in the days after the emergence. They hired steelworkers to build the barrier and bribed armed guards with safety for their families if they promised to keep everyone else out.

When the refugees started crowding in from downtown, the gunmen were told either to shoot the people trying to break through the gate or be kicked outside themselves to join the defenseless. My father and his buddies walked our iron-protected roof with shotguns and cold mint juleps, watching as people were shot or bitten. They refused to let anyone in. Even though there was room for more people, room for a hundred in our house alone.

I wanted to say something, to beg my parents to stop the insanity, but I didn't. I was too messed up. Caroline's body was in the deep freeze in the garage, waiting for the world to settle down enough for us to bury her. I was sixteen and I'd killed my sister. Her death was my fault and my parents weren't speaking to me and the guilt was eating me alive and all I could do when the guns started firing was huddle in the back of my closet and cry. I felt helpless to do more.

Maybe Hitch feels helpless, too, but does that matter? Can I ever respect him again after—

A fairy smacks into my windshield and explodes

in a burst of green. Within a few moments, the glass begins to smoke. The rain and the wipers take care of the corrosive blood before it can bore a hole, but it has the necessary effect on my focus.

I don't have the luxury of dwelling on whether Hitch is "nice" or "not nice," or whether I can respect him again. I need to drive and find a way to get rid of the fairies before I reach the first location. If the lab is at station one, I won't be able to sneak in behind Hitch and help clear the building if I'm being following by acid-spewing fairies.

"You're worse than the Slake," I mutter beneath my breath, wishing I could understand what the freaks are hissing at me as they bounce off the windshield and spiral through the air to land in the swamp below. If Tucker was telling the truth about the location of the Big Man's compound—and I can't imagine why he'd lie, about *that*, at least—then Grandpa Slake is full of shit, but I've learned a lot from him.

But then . . . maybe these fairies have, too. Maybe the old man has been spreading tales, figuring he'd cover his bases in case the Big Man didn't shoot me. Maybe stories of my fairy-controlling, Gentryesque evil were enough to lure this new species out of hiding.

They must have been hiding, being careful to stay off humanity's radar. Either that, or they're a recent arrival on the mutation scene. Considering their numbers and the variety in their age and development, however, that doesn't seem likely. They must have been around for a while, which hopefully means that they don't feed on human blood. If they did, surely humans would have known about them.

The realization gives me hope, but it doesn't help as far as ditching my tail is concerned. There are hundreds—maybe thousands—fewer fairies following me than when I first left the docks, but that still leaves a thousand too many. They buzz around the truck, slamming against the windows, leaving acid streaks that would eat through the glass if the rain weren't falling with such force.

The rain. They don't like the rain. Which I'm guessing means they don't like water, either? Maybe?

It seems strange for creatures that live in the bayou not to care for water, but then again, the Slake can't swim. They lay their eggs in stagnant water and need a hot, humid climate to survive, but they can't swim or stay submerged for more than a few seconds without suffocating. They simply can't hold their breath that long. So maybe . . . if I wait until I'm only a half mile or so from the cave before I drive the truck into the water . . .

"This is a really stupid idea," I assure myself.

Even if I manage to pick the perfect place to drive off the road—one with water deep enough to cover the Land Rover and clear of maiden cane and arrowhead and other masses of floating vegetation—get out of the driver's seat before I drown, swim far enough to emerge somewhere the fairies aren't expecting, and reach the cave on foot without being spotted or sprayed with acid or shot by people guarding the lab, then what?

I'll be soaking wet and poorly prepared for a stealth mission. And that's if I'm not eaten by gators or bitten by a cottonmouth.

But what other choice do I have? I push the pedal to the floor, roaring down the road at a speed that's unwise, praying I'll come up with a better idea before I get to the cave.

Thirty minutes later, I weave off the main road and down a scrawny dirt trail that—from what I remember of the plans—I *think* is leading me in the right direction, I'm pretty certain it's the direction Hitch took, at least, since the low-hanging branches over the road are freshly broken.

I've got a few hundred fewer followers than I did before, but the initial cloudburst has faded to a lighter drizzle. The acid left behind by smashed fairy bodies lingers long enough to melt glass before the rain washes it away. With the rear wiper broken, the back windshield is looking especially nasty. If the fairies get smart enough to start committing suicide in the same spot, they'll be in the truck in a few minutes.

At this point, I can't be more than a mile from the first lab stop. There's a chance I'll run into guards if I wait any longer. It's time, as Fernando says, to shit or get off the pot.

"Okay. I can swim. I'm a strong swimmer," I say, breath coming faster as I round a corner and a decent driving-off place comes into view. The water is plant free and there's a hint of current and it looks deep. Really deep. My arms tremble, sweat breaks out around my hairline, and a sour taste floods my mouth.

I can't do this. *I can't.*

"You can. Just do it!" My knuckles go white on the wheel. I aim the truck off-road and push the gas to the floor.

"Stop! Stop!" The shout comes from the backseat, scaring the shit out of me.

I stomp the brake, but it's too late. The truck zooms off the edge of the road, hanging in mid-air for a gut-shriveling second before nose-diving into the bayou. The impact sends my chest slamming into the steering wheel. I don't do seat belts if someone isn't there to make me buckle up, and staying unbuckled seemed like a good idea when I was plotting how to get out of a sinking vehicle without drowning.

But now, as my skull strikes the windshield with a dull pop and blood leaks into my eyes, I rethink the wisdom of eschewing beltage.

"What the hell, Red?" Tucker's breath is hot on my neck. He grabs my shoulders, pulling me off the steering wheel as the truck begins to sink and water floods in through the cracks in the doors at an alarming rate.

"What the hell, *you*." My words are slurred. I smack my lips. The salty-sweet taste of blood rushes through my mouth. "I bit my tongue."

"You also busted your forehead open." He smears into visibility, his eyes doing a weird jump-cut thing I've never seen them do before. "And probably killed us both," he says, cussing as he swipes the blood from my face and smears it onto the passenger's seat.

"That's going to stain."

"Who gives a shit?"

"It's a rental."

"Are you insane?" he shouts. "What the fuck were you—"

"Don't yell at me!" I shout back, wincing at the pain that shouting stirs up in my skull. "I didn't know you were back there," I add in a softer voice. "Why *are* you back there?" I pull my feet from the floor. The water is up to my ankles and some stupid instinct urges me to "Stay dry!" despite the fact that my plan is to submerge myself as soon as the truck goes under.

"I followed you to the docks and snuck into the garage. I figured you'd end up at the lab sooner or later and I could help you out." He cusses as the water creeps toward his knees. "Show me to be a Good Samaritan."

"You're not a Good Samaritan. You're a spy. You're here to make sure Hitch does what the Big Man told him to—"

"I'm not a spy." Tucker cusses again as the unexpectedly cool swamp water rises higher, soaking the seat of his pants. "I'm trying to help you, you stubborn, crazy, redheaded—"

"We don't have time for name-calling, you spying, lurking jerk." I crouch in my seat and crawl over to the already soggy passenger's side, figuring it will be easier to climb out the window without the steering wheel in the way.

"Hell, yes, there's time," Tucker says. "I want to get it all out. In case I don't live to tell you how crazy you are."

"I'm not crazy. I have a plan." I scan the windows. We'll be under in a few minutes. I need to figure out where the fairies are gathered. Looks like most of them are hovering directly above the truck, with a few still straggling in from the road behind. All of them are being careful to stay above the bayou's surface as they hiss and spit and knock their tiny fists against the glass.

What satisfaction I feel in accurately judging their lack of affinity for water, however, is banished by the fact that I'm *in* the damn water. And it's up to my chest and it's almost time to take this plan to the next level and swim out into gator-infested waters and hope I can hold my breath long enough to emerge somewhere the fairies won't be looking. And hope Tucker can, too, because even though his presence here isn't my fault and it's creepy the way he hangs around *watching* me all the time, I'll still feel guilty if I get him killed.

Unless I'm dead, in which case I won't feel guilty—or anything else—about anything. As appealing as *that* sounds, I'm not ready to go out just yet.

"We're not going to die," I say. "We'll wait until we're under, drop the window, and swim downstream as far as we can. If the fairies haven't noticed us, we'll crawl up on the bank and circle around until we find the cave."

"And if they *have* noticed us?"

"We swim some more," I say, heart bobbing in my

throat as the water inches higher. "And hope we lose them while we're under water."

"With the gators and the snakes." Tucker makes no effort to hide how dumb he thinks my plan is.

Negative Nancy.

"At that point we should split up," I continue, ignoring his dubious grunt, "and hope one of us gets to the lab in time. If this is where it is. One in five chance, anyway, and—"

"I can disappear, Red," Tucker says. "I can get away. You're the one—"

"I'll be fine. Just promise me you'll stop Hitch from killing anyone if you can. He won't be able to live with it if he does. He's not himself right now."

"He doesn't deserve you," Tucker says. "Never did."

My eyes flick to his in surprise.

"You're a good woman. Like the chance to know you better." He gives me a tight nod that looks an awful lot like good-bye.

I clear my throat. I can't think about good-bye. Not yet. "You have any idea where these new fairies came from?" I turn to catch one last glimpse of the outside world. Staring into Tucker's worried face isn't the best idea right now. I'm already seeing my life flash before my eyes; I don't need to see it flashing before anyone else's.

"They're not fairies. They're pixies."

Pixies. It rings a vague fairy-tale bell. "Like troublemaking fairies?"

"No, nothing like that. Different species. Vegetarians."

"Then why are they trying to kill me?"

"Don't know. I've never seen them like this."

"I've never seen them at all."

"Not surprising," he says. "They haven't been out here long."

"Really? They mutated recently? Because I—"

"I didn't say that."

"Then what—"

"That's a story we ain't got time for," he says. "Just trust me, they don't usually hurt people. And there aren't as many out there as you think. They work in illusions. They're making themselves look scarier." Tucker crawls into the passenger's side in back and plunges a hand into the water, looking for the window crank. I reach down, searching for my own. The water is up to my chin now, and I have to strain my neck to keep my face above water.

"How do you know about pixies?" I ask. "Did the Big Man—"

Tucker curses. "Tell me this car has crank windows, Red."

Crank windows. I thought it did, but . . . Did I check? I thought . . .

I fumble below the water, my fingers brushing against the door handle and the armrest and some buttons. Lots of buttons. I jab them. I jab them one at a time and all at once and nothing happens and I pat down the entire door and there is no crank and still no crank and oh *holyshitfuck*!

"Tell me, Red!" Tucker shouts. The water is up to our ears. There are only a few inches of air at the top of the cab. The truck is under. It's time to go, but we won't be going anywhere because I drove a car with power windows into the water and we can't open the windows and we'll never be able to open the door with the amount of pressure bearing down all around us.

Unless . . .

I gather all my internal forces. The familiar knot of potential energy balls at the base of my brain, but even before I send it punching into the window, I know it's not going to be enough. My headache is back—probably because I Suck at Safety and just got my head slammed into a windshield—and now Tucker and I are going to die.

I try one more time—hoping sliding the glass down might be easier than smashing it—but still, nothing happens.

"My head's messed up," I pant. "You'll have to break the glass."

"I can't," Tucker says.

"Yes, you can, you—"

"I can't," he repeats. "I can move shit around, but smashing things isn't in my bag of tricks. Can't work up that much force. Already tried to work it down and got nothing."

"Shit," I say, then decide I'd rather *shit* not be my last word, and try to think of something else to say, something other than "I'm sorry." Because the only thing shittier than *shit* is *sorry*. I'm tired of being sorry, I'm tired of other people being sorry. I just want *something* in my damned life to work the hell out for once! Argh!

The water level surges. Swamp water burns my nose and I taste mud and rotten things and choke on them. "Shit!" My face presses into the ceiling. I pull in my last gasp of air.

This is it.

Shit for a final word it is.

24

Big breath." Tucker's voice is strained from keeping his head tilted back far enough to breathe.

His hand curls under my armpit as he pulls me through the front seats into the back. There's more room at the top here—the truck's going down nose-first—but not much. I brace my foot against the floor, keeping my head above water when Tucker pulls away.

"I'll kick out my window and push you through first," he says. "Got it?"

"No. You should go—"

"Don't argue with me!" He sucks in a breath and starts kicking the crap out of the back window. Even with water resistance working against him, it's a manly display. The window creaks and jumps in its grooves and the truck dips on the right side, but no slivers break the smooth surface of the glass.

We're over. We've got less than ten seconds to breathe; maybe two or three minutes of consciousness before we pass out from lack of oxygen.

No matter how hard he pounds, there's no way

Tucker's going to bust through with his boot. He needs something sharp enough to shatter the glass, or at least a weak place in the—

"The back," I gasp as the water closes over my head.

The back glass with the broken windshield wiper, where the acid from the pixie bodies lingered long enough to start burning holes. It might make it weak enough to break.

Too bad I'm not sure Tucker heard me. I open my eyes, but the water is so filthy I can't see. Not like seeing is going to help much at this point. Neither will floating here with my lungs starting to burn, hoping Tucker was listening in that last second.

I squeeze my eyes shut, grab hold of the headrest, draw my knees to my chest, and drive them at the back window. I hit hard enough to jar my bones, but the glass holds strong. Water swirls around my legs as Tucker's feet hit a second after mine, but there's still no change in pressure in the cabin.

Maybe together, maybe if we—

I pull my knees in and wait until Tucker's energy shifts before kicking my legs as hard as I can. We hit the glass at the same moment. The surface weakens, crumpling under our feet. Hope makes my heart beat faster, but I know we haven't broken through yet. I pull in and kick out again.

And again. And again.

By the fifth kick, my pulse is racing and my body screaming for breath. I can't keep up this level of physical activity without oxygen for long. I need to breathe, and sooner or later my nose and mouth are going to stop listening to logic and—

On the sixth kick, my feet smack the window and keep going, sending chunks of glass floating into the bayou. Tucker and I dive for the opening, knocking elbows and knees as we push through and kick toward the surface. Screw the pixies and their acid spit, I can't stay under water for a second longer.

I break first, sucking in a desperate breath that makes my lungs feel the most wonderful kind of horrible. They ache and burn and tremble—but air! Sweet air! I pull in another breath, relishing the tingle as oxygen races through my blood before catching a blurry glimpse of bluish green bodies and frantic wings. I dive back under. Once I'm a few feet below the surface, I swim hard in what I hope is the right direction.

I'm disoriented after the near escape and still light-headed and panicked, but I force myself to take ten long underwater strokes with my arms and legs before floating back to the surface and sipping in a breath as quietly as I can. This plan isn't going to work if I make a bunch of noise as I swim away. I peek to the right and left. This time there are no pixies in sight, and, as I slip back under, I've recovered enough to look for Tucker under the water.

I open my eyes, though the water is murky and for all I know Tucker could be invisible again. It's instinct, and I know I'm headed toward shore, so it's probably a good idea to keep an eye out for tree roots and rocks and snakes and gators and . . .

And strange metal and rubber portal–type things set into the side of the bank.

My arms reverse their circle, stopping my forward motion. I'm not sure what I'm seeing, but I know I want a better look. I kick closer. The circular shape resembles a giant drain cover—at least four feet in diameter—but at the center, the metal gives way to black. Algae-covered rubber puckers in a circle with a swirl at the center, like a giant, menacing cervix waiting to give birth to anything brave enough to push through to its other side.

I have an idea.

A bizarre idea about the cave and why no one has found the entrance and why the people working here might not be worried about posting a guard on the road. The idea also involves heading straight for that thing and leaving Tucker behind. I didn't ask him to join my mission, and I don't believe for a second that he isn't spying for the Big Man. I do, however, believe he thinks I'm a good woman.

And I'd kind of like to believe he's right. And a good woman doesn't swim off and leave a friend to find his way out of trouble alone, even an invisible, manly, immune-to-fairy-venom friend who's equipped to take care of himself. I would have drowned without Tucker. I owe him the chance to play.

Play. As if this in any way resembles play.

But as I poke my head up and scan the surface of the water, I can't deny that the electricity buzzing along my skin isn't entirely unpleasant. Great.

I'm becoming an adrenaline junkie. As if I don't have enough dependencies.

A man-sized ripple appears in the water a few feet away, making my heart beat faster. "Tucker!" I hiss, not wanting to attract the attention of the pixies spreading out to scan the area around the truck.

Tucker doesn't respond, but the circle ripples caused by his emergence are replaced by a double-V shape that cuts my way. He stops in front of me, treading water, brushing my leg with his a few times until we figure out where our bodies are in relation to each other.

"I think I found the entrance to the cave," I whisper.

"Where?"

"There's an underwater portal thing down there." I jab a thumb over my shoulder. "Set into the bank."

"Jesus Christ," he says, becoming visible with another startling jump cut. "Creative bunch, aren't they?"

"Very."

"Think there are guards on the other side?"

I shake my head. "I couldn't tell."

"I'm bettin' there are guards."

"The lab might not even be here right now."

"Might not matter. Could still be guards."

My breath huffs out. "It looks like a big rubber cervix, I don't think—"

"You seen a lot of cervixes?"

"I was in med school. I've seen my share," I pant, falling silent when a pixie flies within whisper-hearing range. Tucker and I sink lower, until only our eyes are above the waterline.

I widen mine in a way that asks, *Are we going to do this, or not?*

He rolls his in a way that answers, *Fine, let's go, nutjob.*

With a final nod, I sink below the surface. Once under, I turn back to Tucker—planning to point the way—but he's already kicking toward the portal, determined to be born into danger before me. I swim after him, dodging his paddling feet, giving his butt a push when he has trouble getting his shoulders through the rubber seal. I stay close as his feet disappear—not wanting the hole to close again before I start through—and stick my fist through before his boot clears.

I shove my other fist inside and spread my arms. The rubber seal is tight, but the force of the water trying to push in behind me shoves me forward. I find slick handles on either side of the portal's interior, and use them to pull my head—chin tucked for protection—through the hole. Like a newborn baby, the rest of my body spills out in a rush. My hips stick for a second, but a wiggle frees them and soon I'm lying on a cold metal platform next to a drenched Tucker.

He's not lying down. He's crouched like a cat about to spring, and he looks *pissed*. I flip onto my stomach, following his glare to the edge of the platform, where two men with rifles stand staring at us.

Guards. Check another point off for Tucker.

We're facing armed opposition, but the pair—
a lean black kid who doesn't look a day over eighteen, and a thicker black man with a soft middle and
pudgy cheeks that give testimony to how cushy this
guarding-the-portal job must usually be—haven't had
time to use the walkie-talkies hanging on their belts.
And their guns are still pointed at the floor. They're
thrown and the best thing we can do is take advantage of their confusion.

"Hi." I pull my knees up and push onto my hands.
"How y'all doing?"

The younger kid's forehead furrows like an angry
puppy's, but the pudgy man only blinks and stares. I
smile and flip my wet hair over my shoulder.

"Sorry. Didn't mean to surprise you. We're here
to see Bill?" I plop onto my bottom cross-legged, trying to look nonthreatening as I inch across the drain
at the edge of the platform, closer to Pudge. Tucker
tenses beside me. He's going to go for the kid; I can
feel it. Pudge is bigger, but the kid is smarter and he's
on his way through Surprise to Action.

"Who are you?" Pudge asks.

"Bill's friends." I bounce off the platform. The
unruly boobs Fernando teased me about yesterday
bounce with me and Pudge's eyes shift. My moment
has come.

I dive for him, grabbing his rifle at both ends, using
it as leverage to pull him close enough for the knee I
lift to connect with his groin. *Hard*. So hard I wince
myself as he groans and crumples to the ground.
Pudge's hands spasm, and I rip the rifle away. Beside

me, Tucker already has the kid on the ground with his own gun pressed tight to his throat.

"Knock him out," he whispers. "Use the gun."

I look down to where Pudge writhes on the floor. What if I hit him too hard? What if I kill him? I don't want to die or be caught by whoever Pudge works for, but my entire reason for being here is to make sure people aren't indiscriminately murdered, and Pudge hasn't proved himself a person who has to be taken out.

I'm scanning the ground—looking for something to bind and gag the men with—when Tucker lets out a frustrated sigh. He hauls the kid beneath him to his feet like he's pulling a baby out of a crib, and with much rippling of muscles, kneels on the platform and shoves the boy's head through the portal. I gasp as the kid's legs thrash, but then Tucker's hand is on his rump and the boy is out in the water and Tucker is turning back for Pudge.

"Wait," I hiss, as he lifts Pudge with only a bit more difficulty. "The pixies are still out there, what if—"

"Never seen pixies try to hurt anyone but you," he grunts.

"But—"

"We're trying to get people out of here before it blows, right?" Tucker plunks Pudge down on the platform. Despite being in obvious pain, Pudge doesn't put up a fight and when Tucker shoves him forward, he pushes his arms through the tight rubber and slithers eagerly out into the bayou.

After he disappears, Tucker grabs a lever set into

the upper right-hand side of the portal and gives it a tug. Like the cover of an old-fashioned peephole, a metal circle slides down to block the entrance, ensuring Pudge and Kid are trapped on the other side.

"How did you know that was there?" I ask.

"Figured there had to be some way to close it," Tucker pants as he fetches Kid's rifle from the ground. "There's got to be another way in and out."

"What makes you so sure?" I grab Pudge's gun and hope I remember what to do with a rifle. I've been a handgun girl for a long time.

"Nobody's running this way." Tucker points down the narrow concrete hallway that curves darkly to our right.

"I don't think they had time to call for help. I didn't—"

"Listen." Tucker puts a still damp finger to my lips.

I listen, straining my ears until I hear a faint *blerngh*, *blerngh*, *blerngh* echoing down the tunnel. "An alarm?" I ask, lips moving against his calloused skin.

"Sounds like it." Tuckers drops his hand back to his side. "Guess your ex found what he was lookin' for at his first stop."

"It could be something else," I say, but my gut tells me it's not.

"What's the plan now, Red?"

I pull in a breath. "Check this place out, try to get people to safety if they're not already getting to safety on their own. Find Hitch and help him if we can." I shrug. "Don't get shot or blown up?"

"Sounds good." He grins, then bends to press a kiss to my cheek.

It only lasts a second and is as chaste as Marcy's hug, but it doesn't make me feel like Marcy's hug. It makes me dizzy. Must be the oxygen deprivation from all the time underwater.

"What was that for?" I whisper.

"In case I don't get to do it later. But I don't think a peck on the neck is going to be good enough."

Before I can correct him—the "peck" was on my *cheek* not my neck—Tucker's free arm is around me, pulling me into him. Our cold, wet clothes smash together, but the places where we touch warm up fast. He's hard in all the places that I'm soft and something primal inside of me surges to the surface with a purr of approval. I wrap my arm around his shoulder, my free fingers threading through his long, damp hair, bracing myself as he leans down and our mouths finally meet.

And then he's kissing me, rough and wild and abandoned, like we're in a secret underground lab that could explode any minute and this might be the last kiss we ever share with anyone.

I kiss him the same way—lips open, heart open, every part of me reaching out to every part of him because, *god,* have I wanted to do this since the first minute I saw Tucker stretched out on my bed looking so bleeping pretty I couldn't believe he was one of the bad guys.

Screw right and wrong and Cane and Hitch and should and shouldn't and all the rules of relationships that I've never figured out how to live by. Tucker's right, this might be our last chance, our final opportunity to see if we physically parry as well as we verbally thrust.

His hand moves down to cup my ass, my leg wraps around his waist, and we press even tighter together. I think about dropping my gun and going for this with both hands, but I don't. Instead I mumble, "There's something hot about kissing you while holding a rifle," into his mouth.

"It's not the rifle," he says, fingers digging into my hips, pulling me closer to where he is—almost annoyingly—as ridiculously hung as I'd assumed he'd be. "I'm just a damn fine kisser."

"Your ego is enormous." I pull away, breath coming fast.

"That's not my ego, sweetcheeks." His dimple pops and one of those wicked blue eyes winks and I, quite unexpectedly, start to laugh.

I'm laughing hard enough to make my side hurt by the time he *swacks* one last kiss on my forehead and starts down the hall ahead of me. I bite my cheek and follow, trying to feel bad about wasting even a few seconds kissing. But I can't seem to whip up a batch of shame.

"You realize we're going to have to repeat the experiment," I whisper as I draw even with him, my rifle pressed to my shoulder, eyes scanning the hall ahead. "To see if you're that good when you're not under pressure."

"So you admit that I'm good."

"I admit you're better than good."

I see him smile out of the corner of my eye. "Careful, Red," he says, voice husky. "You keep talkin' like that, and you're going to make that ego you hate even bigger."

"If that ego were any bigger, it would be obscene."

He laughs. "I like it when you talk about my ego, and you're not really talking about my ego."

"I don't know what you're talking about," I say. "And I . . ."

My smile fades as the hall ahead opens up. Tucker and I press against the right wall, creeping forward, slowly bringing a locker room into view. Two long benches occupy the center of the space and shiny metal lockers line the walls. A labeled brown door on the left side leads the way to the showers, but it doesn't sound like anyone is washing down and the rest of the area is deserted.

The *blerngh, blerngh* of the alarm is louder here, so loud that at first I can't hear what Tucker whispers over his shoulder.

"What?" I hiss, pressing up onto tiptoe to get closer to his mouth.

He smiles down at me. "Uniforms." He points to a row of hooks near the shower door I hadn't noticed before. White hazmat suits hang limply against the wall, looking a little worse for wear, dribbling something greenish brown onto the concrete floor.

"They look used," I say.

"Also looks like they've got hoods." He steps farther into the room.

I catch his arm. "Do we really want to go in there looking like the bad guys?"

"Think your boyfriend might shoot us?" he asks, staring at something I can't yet see.

"He might." I can't resist adding, "And he's not my boyfriend."

"Really?" Tucker grunts. "Looks like your boyfriend. Big, beefy detective-type without a sense of humor? Bald and—"

"What?" I push around Tucker, getting a clear view through the locker room to a larger space where flashing blue strobes cast rows of computers and monitor-covered walls in an eerie light. At the center of the room, with his gun drawn and his scariest expression on his face, stands the closest thing I have to a boyfriend.

Cane. With Marcy by his side, leaned over a computer monitor, typing faster than I knew her fingers could move.

25

How did they . . . ?" I start past Tucker, but this time he grabs my arm and pulls me back against the wall, out of sight of the control room. "It's okay. They're on our side."

"Right." Tucker looks unconvinced.

"We were going to come here together," I explain. "But they were going through the tunnels and I thought it would take too long. I have no idea how they got here before—"

"I don't care how they got here," Tucker says. "I want to know what they're doing at those computers."

I pause, tempted for a moment to tell Tucker the truth—that Marcy is with the CIA and probably searching for some top-secret intelligence or something. But no matter how much I like Tucker, I can't trust him. "I don't know," I say. "Why don't I go ask them?"

"No chance, Red, I—"

"Cane! Marcy!" I shout, making Tucker cuss colorfully and snap into invisibility.

As soon as his fingers slip from my arm, I hurry

through the locker room and into the heart of the operation, refusing to feel bad for ditching him. In a few minutes, he'll see that I'm okay. Hopefully then he'll do the rational thing and get out of here because I'd really like one less person to worry about.

"Cane!" I step into the cavernous room, but only have a second to notice how immense it is—with several glassed-in labs to the right and a heavy wooden table with seating for twenty or more to my left— when Cane turns my way. His eyes meet mine and his scary expression crumbles, transforming to a combo of horror, pain, and hopelessness usually unique to parents who've just watched their children run into oncoming traffic.

I know I've done something I shouldn't even before another familiar male voice shouts for me to, "Run, Annabelle!" My eyes flick to the left. A few feet behind Cane, Hitch sits tied to one of the wooden chairs from the medieval banquet-sized table. I realize several things at once:

1. Hitch is being held captive.
2. Cane's pointing a gun at his head.
3. Cane's holding the gun, but he's not the one in control.

Now that he's turned, I can see Cane's chest is alive with blinking red lights and rows of red cylinders that I don't need a degree in intrigue to know are explosives. He's rigged to blow. And Marcy is holding the trigger.

She turns from the computers, a stick with a flashing red button on the end fisted in one hand, and my world crumbles for the third or fourth time today. "Put your rifle down, Annabelle, and go stand by Agent Rideau." Marcy's thumb hovers above the red button. "Do it. Or I'll push this and Cane and everybody else in this room will die. There's enough on his chest to blow a hole in the earth a half-mile wide. There'll be nothing left of any of us."

"But, but," I sputter. "But you said—"

"I've already transferred the files I was sent for and corrupted the hard drive," Marcy says. "I was told to consider myself a necessary loss after that. I don't want to die and I certainly don't want to kill any of you, but I will. So put the rifle down and start moving."

As I set my weapon on the floor tears rise in my eyes, surging up from my core no matter how vehemently I tell myself not to cry. "You can't do this."

Marcy sighs. "I'm sorry, baby. I have orders and they don't involve sharing information with anyone. Now step on over."

A strangled sound escapes my throat—part laugh, part protest, part guttural prayer for this all to be a big, hairy misunderstanding. I walk toward Hitch on stiff, numb legs, the adrenaline of the day finally catching up with me, making my entire body feel wrong.

Wrong. This is *wrong*. I stop, spin back to face Marcy. "Please," I beg. "You can't kill Cane. You can't—"

"I'm not going to kill Cane." Marcy plucks her gun

from the table next to the bank of computers. The screens behind her flash an agitated stream of numbers and symbols, as if they're as angry with her as I am. "Cane's coming outside with me. Once we're far enough away, I'm going take off the explosives and send him back home through the gate."

I shake my head, knowing better than to be comforted by her promise. "And what about Hitch? And me? What happens to us?"

Her mouth tightens the slightest bit. To anyone else, her expression would be unreadable, but I can see the pain in her. I can hear the regret when she says, "That isn't my decision to make."

"Then who—"

"I'm sorry," she says, cutting me off. "Back toward me, Cane. Keep the gun on those two until we reach the hallway, then drop it to your side nice and slow." She backs toward the entrance of another concrete hallway about five feet to the left of the one Tucker and I crept down a few minutes ago.

Tucker. For a minute I imagine he might rush in and save the day, that he'll take advantage of his invisibility, snatch the trigger from Marcy's hand, save Cane, and give our side the upper hand.

He doesn't, and Marcy disappears into the darkness, followed by Cane, whose sad brown eyes are almost too much to take.

"I'll come back if I can, Lee-lee," he says. "I promise, I—"

"Don't come back." Tears crowd my eyes and spill down my cheeks. "Be safe. We'll be okay."

"I love you." I can tell by the way he says it that he thinks it will be the last time, and that none of us are going to be okay. Before I can reassure him or even tell him I love him, too, he's gone, pulled away into the darkness by Marcy's firm hand.

I take an instinctive step after them, but stop myself with a clench of my fists. I can't help Cane right now; I *can* get Hitch untied and started toward safety. I have no idea what Marcy meant by Hitch and me "not being her decision to make," but I don't want to stick around to find out. Hitch's suit is gone and he's down to his jeans and T-shirt, but maybe we can find some protection on the way out. Bare minimum we can zip him into a hazmat suit from the locker room, head back through the tunnels, and hope we come out somewhere close to the iron gates.

"Tucker?" I call out, though I'm pretty sure he won't answer. "Tucker?" I pause, giving him a chance to prove he's not as full of shit as almost everyone else in my life. "I thought you said you were going to help me!" I shout over the still blaring siren. "Tucker!"

Nothing. Not a peep or a flicker in the air or a flash of blue eyes.

"Bastard," I cuss as I circle Hitch and kneel down by his bound hands.

Screw Tucker. I silently vow never to weaken toward him again. He's a coward and a minion and under the Big Man's thumb and I was a fool to let his country-boy charm make me forget it. Even for a minute.

"I'm sorry," Hitch says numbly, staring at the ground in front of him as I start working on the knots binding his wrists. "I'm sorry I asked you for help."

"It's okay. We're going to get out of here." I pull at the knots, cursing my inability to grow real fingernails. The knots are tight and I'm having a hard time getting them started. "Eventually."

"I already set the explosives in the lab. They're going to blow in twenty minutes. Maybe less. You should go."

My breath comes faster and my hands shake. "No. I've got you. Give me a second."

"I took time to evacuate everyone. All the prisoners in the holding cells and the people working here," Hitch says. "I shot a few people, but nothing they can't recover from if they get treatment."

"Good," I say. "I'm glad."

"I knew you were right. I'm losing my mind." He drops his head back and searches the ceiling, as if seeking wisdom from the heavens. But we can't see the sky down here, and I'm not sure the heavens are paying attention. "I can't believe I killed those men at the docks . . . I can't . . . I . . ."

"It's okay."

"No, it's not. I *killed* two people. I could have killed you, too. And I'm so—"

"Don't apologize," I say, cutting him off. "You're thinking clearly now and you did what you were sent here to do and Stephanie and the baby will be fine."

Even if we won't, I add silently. Sweat drips down

into my eyes and the insanely tight knots slip through my fingers once again.

"Maybe," Hitch whispers. I can barely hear him over the *blerngh, blerngh, blerngh*ing of the alarm.

"The Big Man will keep his word," I say with more confidence than I feel. There's no reason for Hitch to go out as hopeless as I am right now. I don't trust half my friends or surrogate family, let alone a murdering mad scientist with a god complex. Stephanie is probably a dead woman, and her baby right along with her. But maybe Hitch hasn't reached that conclusion. Maybe he—

"I don't trust him," Hitch says. "I can't trust anyone."

"Weren't you just telling me that—"

"I'm the one who hacked into the system." Hitch turns to look at me over his shoulder. "I read some of the files before Marcy and Cane showed up. This lab is legit."

"What?" I glance up, wincing at the red surrounding Hitch's blue eyes and the haggard look on his face. "What do you mean?"

"This is a top-secret FBI facility. Funded by the government."

My fingers slip off the edge of the knot again. "You're kidding me."

"No. I'm not. There were presidential signatures on some of the orders," he says. "And the prisoners I freed? Convicted felons. Supposedly already executed in other states."

"So they—"

"Faked the executions of men on death row so they could test their weapons. I set free a bunch of killers and rapists, half of them already infected."

Fuck. I definitely don't like hearing convicted felons are loose in the bayou near my town, but that doesn't change the core of what's going on here. "It doesn't matter what kind of crimes they committed." I return to the rope with renewed intensity. "That doesn't give the government the right to experiment on them."

"No, it doesn't," Hitch says. "Or the right to kill Steven to make sure he didn't talk. Who knows how many people they've killed to keep this a secret?" His voice drops. "You should go."

"No." I abandon the knots and hurry to the banks by the computers, searching for something sharp enough to cut through Hitch's bonds.

"There's something else," Hitch says. "I want to tell you and then I want you to go. Save yourself. Find someone you can trust and—"

"Shut up!" I knock keyboards to the ground, sending piles of paper floating into the air as I hunt for something, *anything*. Even a stupid ink pen might help me pry open the knots.

"Annabelle, you—"

"I'm serious. Shut up," I shout, panic rising as I circle around to the other side of the computer bank and there's still no sign of a pen or a pencil and the damn alarm keeps blaring like a sledgehammer to my face. "You have a wife and baby waiting for you. You can't—"

"Stephanie's signature was on one of the orders."

I freeze midriffle through a stack of medical charts. Suddenly, Hitch's empty eyes make a terrible sort of sense.

"I only saw it once, but I didn't have much time to look," he says. "She approved a series of tests on Subject J, a child killer from Kentucky."

I walk back around the bank, my hands still horribly empty. "You're sure."

"I'm sure." He drops his head, mumbling his next word into his lap. "Leave."

My shoulders sag, my entire body going limp with pity for him. Even a week ago, I might have been secretly pleased to learn that Stephanie was keeping something so enormous from Hitch. Now, it only makes me sad. For him. And, surprisingly, for her.

"He was a child killer," I say.

Hitch looks up. "He was deliberately infected with fairy venom."

"So what?"

"And she kept this from me. She let me come out here without—"

"Maybe she didn't know. Maybe—"

"Fuck it, Annabelle. It doesn't matter," he shouts. "I'll *never* know and you need to get out of here."

I shake my head. "No. I'm not leaving without you."

"Go!" he shouts, so loudly he momentarily eclipses the siren.

"No!" I spin in a frantic circle, looking for something, anything—

My rifle. It's still on the floor. I'll shoot through the ropes. There's a chance I might hurt Hitch, but I probably won't kill him and he's definitely going to die if he stays here.

I rush over, squat to grab the barrel, but when I try to stand, the gun doesn't budge. I pull again, hard enough to make my shoulder ache, but it's like the damn thing's superglued to the cement.

Or like someone very heavy has their foot on it. Their extremely large foot, the foot that made monster footprints outside Grace Beauchamp's window, the foot that belongs to one of the last people I want to see—or not see—right now.

Even before the foot and the leg and the rest of the Big Man slowly drift into visibility, I suspect it's him. Maybe it's the smell. He's got a particular stink about him, an earthy, bayou scent accompanied by the faintly sour odor of a man who spends most of his life sweating.

And really, who else could this be? I've never seen the Big Man before, but the behemoth looming over me has to be the man who put the Harley in my kitchen. How many other six feet four, four hundred plus pound invisible men with clown feet can there be in Donaldsonville, Louisiana?

"Annabelle." He smiles.

"Big Man."

He chuckles, making his fleshy neck shake. He doesn't look anything like I imagined. His khaki pants and white short-sleeve button-down are too business casual for roaming the swamp, and his curly mop of red hair and freshly shaved chins—he has at least three, maybe four—make him look like an overgrown kid despite the wrinkles that make me guess him somewhere north of forty. He's got the same pale, redhead skin I have, but a bigger crop of freckles, riots of brown spots that cover his nose and forehead and dribble down his cheeks. On the whole, he's much more Dennis the Menace than Charles Manson.

But when he speaks, his voice is as deep and dark and shiver-inducing as I remember. "I think you been keepin' things from me, *mouche à miel*," he says, proving Cajuns do produce their share of pasty white people.

Honeybee. He called me "runt" last time. Hopefully the change indicates an improvement in our relationship. I pull my hand from the gun and come slowly back to my feet. "Nice shoes. Converse?"

"Gotta have my Converse."

"I thought you were a work boot kind of guy."

"Only when I'm working." A grin blooms at the center of his corpulent face like a toothy flower, lips curling until I can see his cotton candy pink gums. He's a flosser, this one. His mouth is practically glowing with health. I think about complimenting him on that, and maybe thanking him for the Harley while I'm at it to butter him up really good, but Hitch takes that moment to remind us of his existence.

"This cave is going to blow in five minutes," he shouts. "Get out of here. Now!"

The Big Man casts an amused glance in Hitch's direction. "High-strung, ain't he?"

"Um . . . yeah." I nod too long, caught between playing along with the Big Man's low-stress, cheery vibe and catching Hitch's much more reasonable terror. On the one hand, it seems best to keep the tension level low and the Big Man happy. On the other hand, I've heard this man sound perfectly pleasant while strangling people to death with his bare hands, so his chumminess right now might mean less than squat.

"But Hitch did rig the labs to explode," I say. "We should probably get while the getting's good."

"Hitch did a good job. He proved he's willing to do whatever it takes to save his family. Followed orders pretty much to a T." The Big Man stuffs his meaty hands in his tentlike pockets. "Except for telling a few stories to you."

"But I don't count, right?" I force a grin. "Since I'm on your side and all?"

"You made that sound like a question, Annabelle."

"I didn't mean to." My smile wilts at the warning in his tone. "Bad habit."

"Lifting your voice at the end of a sentence makes you seem like a person lacking in confidence." He stalks around to my right. I turn, keeping him in front of me, memories of Libby's last moments making me unwilling to be any more vulnerable than I already am.

"Low self-esteem," I say. "I'm working on it."

"You should. No reason for a smart, pretty thing like you to feel dat way. Plenty of people would kill to be you."

I nod again, acutely aware of the sweat gathering at the base of my neck. The siren seems to have faded in volume, but the urgency behind it feels more intense than ever. If Hitch's estimate is right, we'll all be blown to pieces in a couple of minutes, maybe less.

"Can we continue this outside?" I squeak, edging toward Hitch. "Maybe after you help me carry Hitch out to—"

"No need to carry him. Let the boy walk." He wanders with maddening slowness over to where Hitch sits slumped in his chair, eyes closed, chin tucked, his defeat complete. He's certain we're going to die, and his certainty makes my tongue feel like it's going to crawl down my throat. "You and I are on the same side, Annabelle. From now on, you come to me when you've got a problem. Especially a fairy problem. I understand you know where to find me."

"Okay." My knee jogs, my hands shake at my sides. We're running out of time. Fast. So fast.

"I killed that fairy bastard Tucker said was messing with your head."

Grandpa Slake is dead? I know I should be relieved, but all I can think about is the explosives in the other room and the seconds ticking away and what it's going to feel like to blow up.

"Past time for that one to meet his maker," the Big Man continues. "He's got a history of stirring up trouble. After he worked them pixies into a frenzy, I couldn't see a truce with him being worth diddlyshit. He knew better. We've been trying to round those things up for a damned month."

A month. Round them up.

I store the information away for later. If there *is* a later.

"Besides, you're one of mine now."

Sixty seconds. We can't have more than sixty seconds. "Please, I—"

"Don't worry. We're working on the problem, and the pixies will lose interest. They've got a short attention span, and the fairies got other things to worry about with their leader dead," he says. "So you go home and lay low, you hear me? Don't work any magic, don't talk to fairies, don't cause any more trouble."

"Yes, sir."

Dead. We're dead. It's over. My every muscle strings tight, braced for the explosion I know is coming. I could make a run for the corridor and be out before the Big Man catches up with me, but I can't leave Hitch. I just can't. So I stand and stare into the Big Man's freckled face, cursing the universe that his ugly mug is the last thing I'm ever going to see.

"Take a few more weeks off, have a barbecue, have your kissin' cousin over for a few beers," he says. "I think you and Tucker are going to—"

"Please," I beg, voice hoarse with fear. "We're all going to *die* if we don't leave now. *Now!*"

"All right. Settle down there, *Beb*." The Big Man pulls a pocketknife from his pants, leans down, and cuts the ropes at Hitch's wrists. Hitch flinches as the tension releases, his head jerking up like he's waking from a bad dream. "There you go, son," Big Man says. "Think you'd better grab Ms. Lee and head toward the exit."

Hitch launches out of the chair, closing the distance between us at a run. His hand finds the spot between my shoulders and shoves me—none too gently—toward the corridor where Marcy and Cane disappeared a few minutes earlier. "Run!" he says, urging me in front of him as he takes off at a sprint.

I dash for the entrance to the hallway, casting one last look over my shoulder as I haul ass. I half-expect to see the Big Man standing in the middle of the room with a grin on his face, confident in his ability to withstand an explosion. But by the time I turn back, he's gone. He's light on his feet for an obese man, and he knows his way around. Chances are he'll make it out alive.

I'm not sure the same can be said for Hitch and me.

The corridor ahead of us is long. Very long. Longer than the one Tucker and I walked through to get to the main room. And wider, with oversized railroad tracks set into the floor. We run for what feels like three or four endless, adrenaline-mangled minutes, but there's still no end and no exit and every second is a second of borrowed time and I can feel death crawling up my spine on razor-tipped feet.

"How much further?" I gasp.

"Almost there. There's a staircase. Exit through the roof."

"Comes out in the swamp?"

"Yeah. But no fairies. Iron mesh on the ground. Parked the cruiser close," he says, his sentences getting shorter as he sprints faster. Overhead, the lights set into the ceiling flicker and go out, leaving us in near blackness.

My heart leaps, and I falter, not sure if I can run on through the dark.

"Come on. Almost there. Don't stop."

I recognize the thinly concealed terror in his voice and pour on another burst of speed. Beside me, Hitch matches my pace, his breath coming in long, even draws that make me suspect he could push harder. He's holding back, sticking with me the way I stuck with him.

I want to say "thank you." I want to tell him that I'm glad I knew him—at least for most of the time I knew him. I want to tell him that I love him. Because I do. In a way that isn't healthy and I'm not even sure is *still* romantic anymore, but is *still* love. He was my friend, my lover, and for a long time the only person who knew me. Hitch took the time to see every part, to learn every secret.

Even now, when his presence causes more pain than pleasure, when he's become a stranger and the ties binding us together are shredding at the seams, there's still something incomparable about looking into his eyes. More than anyone else in the world, Hitch is a part of me, and he always will be.

I pull in a deeper breath, deciding to let whatever comes out, come out, but I don't get to say a word.

One second we're running like hell through the near dark, the next the world is eaten alive by a boom so big and bad that the ground jumps beneath our feet and the hallway begins to crumble.

26

Hitch grabs my hand and holds tight, pulling me hard to the left, pressing me against the wall as a piece of rock ceiling comes down where I was standing. I whip my head around to face him. My eyes have adjusted enough to the black to see his lips move, but I can't hear a thing. The first boom is followed by a series of baby booms that make speech impossible.

Still, I scream, "I can't hear you!"

He yells something back, but all I catch is a rogue vowel and maybe a *p* sound. Or a *d*?

I shake my head as another boom hits, buckling the ground, sending me crashing into Hitch. His arms go around my waist, my legs tangle in his, and he stumbles. I try to regain my footing and pull him upright, but sharp chunks of rock and twisted rail jut up from the floor. My shin slams into something hard, my center of gravity shifts, and Hitch falls backward.

I'm tumbling after when large hands grab my elbows and pull me back against damp clothes and a solid stretch of man.

"Fuck you, Tucker!" I wrench my arms away. It's

too dark to see much, but I'd be able to see *something* if there were anything there to see. If he weren't in invisible-coward mode. Yet again.

Still, I *know* it's him and not the Big Man or some other invisible. Even a second of contact was enough for my body to recognize his. *Blargh*. I can't believe I kissed him. As soon as we get back to Donaldsonville, I'm going to wash my mouth out with soap. A fresh bar, one a fairy hasn't pooped on.

I reach back to help Hitch, but he's already up and reaching for me. I take his hand and hold tight, following him over the increasingly jagged floor, shoulders hunched against falling debris, ignoring the pocket of body heat that follows behind. Even when a hunk of rock is magically knocked to the side seconds before it hits my shoulder, I don't look back. Tucker had his chance to help and he blew it. Now he's just another name on the Betrayal List.

What a list *that's* becoming.

I can't believe Marcy strapped *explosives* to Cane's *chest*. What the *hell* does she think this is? Some 1980s spy movie? An episode of fucking *MacGyver*? You don't go around strapping *explosives* to people in real life. Especially not people you care about. Especially not people who—only weeks ago—you advised your surrogate daughter to marry.

Not anymore. Not family anymore. I wince, but I can't tell if it's because of the second supersized boom that shakes the earth, knocking Hitch and me into the wall, or the inescapable truth that hits so much harder.

Marcy's not my family anymore. She left me for

the Big Man. That had to be what she meant when she said I wasn't "her decision to make." The CIA story was a lie. Either that or she's a double agent, working for the CIA *and* an invisible psychopath. A psycho she wasn't sure would allow me to live. I could see the uncertainty and pain in her eyes when she walked away. She didn't want to leave me to him, but she did. She made her choice. And now I've made mine.

No matter how much I love her, if I see her again, I won't pull any punches. I won't protect her; I'll do what it takes to make sure she can't hurt anyone. Ever again.

Hitch drops my hand to push away a falling rock and Tucker makes his move. His arms wrap around me from behind and suddenly I'm in the air, feet thrashing in front of me.

"Put me down," I scream, loud enough that I can hear myself over the next explosion. Guess Hitch can, too. He turns—body tensed, fist lifted.

Before he can deliver his punch, a door flies open in the wall. Tucker pulls me back into a small, dark room that's holding up better than the hall outside. Hitch follows close behind. My hand flies out. Rough, cool, metal—like the bottom of a cast-iron skillet—brushes my fingertips. Metal walls. We must be in a safe room, one of the thousands sold after the fairy emergence.

"This way." Tucker's arm slides from my waist. A second later, a fluorescent light flicks on overhead, casting Hitch and me in a faint blue glow. "There should be an escape hatch in the back. Follow me."

"I can't see you," I snap. "How can I—"

Tucker flickers into visibility next to Hitch, making Hitch jump and his hands ball into fists. "Howdy." Tucker grins that same good-old-boy grin, and holds out a hand. "Tucker."

Anger and Confusion wrestle on Hitch's face before Understanding swoops in and knocks them both out of the ring. "Your cousin?" he asks, lifting his brows in my direction.

"Not my cousin," I confess.

"No shit." Hitch ignores Tucker's hand. "I knew you were lying about that. I didn't know you were lying about—"

"I wasn't lying."

"This is the guy from the road today, isn't it?" Hitch asks, putting the pieces together pretty quickly for a man whose life is in imminent peril. "I can't believe you didn't—"

"All right, lovebirds." Tucker strides toward the far wall. "Let's save the arguments until we're out of this hellhole."

"We're not lovebirds," I say, glad it's easier to be heard in here. "And in case we die, I want you to know that I hate you. A lot."

"No, you don't."

"Yes, I do. You left me hanging in there."

"I didn't leave you hanging."

"Yes, you did!" I ignore Hitch's narrow look. "I—"

"We'll talk about it later, Red." Tucker reaches for the ceiling, taking hold of the black wheel that operates the escape hatch and turning it to the left.

Or *trying* to turn it to the left. The wheel creaks a few inches and sticks, refusing to budge, even when Tucker intensifies his efforts, straining until veins stand out on his neck and arms and his face turns red. Beneath us, the ground continues to shake while the hallway behind us crumbles. Pretty soon we won't be able to get out of here. We'll be stuck. If that wheel won't budge we're as good as buried alive.

"Let me help." I start forward, but Hitch is already in front of me.

"Superior arm strength," he mumbles. He grabs hold and together he and Tucker wrench and grunt and wrench, but the wheel holds tight.

I stuff my panic back down into my stomach and focus. My tongue curls and my shoulders lift and for a second I think I feel magic stirring somewhere inside of me, but when I shift my attention to the wheel, it vanishes. I'm tapped out, and the only way I'm going to be of any help is with my hands.

I shove past Hitch to the other side of the wheel, standing on tiptoe to reach. Clearly this escape hatch was designed for the male of the species. I'm five eight—a good four or five inches taller than the average woman—and I can barely get my fists wrapped around the metal bar.

"Come on," I shout, recognizing the hopeless look creeping onto Hitch's face. He doesn't think I can help. He thinks I'm too weak. "Let's try again. All three of us."

"It's not going to work," he says, backing away.

"The wheel must be stripped. We should get back out there before—"

"Just try! One more time! I—"

Another boom shakes the room and we all shuffle before regaining our balance. "Come on, Doc," Tucker says. "Let her show you what she's got."

I glance at Tucker, torn between thanking him and telling him to go to hell. Instead I say, "On three." I turn to Hitch, willing him to give this one last chance. After a second's hesitation, his hands grip the wheel next to mine.

"One, two, three!" My last word becomes a groan. I throw my weight and squeeze with my fingers and tug until my shoulder blades burn and it feels like my neck is going to snap in two.

On either side of me, Hitch and Tucker strain and pull, but it seems all our grunting and groaning will be in vain until finally, *finally*, we're rewarded with the tiniest *squawnk* as the wheel turns a quarter turn before sticking tight. Again.

"See there?" Tucker pants, propping his hands on his knees as he recovers. "Few more like that and we'll—"

"We're not going to get it open," Hitch says.

"We might." But I'm starting to agree with him. It didn't feel like the wheel was going to budge an inch past where it stopped the last time.

"It's worth one more try," Tucker says. "If we get it open, we—"

"If we get it open we have no idea where we're going to end up." Hitch swipes a frustrated arm across his forehead. "The way I came in was at the top of a two story staircase. This isn't high enough to put us out above ground."

"It might let out underwater," I say. "Tucker and I came in through a—"

My words are cut off as the wheel turns and the room fills with metallic screeching. My hands fly to cover my ears. Tucker's hand flies to a handgun shoved in the back of his pants. When he traded his rifle in for something smaller is unclear, but I'm glad he did. I'm sure we'll want to be armed against whoever opens the hatch.

Unfortunately, Hitch and I aren't going to be able to offer backup, aside from our fists and those won't do any good unless this person decides to jump in and join us. Still, I try to look menacing as the wheel is pulled up into the ceiling, revealing a black opening two feet above.

"Annabelle Lee?" I pin the voice even before the yellowed eyes and sharp face appear in the hole above us. "What are you doing down there?"

"Amity!" I smile, hoping she's forgotten the circumstances surrounding our last interaction. The one where she and her friend beat me up for presumably stealing Amity's Breeze stash. She *was* rather messed up at the time.

Maybe she hates me less now that she's sober.

"I should leave your ass down there to die," she says, stabbing a finger in my direction.

Maybe not.

"You're a fucking bitch." She leans in far enough

for me to see she's still wearing the regulation jumpsuit required for the infected at Keesler. "I heard what you've been doing to my brother, playing with his fucking mind when all he's got is love for you. He's a fine, beautiful-hearted, champion of a strong, proud black man and I—"

A hand touches her back. Amity breaks off, curling into herself, casting a feral look over her shoulder. "Get back off me, dick," she snaps. "I ain't got nothing for you."

"It's okay," a deep voice answers. "It's me. Abe." Abe meets my eyes over Amity's crouched form and does a double take. He seems surprised to see me, but not *that* surprised. Cane must have told Abe I was out in the bayou when he contacted him about taking over Amity's pickup.

But how did he and Amity end up here? It doesn't seem like enough time has passed for him to have picked her up at the docks and gotten this close to Donaldsonville. There must be some kind of transportation system in the tunnels, something other than the scooters Cane mentioned.

"What's happening, Annabelle?" he asks. "We heard—"

"Cane might be in trouble. We need to find him. And there was an explosion."

"We heard. We—"

"You know this guy?" Tucker interrupts, stepping closer, gun trained on the faces peering down at us.

"Abe Cooper. Cane's big brother. He's on the Donaldsonville police force."

Tucker's gun dips. "Can we trust him?"

"Of course," I say, hoping I'm telling the truth.

"Good." Tucker's hand comes to my waist. "Let's lift you up there and—"

"No, I'm not going without you and Hitch." I shoo his hand away.

"I'll lift him up, too," he says. "He's scrawny enough."

I resist the urge to roll my eyes. "Then you'll have no one to lift you, and it's too far to jump." I look up again, surveying the slick sides of the hole. Even if Tucker reaches the opening, there's nothing to hold on to. His hands will slip right off the sides. "We need a rope or—"

"Bring a rope!" Abe shouts over his shoulder, my request spurring him into action. He's going to help us. *Thank god*. I really didn't want to add another name to the betrayal list. "There are people down here! We need to get them out before this area is compromised."

"I won't comprise with you." Amity shrugs his hand off her back. "You can't have none of my pussy."

Abe turns back to her. "Amity, please. It's your brother, Abe. You knew me just a few minutes ago. You remember?"

"Abe," she repeats in a listless voice.

"Yes," he says gently. "Your brother."

"Abraham Lincoln freed the slaves. But he can't help us now." Amity starts to shiver, though the air is hot and thickening with smoke. The explosions must have caused a fire, one that's filling the air with an acrid, toxic smell.

"There were chemicals down here, Abe," I say. "They might be on fire. We need to—"

"I hear you." He calls more urgently to whoever's behind him. "Where's the rope? There's a chemical fire, we need to evacuate." I hear some faint mumbling, but can't understand what the person is saying. Abe must be able to, however. His forehead bunches and he shouts in his best police captain voice, "I don't care about the damned goats."

Goats?

I decide not to ask.

"Let the goats go, we've got *people* down here." Abe sighs and lifts a hand in the air. "Just a second, Annabelle. We'll get y'all out. Then you can tell me what's happened to Cane."

"Thanks, Abe." He disappears into the darkness. I wish I could feel relieved. But the smoke and the devil smell creeping into the room are only getting worse.

"Abe, Abe, Abe," Amity repeats, rocking on her haunches at the edge of the hole, her movements so intense I worry we might soon have one more person in the pit. "Where's Abraham Lincoln when we *need* him? Why has he abandoned the people he promised to protect?" she asks, tears welling in her jaundiced eyes.

She seems sober, but she's definitely not sane. The fairy venom coursing through her veins has already started to erode her neural pathways. For a second I think about telling her that Abraham Lincoln is dead, and that she shouldn't take the abandonment personally, but decide that wouldn't make her feel any better.

I bite my lip, and turn to check in with Tucker and Hitch. Tucker is leaning against the wall with arms crossed, gun still drawn, but partially hidden behind one bicep, looking cautiously optimistic about the rescue. Hitch is lingering near the rubble-blocked entrance to the safe room looking concerned.

Very, *very* concerned.

"What's wrong?" I walk over to hover near his elbow.

"You see that?" He points out into the hall. Even in the dim light, I can see the green-tinged mist creeping between the rocks like an evil spirit rising from the grave.

"What is it?"

He takes a step back, guiding me away from the doorway with one outstretched arm. "While I was looking through the files, I saw something about a Fey mist."

"Like a flu mist?"

"Right," he says, "But instead of vaccinating . . ."

"It infects," I finish. My fingers find his forearm and squeeze, as if I can keep him safe from the foul green air if I hold on tightly enough. "So if you breathe any of that—"

"I'll be infected," he says with surprising calm. "If I'm anything like the rest of my family, I'll be dead within a few minutes."

27

I whip my head around. "Hurry, Abe! Hurry! There's—"

I almost blurt out that there's a venom-infection biohazard floating around down here, but stop myself at the last second. Abe isn't immune and I have no idea who else up there might be at risk. If they know what's coming, they might run first and think about saving us never. For Tucker and me that wouldn't be a problem and Amity's already infected, but for Hitch . . .

The green mist surges forward, billowing close enough that I catch a whiff of fairy stink, the sickeningly sweet scent of a swarm in midfeed, when the poison is flowing from their gums.

"We can't wait for the rope. Tucker, help me!" I pull Hitch toward the hole in the ceiling, where Amity is still rocking and shivering and muttering about Abraham Lincoln.

"What's up?" Tucker asks. "What did you see?"

"The explosion must have released one of the bioweapons from the lab. It's a mist that causes venom infection," I whisper. "Anyone up there who's not immune needs to get away from here, but we need to get Hitch up with them first."

Tucker nods and tucks his gun into the back of his jeans. He grips Hitch's shoulder in a way that's almost friendly. "Come on, brother."

"I'm not your brother."

"And I'm not her cousin, and she's not your mama," Tucker says. "I think we—"

"It's here!" I hiss, bouncing on the balls of my feet as a wisp of green curls into the room. "Come on. Move! Now!"

Tucker bends his knees and makes a basket with his hands. "Step in and jump, we'll push you up."

"Promise me you'll keep her safe." Hitch stares Tucker in the eye, making no move toward safety.

"I swear it, man," Tucker says, worry in his voice for the first time. "Now come on. Get out of here. I got better things to do than watch you die."

With one last look at me—a look so full I couldn't carry it in a bucket without spilling—Hitch braces himself on Tucker's shoulders and steps into his hands. Tucker heaves him up. I move in to help push at his feet, but Amity's arms are already around him, pulling him through the hole. He scrambles up beside her and, with a whispered word in her ear, somehow convinces her to let him take her arm and help her stand.

He glances down, but I wave him away with a frantic flap. "Go, go! Get them out! Leave a rope up there if you can. Tucker and I will be fine."

Hitch nods and leads Amity away. She doesn't say a word, still too lost in despair to gloat about her nemesis being left in a pit filling with poison. A second later, I hear Hitch shout out a warning about the infection risk and my shoulders drop. He's going to be safe. He'll keep Abe safe.

"Now you gonna let me lift you up?" Tucker stands beside me, staring up into the dark as the voices above grow distant.

"Yeah. I'll find a rope and come back for you," I say. "Even though you're a sorry excuse for a partner."

"I was trying to disarm the bombs." He lifts a booted foot, stirring the mist now swirling around our legs. "I stopped the timer for a few minutes, but it started back up again. I came looking for you, but you were talking to the Big Man." His eyes flick to mine. "I've seen him mad plenty of times. He wasn't going to hurt you, and I knew it'd be better for me if he didn't know I was around."

"He didn't tell you to follow me?"

"No." Tucker steps closer. His hands grip my waist. "He told me to head back to town and break things off with Barbara Beauchamp."

"Why?"

"I told him the leader of the Slake was fucking with you. I couldn't think of any other way to keep your people safe." His grip tightens, and his thumbs press lightly into my stomach. I resist the urge to curl my hands around his arms. This isn't an embrace, this is Tucker preparing to lift me up, and I don't want to encourage him to think of it as anything else. "Big Man has ways of finding a fairy when he wants to. I knew he could take out the leader. Now, with the old guy gone, the rest of the Fey will be too busy fighting for chief to mess with you. At least for a while."

"What about the Big Man? I thought I—"

"I didn't tell him you can work the fairies." He looks down again. The mist coats the floor, but it doesn't seem to be rising. "Just said you could talk to 'em a little, mostly in the dreams the old one was sending you."

"So I'm . . . good?" I soften toward him in spite of myself. If he's really managed to keep Deedee and everyone I care about safe and spared me the Big Man's wrath at the same time, I'll owe him one. Maybe two. I'm at least going to have to work on an apology.

"The Big Man's not afraid of you yet," Tucker says. "As long as you stay out of trouble, I don't think you'll have anything to fear from him. Not unless he really decides to trust you."

I shake my head. "But what does any of that have to do with you and Barbara?"

"The Big Man thinks I should find a new girl." Tucker pulls me closer. "He told me I should keep a close, constant eye on this woman. Wants me to eat, sleep, and breathe with her. Even if she is my cousin."

"He wants—" My eyebrows shoot up. "That's why he called you my kissing cousin?"

"You did say 'distant' cousins. That's legal in most states."

"Is that why you kissed me?" My hands curl into

fists against his chest. "Because the Big Man told you to seduce your way into my life?"

"What do you think, Red?" He leans so close his nose brushes mine.

My breath rushes out, memories of our one kiss warming my lips. "I don't know what to think."

"I think I should give you a boost," he whispers. "I don't like the look of this shit. Even if it won't infect us, I don't want a lungful."

I swallow. "Okay. Boost me up. I'll go find—"

"If you leave me, I'll understand," he says, a vulnerable note in his voice. "But I promise I'm on your side. And my reasons for that kiss were my own."

I look up, meeting blue eyes that seem even more piercing than usual. If I didn't know better, I'd think Tucker really cares. Maybe a lot. "Why?" I ask. Hitch and I have a past and Cane and I might have a future, but I don't understand why I've attracted Tucker's attention. "There are a lot of women in Donaldsonville. A lot them better-looking and most of them easier to get along with and all of them with less baggage."

"Not women like you," he says. "I've been stalking you for a while, Red."

"That's creepy. You get that, right?"

"Also a great way to learn a lot of truth about a person in a short amount of time," he says. "I probably know more about you than your mama."

"That's not saying much."

"I know you," he says, refusing to joke around for once. "I like what I know, and I'd like to learn more."

I hesitate, torn between demanding he quit talking feelings like a damned girl and lift me up already, and taking his crazy confession seriously. Because I like him, too. Maybe I'd like him even more if I knew half as much about him as he does about me.

"I'm not going to leave you here," I say. "But you're not learning anything about me until you give some quid pro quo."

"I can do that." He smiles. "You ready?"

I lift my hands to his shoulders. "Ready. How are we—"

"Bend your knees and put your feet in my hands. Then stand up straight with your muscles tight and I'll push you through."

"Standing? On just your hands?"

"Just like in cheerleading back in high school."

"Do I look like I was a cheerleader back in high school?" I ask, with the requisite amount of scorn.

"Nope. But I was. I've got this."

I snort. I can't help myself. "You were a cheer-leader? That is . . ."

"Manly?"

"Strange."

"I got my hands up a lot of skirts, Red. Nothing strange about that." He grins his panty-melting grin and bends his knees. Before I can whip up a come-back, I'm in the air.

I manage to find his hands with my feet—more like he finds my feet with his hands—and do my best to follow the rest of his directions. I tighten my muscles from head to toe and reach for the opening, but I'm still shocked when I slip smoothly through, my body rising until I'm in the new space from the waist up.

I cast a quick look around, taking in what looks like a subway tunnel without tracks stretching away in both directions. White tiles line the walls, with black tiles on the ceiling, and dim lights set into the side of the tunnel every few dozen feet. There's no sign of Hitch or Abe or Amity, but a coil of dirty white rope sits on the floor not far away. Someone took the time to leave it, and I'm grateful. I really didn't want to leave Tucker down there, even if I was intending to come back.

I drag one leg over the edge and then the other and reach for the rope. It smells funny—musky in the way of barns and freshly fertilized fields—but it feels strong enough. I lean over to peek at Tucker, holding it up for him to see. "They left a rope. Let me find something to loop it around so I won't drop you."

"Sounds good." With his head tilted back and the green swirling around his feet, he looks like a Norse god arising from enchanted mist. He's beautiful, I'll give him that, but I don't—

"Hurry, will ya?" he says. "I think this stuff is starting to burn through my jeans."

"Right." Now isn't the time to admire Tucker's man-pretty. I spin to search for a pillar or a rock sticking up from the floor, something I can wrap the rope around to brace it. But there's nothing. The floor is gravel and the walls of the tunnel are smooth. I spot the dull remains of a campfire down the tunnel to my left, but there's nothing there that will help.

"Red? You still up there?" Tucker sounds a trace hysterical. Just a trace, but for Tucker that's practically a screaming, wailing, teeth-gnashing cry for help.

"I'm here. The rope's coming down." I loop the end of the rope around my waist and knot it, then twirl it around a couple times for good measure. I roll the extra around my hands, kick the end through the porthole and bend my knees deep, bracing myself as best I can.

A second later, Tucker grabs the other end and my feet go sliding across the ground. I scramble to get purchase while throwing my weight backward and fisting my hands with everything in me. If I let my hands relax the slightest bit, Tucker's weight just might break my fingers.

"Crap!" My pulse leaps as my tennis shoes finally stick in a dip in the floor.

"You all right?" Tucker grunts from below.

"Yes. But hurry! You're *sofuckingheavy*."

The rope jerks as Tucker climbs faster and my knucklebones grind together hard enough to make me whimper. Sweat breaks out on my neck and chest and the small of my back and my brain sends out panicked messages about letting go of whatever I'm holding before I lose a hand while my leg muscles tremble and my biceps twitch and threaten to abandon the fight altogether.

But finally—when I think I can't hold on for

another minute—Tucker climbs through and the tension on the rope ceases. Abruptly. So abruptly that I can't shift my weight fast enough, and my ass makes a beeline for the floor. I brace myself for a spine crunch, but something breaks my fall.

Something soft and warm. And hairy.

"Bleeeair!" The animal kicks as I roll off its back, and I barely avoid a cloven hoof to the face.

"Holy fucking—Goat!" I scramble away as the pink-eyed beast delivers another series of kicks worthy of an evil ninja, its white hair ruffling majestically as it tries to crack open my skull.

Tucker slams the porthole cover closed. "Looks like a normal goat to me." His movement seems to startle the monster, making it prance away toward the far wall.

"What's a goat doing down here?" I let Tucker unwind the rope from my hands, trying not to wince as he frees my fingers and gives them a squeeze.

"Probably helping people stay alive. Goats give a lot of milk. Easier to manage than cows." He traps my hands between his and applies gentle pressure. "Thank you."

"You're welcome." I pull away, not wanting him to know how much my fingers hurt. "You think people are living down here?"

"I'd guess so." He points down the tunnel. "Looks like someone's been camping over there for a while."

Beyond the campfire I spotted earlier are several lean-to shelters set up against the wall. They're made of old two-by-fours and fallen limbs gathered from the swamp, but they're sturdy-looking. A few of them even have chimneys built into the side and decorations painted on their exteriors. Flowers and vines on one, stick-figure cartoons on the other.

Tucker heads for the minisettlement and I follow. Beyond the lean-tos is a long table with benches on either side and a makeshift stove built out of bricks and concrete. The table is clean, but the stove is covered in crusted dribbles of old food. A plastic bucket of cookware sits next to it, with a second bucket filled with compost not far away. It's nearly full and already starting to squirm a little.

Ugh. Maggots. I glance away. Quickly.

"They've definitely been here for a while." I follow Tucker around a curve in the tunnel, where a wooden fence forms a small paddock. The ground is covered with wood chips and piles of fresh-looking hay sit on either side, but there are no animals in sight. "Looks like room for more than one goat."

"Guess they took the rest with them." Tucker walks past the paddock, scanning the ground beyond. "Looks like they went this way."

I hurry over. "We should follow them, find Hitch and Abe and—"

"Nope." He turns back. "The ground rises in that direction. We're heading that way."

"But what about—"

"Hitch is a big boy. He can take care of himself." Tucker starts walking back the way we've come. "And he made me promise to keep *you* safe, not save his ass."

"I don't care what he made you promise. I can't leave him down here."

Tucker stops. "He'll be fine. He'll get out. And as soon as he does, he'll be on his way back to New Orleans. I'm bettin' the Big Man's halfway there already."

"You think?"

"He'll keep his word. He'll give Mrs. Hitch the antidote, and she'll be back to her old tricks in no time."

Which reminds me . . .

"She was involved in the experiments." I watch Tucker's reaction, wondering if his earlier comment about the FBI was meant to be about Stephanie, in particular. "Hitch found her signature on some paperwork. Did you know about that?"

"Nope, but I told you FBI agents can't be trusted. Wouldn't trust that boyfriend of yours, either."

"You can't talk about Hitch's wife one minute and call him my boyfriend the next."

"Why not?" Tucker asks. "I know lots of married men with girlfriends."

"I'm not interested in getting between Hitch and Stephanie."

"Might not be a Hitch and Stephanie. Either way, it sounds like he's got plenty of shit to work through before you two have a conversation."

"I don't need to *have* a conversation!"

"Good, then start walking." He cocks his head, urging me to follow. "We should make sure that Marcy woman set your other boyfriend loose the way she said she would."

My right foot steps forward without my conscious permission. "She did. She had to."

"And if she did, he's probably going to do something stupid. Like come back out here looking for you. Best if we get to town and let him know you're okay."

I sigh and trot to catch up to him, matching his long strides. "Fine. Let me see if I'm getting a signal. I can try to call them both on the—"

"Your cell's toast, Red. We were underwater. Remember?"

"It'll be fine. It's waterproof." I pull my phone—which is indeed still functional—from my pocket.

"Waterproof." Tucker snorts. "You paid that kind of money for a damned phone?"

"I work in the swamp. It makes sense."

He grunts. "That's more money than I spend on clothes in a year. Two years."

"Shocking. Those wife-beaters look so expensive."

"A man don't need fancy clothes when he looks like this, sweetcheeks."

"Right." I roll my eyes and flick my phone off silent mode, but don't dare look down until we're past the white goat stalking the area around the portal, pawing at it with his hoof. Or *hoofing* at it with his hoof, since he has hooves and not . . .

What . . . the . . . ?

"Wait up." I veer toward the animal. It lets me get close enough to see the blue tag with the white *M* stuck in its ear before prancing away. "Shit."

"You say that a lot."

"Shit goes down a lot, Tucker."

"Amen."

"That's one of Mrs. Malky's goats." I point after the animal trotting down the tunnel in the opposite direction. "She used to brand them, but she starting using those tags a few years ago. They changed directors at Sweet Haven and the new guy got all het up about human-rights violations."

"Do goats have those? Not being human and all?"

"Right. But that's not the important part." I start walking again, figuring this story is best told on the move. Tucker's right. As soon as Cane gets free, he's going to come looking for me. I have to make sure he knows I'm safe. I check my phone, but there's no service yet. I guess we need to be closer to the surface.

"What's the important part?" Tucker asks, falling in beside me.

"The woman who owns that goat works at Sweet Haven. And Deedee was saying the other day that she doesn't have any trouble sneaking out because Mrs. Malky's always off campus on goat business."

"So this woman might be involved with the people living down here."

"People I'm assuming are the 'good' people Cane said were going to take care of Amity, but still . . ." I run a hand through my nearly dry hair, grateful my fingers are starting to feel normal again. "I don't like this. That woman is supposed to be taking care of Deedee, not wandering around in the bayou above a lab where bioweapons are being developed. What if she'd caught something and brought it back to the kids?"

Tucker grunts. "Shouldn't be a problem now. The lab is gone."

"It might be an even *bigger* problem now. Look at the room we just left. If anyone opens the porthole, they could be infected. Who knows how long that mist is going to hang around? There could be chemicals leeching into the rocks and seeping into the tunnels and—And you know what?" I ask, getting angrier the more I think about it. "Even if it's safe down here, that woman should be at the fucking home looking after the kids. There are children *in need,* and they're a hell of a lot more important than that stupid goat. I *hate* that goat."

"Good," Tucker says. "I like it when you're hating things other than me."

"I don't hate you." Great. Now I feel bad again. "I'm sorry. I . . . I thought . . ."

"Quid pro quo."

"What?"

"I think you should get your quid pro quo," he says. "Ask me a question. I'll answer it, whatever it is."

My lips part and the wheels start spinning in my head. "What do you know about the pixies?" Might as well start with the most recent mystery. "How is the Big Man involved?"

"That's two questions."

"No, it's one question with two parts. He said he'd been trying to round them up for a month."

Tucker nods. "That's about right. They broke out a few days before Grace's body was found. At first the Big Man thought one of them might've killed her."

"Why? I thought you said they weren't violent. Broke out from where?"

"Four questions."

"Subsidiary inquiries under the umbrella of the first question."

He grunts. "You sound like my lawyer."

"Why do you need a lawyer?"

"That's definitely a second question."

I sigh. "Why did you think the pixies killed Grace?"

"I never said I—"

"Just answer the question Mr.—" My lawyer impression falters as I realize I don't know his last name.

"Mr. Tucker." He grins. "First name's Jamie."

"Jamie." That's unexpectedly . . . adorable. "I like it."

"Don't think it's too young sounding? Takes away from the raw sex appeal?"

I bite my lip, refusing to smile. "I don't know. Why don't you answer my question, then I'll answer yours."

It's his turn to sigh. "From what I've heard, the pixies and fairies mutated around the same time. But there weren't ever as many pixies. The people working here rounded them up and kept them contained, males separate from females."

"They escaped from this lab?"

"No. When the Big Man and his partners left, they took the pixies with them."

"Stole them?"

"Had to. He uses a chemical they produce during digestion in the shots. But he can only take a little at a time. That wasn't a problem when there weren't that many people needing injections, but now . . ."

"How many of us are there? You said—"

"So a couple of months ago, the Big Man started letting them breed," Tucker says, making it clear there are some questions he still won't answer. "Big mistake. Turns out their magic is stronger when they're mating. We thought illusions were all they could do, but they've got . . . other talents."

"Like . . ."

He hesitates for a second. "We thought they could shapeshift."

"Shapeshift." I know this stuff shouldn't faze me anymore, but it's hard to keep the skepticism from my tone.

"You grew up around here. You've heard the stories about alligator men and the rugaru."

"Yeah, but I assumed they were only stories."

He lifts one shoulder. "Maybe, maybe not, but the pixies aren't shapeshifters. They're parasites. They use magic to enter a body, then set up shop in their host's stomach lining."

Ugh. Shudder. "I thought you said they were vegetarians."

"They are. Usually. But they can live off what their host eats, too."

"Like a tapeworm."

"But they don't just steal food," he says, sounding

as creeped as I feel. "When a pixie's inside something, the pixie helps call the shots."

"Mind control." My mouth goes dry. "What about humans? Can they—"

"They can. That's how they got out, but they can't live inside a person for long. The pixie dies after a day or two, and takes the host out with them. They do better inside animals, but most critters start acting out if the pixie stays inside them for any length of time. That's how the Big Man's hunting them. He sends teams out looking for animals doing things animals don't usually do, traps 'em, and cuts the pixie out of their stomachs."

"Sounds like fun."

He laughs beneath his breath. "I wasn't complaining about spy detail, I'll tell you that."

Hm. Spy detail. "Why *were* you spying on Barbara? What's the Big Man—"

"Nope. You're turn."

"You've spied on me for weeks. I think I deserve *one* more question."

"You know what I think?"

"What?"

"I think we should haul ass back to town and make sure your boyfriend's all right. Then we'll pick you up a shot from my stash, and grab some supper at your place." I'm about to remind him I don't cook, when he adds, "Then I think we should make a trip out to Sweet Haven."

"What? Why?"

"You said the goat lady wasn't taking care of

Deedee the way you'd like," he says. "You going to do something about that?"

I shake my head. "I can't confront Mrs. Malky. Not until I know more about—"

"I didn't say you should confront her," he says. "I think you should take Deedee off her hands."

28

I freeze and turn to shoot him a dirty look. "I can't take Deedee."

"Why not?"

I laugh, but he doesn't join in, apparently not understanding how absurd this conversation is. "They'd never let me. There are forms and rules and hearings and shit."

He shrugs. "Then we'll go pick up the forms."

"You're serious."

"I'm serious. You can at least get things moving."

"I don't want to get things moving." I start walking, faster than before. We're getting close to the outside world. I can smell bayou and the tang of fresh rain. I should have cell service soon.

"I think you're lying," Tucker says.

"I'm not lying. I'm not foster-mom material. I can't take care of Deedee. I can't handle my own life, let alone someone else's."

"You don't have to handle her. You have to love her. I think you do that already."

I swallow, ignoring the burning feeling at the back of my throat. "I'm not sure love is enough."

"You know . . . I gave you some bad advice. Love isn't a mistake, not when someone needs you as much as that girl does. I saw her huggin' on you in the Quik Mart. The way she was looking at you . . ." He trails off with a wistful hum. "It was almost as sweet as the way you were looking at her."

"You have to *stop* spying on me." I keep my eyes on my phone, praying for bars to pop up and give me something to do besides talk about Deedee. "It's disturbing."

"Life is disturbing. Love makes it worth it. I'd give anything to hug my kid again."

I look up, phone forgotten. Tucker's eyes meet mine for a bare moment that assures me he's not joking.

"My son's name was Ike."

"Ike."

"Weird name, but it fit him."

Tucker. A dad. My mind boggles, but I manage to say, "It's a nice name," in something resembling a normal tone.

"It was his mama's Daddy's." The side of his mouth curves up. "He was the most beautiful thing I've ever seen. I know you think I'm pretty, Red, but that kid was . . ." He takes a long, slow breath. "He was something else. The way he smiled . . ."

"What happened?" I ask softly, already knowing it was something awful.

"Doesn't matter." Tucker's expression hardens. "He's dead. Been dead for a while."

I put a hand on his shoulder. "I'm so sorry."

"Not your fault." He takes my hand and holds it. I let him.

We walk on in silence as the air around us grows lighter. Around the next bend a wink of daylight appears at the end of the tunnel.

"What about your wife?" I finally ask, wondering if she's the person Tucker's protecting from the Big Man.

"Never had a wife. You don't have to be married to make babies. That's something you should remember, Red, when you're rolling around in bed with one of those—"

"Don't talk about my sex life," I warn. "It really grosses me out that you've watched that kind of thing. *Really*."

"I have a confession to make." He squeezes the hand he still holds. "I never watched you through your bedroom window. I was messin' with you."

"I don't believe you."

He laughs. "Believe what you want, but I'm not all bad. I could even help you with the kid."

"With Deedee?"

"I'm good with kids. And you're going to need someone to work that front room over for her. I could put in a door, build a loft bed with a desk underneath so—"

"No." I pull my hand from his. "I'm not ready for that kind of help from you. Not yet."

He laughs again, a longer, happier laugh.

"What's so funny?"

He turns to me, dimple popping. "You said 'yet.' I'm growin' on you, ain't I?"

I sigh and turn back to my phone, relieved to see one tiny bar. "I'm calling Cane." Tucker *is* growing on me, but not nearly enough to trust him around Deedee. If she comes home with me, he's going to be even less welcome than he is now. I can't have invisible men popping up in my bedroom if I've got a kid in the next room.

A kid. Deedee. In the next room. It scares the shit out of me, but I might ask her if she's up for it. I might ask her today.

The thought is so simultaneously frightening and awesome that I barely have time to stress about Cane answering his phone before he's picking up.

"Annabelle? Are you okay?" he asks. "Abe called a few minutes ago and said you were—"

"I got out. I'm fine and headed back to town. Are you okay?"

"I'm fine," he says. "I'm at the station. She let me go by the gate. Like she said she would."

"Thank god." I take a deep breath. When I let it out my chest feels looser. "I can't believe she—"

"I can't either, but we shouldn't talk about it on the phone. I'm getting ready to head to Mama's for dinner. Want to meet me there?"

"What?" My forehead wrinkles. "Don't you have a ton of paperwork to do?"

"Nope," he says. "Other than those new fairies, it was a pretty quiet day."

Pretty quiet day, *my ass*. I guess this means Marcy convinced Cane to keep quiet about the lab and everything else. Maybe she used the CIA card, maybe she threatened him or someone he cares about, maybe she asked nicely while Cane was strapped with explosives and he just couldn't say no. No matter how she got the promise out of him, it seems Cane is ready to break a few more rules.

No, not rules. Laws. He's breaking federal laws, including the one demanding he report the deaths of the two dock workers and everything he knows about their murders. It's so . . . *not* him.

Even though I think it's best we keep everything that happened today quiet until we learn more about what the government and the Big Man are up to, it troubles me. Walking the line is part of who Cane is. A big part. Will he know how to be himself with all these dark secrets on his conscience?

"You want to meet me at Mama's in half an hour?" he asks. "We can go for a walk on the levee, talk about . . . things. Have some dinner."

"Dinner. Right." I pull the phone away to glance at the display—checking the time and the box warning I have three messages, at least one of them from Jin-Sang—before putting it back to my ear. "I can't believe it's only four o'clock."

"Tell me about it," Cane says.

I lean against the last patch of tiled wall. We're close enough to see the opening to the outside world about fifty feet ahead, but the tunnel narrows significantly between here and there, becoming a tight, rough-walled cave that we're going to have to crawl through to get out.

I hold up a finger to Tucker. He nods and wanders away, giving me the illusion of privacy.

"What's going on with the FCC?" I ask. "Did they put out a code red? I've got a message from Jin, but I haven't listened to it yet."

"Yeah, they put out the code red. All the shuttles out of town are cancelled until tomorrow morning, and I saw a couple helicopters circling on my way back," he says. "I haven't talked to anyone, but Dom took a call from the FCC central office. They said the air looks clear, but they're sending a team out tomorrow, anyway. They're going to conduct an investigation into the possibility of a new species. I'm sure they'll want to talk to us."

"I'm sure they will," I say. "But what are we—"

"I told them you were helping me answer an anonymous tip at the Gramercy docks when we spotted the swarm and took shelter in the garage," he says, answering my unspoken question. "I'm writing up the report on the dead men we found right now. Putting it down as accidental poisoning until I learn different."

He's not completely ignoring the bodies. It makes me feel a little better.

"This might end up being a federal case, but even if it isn't, Dom and I aren't going to be able to finish the investigation or remove the bodies until the FCC lifts the code red. So there's not—"

"You and Dom can't go out there. You've only got one iron suit and didn't you leave it—"

"I'm going to borrow a couple of suits from the FBI," he says. "Agent Rideau said he'd have some sent up from New Orleans when he sends the car back."

"What?" Surely I heard him wrong. "He did? When did you—"

"Talked to him a few minutes ago. He's giving Abe a ride back to town before heading to New Orleans in my cruiser. Said he figured a suit loan was the least he could do." He pauses, then adds in a stiffer voice. "He wanted me to tell you he'd talk to you soon."

"Oh. Okay," I say, not knowing quite how to feel about that.

It makes me crazy that Hitch had the balls to leave a message for me with Cane, but it's also kind of a relief. He's taking a step away, back to Stephanie and the baby and his life in New Orleans. I know there will come a time when we'll have to talk about the lab and Stephanie's part in it and where we go from here, but I've got my own life, and it feels like our past has finally been put to bed.

Bed. I'm going to need another one. I can probably find a frame in the junkyard, but I'll have to special order the mattress from New Orleans. But maybe—if I file the paperwork tonight and Deedee gets to come home with me in the next week or so—I can borrow a mattress from Bernadette. I know she has a daybed in her guest room.

"Annabelle? You still—"

"Cane?"

"Yeah?"

"I'm going to skip dinner and go start some paperwork at Sweet Haven." I don't know where he and I are going from here, but he deserves to know Deedee might be along for my half of the ride. "I want Deedee to come live with me. Assuming she'll still have me after—"

Cartoon cats crying crystal tears flash on my mental screen.

"Gimpy! Shit!"

"What's wrong?"

"Gimpy's at the vet again," I say, pacing away from the wall. "I totally forgot. I have to go check on him, too, so I really can't—"

"Don't worry about it," he says. "Do what you need to do. I'll swing by your house tomorrow morning before work. We can talk then."

"Okay. Sounds good. We should talk."

"Yeah," he says. "Maybe . . . You want me to come over later tonight instead?"

"Tonight? When?"

"Around nine?"

I dart a quick look over at Tucker, who's not even making an effort to act like he's not listening anymore. He lifts a brow, issuing a silent challenge. "That's okay," I say. "Tomorrow morning would probably be better."

Tucker smiles and I scowl, hoping he realizes that Cane's loss will not be his gain. I have enough on my plate tonight. And I'm exhausted. I need a nice, relaxing evening with *no* men in it."

"All right," Cane says, concealing any hurt he might feel. "I'll see you then."

"See you." I'm about to hang up when he says—

"I meant what I said, Lee-lee. I love you, and . . . I'm sorry."

"Me, too," I say, throat tightening. I'm not looking forward to telling Cane what I learned from Fernando. I have a feeling that confrontation is only going to make the motivation for his visit last night more upsetting. "See you in the morning. Knock at the back door, okay? If there's a miracle and Deedee gets to come home with me tonight, I'll put her in the front room."

"I'm proud of you," Cane says. "You're going to be a great foster mom."

I hear his hope for babies of our own in his voice, but refuse to take it too seriously. I'm not going to be taking anything seriously for the next several weeks. As soon as I get my cat and work things out with Dee, I'm prescribing myself a full month of laying low.

Even if the Big Man hadn't demanded it, I need it. It will be good for me. And Deedee. And god knows Gimpy needs some downtime. I'm going to have to catproof the house. Maybe Deedee will help. Something like that seems like it would be right up her alley.

"See you in the morning." I end the call, and am pulling up my first message when Tucker wanders over with a sigh.

"We should go," he says. "We've got a few miles to walk and—"

"Let me check my messages. Two seconds." I close my eyes, making a great show of listening hard as Jin-Sang's voice whispers in my ear.

Really *whispers*. Why the hell is he whispering? He *never* whispers. Jin's an all loud, all the time kind of guy.

"I don't have much time," he hisses, his accent thicker than I've ever heard it. "An armored car is waiting. I erased your warning. You'll be having interviews soon, but when you are, say nothing about the new species. It is *very* important this big concern goes away. I'll call when I can. Delete this message as *soon* as you are hearing it."

Jin's voice cuts off with a rattle. I scowl down at the phone as I hit delete and start the next message. Why is he so upset? And why does he want me to cover up the new species? Jin's even more of a line-walker than Cane. He lives for regulations and protocol. There has to be something very wrong for him to advocate prevarication.

"What's wrong?" Tucker asks. "Who was—"

"Nothing." I'm not ready to discuss this with Tucker, not until I get more information from Jin. Hopefully he'll be in touch before my interview so I can get the dirt.

I plug my ear as Deedee's voice comes on the line. "It's me. Gimpy's sleeping. I'm goin' back to Sweet Haven, but I'm comin' to visit him tomorrow. I can. I take back my promise not to sneak out. It's okay to break promises to people who don't keep *their* promises." She sighs a long, labored sigh, but she doesn't sound as angry as she's pretending to be. "Bye. Call me if you get this before lights-out." I delete the message, secretly hoping we'll be picking the Gimp up from the vet together.

The last message is from Dr. Hollis, saying she wants to keep Gimpy overnight for observation. She thinks he'll be fine, but that we should talk about antidepressants.

For a second I think she's talking about medication for me, but then she starts extolling the benefits of Prozac for cats and I have to laugh.

"I'm serious, Red," Tucker says. "We aren't the only people trying to get out of here. We need to move before we—"

"I'm done." I shove my phone back into my pocket. "Keep your panties on."

"I don't wear panties."

"Boxers?"

"Wouldn't you like to know?" He loops a finger through my empty belt loop and tugs me closer. "Maybe we'll have time for you to find out before supper."

I cover his hand with mine. "I'm not going to sleep with you."

"Maybe not tonight."

"Not any night. I'm swearing off men."

"Is this like the time you swore off booze?" he asks with a grin. "How long did that last? A day?"

"A day and a half," I grumble, shoving him away

when he starts to laugh. I turn and start down the last stretch of the tunnel, a still chuckling Tucker on my heels.

Within a few moments, I have to stoop down, and not much later I'm crawling, wincing as rocks dig into my knees. This can't be the main entrance. A person much larger that I am would have a hell of a time fitting through. Tucker's on his belly by the time we reach the end, his broad shoulders scraping rock on both sides.

"You going to make it?" I ask.

"Yeah," he grunts. "But hurry it up, will ya? I'm not a fan of tight places."

"Learning so many fascinating things about you today, Mr. School Spirit." I deliberately slow my pace. "I bet you were the cutest thing, in those tight little cheer shorts."

"I'm serious, Red," he says. "Move it!" He slaps my ass, but his awkward position ensures the smack is more symbolic than painful.

"Okay, okay." I gingerly stick my head out into the world, ready to draw back inside should I spot a swarm of pixies or fairies or any recently liberated, venom-crazy felons wandering around looking for a crime to commit. But of course there's nothing that *reasonable* waiting for me, only a quiet clearing with a peek of bayou visible through the cypress trees.

And my shiny red and black Harley propped up in a patch of grass.

I scramble out of the hole and up into the light, with Tucker close behind me. He shoves his shoulders free, but pauses when he gets an eyeful of the motorcycle. "Well, well," he says, a sly smile creeping across his face. "Guess we won't be walking after all."

"How did he get it out here?" I keep my distance, leery for some reason.

"He has his ways." Tucker pulls himself free and jumps to his feet, shaking his head and arms like a dog fresh out of water.

"But how did he know this is where we'd end up? There are at least two other ways out."

"You ever heard that phrase about not lookin' a gift horse in the mouth?" Tucker throws an arm around my shoulders and pulls me in for a celebratory bear hug. I can feel how glad he is to be out of the tunnels, and laugh in spite of the bad vibe I'm getting from the bike.

"Yeah. I've heard it."

"Same applies to gift choppers." He ruffles my hair before starting toward the Harley. "I'm driving. You can ride bitch."

"You are obscenely politically incorrect."

"One of the things you love about me, right?" He smiles as he straddles the seat in a way that's both sexy as hell and silly at the same time.

"What about helmets? Don't we—"

"We'll be all right. I'll dig a couple out of storage before we go riding again."

"You're assuming I'm going riding *now*. I don't—"

"Trust me, Red. You're going to love this. By the time we get back to your place, you'll be begging me to take you out again." He turns a dial and pulls a knob and fusses with enough switches to make me certain I'm never going to learn how to drive the stupid bike, before turning the key and jabbing the red starter button.

But instead of rumbling to life, the engine makes a high-pitched whining sound, and something under the gas pan rattles like a snake ready to strike.

29

Run!" I shout, but Tucker's already on the move. He shoves away from the bike and sprints toward me as the rattling becomes a roar and the bike goes up with an air-scalding blast.

His body slams into mine and we hit the ground hard enough to knock the wind out of me. I cough and flinch as pieces of flaming metal fly through the air and the heat of the explosion warms my feet. I try to roll over and run, but Tucker has me pinned.

"Get up," I shout. "We have to—"

Something hits his back, sending a shudder through us both. There's a sick-sounding thunk and his eyes close with a groan. He collapses on top of me, squeezing the wind out of my lungs a second time, leaving me breathless as the last pieces of the Harley fall to the ground.

And then the swamp is quiet, but for the cries of frightened birds and the hiss of the fire licking at what's left of the Big Man's present.

The Big Man. He has to be responsible for this.

Tucker was wrong. I'm not safe. And neither is he. In fact . . .

"Tucker?" I ask, voice muted and strange in the ringing silence. I run my hands up his back, pulse slowing when I feel the gentle movement of his ribs as he draws breath.

He's not dead. My arms tighten around him. *Thank god.*

Trembling with relief, I continue my exploration, tracing his spine up to his neck, pushing aside his tangled hair until I touch something hot and wet at the base of his skull. I apply gentle pressure. Within a few moments, my fingers are sticky and slick. He's bleeding. A lot. But head injuries do that. It's probably not as bad as it feels.

"He's going to be fine," I say, then repeat, "you're going to be fine," in case he can hear me.

We just have to get back to town and everything will be okay. I'll get Tucker patched up and then . . . then . . .

Then what? I come out here and hunt the Big Man down? Kill him before he can kill me? Even though he's invisible and powerful and has a small army of people doing his bidding? It's impossible. He'll find me first and he'll finish the job he started and—

"Is it her?" The question is distant, hushed, but I hear it. I freeze, fingers going slack in Tucker's bloody hair.

"It is. It's the ginger woman," says a second voice, more guttural than the first. It's coming from the other side of the clearing, not far from what's left of the Harley.

"Is it dead?" asks the first.

"Not yet. Soon. We wait."

"We finish it," the first voice replies with a screech I'm guessing is the monster's version of laughter.

Fairies. Fucking *fairies*. And I'm all out of magic. I might be able to shove Tucker off of me and make a run for it, but I'd never make it back to town before the Fey caught up with me and I can't leave him here unconscious and maybe bleeding to death. There's no way out. This is it. If they're willing to die to kill me, then I'm dead. The end.

I feel a sob rising in my throat but swallow it down.

I had a life before I started catching magic. And in that life I managed to get into more than my fair share of trouble. But I almost always got out of it, and I didn't use magic. I used my brain. And I still have that. Mostly.

I also have an idea.

"I'm not dead!" I make sure I'm loud enough for the bastards on the other side of the clearing to hear me. "If you try to finish me off, you'll only be killing yourselves."

"Gentry," the first voice says, sounding a touch frantic. "Gentry!"

"That's right," I say, hoping I won't have to prove myself. "But I don't want to hurt you. I want to help. I know your leader was killed."

There's some mumbling from the fairies and I

think I hear a few new voices I haven't before, but no immediate response.

"I talked to Grandpa today, and—" Tucker moans and twitches, nudging his face closer to my neck. He's still unconscious, but he's present enough to be bothered by someone screaming in his ear. I decide to take that as a positive sign and continue in a softer voice. "He was worried about what's going to happen if the invisible people are allowed to stay in the swamp. He was right to worry. One of them killed him today."

More mumbling, more agitated this time, and finally the gravelly voice asks, "Who killed the leader of the Slake?"

"Who do you think?" I ask. "The Big Man thinks he's untouchable, but he's not. I know his weakness. And I want him out. I think you want the same thing."

A whisper and hiss later a soft whumping sound stirs the air above me. An ancient Fey woman appears over Tucker's shoulder, beating fragile-looking pink wings. Her face is creased with wrinkles and her breasts droop like shriveled apricots over a softly rounded belly, but I can tell she isn't as old as grandpa. Not quite.

"What is his weakness?" she asks, confirming she's the owner of the huskier voice.

"Me. He doesn't like Gentry women. He's scared of what we can do."

She considers me for a moment, a hard smile on her tiny face. "So are we. Perhaps he and we are the ones who want the same thing."

Smart. This one. "He also wants you in a cage.

Like the pixies. You know he had them, and he's hunting them again. As soon as they're back under wraps, you're next." It's a bluff, but it's a good one. I can see the fear the words inspire in her flat eyes. The fairies I've seen in containment units at Keesler are pale, feral shadows of their free brethren with a life span of six to eight months, a year at best. Captivity doesn't agree with many creatures, but it truly doesn't agree with the Fey.

"And what do *you* want?"

"I want him and everyone creating weapons with Fey venom out of here. For good. The only way to do that is for us to work together. You help me, and I'll help you. You leave the people of Donaldsonville alone and in exchange, I'll leave you to your breeding and mosquito killing and . . . whatever else you're up to."

She scrunches her nose, baring the top layer of her fangs. "We had a truce before. And now, if you are to be believed, that man has killed our leader. Why should we trust another human?"

"Because I can kill you with a thought," I say, willing myself to believe it. That I'm capable of doing it. That I have the magic to make her evaporate. Right here. Right now. "I will kill you and the fairies over there and keep killing and killing until every one of you is dead. Then I'll gather your eggs and use them to make really stinky mayonnaise that I'll eat on a turkey sandwich when the Fey are extinct."

"You'll kill yourself."

"I don't care."

She flutters closer, until her feet touch down on Tucker's filthy wife-beater. Her wings still and sag, wilting around her hunched shoulders. When she crouches down to bring her wee nose closer to mine, her knees tremble. "Our leader is dead. We will not easily choose another. But . . ."

"But?" I whisper.

"When we do, I will present your offer."

I take a breath. "Until then we have a truce? You won't come after me or my friends?"

"I lack the power to make that promise," she says. "I can give you safe escort to the gates tonight. That is all."

Shit. That's not good enough. I need to know Deedee's safe, and how am I supposed to get Tucker back to town? He's too heavy. I'll never be able to carry him with my muscles and when I can't carry him with my mind, the fairies will know I'm full of shit. *Shit!*

"All right," I say, sounding remarkably calm.

"But if you harm me or my flight, we'll tear you apart." She leans even closer, until I can see my pale, frightened face reflected in her bug eyes. I don't look tough. I look like a little girl who's seen the monster under her bed. "I don't care, either."

I nod. Swallow.

"Come."

I nod again. And poke Tucker in the stomach. Once, twice, three times. He moans and shifts his legs, but doesn't wake up. I poke him again. More moaning. Less shifting. I start to sweat. All over. All at once. "One second," I tell the fairy. "Let me see if I can wake him up. He could have a spinal cord injury. I don't want to move him with magic unless I have to."

She flutters into the air. "I'll go convince my flight not to eat your heart."

"Thanks," I say dryly.

I swear the old lady smiles before she flies away.

"Bunch of smart-ass, blood-sucking, flying vamp—"

"Blood," Tucker interrupts, his lips moving sluggishly at my neck.

He can hear me! "Tucker!" I hiss into his ear. "Wake up! You have to wake up."

"Mmm."

"There are fairies here. They are going to *kill* us if you don't get up."

"Mmmm." It's a longer sound, but vaguer. I can feel his spirit pulling away, sinking back into an oblivion he might never crawl back out of unless I do something.

"Tucker, listen to me. I have a proposition for you," I whisper, letting my lips kiss his skin with the words. I shift beneath him, rolling my hips as I move my hands around to the small of his back. A part of me feels ridiculous for thinking this might work—the man has a head injury and no amount of sexing or promise of sexing is going to help my cause.

But the other part of me knows Tucker better than that.

"If you get up and walk, I'll take you home, and do sick, wonderful things to your body. All. Night. Long." My hands slide down to his ass, and his breath comes faster. "First we'll take a shower. I'll wash your back . . . You'll wash . . . whatever parts of me you think are *dirty*." His lips part and his eyelashes flutter. "And you know what we'll do after that?"

"Mmm?" His moan has a question mark at the end. I'm sure of it.

"Then, we'll dry off, and you'll show me you know what to do with that ego of yours. And I'll show you how good redheads are in bed." More eyelash fluttering and a sliver of blue peeks through before his lids slide closed. "And then we'll do it again. And again, until you come so hard you forget your own name. Sound good, Jamie?"

"Tucker." He blinks in slow motion, and his lips twitch at the sides. "Call me . . . Tucker."

"All right." I cup his face in my hands, willing him to stay with me with my sexiest sex eyes. "I'll call you Tucker," I whisper. "I'll call you baby. I'll call you He-Man Master of My Vagina. But you've got to get up and move. Now."

It's like he's been Tasered. His abdominal muscles clench and his arms move and his knees slide through the singed grass and a minute later—with a little help—he's on his feet. His arm lies heavy around me and I feel at least fifty of his two hundred and whatever pounds bearing down on my shoulders, but he's up.

"We've got a fairy escort back to town," I hiss. "Think you can walk two miles?"

"I can walk to . . . New Orleans," he says, voice only slightly slurred.

"Good. Because if you fall down before we get there, you won't be getting up again," I whisper. "The fairies will kill us."

"I'm not falling down." He takes a stiff step forward and then another, gait growing smoother as we cross the clearing to where the fairies hover beneath a peeling cypress. "I'm Tucker, Master of Your Vagina."

My laugh sounds slightly hysterical, but only slightly, which is pretty good given the circumstances.

30

Six weeks later

It's the perfect day for a wedding. Eighty degrees, with a pale October sky overhead and a breeze blowing through the live oaks, keeping everyone cool in their Sunday best. The wide drive leading up to Camellia Grove is dissected by a blue runner a shade darker than the sky, lined on either side by rows of white wooden chairs. The columns on the plantation house at the end of the drive are strung with blue and white ribbon, and explosions of hydrangeas in antique copper kettles sit at the end of each row of chairs.

There are a *lot* of chairs. Half the town has turned out. People mill around the drink tables with mimosas or Cokes in hand, visiting and laughing, ordering children to "go play" until it's time for the service.

Until I have to walk down that aisle and do what I've promised to do, no matter how much I wish I could run home and hide under my bed until this is over.

"You go play, too," I say, giving one of Deedee's braids a nervous tug. Her hovering is only making me more anxious.

"But I'll get my dress dirty."

"You're a kid, you're supposed to get your dress dirty. No one's going to care."

"I care. I'm the *flower girl*." She stands up straighter and sticks her nub of a nose in the air, pretending she's not watching as two girls about her age walk by holding hands, talking very fast about cake.

Deedee's doing fine in school, but she hasn't been getting along with some of her old friends. Apparently, third grade is the time when girls start the cliquey, tormenting-each-other-for-fun thing these days. Sad. I think it was at least fifth grade when I was in school. Maybe sixth. And I always had Caroline.

Caroline . . . whose dying face I'm beginning to think it's okay to forget. Maybe she'd even *want* me to forget. No matter how we fought as teenagers, she loved me. We were good sisters. And good sisters don't wish suffering upon each other.

Deedee made some noise about wanting to adopt a baby sister last week—observing that we have enough room now that we've moved in with Tucker. I gave her the evil eye and reminded her that we already have a cat. An *insane* cat, that would probably eat our baby if we were crazy enough to get one. I almost warned her not to get too comfortable at Tucker's house, either, but I didn't. She's been through enough. I want to give her at least the illusion of stability. I don't plan on saying a word about leaving Donaldsonville until the day we pack the armored moving van.

Six more months.

Six more months of proving myself as a foster mom and I'll be able to adopt Deedee and whisk her away from all the deadly drama. Until then, I can't take a foster kid out of state. And I can't let down my guard. And I can't let anyone know that I'm planning to get as soon as the getting's good.

"Can I have another Coke?" Deedee asks.

"You already had a Coke."

"So? I'm still thirsty."

"You don't need another Coke." I stand on tiptoe to see over Dom's and Dicker's heads. They're camped out by the booze table, too. It's good to see them enjoying themselves—especially since I wasn't sure they'd be on board with these particular nuptials—but I hope they won't be too smashed by time for the ceremony. Dom is one of the groomsmen.

"Why not?" Deedee whines.

"Too much sugar." I lean to the left and the right, but there's no sign of the man I'm looking for, the man who *promised* to come talk me down from the ledge before the ceremony.

"What about you?"

"What about me?" I ask.

"That's your third mimosa, ain't it? Haven't *you* had too much sugar?"

I shoot her my best I-am-not-amused look. "I can handle it."

"So can I."

"Why don't you put Gimpy in his basket and go play?" I ask with a tight smile, giving her braid a firmer tug. "I can keep him out of trouble."

"No you can't. You have to concentrate." Deedee hugs the Gimp tighter. He growls and slits his eyes, but doesn't make any move to jump out of her arms. He's been like a furry growth on her side lately. He even let her tie a white bow around his neck this morning to match my dress.

It would be sweet. It *was* sweet, until I found him in her room last night, trying to eat one of her braids while she was sleeping. Seeing him crouched over her little body in the moonlight streaming through her window . . . disturbed me. A lot. Enough to lock him up in the old chicken coop behind Tucker's house for the night, and to start thinking about who might take in a deranged animal when it's time for Deedee and me to hit the road.

I love Gimpy, but I love Deedee more.

"And I don't want to leave him with someone who's doing drugs." Deedee glares at the drink in my hand. "I'll be in charge of him today."

Man, do I love her. I also love Donaldsonville Elementary's "Say No to Drugs" program, which has turned her into a pain in my ass every day around beer thirty.

"That's probably a smart idea," I say. "Why don't you go be in charge of him over there? In the *grass*. While you *play*."

"I don't—"

"Play!"

Deedee huffs and rolls her eyes. "Fine. But I'm going to play in the garden. Grass smells." She stomps away with the Gimp in her arms.

"Love you," I call after her.

"You, too," she grumbles, sticking her tongue out over her shoulder.

I wait until she's through the garden gate before tipping my glass back, letting the other half of my mimosa fuzz down my throat. I drop my empty glass on the booze table and circle around the rows of chairs, waving to everyone who calls out a greeting, but not stopping to talk. I can't smile and chat with people with *that* light in their eyes, that weird light people get when they're looking at a woman wearing a wedding dress.

I stop, scanning the crowd, but there's still no sign of Tucker. Where is he?

I should never have agreed to this. I should have worn my brown pantsuit. Even a simple wedding dress—white, sleeveless sheath that ends above the knee, with a blue sash at the waist to match the flowers—is too much wedding dress.

I feel like a virgin being offered for slaughter. I feel like I'm going to puke. I feel like—

"Drink?" Fern's voice comes from behind me, so close the heady scent of Le Male engulfs me in its manly fog. A second later, a fresh mimosa floats over my shoulder.

"I've already had three."

"Then you better drink up. You'll want at least four in you before the ceremony."

I take the glass, gripping the stem tight as he comes

to stand beside me, staring out at the assembled witnesses. "If I'm too wasted to remember my lines it's your fault."

Fernando laughs. "All you have to remember is the last part. That's the important part. It won't be legal until we hit city hall in New York tomorrow, anyway, so . . . no stress."

Then why do I have to do this? I want to ask, but I know why. It doesn't matter that gay marriage is still illegal in Louisiana. Fern wants a ceremony here in town with his friends and Abe's family, he wants to start his new life out in the open with a celebration, and he wants his best friend to officiate.

"Thanks for doing this," he says, nudging me with his hip. "I appreciate it."

"I'm honored you asked."

"I'm honored you said yes."

"So much honor." A strained silence falls, but I smile through it. I'm not sure Fern and I will ever have the easy relationship we once had, but we love each other and when it came down to choosing grudge or forgiveness, there was no choice to make. My grudges these days are reserved for people who've tried to kill me.

"You look smoking," he finally says.

"You, too." He's more than smoking. He's elegant and poised and completely stunning. The man was made to wear a tux.

"I love that dress."

"You should, you picked it out."

"Somebody needed to wear a dress," he says. "It

doesn't feel like a wedding without a dress. I bet you'll get that proposal out of Cane today. I can feel it coming, like a zit ready to pop."

"That's disgusting."

"But evocative."

"Right." I cover my awkwardness with a long drink. No need to tell him that Cane already proposed about a week ago. Or that I said no.

He was asking for the wrong reasons. His mom handled Abe's highly unexpected coming out better than I thought she would, but I can tell Cane is feeling the pressure. With Amity infected and Abe marrying another man, Cane is the last chance for grandbabies and he's pushing forty. He's desperate for a family, but I'm not sure he's desperate for a family *with me*. No amount of talking seems to be able to make things right between us, and he's been . . . distant. But then, so have I.

There are things he still doesn't know about my life, that he can *never* know. The secrets I have to keep color things between us.

Then there are the things that I've done . . . Things I did a week or so after dragging Tucker through the bayou—caving under his seductive pressure—and that I've continued to do on a *very* regular basis despite the fact that everyone in town, Deedee included, still thinks Tucker's my cousin. My friends, even Cane, believe I moved into Tucker's two-story house so Deedee and I could have our own bedrooms, more living space, and a yard for her to play in. Bernadette is the only one who even suspects there's something fishy going on, and she's too excited about being a surrogate grandma to Deedee to say anything.

But it doesn't matter what the town thinks. In reality, I know I'm involved with Tucker. It's more than sex, and I wouldn't have let that happen if I loved Cane the way I should. At the very least I'd feel guiltier about it than I do.

But I'm not drowning in guilt. I miss Cane, and I'll always love him, but I'm also . . . happy. As happy as possible considering at any given moment a part of me is expecting to be murdered.

The Big Man swears the explosion was an accident. He says he gave the order to remove the bomb after we chatted in the lab, but that the guy in charge of disarming bombs was busy being eaten by a pixie-infested gator at the time.

Nobody's fault. Just bad luck. The Big Man gave us replacement Harleys by way of apology—his and hers 1984 Harley FXRTs in red and black, great engines, ride like badass tractors—and everything is allegedly fine.

But Tucker and I still sleep with guns by the bed. He still plans to spend the next six months hoarding shots—enough to keep us from going venom mad until we figure out how to make our own—and I still hang iron netting over Deedee's door at night, adding an extra barrier against any fairies that might make it through the gate.

So far it's been a quiet fall. The fairies are too busy fighting for control to mess with me, the Big Man has rounded up most of the pixies, and the team investigating the new species should be wrapping up their fruitless investigation any day now.

Jin-Sang never did explain why Cane and I were supposed to lie about the pixies. By the time he called, the lies were already told and he was no longer my supervisor. According to the rumor mill, he was spectacularly fired during a four hour meeting at the FCC central office. No one knows why—and he refused to dish—but it gave me a good excuse to hand in my resignation. I said I was tired of supervisors coming and going and that I wanted to spend time with the little girl I'm hoping to adopt. No one batted an eye. They simply wished me well and sent a new recruit to pick up my official orange vest and sample-collecting kit.

Things could be a lot, *lot* worse.

Still, it feels like danger is perpetually hanging over my head, a two-ton weight on a fraying rope. Even today, when the sun is bright and my friends are happy and my tummy is gurgling with good champagne, something feels . . . not right.

"You okay?" Fern asks.

"Nerves." I force a smile. "Why am I the one who's nervous?"

"Because you're giving away your best friend."

"Which is not fair." I lean into him as he puts his arm around me. "I shouldn't have to give you away *and* marry you. Entirely too much responsibility."

"I know, but I appreciate it," he says. "Thanks for being my friend."

"I love you." I wrap my arms around him, squeezing tight. "I wish you only good things."

"You too, girl." Fern sniffs and pulls away with a breathy laugh. "I better go hide out in the front hall. Cane called. He should be getting here with Abe any minute."

"Okay." I give him a thumbs-up as he backs away. "I'll get Deedee and have Dom tell Barbara all systems are go." Barbara Beauchamp still isn't speaking to me—despite the fact that she's Fernando's wedding planner, a gig she's picked up to afford the lifestyle to which she is accustomed—but that's fine. I don't enjoy chatting with people who once slept with people I'm currently sleeping with.

Hm. Maybe *that's* why Tucker is MIA. Maybe he's hiding from Barbara, who, a month after he stopped calling, still hasn't gotten the hint. The last time he ran into her at the liquor store, she grabbed his crotch.

"Crotch," I mumble as I slug back the last of my mimosa and head off to the garden to grab the flower girl and her cat.

I'd like to grab Tucker's crotch. A quickie in the bathroom—skirt up around my waist, Tucker's fingers digging into my hips while I brace myself on the sink—would really take the edge off. It would be good. Sex with Tucker is always good. The man is quickly becoming my drug of choice.

I keep an eye out for him as I give Dom the message, but there's still no sign of "my cousin." If he doesn't show up soon he'll miss the wedding. Fern won't care—he's not a fan of Tucker, thinks he's too pretty to be trusted—but I was looking forward to seeing him in his new black suit.

But the only black suit I spot on the way to the garden belongs to an FBI agent. Howard. He rolled into town a few weeks ago with a letter from Hitch that said everything was under control, that I should sit tight and stay quiet and he'd be in touch when it was safe. It also said thank you, and that he and Stephanie were good and having a boy.

It was a nice letter. And only the tiniest bit painful.

"Howard." I lift a hand as I walk past. Howard nods, but doesn't say a word. He's the quiet, crusty type, a fortysomething man whose skin seems to constantly be flaking. But for an FBI agent he's not too bad.

At least he's not my ex or having my ex's baby. Both pluses.

Inside the garden, the air smells of roses past their peak; a sweet, slightly rotten scent that is, nevertheless, kind of nice. There are other things blooming too—pansies and orchids and a patch of burnt orange calla lilies that make me wish I could have convinced Fern to go with a more autumnal color palate for the wedding. I don't know when he developed such a love for baby blue. Maybe it's Abe's favorite.

Big, bad Abe, the chief of police, has an abiding love for baby blue. The thought makes me smile.

"Deedee?" I call. "It's time. You ready?"

No response. The garden is quiet. Almost unnaturally so.

"Deedee?" More silence. My smile fades as I

move deeper into the garden, past water features and empty benches, sticking to the path. Deedee wouldn't veer from the path. She grew up here. Fear of stepping on Miss Barbara's plants was ingrained in her right along with fear of god and strangers and fairies.

Fairies.

"Deedee!" Hysteria creeps in, and my walk becomes a jog. The plantation is close to the gate—only a couple hundred meters away. If a fairy were going to slip through and attack, this would be the place to do it. They wouldn't have to fly through the iron grid work in town, just slip through the bars. Grandpa Slake could have done it. He's dead, but one of the older fairies could probably survive inside the boundary, too. I should never have let Deedee come here. I should never have let her go off alone.

"Deedee! Answer me! Answer me right now!" My words end in a gasp for air as I reach a fork in the path. I take the one that curves to the right, back around to the house. Maybe she decided to go inside. Maybe she had to use the bathroom or something. Until recently, this was her home. She'd probably feel comfortable—

There! A puddle of blue on the paving stones. She's sitting cross-legged just outside the kitchen, neck bent, petting the cat in her lap. I let out a ragged breath and press a hand over my heart.

"Jesus, Deedee," I say as I cross the few feet left between us. "Why didn't you answer me? I was scared to—"

She lifts her tear-streaked face and my anger evaporates. She's crying. Hard. Full-on eye leaking with a side of runny nose. "What's wrong?" I squat down beside her, smoothing her braids away from her face. "What happened?"

"I . . . I miss my mama," she says, shoulders shaking with a fresh round of sobs.

Oh, man. I *knew* this was going to happen. I should have trusted my instincts and told Fernando Deedee was going to stay with Bernadette during the wedding, no matter how thrilled out of her goddamned mind Deedee was to be the flower girl. It's too soon for her to be back in the place where her mother was murdered.

"I know you do." I lay a hand on her back, ignoring Gimpy's low growl. "I'm so sorry. I shouldn't have brought you here."

"No." Deedee shakes her head.

"It's all right. Let's go call Bernadette. She said she'd watch you. I can run you back home and—"

"No! That's not it." She shrugs off my hand, her movement summoning another dangerous sound from the Gimp. Damned cat. "I don't want to go. I'm the flower girl."

"Okay," I say in my most soothing voice. "Then let's go get you cleaned up. The ceremony is about to start."

"I can't," she whispers.

"Okay, then we'll call Bernie. Fern won't be mad. We—"

"No! You don't understand."

Of course I don't! *Argh*. Kids. Why did I think
would be able to pull this parenting thing off? I start
to run a hand through my hair, then remember it's
pulled up into a knot and rub my neck instead. "I'm
sorry, Dee," I sigh. "I don't understand. I need you to
help me. Remember we talked about this, how I'm
going to suck at this sometimes and I'll need your
help?"

"My mama would know what to do."

"I know she would."

"She knew all about cats. She knew they were bad
sometimes."

Cats? I cast a glance down at her lap, where the
Gimp is glaring at me with more mean in his eyes
than usual. "Is something wrong with Gimpy? Did he
eat something again?"

"No," she says, then adds in a whisper. "I think he's
turned bad."

"He was always bad, honey. So let's leave his fluffy
butt in his basket and—"

"I can't. He won't let me go. I tried to get up before,
but he wouldn't let me."

I look back down to where Deedee's fingers tangle in Gimpy's fur, unable to imagine any reason she
can't move her hands. This is weird. But Deedee's a
weird little kid. It's one of the things I love about her.
I'll play along and get her back to the wedding and
hope another Coke or three puts her in a less melan-
choly mood. "Okay," I say with a nod. "I'll take care
of this. When a cat turns bad there's only one thing
to do."

"What?" she asks, eyes wide.

"A dish of half-and-half," I say reaching for Gimp. "It gets rid of—Shit!" I curse as Gimpy lashes out with his claws, leaving scratches that fill with red on the back of my hand. "You little rat!" He's never scratched me before. And I'm not about to put up with it now. I reach for him again, but he stops me with fully bared fangs.

"See?" Deedee sobs. "He's bad. He's turned evil."

Something is wrong with Gimpy. Something is very wrong. I worry that he's eaten something that's finally tipped him from lovable crazy to feral crazy. I worry that he's caught rabies.

I *don't* worry that he's turned evil.

Even when I dive for his shoulders and pull him, hissing and clawing, away from Deedee, dragging him across the paving stones, I don't consider the validity of her argument. She's just a kid with an oversized imagination jumping to weird conclusions.

And then I look down and see the ripple across his fuzzy underbelly, the thing pressing against his stomach from the inside, the thing that looks a lot like a tiny hand.

"Shit!" I hurl Gimpy into the flowers and reach for Deedee. "Come on!" She grabs my hand and I sprint for the kitchen as fast as I can in high heels. We slam inside and shove the door closed seconds before Gimpy hits the glass with a growl.

"Shit," I pant. "Fu—Fudge."

"You already said *shit* three times," Deedee says. "Don't cuss."

"It's not cussing if you're repeatin' what somebo~~dy~~ else said."

"Not now, Dee." I back away from the door, pulling her with me. Gimpy's trying to dig through the glass. I know he can't, but I'll feel better with some distance between us.

"Are we going to have to shoot him?" Deedee asks in a small voice.

"No." I squeeze her fingers. "He's just . . . got . . . an infection. I know someone who can help." I think so, anyway. The Big Man usually kills animals to get the pixie out, but there has to be another way. "I'll go talk to him. Right after the ceremony. Come on, let's get back out front."

"What if he comes after us?"

"He won't." I hope I'm telling the truth. Gimpy isn't a fan of large gatherings—or the pixie inside Gimpy isn't, anyway.

Pixie. Inside my cat. How long has the damned thing been there? Weeks? Months? Since the very beginning? Did I adopt a pixie back in August? Who *is* Gimpy? Do I even know him at all?

"This is nuts," I whisper beneath my breath as Deedee and I hurry through the long hall leading to the front of the house.

"Your life is nuts," Deedee says.

I freeze, only realizing we're still holding hands when she jerks to a stop beside me. "I know. God, I know . . . Do you want to go back to Sweet Haven? If you do, I understand. I don't want you to go, but—"

"I don't want to go. I want to stay with you."

'Even though my life is nuts? And probably going ⟩ stay nuts?"

She cocks her head, and shoots me that look she gives me when I'm being especially confusing. Like when I tell her I don't care if she makes her bed because it's going to get unmade, anyway. Or that she can leave her clothes on the floor as long as she keeps track of which ones are clean. Or that it's fine to drink out of the same water glass for a day or three in the name of dirtying fewer dishes. "Don't you like me anymore?"

"I *love* you." I wipe the tear streaks from her face with my nonbloody hand. "I just—"

"I love you, too." She sniffs, and shrugs her narrow shoulders. "Nothing else matters."

Nothing else matters. I'm not sure she's right . . . but I'm not sure she's wrong, either. I only know that I'm strangely relieved. Deedee is a terrifying responsibility, but she's also slowly making me someone stronger than I thought I could be. "You're right." I nod. "We're family. You and me and Gimpy. Once we get him fixed."

"And Tucker," Deedee says.

"Yes, and Tucker." *For now,* I silently add. But what else is there, really? There's now and what we make now, and for now Tucker makes my now a lot nicer. "Come on." I shake her arm. "Let's go marry some people."

She starts to walk, but stops a second later and swipes her arm across her face. "Do I look okay?"

I glance down at her—her slightly fuzzy braids

and the cat-hair-covered front of her dress and th⸱ fresh snot trail on her arm—and say, "You're beauti- ful," and hug her tight. "The beautifulest."

She lays her damp cheek on my stomach and hugs me back and it's the sweetest hug I can remember. And when it's over we hold hands all the way through the front hall, past a smiling, anxious Fern, and out into the sun.

Fantasy.
Temptation.
Adventure.

Visit PocketAfterDark.com, an all-new website just for Urban Fantasy and Romance Readers!

- Exclusive access to the hottest urban fantasy and romance titles!

- Read and share reviews on the latest books!

- Live chats with your favorite romance authors!

- Vote in online polls!

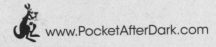

www.PocketAfterDark.com

26119

More Bestselling Urban Fantasy from Pocket Books!